ADRIANA ANDERS is an award-winning author of romantic suspense, contemporary romance, and erotic romance. Her books have received critical acclaim from the *New York Times*, *Entertainment Weekly*, *USA Today*, *Publishers Weekly*, and *Kirkus*, among other publications. Today, she resides with her husband and two children on the coast of France, writing the love stories of her heart. Keep in touch with Adriana at www.adrianaanders.com/newsletter.

DOM COM

PIATKUS

PIATKUS

First published in the US in 2026 by Forever,
An imprint of Grand Central Publishing, a division of Hachette Book Group, Inc.
First published in Great Britain in 2026 by Piatkus

1 3 5 7 9 10 8 6 4 2

Copyright © 2026 by Bittersweet Books LLC
Interior design by Marie Mundaca

The moral right of the author has been asserted.

*All characters and events in this publication, other than those
clearly in the public domain, are fictitious and any resemblance
to real persons, living or dead, is purely coincidental.*

All rights reserved.
No part of this publication may be reproduced, stored in a
retrieval system, or transmitted in any form or by any means, without
the prior permission in writing of the publisher, nor be otherwise circulated
in any form of binding or cover other than that in which it is published
and without a similar condition including this condition being
imposed on the subsequent purchaser.

A CIP catalogue record for this book
is available from the British Library.

ISBN 978-0-349-44686-8

Printed and bound in Great Britain by Clays Ltd, Elcograf S.p.A.

Papers used by Piatkus are from well-managed forests
and other responsible sources.

Piatkus
An imprint of
Little, Brown Book Group
Carmelite House
50 Victoria Embankment
London EC4Y 0DZ

The authorised representative
in the EEA is
Hachette Ireland
8 Castlecourt Centre
Dublin 15, D15 XTP3, Ireland
(email: info@hbgi.ie)

An Hachette UK Company
www.hachette.co.uk

*To my Good Girls, Bad Girls, Brats, Dommes, subs, Baby Girls, Little Girls, and every other iteration of women doing whatever they want with their bodies.
This one's for you.*

DOM
COM

CHAPTER ONE

Rae

I can't possibly do another walk-by. At some point, I've got to just bite the bullet, march up to the door, and go inside.

Half a block away, I work up the courage and scrub my clammy palms down my thighs. *Be Mimi in* Rent, I think, the way I always do when I need to kick my butt in gear. *Forget regret and just move on. Okay. This is it.*

I eye the building as I make my final approach. It's pretty. Red brick. Originally a warehouse, I'd guess, like most of its neighbors, with lots of big windows, mostly dark now. The comedy club on the ground floor is open for Friday-night business, judging from the sickly green cast of its neon sign and the stink of cheap beer.

Where I'm headed—if I can make myself take that final step—is in the basement. Off the Cuff, it's called, though there's no visible sign. I like the name. It feels right in a way I can't entirely describe. Sexy, but also not too serious. Like maybe if I get the giggles my first night, they won't run me out of town and cross my name off the permanent, forever, etched-in-stone kinky person list.

I concentrate hard on taking one step after another, regretting the stilettos I finally chose. Yes, they're cute, but limping into a

BDSM club for the first time with a blister and a sprained ankle isn't exactly the look I'm going for.

I'm maybe five yards away when I catch the eye of the bouncer standing in the alcove between the comedy club's plate glass window and Off the Cuff's wholly unremarkable front door. She's wearing all black with the requisite earpiece and that bland, vigilant look I remember from the few times my friends and I ventured out to dance in college. Before I met Brendan and became—

Nope. Not thinking about the ex tonight. Tonight is for me. My night. There's no room for thoughts of Brendan and the way he'd steel himself before going down, like a man headed into a burning building instead of a guy about to give oral sex to his girlfriend.

No room for thoughts of work and how the new mystery consultant—Grant Bowman—is dragging us all back into the office on Monday, after three years of doing fine working from home.

Just thinking about it is giving me anxiety.

Three years of never once having to remove old tuna fish sandwiches from the break room fridge or telling Dani down in graphics that roasting lamb in an Instant Pot on her desk isn't workplace-appropriate or figuring out how to politely let Stinky Phil know that he's got to leave his shoes on in the office or risk general mutiny.

Three years of work-from-home bliss brought to a screeching halt by Grant Bowman, the executive consultant ostensibly brought in to "help us transition back to the office," which is one hell of a vicious cycle if you ask me.

I've got a real bad feeling about the man. Like that indescribable, life-changing, *Something wicked this way comes* bad.

It's half the reason I'm here tonight. To let off steam and face my fears and just bite the bullet and do this *one* thing I've dreamed of for so long.

So that's it. No thinking about exes or the office or checking the family chat or asking Dad for the umpteenth time if he's taken his meds. None of it.

In fact, there will be no thinking allowed at all beyond this point. Nothing but me and this Friday-night foray into my fantasy world.

A car honks a few feet away, and I look up, startled to see that I've reached the door. The bouncer leans against the wall, staring at me with a look that says she knows exactly why I'm here.

To be dominated by a stranger. And maybe even to do some sexy stuff while I'm at it.

Oh no. What was I thinking? I can't do this.

Doing my best to pretend I stopped randomly, I tap my phone and walk on, opening apps like I mean it. Nothing to see here. Just a busy woman in a trench coat, tiny little dress, and killer heels, being busy, busy, busy. Not even a little interested in what's happening beyond that sleek silver door.

A group of fratty guys charge past, smelling like booze and AXE body spray. One of them bumps my shoulder, and my phone flies from my hand to land on the cobblestones directly in front of the club. My indignant yelp is eaten up by a wave of bro laughter, and of course—of *course*—Siri chooses that moment to scream at the top of her lungs, "I'm sorry, Rae. I didn't quite catch that. Do you mean Pops and Stuff on Broad Street or Off the Cuff on Cary Street?"

Busted.

Resisting the urge to bolt, I pick up the phone with as much grace as the heels and too-short dress allow.

"Done scoping us out?" One side of the bouncer's mouth kicks up to make her look only slightly less stoic. She's got Ilona Maher's tall, wide, intimidating stance. A woman used to being obeyed.

I shiver. "Guess so."

"Your recon skills could use some work."

"Yeah. I figured." I scuff one heel to the sidewalk, feeling exactly like a little kid caught doing something naughty.

"You already registered?"

"Yes."

"Name?"

"Jensen."

She pulls out a phone, checks something, and nods. "Need to take a few more laps or—"

"I'm good."

"All right."

When she doesn't immediately move, I experience a moment's panic that I overlooked a secret passcode or the complex handshake that everyone in the fetish world must learn in order to get into their clubs. After a beat, she shifts over to press a finger against a keypad.

The door opens. A sliver of warm light spills onto the cobblestones.

"I'm Harlow. She/her." She twists to hold the door for me, in the process baring a black BDSM triskelion tattoo inked into the skin behind her right ear. Not just a bouncer then. Maybe a member too. "Welcome to Off the Cuff." She grins, momentarily dropping the bouncer persona. "Unless you were actually looking for Pops and Stuff."

Snorting, I step past her and wait for the door to close with a solid finality before leaning against it and just breathing.

It takes a moment for my eyes to adjust to the light, which is low, though nowhere near as dark as I'd imagined. I expected a moody, industrial vibe or a gothic vampire's den with reds and blacks. Definitely not the warm gray painted brick walls or these artfully tarnished sconces casting an almost-natural light over the wide hardwood steps.

Slowly, I make my way down, expecting the floor to shake under my feet with some heavy bass and an occasional scream or two rising from the dungeon's depths. If nothing else, I brace myself for a smell.

When I get to the bottom, I look around and decide that this place isn't seedy or gross at all. It's really nice. It smells expensive, like something floral and spicy.

There's a little seating area with a sofa and two big chairs upholstered in a warm cognac, inviting me to come in and get cozy. Beyond it is a desk, where a very pale-skinned platinum blonde sits, wearing a patterned bustier and one of those tiny hats with a veil. A fascinator, I think it's called. "You joining us tonight?"

"Yes." I move in, noting the low, tasteful thrum of music, electronic but somehow vintage-sounding. A dark, sensuous tango. "I um, registered for a guest night? And paid online. It's…" Crap, am I supposed to give my real name? "Uh…Jensen."

"Rae! I'm Mistress Daff." She stands up, clapping. "So, so excited to meet you. I did your intake." She towers at least a foot and a half above me, her thick, perfectly shaped eyebrows animated as she talks. "We've got so many Doms in tonight, my friend. It's a veritable smorgasbord up in here."

"Really?" My nerves ramp up, buzzing through to the tips of my fingers.

"You'll have the pick of the litter," she says with a low giggle.

I blink, feeling almost outside of my body for a second as I imagine what that would look like. Doms everywhere. Big ones, little ones, mean ones, nice ones. On a rock. In a sock. With a—

Whoa. Simmer down, Jensen.

"You know it's Dom/sub speed dating this evening, right?"

"Oh, wow. No. I didn't."

"Ah. Well, you're in for a treat. Come on, lovely. Let's get you squared away."

I hand over my phone—which isn't allowed inside—along with my jacket and purse. I don't get a tag or a number in return. This club, apparently, is too posh for that.

"Your intake says you're a sub, cis, looking for men. Has that changed?"

"Oh, yeah. I mean, no change."

"Pronouns?" Daff asks.

"Oh. Um. She/her is fine. And you?"

She shows me the back of her hand, where it says *She/her* in red. "Want a stamp?"

"Sure."

I watch as she presses the ink to my skin, excitement fizzing through me like bubbles.

"If you could just sign this waiver?"

The slight shake to my hand makes my regular signature look like a five-year-old's. Oh well. No one's seeing that anyway. One big selling point on the club's website is how cutting-edge their security apparently is, both physical and online. My identity is safe here.

"What do we call you?"

"I don't know." Oh, right. I need a kink name. Something that represents me, but I don't even know who I am at this point. "I hadn't planned on anything. I'm just curious, you know?"

"Newbie sub...Alice? Like Wonderland? Or just, like Ray? Ray of Sunshine? Or, oh, hey, how about Little Miss Sunshine? No, no, no, I got it. *Sunny!* That works, right?"

"Sunny," I repeat under my breath, feeling a little less like a fraud under Daff's care. "I like that."

"Here you go, lovely." She hands me a matte black name tag. In silver, she's written:

SUNNY-SUB
MEN
BE NICE, I'M NEW.

"Oh, here's a copy of the checklist you filled out on our website. In case you decide to share it during speed dating. Sometimes helps to know right away if someone's a match."

"Oh, great idea." The club provided eight pages of *want*s and *maybe*s and *hell, no*s to go through before I could even sign up for tonight. I look down at the list, my eyes snagging on Blindfold (yes), skipping to Breast Bondage (maybe), Cages (hard no), Collars (maybe), and then on down to Spanking (yes) before I meet Daff's gaze again.

"Alrighty then. Come on, Sunny." She pushes through a heavy steel door. "Let's find you the Dom of your dreams."

CHAPTER TWO

Grant

"How's it looking back there?" asks Lucas, aka Tank, as I crouch to shove the tools behind the bar.

"It'll survive the night," I say, ever the optimist.

"That good, huh?"

"I took care of the leak. For now. But we can't get the private playrooms up and running again until we replace the plumber's mess." Which isn't in my damn budget. Standing with a groan, I stretch my back and wash my hands at the bar sink. This is why I hate subcontracting, and so often end up doing things myself. At least I know it'll be done right.

He gives me a sidelong glance. "You want me to fire the guy who did the work?"

I snort. Lucas is the closest thing I've ever met to a human teddy bear. Firing people just isn't in his wheelhouse. Thankfully, with someone like me around, he never has to be the bad guy. Unless he's playing, of course. In which case, being the bad guy is exactly his thing. "My building, my responsibility."

"Thanks, man. We talking a lot of work?" The look I give him makes him flinch. "Shit. I know being a landlord wasn't the plan."

And yet somehow, here I am, property manager and fix-it

man to three different businesses. Definitely not what I envisioned when I bought this building. I'd planned to buy, renovate, and sell. Short-term, low commitment. Just the way I like things.

I grab a beer before glancing up at my friend, who's standing there, arms folded, legs wide, looking even more tanklike than usual in his uniform of matte leather pants and tight black muscle shirt. "Geez, Lucas, how much time you been putting in at the gym?"

He shrugs one massive shoulder. "Been working a ton outside."

"Doing what? Crushing rocks?"

"Just some yard work."

I pull hard on the beer and cast an eye over the club, which is pretty busy for this early on a Friday night. Every seat appears to be occupied, and there's not a familiar face in the bunch. "What's with the crowd?"

"Can't you guess?" Lucas's smile widens. "Wasn't this your idea?"

On second look, I notice the group has broken into mini-clusters of two, leaning in to each other, face-to-face, chatting animatedly. "You didn't."

"What?"

"Dom/sub speed dating?"

"Bingo."

"My idea?" I snort. "I recall saying something like, 'Whatever you do, please no speed dating.'" Just the concept annoys me. When it comes to kink, I believe in taking the time and doing things right. Speediness is the literal opposite of what a scene should look like. But, as Lucas has reminded me more than once, the club's success could very well hinge on thinking outside the box. Which is precisely why he and Harlow are in charge of events. I'm just the landlord. "Pull in any new members?"

"Quite a few."

At least there's that.

"You stickin' around to play tonight? Zelda was askin' about you."

I say, "Nope," but what I really mean is *hell no*. Zelda wants a relationship, a collar, and a Dom to call her own, and that is not me. Which Lucas very well knows. Everyone here knows it. Play, Don't Stay is my motto.

I suppress a yawn, already planning my exit, when my gaze is drawn toward the front door as it opens. In comes a shaft of mellow light from the anteroom, then Daff, and behind her...

"Oh, hello." Lucas's head tilts at an interested angle. "Would you look at that."

I am looking. I can't stop looking. Can't breathe, actually, for the handful of seconds it takes my mind to catch up to my eyes. The woman who's just walked in is fascinating, though I can't say exactly why. I'd call her cute if it weren't for the slightly too-strong nose bisecting her face with its sharp edge. That nose takes the big eyes, round cheeks, and plush lips and makes them arresting, even beautiful. A classical painting instead of a manga cartoon. Something about the way she walks, and that body, all soft looking and round with pale, freckled skin, has me perking up for the first time in ages.

"I'll go say hi." Lucas's thick brows do a little dance.

"Don't bother."

"Why not?"

"That woman's not into what you dole out."

"Oh, please. You can't read that from here." He breaks into a grin. "I better go find out," he says, taking off. I'll give it to the guy. Never wastes time.

I, on the other hand, trudge around the bar and turn my back to the room. Because yeah, the newcomer's absolutely stunning—and I mean that literally as well as figuratively given how I lost my breath when she came in—but between this place, my other properties, and the new project I'm starting on Monday, I don't have time for distractions.

And that woman would absolutely be a distraction.

I'd bet anything she's a sub, though. No, I couldn't see her name tag from that distance, but I'm getting a vibe. Sometimes you just know.

I can't help but watch over my shoulder as Lucas reaches her side, puts his hand out for a fist bump, and chats her up, all easy smiles. She hands him a few sheets of paper—probably the standard club questionnaire. After a quick scan, he throws me a disappointed look and a subtle shrug. My breath quickens. Dammit, I was right.

Lucas, ever the ingratiating sadist, walks her to a table, pulls out a chair, and after a minute's discussion, comes my way.

"Sunny does not, alas, wish to be treated like a filthy slut by a man twice her size. You're in luck, though, because she does wish to be dominated." He steps behind the bar and reaches for a glass. "This is her first kink event, and she's nervous." He pops a champagne bottle with a practiced flourish. "Celebratory bubbles." The wink he gives me as he pours is equal parts friendly and lascivious. "On you."

"I'll pay, but I'm not walking that over there."

"Oh?" His thick brows flick up. "You scared of a fresh, brand-spanking-new, bright-eyed little subby-sub?"

"Scared, no. Wary, yes."

"Oooooh, that's right. The General doesn't do newbies."

"They require time, attention, care..."

"Not to mention commitment. God forbid." Humming his

disapproval, Lucas swans back to her table, where he places the glass in front of her with exaggerated care before pointing my way.

The dick.

Rather than lead Sunny on, I turn my back to the room again and pick up my beer, surprised to find it empty.

The music changes, slow and sensuous replaced with something more upbeat. Behind me, a whip cracks, making me tense up before I force my shoulders to relax again.

"Allllll right, kinksters. Doms, get up and move on to your next lucky partner!" Lucas is having a blast with this speed-dating thing.

Which is exactly why I thank god every day for my business partners. If I'd been the one to open this place instead of Lucas and Harlow, the club would be a big, utilitarian black box. No bells or whistles. None of the fancy paint colors or plush velvet furniture. No shockingly expensive baroque murals painted by avant-garde artists or hidden lighting to warm and soften bodies and turn sexy into sultry.

They're right, as always. And like Lucas said, if gimmicks like speed dating are what it takes, then speed dating is what they'll do. Along with auctions, leather nights, burlesque shows, costume parties, and whatever other extraneous crap keeps membership growing.

The fact is that the club isn't really mine. I'm a silent partner, an investor with a personal interest in its continued existence.

I agree that the club is important. This *community* is important, and these people will do whatever it takes to keep the club alive and thriving. Including hosting kinky bachelorette parties or, in my case, giving them the space rent-free until they turn a profit.

Which had better be soon. Because between this place and the company moving in upstairs, I'm not making a goddamn dime.

With a sigh, I stretch over the counter and snag another beer from the cooler, knock the cap off against the edge of the glowing wood bar I salvaged and refinished myself, and do my best to ignore the question-and-answer session happening between some lucky Dom and that fascinating little sub at the table right behind me.

CHAPTER THREE

Rae

"Good meeting you, Sunny." My seventh or eighth Dom of the night slides me a business card as he shakes my hand, and then clasps it in both of his. Very, very heartfelt. "Let me know if your place of employment's ever in the market for a new printer/copier."

Right. Okay, then.

With a nod and a smile, I wave goodbye as Master...Frank, was it?...moves on to the next table. I then cross another number off my little cheat sheet. He was fine. Nice. Just not what I had pictured.

None of this is what I imagined when I left home tonight.

I mean, the space is amazing, and there are more than a few interesting people, including Tank, the really handsome guy who's leading tonight's event, whip in hand. He seems nice, friendly, smiley, but then his name tag says that he's a Daddy and a sadist, and that's not what I'm looking for. Bossy, yes. Mean? No, thank you. I get enough of that in the real world.

Then there's the brooding man standing at the bar in his dark pants and crisp button-down shirt, sleeves rolled up to show thick, veined forearms and impatient, long-fingered hands. His dark hair curls a little long around his ears and his nape. It looks soft and thick. His face, though youngish, is sort of craggy and worn. Like he's lived. He's seen things. And he's maybe a little pissed about it all.

His eyes meet mine, and I quickly turn away, only to find myself sneaking glances at him a few seconds later. He's interesting. More than interesting, actually. Intriguing, intense, mysterious.

Funny how, all night, with every Dom I've sat with, I've barely been able to muster a *meh*, but somehow this man gives *all* the adjectives.

Annoyed. I add that to the list when our eyes meet again.

Maybe he's just bored.

Which I get. I'd expected a whole lot more excitement when I gathered up the courage to come here tonight. Not quite people hanging naked from the rafters, getting whipped and flogged, but something close to it.

Although there is a definite buzz in the air.

I cast a quick look around. There are a few vinyl- and leather-clad folks not involved in the speed dating, lurking in the corners on sofas or in clusters around funky pieces of furniture. That bench over there, for instance, is that really a sculptural table, or is it meant for something painfully sexy? Right now, a couple's cuddling on a sofa beside it, their drinks resting atop its shiny surface, but I can picture myself stretched over it, ass in the air, ready for a spanking or—

"You're cute."

I look up as my newest speed date takes a seat across from me. "Oh, thanks."

Daddy Brice, his name tag says. Okay, another Daddy.

I've met three sadists, a couple of new Doms who, like me, are maybe a little out of their depth. One guy—Sincaid?—who said all the right things, but just, I don't know, smelled wrong or something. He was also a Primal Dom, which I'd never heard of. The whole time he described his fantasy of chasing a submissive through the woods and having his way with her on the ground, I pictured gnats and mosquitos and just how bad poison ivy would feel on my nether regions. Huge no. Then there was Master Ev, dressed head to toe in leather, whose ideal partner would submit to him 24/7. I can almost see the appeal. I mean, making decisions is exhausting. But nope. There was Pedro, the rope guy, who was attractive and seemed pretty fun. Maybe I could do the suspension thing if it's low-key and doesn't put too much pressure on my knees or cut off my circulation or hurt in any way at all. Oh, then there was Thor, who called me *dear* even though I'm pretty sure I'm ten years his elder.

This new man's nice looking in a straitlaced, older-dentist way. His wire-rimmed glasses don't exactly go with his mesh top and tight, squeaky vinyl pants, but that's okay. A Dom's a Dom, right?

Wrong.

Yeah. I'm learning very quickly that there are a few things the romance novels—not to mention my favorite kinky subreddit—have gotten wrong. First off: most Doms are *not* sexy. Or smooth. Or even, if I'm being honest, very dominant.

Maybe he'll—

"You a good girl who wants to kneel for Daddy?" He rifles through the list I put face down on the table.

"Not today." I slap a hand on my list and tug it away from him.

He tugs back. "Come on. Let's see it."

"I don't think so."

"Awwww, look at you, all rosy-cheeked. You a shy, sweet girl who wants her big Daddy to—"

"You're done," says a deep voice. I look up in time to see Broody Bar Guy grab Nasty Dentist Daddy by the spiked collar of his leather jacket. "Out."

Right away, bodies converge. Massive Tank, a sexy couple from one of the dark corners, Daff from the front desk. Then Harlow, the bouncer from upstairs, swoops in and drags him off single-handedly, which is a level of badassery I absolutely aspire to.

Well, then. That removal—quick and painless—certainly speaks of a well-run establishment.

Broody Bar Guy returns, sets my checklist face down on the table, and smooths it out. "I'm sorry about that."

"Wasn't your fault," I reply.

"That man shouldn't have been here." He watches me carefully.

"It's okay."

"No. A good Dom doesn't impose his will like that. The club should have vetted him better."

I blink up at him, noting the hint of hair just visible at the open V of his collar and the sharp angle of his jawline, shadowed by dark stubble. Above it, his face is deadly serious.

"What, um…?" My voice is embarrassingly squeaky. "What is the hallmark of a real Dom?"

"First off, Doms set up ground rules. Make sure they're on the same page as the sub. A good Dom asks questions and pays attention. Listens to the sub. They'd let you call the shots." The sharply etched lines between his brows deepen as he leans in. "You, for example, don't want to be hurt."

My mouth drops open. How could he possibly know that?

"You saw my checklist?" I lift the now-crumpled pages.

"I wouldn't read that without your consent."

"What would you do? With my consent."

"Maybe a little role play. A little dirty talk." Somehow, he's a step closer, his face lower. "Got the feeling you want to be told what to do." A quick twist of his lips. "And I heard what you told the last guy."

"Which part?"

His mouth loosens into something close to a grin. "Well, not the part about color copies in your workplace."

I huff out a laugh. "Were you eavesdropping?"

"I tried not to listen, believe me. Couldn't help but hear the part where you want someone to take care of you."

Oh. Did I really say that? I guess I must have. "I didn't mean, you know, financially. Like that Sugar Daddy from earlier was into."

"Oh, I know." His voice is a warm whisper. "You meant take care of your pleasure."

He's squatting beside me now, our faces close. He smells like beer with maybe cedar and cloves and hints of something metallic. I want to bottle that scent, spray it all over my sheets, and roll in it.

"Are *you* a Dom?" I whisper.

Like a rocket, he's up and about three feet back.

"I'm not in the market for a sub."

I stand. "Oh...oh, sorry. I just. You seem to know all the things, and I thought—"

"Doms up," Tank bellows. "Say bye-bye to your current subs and head to the right!"

Someone approaches my table, looks at me, at Broody Bar Guy, and moves on.

"You scared the next Dom away, Gen," Tank yells from a couple of tables off. "Looks like you owe the woman her speed date."

For what must be a good fifteen seconds, Broody Bar Guy

seriously considers hot-footing it out of here. I'm sure of it. Finally, with a sigh, he casts a narrow-eyed glare at our MC and holds out my chair.

"Honestly, I could use a break anyway." I stay standing. "Carry on."

"Carry on?"

"Yep. I'm good. No need to play Dom with me."

A hint of humor warms his eyes. "Come on." He sweeps a hand at the chair. "Give me a chance to be less of an asshole."

"I think I'll go. This isn't my scene after all, and—"

"No!"

Everyone stops talking. And dancing and spanking, or whatever that couple in the corner just started doing. In my peripheral vision, I catch Tank folding his massive arms over his chest and giving Broody Bar Guy the kind of raised-eyebrow stare that would make me want to run and hide.

BBG sighs. "Please."

After a second, I sit and watch him head to the bar and return with the open bottle of champagne and a beer. Around me, people have gone back to their conversations and...yep. That's just a casual, garden-variety spanking happening over there.

Wow. Okay.

I risk a quick glance and turn back as BBG sets a full glass of champagne in front of me and moves to take the chair opposite.

"I'm truly sorry." He squeezes his temples before looking at me, head-on. "Let's start over. People here call me the General."

"Oh! That seems appropriate. I'm Sunny."

"I am bossy." He smiles, and it is...*whoa*. Uh-oh. Big, huge uh-oh. The man is handsome and dimpled, his smile bright and white. Between his almost-beard and the shadow of chest hair, the tailored midnight blue shirt and well-fitted pants, he's the perfect combination of groomed and rough around the edges. "Sunny suits you," he says.

Though I know it's meaningless, the compliment hits warm and solid in my center. "Thanks."

"What brings you to Off the Cuff tonight?"

"Curiosity." At his look, I go on. "I've spent a lot of time reading BDSM romance and how-tos and watching YouTube videos and other fun stuff, so you know."

"Figured you'd check it out IRL?" His smile becomes a grin. The man is way too gorgeous when he's not scowling. It's unsettling.

"Yeah."

"And? What are you into?"

"You want to read this?"

Though he accepts my list of desires, his eyes stay on me. "Why don't you tell me?"

I consider, barely registering as my hand moves to cradle my own throat.

He notices, though. His gaze lingers on that hand and moves up my jaw to my mouth.

"I like the idea of...letting go. No power, I guess? I wouldn't mind being made to do things." An embarrassed sound huffs from my mouth and lingers between us before rising up, lost to the room's happy hubbub.

A slow nod.

"But I don't want to be, like, actually hurt. If that makes sense? Anyway, I haven't seen too much of that here tonight." I can't help but glance over to where a series of light thwacks give way to a long, ragged moan.

When I look back at the General—or as he'll forever be known in my mind, Broody Bar Guy—he's watching me, if possible, even more sharply than before.

"So, you're a sub, not a masochist."

"Exactly. You get it!" Enthusiasm has me lightly smacking his arm and...holy biceps, that thing is solid. Warm. That tiny bit of contact makes my breath come out in hot little bursts. My vision's gone a little fuzzy at the edges. From a bicep. Clearly, it's been a while.

"I want your hands flat on the table," he says, low and menacing. "Both of them."

My belly flip-flops, and before I've had time to consider his words, my traitorous hands obey.

"Here's the thing about a good sub, Sunny." He's close enough that I can hear every word with crisp clarity despite the ambient noise. The atmosphere's changed in the last few minutes, and I can't tell if it's just me—us—or the entire place that's sunk into this deep, sensual torpor.

Is that the sound of flesh smacking naked flesh now, instead of vinyl? Are people taking off clothes? I don't know. And no way am I bursting this bubble of ours to look.

"A good sub listens and learns." His hands are busy, rolling those sleeves a little higher, tighter, with perfect precision, giving me even more of those pornographically sexy forearms. "But so does..." Another fold. More of that strong right arm, lightly flexing muscles, a scattering of dark hair. "A good Dom."

I glance up at his face, which is calm, serious. His rugged features right in a way that twists up my insides and makes me want to say something a young, innocent version of me might have said. *Please, please, please like me as much as I like you.*

Which I don't, obviously. I just met the man. And he said himself that he's not in the market for a sub. He probably has one already. Lots, in fact. A sub for every day of the week. Two on weekends and holidays.

"First of all, a good Dom will *ask* if you want to scene. Unless it's part of a preestablished agreement, he'll never tell you. Got it?"

I nod, my head apparently the only functioning part of my body at this point. The rest is too busy sending hot, syrupy warmth to my nether regions.

"When playing, unless you're gagged, or your mouth is... otherwise engaged, make sure you say everything out loud, okay?"

My insides rearrange themselves at the idea of exactly what's got my mouth in that scenario. Then my imagination moves on to serve up a rousing game of Dom/sub charades in which, bound and gagged, I struggle to express all the sexy things using just my eyebrows and some well-placed hip thrusts.

I suppress the giggle trying to work its way out. Pretty sure a guy who calls himself the General would not appreciate it if I laughed mid–Kink 101 lesson.

But he obviously notices and, instead of getting bent out of shape, appears to take it in stride.

"Look, Sunny. We Doms need as much communication help as we can get," he says, which I don't believe for a second. This guy doesn't need help. I'll bet he can communicate his wants with a single eyebrow. The flick of a lash.

"So..." He leans in, and though I want to look at what his hands are doing, I keep all of my attention focused on his dark eyes, his mouth, and then the dimples playing hide-and-seek in his stubble. "Do you want to see what it's like, Sunny?"

CHAPTER FOUR

Grant

"Yeah," she whispers. And again, louder. "Yes. Yes, I'd like that."

It's been a while since I met someone as unabashedly enthusiastic as Sunny.

I know I should stop.

But look at her, all round and soft, plump and gorgeous. She's pure excitement without a hint of pretense. Sitting in the glow of all this curiosity, I almost feel like my teenage self when I got off on the idea of tying June Cristano—my football coach's college-age daughter—to my bed and making her wait and wait and wait for that orgasm. She'd be writhing by the end of the fantasy. And I'd have made myself come about five times.

I knew, even then, that my soul was a little twistier than others'.

Sunny's eyes are all pupil, her pulse visibly racing in the hollow of her throat, her freckles almost entirely camouflaged by the beautiful bright pink flooding her cheeks.

Cracking my knuckles, I drag myself back to the safety of protocol. "You know the club safe word?"

"Oh. Oh, yes. I do." She smiles, the expression so bright and pretty it tweaks something in my chest. I shouldn't do this. Not tonight. Not with this brand-spanking newbie who might not get that a scene is just a scene. "Red. Yellow if I need to slow down."

"Good."

"You gonna ask me my limits?" she asks, her eagerness drawing a laugh from deep inside me.

"This *is* your first time, right?"

A nod.

"How about we take it real easy, hm?"

"Yep. Yep, okay."

"You still want me to read this?"

"Oh. Um. Sure."

As I go over her wants, and don't wants, and everything in between, my dick goes warm and heavy. Everything she's checked is right up my alley. Restraints, spanking, light flogging, orgasm control. The list goes on. I reach the last page, put it down, and take a moment to gather myself. When I speak again, my voice is rougher. A little raw from excitement.

"Okay. Your list is...good."

I have to shove back the satisfaction I feel when she smiles, her ass wiggling with pleasure. Praise kink? Check.

"Showing me the list doesn't mean you are asking me to do those things. Okay? I'll get your consent every step of the way." That is Kinkster Rule #1, whether you're topping or bottoming. It should be etched in goddamn stone. Her palms are still face down on the table. "Can I touch your hands, Sunny?"

"Oh. Sure."

Gently, I cover her hands with mine, no pressure, no weight. Just heat and presence. I watch the way her expression changes. Her eyes are huge as they drink everything in, and for a split second, I want to see this—to live it—from her perspective. Not to be dominated but to get a hit of that first-timer eagerness.

The song ends. Behind me, Lucas cracks his whip and yells at the Doms to change tables. I ignore him, ignore whoever walks up with the intention of taking my place, and focus on Sunny.

"These." I put the slightest bit of pressure on her hands. "Stay here. Got it?"

Her *yes* is breathy.

I stand, grab my chair, and set it down behind hers, taking in the round curve of her shoulders, the way her chest swells out of the neckline of a dress that's likely meant to be sexy but comes off more sweet than anything. It's black and shimmery and printed with what looks an awful lot like spiderwebs. So damn cute.

"This is pretty." I flick the strap where it hugs her shoulder, careful not to touch her skin.

"Thank you."

"Spooky."

She snorts and cranes her neck to roll her eyes at me. "I don't have a lot of fetishwear in my closet."

"I like how the top's almost a corset."

"Right? I was looking for something a little corset-like, but at the same time, I came alone tonight and didn't really want to walk around Carytown with, like, I don't know, my boobs out in shiny, black…"

"Rubber?" I brush her auburn hair over one shoulder and watch goose bumps trail in its wake.

"Exactly. Rubber." The shudder she gives is theatrical. Not into rubber, I note. Fair enough.

I straddle my chair, lean forward, and let myself breathe her in, not quite touching the nape of her neck but giving my body heat a chance to meet hers somewhere in the ether between us.

Finally, after inhaling my fill, I put my lips close to her earlobe. "Can I touch your shoulders, Sunny?"

"Okay."

"Okay, yes, or okay, I don't really want that, but I'm agreeing because I think I should?"

"Yes. Do it. Whatever it is, I'm into it."

"Do not give blanket consent like that. Ever."

"Ugh. Oh my god, fine. I'm saying yes, Professor Kinkmeister," she grumps, a smile in her voice. "Please, please, for the love of all that is kinky, touch my shoulders."

Oh great. She's a brat. Sweet, eager, and submissive, with an attitude. Somebody's going to have their hands full with this one.

Smirking now, I stroke her satiny skin. "Arms? Back? Neck?"

"Yes, yes, yes."

She shivers as my knuckles skate over the places I've just mentioned, then down her arms until my hands are circling her wrists like shackles. Or rope. Measuring the circumference of her frame against mine. She's thick in places—her ass and her belly, the tops of her arms, those lush tits that threaten to spill over the neckline of her dress. Her wrists, though, are as delicate as her neck. I like that contrast. Big versus little.

I go back to her shoulders and rub them again, putting a little more pressure into the contact this time, offering her the strength of my fingers and taking a little of the tension she's clearly got stored right...there.

As I dig my thumbs into that tender spot beneath her shoulder blades, she moans and drops her head forward, and without fully intending to, I lean in and start whispering in her ear. "Look at what a good girl you are, all warm and relaxed like this. You always moan when you get touched? Hm?"

She shakes her head and then, appearing to remember herself, says, "No. No, I never moan."

"It's a beautiful sound. Goddamn siren's song." I shift my hold and press in again, working out a knot she's probably been sporting forever. "Shit, you're tight. Right…" I press gently but firmly. "Here."

Her whimpers are absolute music to my ears.

"Lean back," I tell her. "I need to see your face."

"Okay," she manages as I nudge her head to rest against my shoulder. Her expression's relaxed and easy until I push that magic knot again, sending her expression into that indescribable limbo between ecstasy and agony.

The kinkster's sweet spot.

"You gorgeous little thing. Look at you, all blissed out." I run my thumbs up, soaking in the way she shudders and grunts every time I hit something good or tight or too tense to handle. "I'm gonna work out every single one of these kinks, you got that?"

With a smile, she shifts, leans forward again, and spasms.

"Sunny, are you hurt? Was it too much pressure, or—"

"No! No, I'm good." Shaking again, she nods and leans back, tears leaking from her eyes. "It's just…When I decided to try out my first kink club tonight to work a few things out, I had no idea just how literal it would be."

"Literal?"

"You said…you said you were gonna work out…" She's giggling now, definitely. Not crying, which is a relief. "You said you'd work out my *kinks*, and I feel…" Another yip of a laugh has me staring down into her face. "I feel like you're doing a bang-up job."

Yep. One hundred percent brat. "Yeah?" Suppressing a smile, I press that hot spot of hers again and watch her groan and sink back with a gasp. "Come on. Let's get you relaxed, sweet girl. Tell me what you think about, Sunny, when you come home from work and slip into a hot bath."

"I don't have a bathtub."

I make an irritated noise.

"Yeah. I miss baths." She turns and stretches when I hit a tough area on the side of her neck. "Just a crappy little shower."

"All right, then. What do you think about in the *shower*?"

"Um... You mean, like this morning?"

"Sure."

"Okay, well, um..." The way her eyes go glassy tells me she's going deep in search of her deepest, most secret fantasy.

I watch my hands work the muscles and tendons of her back, massaging up and down, listening for reactions, concentrating on those needy little sore spots and the exquisite way her breath catches every time I hit one. In my mind, I see her deep in a steaming hot bath, her hands playing with those big breasts, sliding over her soft belly and down, down, hidden by the bubbles.

"Sooooo, I've been having this internal debate."

"Go on." Her skin is so smooth under mine, her body responsive. She'd be all slick in that water, all plush and warm, her plump curves so inviting that I'd have to shuck off my pants and slide in behind her.

"Lion or octopus?"

Convinced I misheard, I stop, hands suspended mid-rub. "What?"

"I can't decide. What do you think?"

My brain feeds me a million bizarre images, each of which I immediately shut down. "About...?"

"It's been driving me nuts. So, like, Pepe, my cat. I'm obsessed with finding this year's Halloween costume. He's been an angry Frenchman twice now, and I really think we need a change. What's your vote? Irate lion or pissed-off octopus?"

"That's...that's..."

My mouth opens and closes a couple of times. Nothing comes out.

"So he'll probably never speak to me again if I put him in the octopus, 'cause it's like absurd."

"*Speak* to you?"

"But the lion's been done. A lot. Then again, he doesn't go out, so who cares, right? It's just for him and me and the trick-or-treaters, which I won't get because I live in a backyard."

"Quite the choice. Could you—"

"You're right. I'm getting both. Intermission costume change." She twists back to look at me and sets her hand over where mine is sitting lightly on her shoulder. "Thank you."

My jaw muscle involuntarily flexes. "I didn't do anything."

"You did, and I appreciate it."

I reach down to her back again, push that tender spot, and watch her go limp. Much better. Clearing my throat, I shove back my annoyance at having been misunderstood and carry on. "Okay. Obviously, I wasn't clear enough. Allow me to set the scene. After work. You come home, tired out. You need candles. No lights on. Music."

"Oh, sure. Right. I get it. You wanted my sexy thoughts. Duh. Not cat costume thoughts. Sorry."

"No. It's my responsibility, as a Dom, to express myself clearly."

"All right, well. Fantasy. I can do this. Candles and music: check. I'd have to take a shower. Oh, maybe a glass of wine, right?"

"Good. That's good."

"What else?" she asks, the eagerness in her voice hitting me low in the belly. Much better. "What else should I do?"

What else?

There it is. That question, more than anything, flips the mysterious little switch that's been lodged hidden inside me for too long. *What else?*

"You touch yourself." My voice is gritty now, almost raw. "You slide your fingers over your belly to that hot, slick spot between your legs."

"Oh. Okay. Yep. That works."

"In the bath or shower. In bed. On the sofa. Let your hands roam, let them make you feel good, like I'm doing now."

"Yes, Mast..." Breathing hard, Sunny pauses and cranes her neck to look over her shoulder at me. "What do I call you?"

"What would you like to call me, sweet girl?"

"I don't know." Her laugh is a sugary delight, her light Richmond accent like music. "Are you a Daddy type? You kind of seem like it, all bossy and nurturing or whatever."

I half shrug. She's not wrong. I've never been into Daddy Dom/little girl play, but I get parts of the role, no problem. "I've got some caregiver instincts, for sure."

"Big Daddy Boss Ma-an," she says, giving the last word two syllables.

"Cute. But no." My hand hovers over her head. "I want to touch your hair. Not too hard."

"You can."

My fingers wind into those thick red curls and tighten infinitesimally. "This okay?"

"Yeah." Tilting her head, she tests my hold. "Oh, definitely."

My fist tightens, drawing a gasp from her pink lips as I pull her back against my shoulder again and look down into those astonishingly bright eyes. "You can call me *Sir*."

"Sir." She stiffens, a soldier going unconsciously to attention. "Oh, that's really good."

Dammit. It's there. Here. In me, her, between us. That Dom/sub chemistry that makes a scene flow, makes playing a pleasure instead of hard work.

Makes it even, sometimes, beautiful.

I can definitely work with this.

That is to say, I could. If I were actually in the market for a sub.

CHAPTER FIVE
Rae

This, this, this.

This is what I came here for. Exactly this. Well, no, not *exactly*. Before tonight, I'd pictured this a dark, sleazy nightclub complete with heavily thumping bass and obscenely writhing bodies. I'd imagined a masked Dom dragging me into a corner, pressing me against a wall, and having his way with me.

Now that I'm here, I get that what I'd envisioned was pure fantasy. Impossible, unreal, and, in the end, completely unsafe. I'd have turned right around and walked out if the place had been skeezy and some dude had tried to *make* me do anything, much less have random, unprotected sex against the wall.

This is so much better. Not once did I dare daydream a fraction of this excitement.

I whimper at the feel of the General's breath against the side of my face.

"Had enough?"

"No way," I whisper.

"What's that?"

"Sir, I mean. No, sir. No. I want more."

"Where do you feel it? The want?"

"I...I don't know." In my brain? Mostly. Other places too, I guess.

"Show me."

Does he...? Does he want me to take off my clothes? Touch myself? I can't tell, and maybe that's what he intends. He's destabilizing me so that up is down, and doing literally nothing while he massages my back has turned me on more than any single sexual act of my life. This man—this erogenous zone wizard—should give lessons. He should become a cult leader. Or at least an influencer. Hell, if the man did a TED Talk, he'd get billions of views.

"In my lungs." I finally eke out an answer. Honestly, I feel what he's doing to me everywhere.

From where he's now sitting at my side, I watch his eyes flick toward the quick rise and fall of my chest. "I see that." The tiniest curve pulls at his lips. "Where else, Sunny?"

"My...um breasts. Nipples?"

Another brief look, down and back up to my face. "Good." He shifts, the movement tilting my face into his neck, where the spice of his cologne is layered with skin, musk, and the tiniest hint of sweat. It's a pure shot of aphrodisiac, whooshing straight to my core.

"Now touch them."

I stop moving, my breath caught in my throat like a trapped bird.

People are seated at tables a few feet on either side of us, but they might as well be miles away for all the attention I pay them. They're the hum of voices in the background, the occasional scrape of a chair. Can they tell just by looking at us how seismic this feels?

"Go on. Take those hot little hands and put them on those tight, aching nipples."

"Uh…uh…" My hands, which I suddenly realize have been squeezing the velour edges of my seat cushion, hover in the air for a moment, above my body, seesawing between the mortification of following this stranger's order with an audience versus the chance of pleasure glimmering just over that horizon.

Do I *do* the bananas thing? Do I?

"*Now*, Sunny. You touch them now. It's an order. You wanted this, right?" Oh, there's something different in his voice. A challenge that's both playful and risqué. He's the devil, armed with nothing more than the ammunition I gave him myself.

Coerce me. Make me do the bad thing.

This, this, this. It's here in full force now, this feeling of right from wrongness, the hot, vivid spotlight shining deep into my inner workings, lighting up all the shadows I've spent a lifetime working to hide.

"You better do it, Sunny."

Oh my goodness. My insides go liquid.

"You listen, you obey, you'll get exactly what you came for. If you defy me…"

What? What happens then? Please, please, please, please tell me!

I guess I won't be finding out, what with how my fingers have a mind of their own and set to tweaking my nipples through my dress, plucking at them and twisting until there's enough pain to make me gasp.

"That's it. Good girl." *Good girl?* My stomach does a little dance. Level unlocked and mastered in one fell swoop. I am a good girl. I really, really am.

Seriously, what is it about his voice? So matter-of-fact as he watches me play with myself through my clothes. He's the serious professor, the concerned doctor. He's all the dirty, dirty, dirty things I've only ever let myself dwell on in the farthest reaches of my imagination.

With masterful precision, he kneads that knot in my back again. My mouth drops open on an embarrassingly loud moan.

"There it is. That's the spot, huh? Goddamn, that looks good." I go half-limp at what sounded like praise, though I've got no earthly idea what for. For groaning while he rubs me? Most people don't find my groaning all that sexy. I groan at the gym. Nobody calls me a good girl for that.

"Did I say you could stop?"

I startle when I realize he's waiting for my reply. "Uh. No. No, sir. I was just…"

"Just what?"

"Nothing." I straighten in my seat, concentrating hard on the here and now.

"No. Truly. Communication is essential." His heat backs off a bit. "Communicate. Please. What were you just doing?"

"Well." I swallow, knowing this is probably not what he means by communicate, but then again…who am I to guess, right? "I was thinking about working out. And then the gym. And then gym class and, from there, I started wondering if they still let kids play dodgeball."

His hands drop from my back. "Dodgeball?"

"You know. In school?" I crane toward him as I explain. "Such a violent game for kids to play, right?" His face has morphed from its original stern expression to something teetering between annoyed and utterly baffled. "Sorry," I say, snapping my mouth shut and slapping my hands back up to my chest like I've been caught shirking my responsibilities instead of doing the important work of feeling myself up.

After a brief pause, he picks up again where he left off. I go as limp as a rag doll the moment his magic fingers hit my back.

"You're easily distracted."

"There's a lot to think about."

"Not here, there isn't. Now keep touching yourself, Sunny. *Or else.*" The threat fills the narrow space between his mouth and my ear, and in a flash, everything disappears but the feel of this moment.

Oh, okay. Yeah. That does it.

"Or else what?" Now that he's shown me this new mystery door, all I want to do is open it. "Sir?" I gasp, shutting my eyes against all the possibilities.

Will he make me do other things? Dirty things? Sexy things? Will he use those big, rough hands on my skin? Spank me the way that person's getting spanked in the corner? What if he made me go down on him in front of this crowd?

The real me wouldn't stand for that. Ever.

A liquid pulse, deep in my core, proves me a liar.

Okay, fine. Outside the club walls, I'd prefer to blend into the background and let someone else have the limelight. Not to mention the whole part where I don't let men order me around in my real life. Or in any way diminish me. No more Brendans making me feel small and silly.

This me, though? Someday, when I've gotten past the initial weirdness of being here? I could maybe see myself being *really* into spanking—public or not.

"If you defy me, sweet girl, you get punished." His voice is close and low, so quiet I can barely hear him.

Wow. None of what he's doing is like the Dom I'd pictured in my head. It's better, so much better. This guy doesn't yell. He doesn't have to. Why raise your voice when a skin-licking whisper does the trick?

Punished.

The word sends a fresh wave of frenzied need through my veins, along with a dozen freeze-frame flashes of possibility. Pain, sex, voyeurism. I didn't want half those things coming in here, but now? I'd take them all. Anything. All of it. Make it rough. Make it last.

He doesn't go that way, obviously. That route is too easy for the man who made massage sexy again. I see now, with every fresh unveiling of his Machiavellian plans, that a real Dom doesn't have to yell or hurt or *make* his sub do a damn thing. A real Dom suggests.

And a sub? A real sub?

Well, based on the current state of my underwear, I'm guessing a real sub begs for whatever her Dom will give her. And then begs for more.

"What's the punishment?" I ask.

"Depends. I could stop."

"No! No, definitely not that."

His eyes crinkle into what could almost be a smile. "Punishments would typically be negotiated before a scene."

"Like spanking? Or... flogging or something?"

He's outright grinning now. "Possibly."

"Wow. Okay. But I mean, I won't defy you," I spit out in a pathetically rushed whisper. "I wouldn't do that."

"Good girl." A slight shifting of my weight in his arms, a gentle stroke on my cheek, just the back of his finger, barely touching, and I'm squirming in my seat. "You like the idea, though."

"I don't... I don't... know. No. I... Yes. Yes, I do." My eyes strain toward him as a huff of laughter escapes me. "Honestly, I'm a mess."

"You're a beautiful mess, Sunny. Gorgeous."

With the next scary flip-flop of my stomach, I get it. All of it. This man's power isn't about being a bully. It's more subtle than that. He's a freaking hypnotist. He gets you with kindness, with care. The compliments, the control, the suggestions...all of it has turned me into a baser version of myself. A little needy, very excited, and, if I'm to believe this man, beautiful.

Here's the thing. I've been complimented before, even told I was pretty, but I never quite believed it the way I do in this moment. This guy wouldn't lie. Why should he? And, even if he were a master at it, he couldn't fake the quick thump of his heart against my ear or the shakiness of his breathing. He's as excited by this exchange as I am.

It feels amazing.

I've just opened my mouth to tell him so when the whip cracks behind me. My shoulders tense up, the General curses under his breath, and the murmur of conversation around us shifts gears.

"That's it for tonight, folks!" Tank's jovial bass breaks through the sexy, warm little bubble in which I was happily basking. "Off the Cuff's first monthly speed-dating night is done!"

And just like that, I fall back to earth with a thump.

CHAPTER SIX

Grant

This was a terrible idea.

It's one thing to play with experienced subs, but fresh new kinksters like Sunny need lots and lots of attention.

And I'm absolutely not in a position to give that to anyone right now. Especially the kind that involves more than one session and hours of gentle aftercare. A bath, more back rubs, candles. Gentle punishment and sweet coercion.

"All done," I say in a much louder voice than intended.

A few people glance at us before looking quickly back to where Lucas is reiterating the dungeon's two-drink maximum rule, along with the club's motto of risk-aware consensual kink, otherwise known as RACK.

"Alrighty then. Yep. Thanks." She's up and backing away in the direction of the door before it occurs to me that she's trying to leave without aftercare. "That was great. I guess I'll see you around. Bye!"

"Hey. Wait a minute." I snag her BDSM checklist and move to intercept her. Just because I don't have time to take on a new sub doesn't mean I won't provide her with adequate aftercare. We're not done. "Don't go. After a scene, we need to—"

"Oh, I'm good." She snags the sheaf of papers from my hand. "Thank you." Her smile is crisp and quick and the complete antithesis of the slow, sensual way she opened up to me just a minute ago. I don't like it.

"Listen, you wanted to know how a scene goes. This is how it goes. Aftercare's part of doing a scene. You can't just take off like—"

"I'm *fine*." Another of those too-sharp smiles. "Oh, I mean, I loved it. It was really great." Her lips turn down a little at the edges, taking her smile from fake to downright condescending, which makes no sense at all. Is she patronizing me? "You are *really* good at that, sir. Great job. I mean it." With a double thumbs-up, she takes off for the door.

I follow her. "Hey."

"What's up?" she says over her shoulder.

"You need to listen to me. I know about this stuff."

She stops with a sigh and looks up at me, her once-sultry blue eyes clear. "Oh, I get that. I just need to get home. I've got things—people—waiting for me." Then she pats my arm and says, "I'll do aftercare there. That's okay, right?"

"Aftercare at home," I mumble.

"Exactly! Aftercare at my place." Her nod tells me I got it in one. It's the kind of nod a kindergarten teacher might give a kid who needs extra positive reinforcement. "Have a wonderful night!" And then, to really drive her point home, she makes a little gun with her hand and winks as she shoots it at me, saying, "You rock!" like I've just earned my first star in class, and she's so very proud of me.

There's not much I can do but watch as she bustles out the door, leaving me standing in the middle of the growing crowd like a moss-gathering stone in a river.

"I do believe you've found yourself a new sub. She leave behind a shoe?" Lucas walks up, wearing one of his evil grins.

"A shoe?"

"Like Cinder...Oh, never mind. That looked like fun."

I ignore the urge to shoulder check him and say, "Absolutely not. No new subs for me."

"But you like her."

"She's fine." A rogue muscle flexes in my jaw. It's been doing that a lot lately, what with the renovations upstairs and my neighbor's troubles and the endless phone calls from my mother, inviting me to attend yet another wedding, bookending a marriage that's bound to end in disaster. What number is this? Ten? Twelve?

Holy shit. Could this be her thirteenth?

Twelve botched marriages and she's still trying. Got to give it to her. The woman has staying power. Or, I guess, trying power. Sadly, no matter what my extremely driven, intelligent mother says, when it comes to relationships, she is genetically inclined to fail. It's written into her goddamn DNA, as surely as it is in mine. Except, unlike my literal genius dentist mother, I was smart enough to figure out the pattern after a single mistake instead of a baker's dozen.

Thinking of my mother is what does the trick. Suddenly, all my tension eases. I go perfectly calm, as if this whole blip never took place.

Because it didn't. Or, at least, what happened didn't mean a thing. I can handle a new sub for a night, but, as I told Sunny from the start, I am absolutely not in the market for anything lasting. And that's a permanent condition.

As an experienced Dom, I may not like when a woman refuses aftercare, but once she leaves of her own volition, it is no longer my problem.

"Fine? Just fine?" Lucas's disbelief rubs me the wrong way. "Bet you anything she'll be back. 'Cause that little scene seemed like a hell of a lot more than just *fine*."

"Yeah? Well, good." I turn to look across the club floor at where members are gathering in groups, some already playing, others planning a session or just hanging out the way people are doing all over the city at this hour. "I hope she does come back. I'm sure she'll make some Dom very, very happy." I give him a bland smile.

"Sure, bud. Whatever you say." Lucas leans in and gives me a long look of concern. "You're tired as hell. Been burning the candle at both ends, man. Why don't you head on home? We got it covered here. Go and get some rest. Give yourself a minute to come down." Giving my upper arm a solid thud, he takes off into the crowd, his head a foot above everyone else's, grinning like a fool.

CHAPTER SEVEN

Rae

I GET OUT, GRAB my stuff from a busy, smiling Daff, and race up the club's stairs like I'm being chased by a pack of rabid dogs, quietly mouthing the lyrics to "Guns and Ships" from *Hamilton* the way I do whenever I move quickly.

I had to get out of there, right that minute. It was all too much. Too intense, too real, and then the speed-dating thing ended, and I snapped out of it and understood that none of it was real at all. It was pure fantasy, and I'd fallen face-first into the deep end. The scene finished, and I was standing there looking at that guy, that stranger, who'd barely touched me and somehow made me feel so much more than I'd ever felt with Brendan or anyone before him, and suddenly, I was drowning.

"Have a good time?" Harlow asks as I burst out onto the brick sidewalk and suck in my first breath of crisp, early-fall air.

I blink at the lights and the traffic and all the ordinary, everyday things that oddly didn't magically melt down while I was downstairs getting my whole world blown wide open. "Yeah." The truth rises up like a fresh sunrise. I did it. I went to a BDSM club, and I did the Dom/sub thing. "It was amazing."

"Guess you're one of us, then, huh? That mean you'll be comin' back?"

I hesitate, unsure if it's a good or terrible idea to regularly partake in something so absolutely cataclysmic. "I don't know."

"No?"

"It was a lot." Understatement of the freaking century.

"You okay?" She steps closer. "Sure you don't want to stick around for a while? Maybe wind down? Just hang out and chill?"

"I need to go."

"Safe to get home?"

"Yep. Parked over there."

"That's right. The Honda." She snorts. "You sat there for like ten minutes before getting out."

"Come on. Give a shy girl a break."

"Shy? More like scared shitless." Smirking, Harlow watches a group of people approach, dressed in club wear and carrying sports bags and rolling suitcases, no doubt full of BDSM and fetish gear. "Next time, instead of lurking all night, you can hang with me until you're ready to go in."

"Next time I'll walk right in." If there is a next time. Do I want a next time? "But hanging out sounds fun too. Thanks."

She gives me a friendly elbow nudge and takes IDs from a couple of the people now crowding the entrance. "See you soon, then."

With a final wave, I head to my car, get in, lock my doors, and let out a long, uneven exhale before turning on my phone. Hands shaking, I text my best friend.

Me: Done.

Samantha: Whut?

Me: The club. The Dom/sub thing. I went.

Immediately, the phone rings. I start the engine, pull out into the late-night Richmond, Virginia, traffic, and accept the call.

"You *skank*, how could you?" Samantha's not happy. She takes her role as my best friend very seriously. More seriously, actually, than her role as Sugar's coms director, which is frankly too bad.

"I needed to do it on my own." Not to mention, Sam's been MIA recently.

"Without even warning me? Who'd you use as backup? Your dad?"

"No!" Dad's liberal and all, but no. "Absolutely not."

"What if they'd been serial killers? Or, like, truly bad people? What if they'd chained you up and had their way with you or tortured you with…? What's your worst thing?" She gasps. "What if they glued your eyes open and forced you to watch the non-equity tour of *Mean Girls*? Or, oh, oh, blackhead-removal videos. For hours."

As always, I gag at the thought of another person's pores up close and personal. "Both of those are terrible."

"Sorry."

"No, you're not. You love the yucky skin stuff."

"Yes, but you hate it. Weird, since you're the masochist. I'm just a simple girl who enjoys a good pop of—"

I barely contain another dry heave. "I'm not a masochist. I told you, I'm a submissive. A bottom. I don't want to be hurt or treated badly or made to watch anything. I want someone to, like…" Rub my back and call me beautiful. "Do things to me," I end on an embarrassed half whisper.

"I could boss you around if you—"

"Ew. Stop it."

"So, how did it pan out? You meet the Dom of your dreams? Did he put a collar on it? Throw you over his leather-clad shoulder and drag you back to his lair?"

"Clearly not, if I'm calling you."

"Yeah, why are you calling? Shouldn't you be getting it on right now?"

I go quiet, the only sound the click of the turn signal as I pull up to my place.

"You didn't even go in, did you? Bet you did a walk-by and chickened out. Am I right?"

"I went in." I look around to make sure the street's empty before getting out of the car and rushing around the house to the converted garage that contains my entire life.

"Selfie or it didn't happen."

As usual, Samantha manages to put a smile on my face. "They don't let you bring your phone inside."

"All right. Hickey or it didn't happen. Or, like, I don't know, lash marks or something."

I laugh outright now, which isn't easy to do quietly as I squint, trying to locate the lock. "It happened."

"Whaaaaaaaaaaaaaaaat exactly happened? Come on, spill!"

"I mean, nothing happened. But I went." I don't even know why I bother prevaricating. She'll get it all out of me eventually.

"So, when can we go? I want to see it. I want the full HD kink experience."

"I don't think I'm going back."

Quiet on the other end. The only sound is the jingle of my keys.

"You home?"

"Yep."

With a deep, relieved sigh, I lock the door behind me and turn on a light, kick off my shoes, and head to my compact kitchenette to wash my hands, taking care not to trip on a meowing Pepe as I go.

"Is that my boy?" asks Sam, who's known—and loved—my cat since the day she went with me to the SPCA and helped me pick out the feline most likely to eat his person before the body goes cold. Pepe's got the eyes of a stone-cold killer and the body of a gelatin pillow. I love him more than anything in the world. "Geez, he's loud."

"I know," I say, cooing as I bend and scratch him behind the ears before filling his food bowl to the brim.

Everyone thinks I'm ridiculous for moving into this place after the split with Brendan, but I don't hate it, at all. Yes, it's about the size of my bedroom growing up, but it's mine. Not Dad's house, where my sisters tried to pressure me to move, more I suspect to keep an eye on him than anything. Not the creepy storage room at Samantha's shared house.

Mine. One space for just me and my babies.

I pick up baby number one, Pepe, who puts up as much resistance as a bowl of slime, and turn to my other babies: book nooks.

What started as a way to blow off steam during lockdown has become a full-on obsession. Despite it being a little wonky, I'm still proud of the very first one I built from scratch. It's a scene from the old Sugar headquarters. Since then, I've done more than two dozen, including a Paris bookshop, a sweet little greenhouse, and a cozy winter cabin, complete with a mountain man, his dog, and Pepe snoring in front of the fire.

Brendan hated my book nooks. Sam thinks he was jealous of all the time I spent on something that wasn't him. My sisters are convinced it's because I was good at something. And he wasn't. What matters, though, is the deep satisfaction I feel as I sit at my workstation now, settle my purring fur ball on my lap, and jump back into the process of putting my real-world problems into itty-bitty bookshelf boxes. Right where I can keep an eye on them.

"What are you working on tonight?" Samantha asks, knowing that I can't go to bed without spending time with my projects. They're my late-night darlings. My actual nightlife.

"My first commission."

"Right. You mean the one you're doing for Hannah," she intones with obvious skepticism.

"Just 'cause it's for my sister doesn't mean it's not a commission."

"That and the part where you're not getting paid," she says around the Blow Pop she's obviously just stuck in her mouth. "Let me see."

I hit the camera button and give her a wide-angle view of the whole piece.

"Oh my god. It's Romero's!"

"You got it!"

"Closer. I can't see anything."

I show her the checkered tablecloths and the tiny candles in bottles and move up to the signed black-and-white photos on the walls. "What do you think? Is it okay?"

"Holy shit, Rae. That looks exactly like Otty." She gasps. "Is this the soda balls incident?"

"Yep." I step back and stare hard at my take on the incident that lost our youngest sister, Otty, her very first job, when she spilled an entire pitcher of iced cola in a diner's lap.

"You need to start selling them."

I don't bother arguing. I've heard it before.

"I'm serious, Rae. You're really good at this."

She can't see my shrug, but she knows me well enough to say, "At least have Hannah pay for supplies. That husband of hers makes money."

"I will."

"Why must you turn your she shed into a house of lies?"

A noncommittal hum is all the answer I give her as I sink into the minute details of creating worlds where everything is fine. Just fine.

"The second someone finds out at work, you'll start getting requests out the ass."

"I'm not telling anyone at work." I glance back at the shelves, where probably two-thirds of the book nooks immortalize infamous scenes from work, including such classics as Pajama Party Friday (highly inappropriate) and Bring Your Pets to Work Day (an epic disaster). "They'd want to see my work and...that wouldn't go over well."

"Do Klaus as a marauding Viking. I'll pay you."

"With what? Blow Pops?"

She snorts. "You start a TikTok yet? You could totally monetize this."

"Oh my god, Sam. Seriously? Let it go."

"I'm not the only one who thinks they're the greatest thing ever. You'd make a killing if you'd just—"

"Can we please talk about something else?"

Another smack of her lips. "Okay. So, why are we not going back to the sex dungeon?"

A message pops up on my screen.

I lean forward and read. My Vitals Tracking alert: Patient heart rate elevated.

"Crap, Dad's heart rate's up again."

"Don't avoid the question. What happened at the club? Do we need to report someone or—?"

"No. No, when I said it was good, I was not kidding. At all." Distracted now, I scroll over to Dad's heart monitoring app and click the heart rate icon. This has been happening a lot lately. "The thing is, the one Dom I'd be into playing with again is apparently taken. So..."

"Bummer."

"Total bummer."

"Too bad you're not the kind of evil wench who'd go back there in twenty-inch heels and transparent booty shorts or something and steal him away."

I pause, my head tilted as I picture that. "Transparent? You mean fishnet or—"

"I was thinking more like a medium-transparency vellum, but plastic wrap could—"

"Ew." I squint. Dad's heart rate's okay, although it's definitely a little elevated for this hour. This is TV time.

Samantha slurps at her lollipop and hums while she, too, lets the image sink in. "Oh, yeah. I see it now. Nothing transparent, then. You'll have to do pasties and one of those—"

"I should call to check in on Dad."

"Wait. Seriously? Now? You haven't even gotten to the good stuff. Can't one of your sisters deal for once?"

I snort. "What, Hannah? No. Between the kids and—"

"The loser husband."

"Come on. Don't say that."

"We all know it's true. I'm just not Jensen enough that I get to say it out loud."

"You're Jensen-adjacent."

"Exactly." She makes a popping sound with her mouth, so familiar I can smell the artificial watermelon as if she were here beside me. "I tell it like it is. What about Otty?"

"What about her?"

"Why don't you ask her to pick her ass up and check on your dad at the crack of midnight, instead of you doing it? What else could she possibly have going on?"

"Well, it is Friday."

Samantha lets out a low, evil, lollipop-muffled laugh that says everything there is to say about my youngest sister without uttering a single word. Otty, we both know, is out getting her heart broken. Again.

"Oh, crap. Got to go."

"Wait. Why?"

"Think you're the only one who's got hot-and-heavy playdates, Rae?"

"Playdates? Hey, who are you—?"

"That was the doorbell. Better run!"

"Who is it?" I yell, though she's already ended the call.

When did Sam start having secret midnight sex dates? I mean, the midnight-sex-dates thing is typical Sam, but the secrecy sure isn't. I know Sam better than anyone on this planet. And that's saying a lot, given how close-knit my family is.

I don't like that she hasn't told me about this new person, whoever they are. Then again, I went to the club without telling her.

But Sam and I have been friends forever. She knows me and my wackadoodle family to a *T.* She has opinions. About everything. So maybe I didn't tell her because I didn't want to have to overdiscuss why I want to be submissive in bed. I just wanted to do it.

If I'm being honest, Sam's been kind of pushy lately when it comes to my life decisions. Like the book-nook thing. If it were up to her, I'd quit my job, move to some island in the sun, and become an Etsy millionaire.

Do I occasionally fantasize about doing something other than HR for a living? Absolutely. Would it be nice to make money doing something creative? Hell yeah. Do I wonder how it would feel to go somewhere or do something just for myself?

Well, yes. And that's exactly why I went to that club tonight. One night. Just to see.

I don't need more than that anyway. I've got everything I

could possibly want here. A job, a family, and my very own she shed without Brendan negging everything from my romance novels and book nooks to the dinosaur-print dress I never got up the courage to wear while he was around.

Somehow, my ex being a jerk about my clothes reminds me of the General's compliments tonight, and then I start thinking about how it felt when he rubbed my back, picturing what might have happened if we'd had privacy, so when another alert comes through, I jump like a startled rabbit, nearly upsetting my entire work setup.

Crap. Dad's heart rate's gone up again.

I call him. When there's no response, I open the sisters' group chat and type out a message.

>Me: Anyone talk to Dad?

>Hannah: What? Why?

>Me: Heart rate alert.

>Hannah: Calling now.

>Me: I just tried. Can you go over?

>Hannah: Schaffer's not home yet.

Still at work at midnight on a Friday while his wife's home with a five-year-old and three-year-old twins? It's about time Schaffer and I had a chat.

>Me: Anything?

Hannah: No answer.

Me: Don't leave the kids. I'll take care of it.

Shaking a little as I picture Dad passed out on the bathroom floor or stuck in the shower, I send him a quick message and video call him again.

I'm about to hang up when he fumbles the phone on and puts it to his head, giving me a screen full of ear. "Rae? That you?"

"Dad? What's going on?" Relief pours through me. "You okay?"

"Yes. Yes, fine. Fine. Why are you calling so late?"

"I got another one of those alerts." *So late?* "It's not even midnight." After a pause, "This is a video call, Dad."

"Oh, oh, crap. Sorry." He holds the phone up in front of his face and squints into it with a broad Dad grin.

"What are you wearing?" I ask, staring at the screen as if my father's grown a set of horns or something. "Is that the Christmas robe?"

His quick downward glance looks almost sheepish, which makes no sense. "I thought I'd pull it out of semiretirement. Give it a little more air time. You know. Poor thing barely sees the light."

"Okay." What's happening here? What is this? There are some things, like Dad staying up to watch TV until 1:00 a.m., that we can always count on. They are as constant as the stars above or rush hour traffic or going on the New Year's Banana Hunt, which I realize isn't a tradition outside our family, but still. For us, it's a thing. Like clockwork, the Christmas robe comes out on Black Friday and gets sent back to the mothballs January 2. It's only September. It's several weeks until holiday robe season. "Are you okay, Dad? Do you need help?"

"Help?" Looking confused, he pushes his glasses up on his nose but doesn't otherwise react. "Why would I need help?"

In a whisper, I ask, "Is someone there?"

He startles and casts a quick glance over his shoulder. "Here? In our house? No. No one. No one at all. Not a soul."

"Are you being held up or something? Did you mention we've got nothing worth stealing?"

"I'm fine, Rae." After a pause, he tilts his head and squints at me. "What about you, sweetheart? You seem a little out of sorts. You need to come over this weekend for some musical theater karaoke or a sweet baby huggle? I can make hot chocolate, and you and Otty can do 'I Feel Pretty' and—"

Oh god, no. No huggles or chocolate or any other old-school Dad comforts. Especially not karaoke, which everyone knows I'm terrible at. I am the musical dud in a family of Broadway-worthy belters.

"So, you feel okay?" I ask.

"Right as rain."

"No excessive physical activity? Are you...jumping or something?"

"Nope! Not a thing. No jumping. Thanks, Beanie." He casts a glance to the side and then looks at me with a long sigh. "You don't have to take care of—"

"I know."

"You going out? What's that you got on? You look fancy." Leaning too close to the phone. "Are those spiderwebs?"

"Just a...a costume thing. I'm home now."

"You sure you're too busy this weekend? I've got the extra-special cocoa mix with the little freeze-dried marshmallows."

The special cocoa in our family is the opposite of what anyone else would consider gourmet. I realized sometime in my teens that it was all we could afford back when we were little, but like everything else, Dad somehow managed to make it shine.

Even now, looking at him in the Christmas robe, I see the frayed collar, the fading red and white stripes, and understand just how much of our upbringing was cobbled together from smoke and mirrors and pure, unadulterated love.

Stifling a sigh that's half adrenaline crash, half affection, I shake my head. "I've got to finish one of my book nooks."

"Let's see it."

Grinning, I turn the camera around and show him the mini restaurant scene.

He *oohs* and *aahs* until I tell him goodbye. He then opens his mouth as if about to say something, but then closes it. "You look lovely, sweetheart. Glad you're going out and having fun after…"

He doesn't finish his sentence, but he doesn't really have to. We both know he means I'm getting out and seeing people after Brendan. Unlike Hannah and Otty, who've unsubtly celebrated since the moment I ended things, Dad has, true to form, kept his thoughts to himself. Even now, see, he turns an incomplete sentence into a full thought without actually saying the awkward thing out loud. It's an art.

"Okay, Dad. Good night. I'll just—"

"I'll let you get back to—"

He hangs up on himself, leaving me staring at my reflection in the black screen.

After a second, I close my eyes and let myself remember just where I was an hour ago and exactly what I was doing.

No regrets. At all. And who knows, maybe I'll work up the courage to go back to Off the Cuff next weekend.

Yes, actually. That's just what I'll do.

CHAPTER EIGHT

Grant

I GET HOME, STILL thinking about the way my little sub took off into the night like a kinky Cinderella.

The abrupt ending to our scene doesn't sit well with me. I get pleasure from giving pleasure, and that didn't happen the way I'd have liked. Nothing irritates me more than sending off a play partner without a happy ending. Then there's the issue of aftercare. It wasn't a particularly intense scene, but it was her first play session. I would have liked to at least provide a check-in. A water. A seat. Time to get her emotions, adrenaline, and hormones in order.

I'm antsy as I trudge up my porch steps, trying to let it go, when every one of my dominant instincts tells me to finish what I started.

Which is why I pull out my phone and shoot a text off to Harlow.

Me: Could you please send my number to one of tonight's new subs? She took off quickly. I want to check up on her.

Harlow: 😈 You couldn't possibly mean the cute redhead, could you?

Shit. What am I doing? They'll never let me live it down if I show any interest at all in this woman. Which I'm not. This is about providing her with a safe experience.

> Me: Never mind. Forget I asked.
>
> Harlow: 😒 Sorry. Just got her number from Daff. I'm texting her.
>
> Me: Please don't.
>
> Harlow: Too late.
>
> Me: FFS
>
> Harlow: 😈

I stomp down the long hall to my kitchen, chuck my phone onto the island, and pull a beer from the fridge, so irritated that the bottle cap goes flying when I smack it off on the counter's edge. I spot the damn thing halfway under the butcher's block, bend to retrieve it, then bash my head when my phone vibrates with a new text.

Cursing, I stand. It's an unknown number.

> Sunny: Hi. Thanks for checking in. I had an amazing time tonight.
>
> Me: Good.
>
> Sunny: Thanks to you.
>
> Me: You get home safe?

Immediately, my mind spins up a cute little house in the suburbs. No. Maybe she's got an apartment. Hell, maybe she's in college? A dorm room? I hope not. Actually, that could be a good thing. I don't do college girls, so that would put an automatic stop to this.

> Sunny: Yep. Thanks. So, I was thinking I'd go back. To the club. Maybe next week.

I sink onto a stool and picture her sitting beside me. I'd make her hold on to the edges of her seat while I drag that dress up to reveal her panties. Lace. No, cotton. Pink or white or, fuck, with little flowers on them. I resist the urge to ask for confirmation and instead gather myself together, and type.

> Me: You should.

Just looking at those words makes me go hard. I shut my eyes and take another slug of beer, imagining how she'd taste. How she'd feel as she came against my tongue.

> Sunny: I will.

> Me: Good.

> Sunny: I'd love to play again sometime.

It's a terrible idea. Which doesn't stop me from imagining her strapped up on the St. Andrews Cross, arms and legs splayed wide, leather straps striping her body, just tight enough to press her breasts out and highlight those generous curves. Thighs and belly outlined, her pussy perfectly framed for my mouth. I'd make her come so many times, she wouldn't be able to walk out on her own two feet.

I force myself to tap another text.

Me: I'm afraid not.

When she doesn't reply, I shove the mental image of sucking her nipples aside, and continue.

Me: I'll show you around, though. Introduce you to a couple decent Doms who'd be happy to play with you.

The ellipsis appears and disappears a couple of times. I resist the urge to make a promise I'll definitely regret and force myself to wait her out.

Sunny: Great. I look forward to it. Take care now.

Now it's my turn to start a message and delete it. Twice. Both times offering up my services in ways I would absolutely regret.

Finally, I force myself to type a message she will in no way be able to misinterpret.

Me: You too. Have a great night.

And then, because I wouldn't be fulfilling my responsibilities if I didn't end on a caring note, I add, Sweet dreams.

Later, I lie in bed, hard as nails, mentally scrolling through every single storyline in my playbook in search of a quick release to help me sleep. It's not until I give in and replace my usual fantasy women with Sunny's sweet face that I get anywhere close.

But when I do—fuck me, it's so good. Her list of BDSM limits and fantasies was so on par with mine that I don't have to look far.

She's on her knees, her hands tied at her back, those long red curls a wild tumble, just begging for my grip. Her spine arches hard as I consume her from behind, forcing one orgasm from her body after another.

She'd beg me to stop, and instead of giving in, I'd tell her just how pretty her pussy is, all puffy and pink and shining with want. When I finally line up and allow myself the mind-numbing pleasure of penetration, the tight, swollen clasp of her body pushes me right over the edge. Hell yes. That's it.

My climax blasts through me so hard I see stars for a few head-spinning seconds. Best I've had in ages.

A few minutes later, I clean up, stretch out in the dark, my heartbeat finally back to its normal rate, and think about how, once Sunny's learned the ropes, grown a thicker skin, and gotten a hang of the kink world, maybe we can play without the worry that she'll get too attached.

In the meantime, I grab my phone with the intention of deleting tonight's text chain. My thumb's hovering over the trash icon when it occurs to me that she might have questions at some point, or hell, maybe I'll come up with a great Dom for her and send the info along. Instead of deleting her number, I save it under Subby Sunny.

Finally, I fall asleep.

CHAPTER NINE

Rae

MONDAY'S ONE OF THOSE bright autumn days I'd be absolutely in love with if I didn't have to drag my ass over to the new office. All because some out-of-touch finance bro says we have to. I can't imagine why Dorothy—the Sugar app's founder, CEO, and acclaimed matchmaking queen—has entrusted our fates into this guy's hands.

He's a consultant who's been pulled in to cull the flock. I know it, even if Dorothy refuses to confirm. This is exactly the kind of thing that happens to start-ups after that initial wave of success dies down and the executives realize they need to trim the fat to stay afloat.

My job as HR manager is to make sure that doesn't happen. Okay, not really, but there's no way I'm letting some corporate toady like the mysterious Grant Bowman come in and slash positions at will. Nope. Not on my watch. I advocate for my team.

From what my phone's telling me, the new office isn't too far. So at least there's that. In fact, it's in Carytown. Maybe if things get really bad, I can swing over to Off the Cuff for, I don't know, another massage or something.

Ha! No. No, as the General told me, that was a one-off—a one-night domination experience. *Not in the market for a sub.*

Whatever. That's fine. There's nothing stopping me from finding another Dom to play with, right? Like he said, maybe the General can introduce me to an experienced Dom like him. Only better. If I'm lucky, the new guy will rub my back and talk sweet and dirty in my ear and make me come apart at the seams. Maybe he'll be all frowny-browed and serious about it, like it's his job to do this one thing right, and by god, he will, come hell or high water. And maybe we'll go further than just a back rub. Maybe he'll go through the list of things I want, like spanking and hair-pulling, and that fantasy where he pushes me into a dark corner and puts his hand in my panties and makes me see stars over and over again and tells me how badly he wants—

No. I promised myself I'd quit thinking about it every second of every day. Quit checking my texts just in case the General changed his mind and decided he was in the market for a sub, after all. Quit picking up my phone and typing out messages asking for just one more Dom/sub experience to slide into the spank bank for posterity.

Seriously, if I don't stop this nonsense right now, someone like Jaffrey Jenkins will poke his oddly square-shaped head into my new office to ask about retirement benefits and catch me squirming in my seat with my eyes rolled back.

Gross.

I park and hop out of the car, juggling my coffee, my computer bag, my office survival supplies, and a teetering mountain of freshly baked chocolate chip cookies as I go. If nothing else, maybe the cookies will soften up Dorothy's Evil Boy Genius.

"Grant Bowman," I mutter. Ugh, even his name has founding families vibes. I can't help but picture a fifth-generation

Ivy Leaguer and CrossFit addict with a wife named Binky and two-point-five children. The kind of guy who thinks of cutting employee benefits as a perfectly viable way to improve the bottom line.

Dorothy insists that he's coming in to help smooth out processes. Could she be any more vague? Will positions be cut or not? The company Slack's become a hotbed of conjecture. As human resources manager, I should, of course, put a stop to that. But I mean, who texts the new office address to their HR manager over the weekend like that? I literally only found out where we'd be working last night and then had to make sure it got out to the full team so they'd actually show up this morning.

I'm half a block from my destination when my phone rings. It's Samantha.

"Hey."

"You're not gonna believe this place," she hisses.

"Crap, am I late?"

"You're always late. Listen. Old warehouse. Just converted. Gorge."

"Okay."

"It's ancient. Red brick and everything. We've got the top floor. The renovation is…" She makes a smooching sound. "Modern industrial. You're gonna die over all the cast-iron fixtures. And the furniture…" She lowers her voice to a whisper, the sound muffled like she's pressing her mouth to the phone, sharing a massive secret. "Herman Miller chairs, Rae. We've got Herman Miller chairs!"

"Samantha, is the new guy in—?"

"Tasteful too, you know? None of the tacky shit Dorothy bought for the Glen Allen office. Probably got that crap off a truck or something. Someone definitely paid her to take it off their h—"

"Samantha, has Grant Bow—"

"Anyway, we're upstairs from a club. Can you believe it? Wonder if they have an open-mic—"

"Samantha Martinez. Has the new guy arrived?" I pause and look up. This street is familiar. I feel like I was just here.

"Ugh. Yes. Yes! And he's…" Her voice goes quiet again. "H… A… W… T…"

I let out a long, annoyed sigh, nearly colliding with a guy in bike shorts in line at the Coffee Hut. Seriously, did I just double back or something? Because I feel like I passed the Coffee Hut just the other…

I glance down at the map on my phone and go absolutely still.

…night. Friday night, to be exact.

My skin prickles. "What was that about a club?"

"Get this. Right downstairs. A literal comedy club. Hilarious, right? Hey. Are you far? Staff meeting's about to start, and everyone's asking about the cookies."

I look up at the street name and over at the cross street. With a burst of speed, I turn the corner. There, half a block up, is the building I spent Friday evening getting… Dommed in, for want of a better term.

"But the office is 2222 Uptown. I'm right around the corner—"

"That's the rear entrance. Parking's back there. Well, for Work Dad and Dorothy. We minions get to fight for a street spot."

Work Dad?

"But the other address? For the front of the building?"

"24026 Cary Street. Geesh, Rae, I know it's Monday morning, but come on. Didn't you look it up?"

Everything inside me tries to sink to my toes.

No, I didn't look it up. I was too busy getting cookies baked and supplies packed up, pumping gas, and then driving a jerry can over to Hannah's because Schaffer forgot to fill up the car over the weekend, leaving his entire family stranded. I still haven't called to bitch him out.

Get it together, Rae. It's just a weird coincidence.

Somehow, I get my mouth to spit out words that make sense. "Okay. Okay. Be right up."

"With cookies?"

"Always."

I walk up the familiar sidewalk to the rough-looking brick of the building that does, in fact, house the comedy club, our new office, and, just to keep things real, the kink club that I spent all weekend trying not to think about.

Look how well that's going.

CHAPTER TEN

Rae

I HURRY UP THE stairs.

So what if it's the same building? It's a weird coincidence. Not the end of the world, right? Richmond's not a huge city. Stranger things have happened.

Could this be a sign that I should absolutely become a full-fledged member of Off the Cuff? Is this fate's way of telling me I haven't yet fulfilled my destiny? Only instead of taming dragons and saving the world, like some elf princess from one of those fated mates romantasies I love so much, my one true path involves being called a *good girl* and getting spanked.

Very noble, I know.

With a final breath, I shove the handle down, lift my chin, and stride into the lobby.

"Yay!" Samantha yells from behind a big wood-and-glass reception desk. "The cookies are here!"

"Staff meeting!" a voice immediately responds from the wide, brightly lit open office area to the right, followed by the sound of about ten chairs rolling back from desks as people stand, whooping. At least two baseball caps take to the air like mortarboards at graduation.

"The eagle has landed. Cookies are here. I repeat. Cookies in the house. This is not a drill," Samantha says into her phone, her voice echoing through a dozen speakers. She eyes my outfit. "Love the skirt. Is that—"

"Vintage. No label."

"And the top?"

"Yes, it's the one Brendan hated." Too tight, he'd said. Too showy.

"May he rot in hell. The top is gorgeous on you."

I smile. "Where's my office?"

"Right there." Wide-eyed, Sam points at a door to my left, directly off the lobby. "But you might want to—"

"Oh, honey! You're here!" Dorothy glides through another door, this one straight ahead. Our boss is a chaotic swirl of colorful fabrics and long gray hair. She wraps me in her patchouli-sandalwood-scented arms and squeezes. "Ugh! I just...missed you, honey!" Releasing me, she pinches one of my cheeks, a thing she's always done. In all fairness, I've got a pretty round face. I'd probably pinch them myself.

Which, of course, makes me think of getting pinched in other places and—

Nope. No. What happens at Off the Cuff—in the basement of this very building, no less!—stays at Off the Cuff.

"Missed you too, Dorothy. Before the meeting, could you and I quickly—"

"Ooooooh, are those the famous new-and-improved recipe?"

"Yeah, I'll just put my stuff down and get these to—"

"Here. I'll help." She grabs the top plate, pulls back the foil, takes one, and shoves half a cookie in her mouth.

"That's gluten-free."

"Listen." Her words come out garbled. "I won't be around for long, so—"

"You won't?" Why does that sound so ominous? Oh my god. Does she mean forever or just this morning? Is this what the consultant's about?

"Goddamn, this cookie's amazing. Wow. Okay. Sorry. Your new office is right over there." She points across the wide, airy lobby, which is currently filling up with staff, excitedly greeting one another as they move down a long hall toward what I'm guessing is the conference room. "Meeting first, though. I want to get you and Grant all set up together."

"Actually, do you think I could have a moment before we're all—?"

She hugs someone hello and then turns back to me as if I haven't spoken. "Oh! You wouldn't happen to have brought an extra butt pillow, would you? I forgot the old one at home, and my tailbone's already acting—"

"Sure." I balance the rest of the cookies on Samantha's desk, slap her hand as she reaches for one, and rummage in the box of survival supplies I prepped over the weekend. "One memory foam desk chair pillow." Special ordered last week, along with three backups.

"*Oooooh.*" Dorothy side hugs me. "You are a gem, Rae. An absolute gem."

"So, could we just chat before the team gets—?"

Not hearing me—or pretending not to?—she calls out, "Treats this way, kiddos!" and absconds down the hall with the entire plate of gluten-free cookies. The quiet swoosh of her vegan-leather, Moroccan-style slippers is drowned out by the clank of dozens of metal bracelets and the pitter-patter of a full team of hungry developers, all following the Pied Piper scent of what might very well be the world's best cookies. Truly. It took me three years, and I literally cried when I finally got the recipe right.

So did Samantha, who declared them almost as good as watermelon Blow Pops.

"Here, let me help." Samantha grabs the next plate from the pile. "We'll be in the conference room. Better hurry." She tilts her head toward me and whispers, "Work Dad's in there. And did I mention he's really, really nice to look at?"

Crap.

Work Dad. How does he already have a nickname? And what an innocuous title for a man whose presence is a sign that things are not nearly as hunky-dory as Dorothy likes to pretend.

The opening strains to "Something Bad Is Happening" from *Falsettos* automatically kick up in the back of my mind.

If only Dorothy would talk to me instead of this avoidance thing.

I zoom into my new office to dump my stuff and lock up the payroll and personnel files, and—

Come to a screeching halt.

Two desks face each other, one already showing signs of occupation. This can't be my office.

"Um, Samantha. Someone's already moved in here. Where's my...?"

I turn. The reception area's empty. From crowded thoroughfare to tumbleweed wasteland in the blink of an eye. That's the power of cookies, I guess.

"Get your ass in here, Rae!" Jamie-Lynn Jones—who once conducted an entire Zoom meeting from the Mechanicsville County Fair Ferris wheel—yells from down the hall. "Oops! Sorry! Meant to say *behind*. Get your lovely little...I mean your... Just...come on."

Armed with the full-gluten, -fat, and -dairy version of my cookies, I grab my things and race down the hall at a fast clip, almost miss the conference room door, spin to make up the difference, bag, coffee, plates and all, and plow into a brick wall.

A living brick wall. A wide, warm, solid brick wall with big hands that steady me.

An alarm bell goes off inside my head, faint but really, really shrill.

"You're late," says the wall in a voice that's deep and rich, though it's got some grit to it. Just a hint, like the finest sandpaper.

Uh-oh. I know this voice. I've felt it against my ear, my nape, and that sensitive place where my neck meets my shoulder.

No. Uh-uh. Nope.

I tighten my hold on the myriad things I should have just left on the desk in the other room and look up in the kind of dumbstruck slow motion that nightmares are made of.

No way. It can't be *him*, him. Not the one-and-done dream Dom I decided I'd never be seeing again, despite having literally touched myself all weekend thinking about him.

There's a moment of relief when I see his jawline. It's square, like the General's, but clean-shaven. Not a hint of that raspy five-o'clock shadow.

My heart sinks as soon as I take in the deeply cut cheekbones, the pissed-off brown eyes, and those hands like live wires on my skin…

Please, no. Please.

"*Sir?*" I whisper aloud, in front of the entire freaking staff, all of whom, for once, have gone eerily quiet.

CHAPTER ELEVEN

Rae

"Uh..." The General's eyes take me in, up and down and up again, until they land on my face. His expression morphs from confused to angry. "How did you get in here?"

He's so magnetic that my internal compass is spinning. "What?"

"What are you doing in my place of work?" Though from across the room he might look self-contained, this close, I feel pure white rage seeping out of him.

Wait. He's pissed at me? *Are you kidding?*

That does it. With the next heartbeat, my poor, electro-shocked brain breaks free from his hold. "How did *I* get in here?" I hiss quietly, right in his face. "I work here. Are you serious with the—?"

"You can't brazenly walk into someone's place of—"

As one, our overlapping voices come to an abrupt stop.

I don't have to crane my head to know that every single pair of eyeballs is laser-focused on us. Hushed whispers. Someone coughs.

Truly, I don't think the Sugar App staff has ever shown this level of decorum. Like, not once have I gotten every person to be quiet simultaneously.

I swallow, the sound a loud, dry click that every single one of them hears. Except possibly for Doreen, whose eardrums have been shot since her days of following the Grateful Dead.

"You must be Rae." The General's tight face twists into an expression that's only slightly less indignant than his initial reaction. Is that his attempt at a smile?

"Yes." I do my best to appear pleasant. "I. Am. Rae. Rae Jensen. Human resources manager." That didn't sound robotic at all.

Pulling at his collar, he clears his throat. Behind him, someone chomps into a cookie. Feet shuffle. Throats clear.

"Good to finally meet you. Rae." He puts out a hand that I know for a fact is thick and strong and calloused. I really, really don't want to touch him right now, in front of everybody. "Grant Bowman."

I look at his hand, hanging there just waiting for a shake, and then down at my fully occupied appendages and say, "Well, that is fabtastic!" Fabtastic? What is my mouth even doing? "I mean, good to meet you," I finally manage through a tight rictus of a smile. "Great! But...sorry. Can't shake." My attempt at an apologetic shrug probably looks apoplectic.

Crap. I've got to get it together or I'm the first person the General will axe. Not the General. This is Grant Bowman. And Grant Bowman is a man who looks like he could file your taxes, change your oil, and give you one hell of a tune-up...without breaking a sweat.

Past his shoulder, I see Samantha, standing there staring at me like I just tore off my clothes and started performing *A Chorus Line* in nothing but stilettos and sparkles.

To my right, Dorothy comes into focus. She's watching, her vague, benevolent smile quickly fading into confusion as the seconds tick by and my brain scrambles to find a conversational gambit that will extricate me from this nightmare.

Finally, my eyes zero in on the platter of baked goods now teetering on my right arm.

"Cookies," I whisper, emerging from my stupor with something like hope. In a louder voice, I proclaim, "Here are the full-fat, glutenous, dairy-rich cookies you've been waiting for!" and shove them at his chest. Blinking, he accepts them and mercifully steps back, taking away his warm scent and that electric thing that sizzles when he's near, leaving just enough room for me to slip farther into the conference room and throw myself into one of the two empty chairs.

All in all, not the best start to my first day back.

CHAPTER TWELVE

Grant

WHAT THE HELL KIND of circus is Dorothy running here?

I'm standing in the middle of the conference room, surrounded by the motliest staff I've ever seen, holding a huge platter of cookies—there must be fifteen pounds here—staring at the beautiful woman I spent all weekend picturing naked. I've got to get control of this situation.

There's a staff member knitting, for Christ's sake. Another's stirring a Crock-Pot. Every single one of them's eating cookies like Chaos Muppets on a mission. This is Dorothy's successful tech start-up?

"Oh, thank god. The full-fat cookies," says coms director and social media manager Samantha, who I'm told will do double duty as receptionist now that I've dragged them back to the office. She scoops up a handful from the platter before sinking back into her chair beside a purple-haired person wearing massive noise-canceling headphones.

Dorothy, wide-eyed and smiling, swoops over to join me in the middle of the room, clapping like she's talking to a herd of first graders instead of paid employees. "I am so glad you could all come in today, my sweeties."

Could all come in? Was attendance optional?

Dorothy knows damn well that there's no time for this nonsense. We've got to locate an alleged data breach and address all compromises before her investor meeting next month. I've got three weeks—exactly twenty-one days—to ensure that any vulnerabilities are taken care of. Frankly, if these people had any idea just how iffy their positions are, not a single one of them would be smiling right now.

A very tall, big-boned man wearing shorts, knee socks, and suspenders and sporting the biggest red beard I've ever seen comes over and palms a swath of cookies from the platter, easily reducing its weight by a third. He then proceeds to sit back down, chomping on them—two at a time—never once taking his lens-enlarged gaze from mine.

The misgivings I'd felt at taking on this job quadruple, and that muscle in my jaw goes tight again. What have I signed myself up for?

Meanwhile, Dorothy side hugs every person who comes to help themselves to a cookie.

"So, yes, this is Grant, my lovelies!" She's still talking, although nobody appears to be listening. "An expert in all things finance, executive management, and human resources, including…"

"Did you put pot in these? I swear there's weed in this one."

I turn to glare at whoever said that. It's unclear, though it's possibly one of the three almost identical, twentysomething white men slouching against the wall in hoodies and beanies.

My god, who are these people? They're like locusts. Or toddlers.

"I can do CBD," someone responds. "But THC gets to me. Hope it's not THC."

"Good morning," I say with all the authority I possess.

"There's no THC," the source, origin, and reason for this cookie mayhem replies, just sitting there with her pale, freckled skin and those clear blue eyes. Rae Jensen is smiling as if this sugarcoated chaos is a good thing.

How can she look so calm when she created this mess by bringing possibly spiked snacks to the first in-person meeting these people have had in years?

It's completely unhinged. All of it. My insides are close to boiling.

No wonder Dorothy needs me. With this killer bunny masquerading as human resources manager, I'm shocked there haven't been issues before now.

"No cookies," I say from my spot in the center of the circle. Firm, but reasonable.

They all freeze, cheeks bulging like chipmunks, and stare up at me.

"Oh," Dorothy starts, "I don't think we need to take away their—"

From out of the blue, Rae Jensen's cheery voice cuts through the hubbub. "Mr. Bowman is right." Color flies high on her softly rounded cheeks. "We should start the meeting."

Finally, a little rationality. That it happens to come from the one who sowed the chaos doesn't matter at this moment.

"Are you saying we can't eat at work?" asks a woman in a T-shirt featuring Pedro Pascal and the word *ZADDY* in all caps. She's clearly gearing up for a fight. "Because that's against the law. Right, Rae?"

"Refusing food breaks is against the law," Rae replies. "However—"

"You can eat the cookies after the meeting," I respond, my tone reasonable.

"We open meetings with cookies and coffee. That's how we do it at Sugar." This from Samantha, who is apparently taking a stand now that she's demolished her pile of treats.

All around, teeth crunch on baked goods while the staff watches me with the wide-eyed attention of a movie-theater audience eagerly awaiting the next zany twist.

My jaw tightens, my teeth grinding together.

"Well, I'm here to fix things, so starting today, we close meetings with cookies. Start with business, end with pleasure."

At those words, Rae Jensen's cheeks turn even ruddier. I watch, unable to tear my eyes from the bright, hot-looking red that mottles her neck before conquering her ample, if modestly covered, décolleté. Her eyes narrow as she folds her arms across a chest I recently watched her fondle while calling her a *very good girl*.

Dammit. I won't go there.

"It's tradition" comes a low voice from the group of entitled young clones in the far corner.

"Not anymore."

More munching around us. Someone steps forward and snags another cookie—or seven—from the dish I'm still holding as if I'm one of those ridiculous butler statues.

This was supposed to be simple and quick. Surgical. Dorothy brings me in as an "executive consultant," a cover for what I'm really here to do. Twenty-one days seemed like more than enough time to find and fix things when I left the house this morning. Now? I get the feeling this isn't going to be easy at all.

CHAPTER THIRTEEN
Rae

I RACE BACK TO the shared office as soon as the meeting lets out, relieved when high-and-mighty Grant Bowman doesn't immediately follow.

It takes a while to settle down as I debate the merits of going through his desk and trying to log in to his computer. Because that would absolutely be a fireable offense, I back off. That and I'm a rule follower at heart. I've never broken into anything in my life. Also, I'm pretty sure he had his laptop with him in the conference room. But still. What is going on here?

I consider switching desks with him, given that a conversation should have occurred, at the very least, before he went and picked a side. First dibs isn't a thing in a work environment. First dibs is for the front seat on road trips or when you get snowed in at the airport with a stranger and have to share a hotel room. Actually, no dibs when there's only the one bed.

Yeah, well, if life were a romance novel, Genghis *freaking* Bowman wouldn't be such a stick-in-the-mud at the office. Also, we would absolutely have had sex Friday night instead of just a massage, making this morning's awkwardness and pheromones out of this world. We'd exchange hot glances across our desks, and he'd get up and shut the door and tell me to lift up my skirt for a spanking—obviously, I wouldn't be wearing these tights and my big, comfortable cotton panties—and I'd bend over my desk and he'd fold up his sleeves like he did Friday night and—

A quick knock on the office door makes me jump, squeaking out a ridiculous "Come in."

When Blake from the design team rolls in, I sag with relief. No way could I deal with Bowman, my face blazing away, with these images running through my brain. I cannot sit here at my desk, all turned on while that straitlaced...sociopath refuses to let employees eat cookies.

"Hey, Rae. Sooooo, the matcha's not there?"

"Good morning, Blake. How are you?"

"Oh, yeah, good. But the matcha's not where it should be?"

I blink up at her. "I'm sorry?"

"You know? I need the matcha chai, *riiiight*? Remember? I know it's been a while, but—"

"I'm sorry. I don't understand what—"

"In the break room?" She sucks air in through her teeth with an exaggerated *sorry* grimace. "Yeah. I always get matcha. Remember?"

Breathe. Deep. Pretend I'm at home, rolling up tiny scrolls and gluing them into place. Hanging miniature lights over perfect balsa wood bookshelves. Slow, infinitely patient. In control of everything. "So, let me see if I get this. You would like someone to order matcha pods for the machine in the break room? Is that right?"

"Yes." She looks at me like I'm somehow at fault for not knowing this. "Also, Phil brought cheese."

"Already?" Come on. "We just got here."

"Right? It's unsanitary. Raw, unpasteurized, sitting there

contaminating my hemp milk as we speak. So, on TikTok, this expert talks about how fridge coexistence leads to microspecks from one..."

Nodding, I shut my eyes, picturing the tiny version of Blake I made during lockdown for one of my first mini bookshelf inserts, steaming hot cup of matcha eternally stuck to the figurine's mouth. Phone forever frozen in front of her face.

God, I miss Zoom calls, with every person contained in their own little screen, drinking their own drinks and stinking up their own fridges and homes with cheeses that smell like feet. I know for a fact that half the guys didn't wear pants during those meetings, and I didn't even care.

"I'll see what I can do." I cave just to get her to shut up.

"Awww, you're the best."

Right.

Nodding, I wait for Blake to leave. She steps out the door, and my relieved sigh makes it halfway out before she's back. "Any chance you brought the blood bag?"

Blood bag is the totally inappropriate name that Samantha came up with for the menstruation product supply I used to keep in a purse in my office. For a while, I put it in the restroom, but someone emptied it daily. In the office, people swing by and help themselves.

I can't believe people remember the blood bag after three years.

"Sure." I dig around in the big bin I lugged in and stack tampons, pads, and a couple of silicone cups on my desk.

She helps herself to a vast selection and pauses again.

"Yes?" I ask.

"So, you in on it?"

"On what?"

She points at the empty desk. "What the mean guy's doing here?"

"We were asked not to discuss this, Blake."

"He says we can't take our computers home!"

"Good!" I improvise. "That'll make for a better work-life balance."

"What? No. My home laptop died, and I use the work one to—"

"You sure you want to finish that sentence, Blake?" I ask.

"Oh. Right. 'Kay, bye!" She takes off, leaving me to settle back into my chair and stare at the other desk.

Another knock comes, this one a sharp double rap.

The door opens to reveal my new office mate. He steps in and shuts it behind him, turning and coming to a full stop when he sees my desk covered in a mountain of menstrual supplies. He looks at me, brows raised. "Got a minute?"

"Sure." I scramble to slide the boxes into a drawer and immediately wish I hadn't. If he can't take the sight of boxed-up menstruation supplies, how on earth does he manage what happens downstairs in that club?

Argh. No! No club thoughts in the office. Only office thoughts.

Immediately, my mind provides that image again—him flipping up my skirt, swiping the surface of my desk clear...period supplies flying everywhere.

Stop it! Suppressing a groan, I sit up taller, forcing a neutral, professional look to my face and, in need of something to keep my hands busy, start emptying the bin of supplies. "What can I help you with, Grant?"

"We need to lay out some ground rules, you and I."

And just like that, my brain goes flying back to the club.

CHAPTER FOURTEEN

Grant

"Oh? Such as?" Rae "Sunny" Jensen watches me, her expression a fascinating mix of annoyance and that wide-eyed curiosity she showed on Friday night. Beside her desk is an enormous plastic bin filled to the brim with tchotchkes.

I focus on her annoyance, wondering how she can be peeved at a perfectly logical request from me after sitting unfazed through that unhinged staff meeting.

Because Rae is an agent of chaos. That's how. She may look all sweet and innocent with those rosy cheeks and curly hair, but underneath all her disarmingly cherubic trappings, she is a wreaker of havoc who has somehow snowed the rest of the world into thinking she's harmless.

I know better, though.

"Are you going to be a problem, Rae?"

"Are you?"

"Very mature."

"I'm not the one treating the team like children. No laptops outside of the building? No one works from home? That's ridiculous."

"We're not discussing company policy, Rae. We're talking about this." I flick my finger back and forth between us.

"Oh, rest assured, there is no *this*"—she stops emptying her bin just long enough to wiggle her hand in a parody of mine—"to discuss."

"Excellent. And no blending professional and personal. Ever."

She takes out a box of adhesive bandages and adds it to the growing pile of medical supplies littering her desk, followed by tissues and a half dozen tiny desk fans. After that comes an animal-shaped bowl, which she promptly fills with three kinds of candy. "Of course not."

Of course not? Of *course* not? I've never seen a less professional environment than this, including companies where my contract ended with half the personnel going to prison. The club's got better boundaries than this hellscape, and people there have literal sex with each other. It may not be in my job description, but there's no reason I can't straighten a few things out while I'm here. Poor Dorothy's been snowed by her own employees, and if I'm not mistaken, this woman's spearheading the whole shambolic thing. She may be, as Dorothy claims, "the heart and soul of the company," but more than anything, I suspect that she's the life of the party.

Rae Jensen is an anarchist in sheep's clothing. This ends now.

"I mentioned to Dorothy that we'd met before."

Finally, she stops unpacking things from that damn box, like some demented Mary Poppins, and gives me direct eye contact. Those freckles do things to me. All over her nose, a few on her cheeks, and others scattered toward the neckline of that sweater. With those massive blue-green eyes, she's like a killer bunny. Cute and unbelievably dangerous.

"Oh, really? You just went and did that, without first discussing it with me?"

"I didn't tell her the circumstances. Just that we'd met."

"Great. Fine." Her smile's so wide and fake that it's atrocious. A clown smile on a baby deer. "Thanks. I'll make sure to put it in our personnel files." She opens her laptop and types furiously.

"I'd like to—"

A blue-tipped finger goes up, stopping me in my tracks while she continues to tap out notes about our previous relationship. Or whatever she's chosen to call it. Doesn't matter. I won't be here long enough for that to affect me.

Wait. How do I have a file? I'm not an employee.

With a final flourish, she looks up, her expression polite. "Go ahead."

I blink, my mind blank before remembering what I was about to say. "As I was saying, we need to make sure we're on the same page about how things work around here."

"What page is that?"

"As you know, Dorothy's asked me to come in and help her out with a special project. Once it's done, I'll be out of your hair."

"And when will that be?"

"Depends on how much cooperation I receive from HR while I'm here. Will you cooperate?"

"Certainly." Another fake smile before she digs back into the big box. Clothes start to come out now. Sweaters, followed by a pile of doughnut-shaped cushions. Umbrellas. "Anything else?"

"You do not go back to the club."

This time, when her head snaps up, emotion has broken through. She's pissed, and man, is she gorgeous. "What?"

"The club is my domain, and I'd prefer that you not—"

"I don't think so."

"Excuse me?"

"You don't get the club."

I'm a silent partner in the club, and the building is literally mine. Given the circumstances, I mention neither. "I'm a member" is all I go with.

"You just said we're keeping private and professional separate. Maybe I've decided to become a full-fledged member of the club. Are you saying that, in your short-term capacity here at Sugar, you have a say in where I go on my nights off?" She leans forward. "Because I didn't hear you complaining last Friday. In fact, I happen to have a text on my phone offering to show me around next time I—"

"You don't want to go" is the only thing my brain can come up with.

"Oh, I do."

"You don't."

"I really, really do."

"Why?"

She pauses, mouth open, cheeks blazing again, those eyes flashing fierce and green. For a handful of seconds, I have to work to get my breathing back to normal.

"Whatever, Genghis. I'm done talking about it."

"What was that?"

"I said whatever. I'm not—"

The conversation is saved by a knock on the door. "Quick question, Rae." Dorothy slides inside, smelling like a marijuana dispensary. "I've been thinking about benefits."

"Okay." Rae sets down the clothing stain pen and wipes she's just unpacked from her magical mystery box and, after a scathing glance my way, gives Dorothy her full attention. "Shoot."

"You know how McGruntcakes got sick last year?"

"I remember. So glad he's better."

My attention bounces between the two of them, wondering why on earth they're talking about Dorothy and Malika's dog.

Dorothy comes over and perches on the corner of my desk. "Weeeell, I was thinking we should give the employees paternity leave. In case of pet sickness."

I lean forward. "What leave?"

"*Paw*-ternity. Isn't that cute?"

"It really is." Rae slowly nods. "And how long were you thinking?"

"Oh, you know. Very flexible. Like, Grunty was sick for a couple of weeks, so..." She shrugs. "As long as it takes."

"Right." Rae appears to consider. "Um, so, would there be, like, a limit on what kind of pet?"

"Oh, no. Of course not! We don't discriminate."

"Definitely. Obviously. Cool. Yes. Right away. I'll look into it and get back to you with details."

Dorothy stands up with a tinkle of bells and bends to give Rae a big kiss on the cheek. "You're a delight." She turns to me. "Isn't she? Come on. Look at her. Isn't she just freaking gorgeous?"

"Ahhhh." I glance wildly over at where Rae's watching me with an expression that says, *Go on, agree with her. I dare you.* "Rae seems great." I settle on neutral ground, relieved when Dorothy mumbles something about just being so happy to have us both in the office as she jingles her way out, closing the door behind her.

"What the hell was that?"

"What?" Rae goes back to emptying the box.

"How could you say yes to something so patently idiotic?"

"You're talking about the paw-ternity leave?"

"Yes. Why on earth would you agree to that?"

"I always say yes to Dorothy."

"That's ludicrous!"

"Really? Is it? Look." She sets a miniature bottle of mouthwash on her desk and gets up, goes to our office door, and opens it. I don't allow my eyes to follow the roll of her hips. "Do you see a foosball table out in the lobby? Ping-Pong?"

All I see is a comms manager tapping at her phone and sucking on a lollipop. "No."

"A row of those footbaths with the fish that eat calluses?"

"Of course not. That's disgusting."

After shutting the door, Rae starts moving items from her desktop to the cupboards. "Well, you can thank me because Dorothy wanted those things."

"Seriously?"

"You have no idea."

"She's a menace." Maybe I should talk to Malika. Dorothy's wife might know how to curb her more absurd requests.

"Don't you want to know how I did it?"

I sigh. "Go ahead. I can tell you're dying to school me."

She stops what she's doing, turns, leans back against her desk, and folds her arms across her chest, which pushes up her ample breasts. For a handful of seconds, the edges of my vision literally go dark.

"Like I said, I always agree to Dorothy's shenanigans. Always. Bring Your Pets to Work Day? Bagel of the Week? Best Zoom Background awards... I said yes to every one of those suggestions."

"That's silly. Just tell her no."

She shakes her head, making that little librarian, you've-been-a-bad-boy *tsking* sound, and I'm suddenly not so sure this shared-office thing was a good idea. "See, if I agree, she forgets and moves on to the next outlandish request. If I refuse, it becomes a thing." She leans toward me conspiratorially. "Trust me, refuse and you wind up with a pair of llamas disturbing the peace and a summons to appear in court."

"You're saying that happened?" I'm beginning to suspect that I don't know Dorothy at all.

"Yep. The llamas were aggressive. We paid fines." The sparkle of humor in her eyes makes me want to, hell, tickle her or something. I do not fucking tickle. "Try it sometime. Agree to one of her ideas."

"Harebrained nightmares, you mean."

"I'm serious. Agree, write it down, and walk away."

"What if she asks about it later?"

"Oh, she might." She gives a wicked grin that I want to lick off her face. "That's when I pull out the list."

"The list."

As she bends to grab something from the mystery bin, her skirt goes taut around her hips, sending a jolt to my cock. The fact that she emerges holding a clipboard in no way diminishes my body's inappropriate reaction. "The master list—or as I like to call it, the *mistress* list—of all requests made to date." With long, crystal blue fingernails, she points at one column and then the other. "Those fulfilled and those pending."

I watch, slowly filling with something like awe at how this woman has managed to hide an entire Machiavellian underbelly beneath that Strawberry Shortcake facade.

Then again, she did come into a kink club on her own the other night, shopping for a Dom, so there's definitely more than meets the eye with this one. What worries me now is this urge to scratch the surface for a glimpse at the other good stuff within.

"And?" I finally prompt.

"And nothing. I hold up the clipboard, flip through the many pages." She does it now, wide-eyed and cheerful as a Costco hostess hell-bent on getting rid of her last pig-in-a-blanket sample of the day. "I mention the budget and how we've got to whittle it down. Maybe, in this case, I'll let her know that if I stop getting her butt cushions, we can afford the paw-ternity leave. For one pet. But I'd be happy to go over all the line items with her. One at a time."

"I'll bet she hates that."

"She really does. Nothing gets her out of the office faster than bringing out the list. Works like a charm. And…" Rae lifts that bossy little finger again. "Every once in a while, when something's not too egregious, I give it to her."

"Such as?"

"Such as homemade cookies at staff meetings," she deadpans.

"Baked by *you*."

"Yeah, well. I've been upping my baking game anyway, so…" With another half shrug, Rae goes back to sit at her desk, bends down, and pulls out a handful of phone chargers.

It's not until I tear my gaze away from her that my lungs finally fill back up with oxygen. Yet again, I'm kicking myself for this shared office setup.

This is going to be hell on my libido.

CHAPTER FIFTEEN

Rae

I'VE NEVER FELT SO watched in my life. I keep thinking Grant's staring at me, but when I look up, he's innocently typing away, that little frown between his eyebrows reminding me of how he looked Friday night, all serious and interested.

What is he working on that's making that muscle tic in his jaw right now? Is it the employee evaluations I was forced to give him access to this afternoon? Is he checking off pros and cons for all of us, preparing reports? Getting ready to slash, slash, slash?

Has a workday ever felt so long? I swear we've been here for a month when I glance at the time and see that it's only 5:48 p.m.

Oh, thank god. I just need to finish updating my benefits files, and then I'll go.

Someone knocks on the door.

"Does it ever stop?" Grant grumbles, without looking up.

Ignoring him, I call out a cheery "Come in!"

Dani, one of our graphics people, sticks her head around the door, expression apologetic. "Hey!" She looks from me to Grant and back, her eyes big. "Sorry, Rae, but the dev team's in a meeting, and most everybody else is gone. I've got to skedaddle, and..." She pushes the door wider so I can see the new water cooler, along with several of those huge jugs dumped in the middle of the reception area.

"The delivery person just left it there?" I ask.

"Yeah. And Sam took off." Without saying goodbye? That's weird. "I'm late for something, so I figured you'd be good with… You know. Got it?" She's backing out of the room.

"Sure. Fine. Yes."

"You're the best." She's making her exit. "Have a great one, you guys. See you tomorrow!"

With a sigh, I save my document and go out into the lobby. Grant doesn't glance up from whatever he's doing at his computer. Top secret things, clearly, that involve bursts of typing and the occasional grunt. He's wearing what are likely noise-canceling earbuds, and aside from a couple of quiet, curt calls that divulged absolutely nothing aside from he's performing some kind of audit, he's barely interacted with anyone all day.

The water cooler, it turns out, is heavy, but by shimmying it from corner to corner, I manage to get it up against the far wall. I go back for the bottles. They're easy to slide across the floor, one at a time. The issue's going to be getting one of these big bottles open and then into the cooler, which is chest high on me.

For a second, I consider bringing Grant in on this but immediately decide against it. He's muttered a complaint every time someone's knocked on our door today. I'll admit that it's a lot of interruptions, but that's just a day in the life for me. First Klaus needed tissues for his office, and then Dorothy asked if I'd consider pet sitting for her and Malika over Thanksgiving. I said yes, even though I'm not sure how I'll make it work around getting dinner ready for the family and putting up the office holiday decorations. Samantha came in to ask if I'd get lunch with her—I couldn't, but she brought me back Tater Tots and lettuce cups from Sticky Rice. *Oh my god, yum.* Two people got me to buy Girl Scout cookies from their kids, three needed benefits account log-in info, and one wanted to know how to turn the temperature down in the break room. Weirdly, Grant was able to answer that last one.

I'm tired, I'm hot, and, yes, I'm more than a little bothered by that man's constant presence. Because, though he's grumpy and grumbly and can't seem to crack a smile to save his life, he sure is nice to look at.

At least he hasn't caught me staring. That would be mortifying.

Ugh. What is wrong with me? You know what? That's it. From this moment forward, I won't even look. There. A solemn promise to myself. No glancing at the living thirst trap Dorothy's saddled me with.

It is hot in here, though. Sweaty from all the effort, I wrench my turtleneck up and off, only belatedly remembering that I've got on just a bra and tank top beneath. Whatever. I've seen at least three people here in crop tops today.

Okay. Focus. Water.

The problem, I realize, the second I lug an open jug up and into my arms, is that the office is so overheated that even my hands are slick, and this bottle is way heavier than it felt when I pushed it across the floor. Tilting the darn thing's not easy, but now I've got to heft it up and stick the end in that hole. I shimmy it higher, hugging it like a child, roll it to lean on one hip, try to lift the bottom without spilling, and then make the mistake of attempting to use my knee to lever it higher.

It's the pencil skirt that really gets me into trouble. In the thick of the action, I've forgotten how hip- and knee-hugging the fabric is, so when I kick up—or try to—I lose my balance, the bottle shunts forward, and instead of pouring into the open top of the dispenser, it sloshes my face, straight down my front, soaking my shirt, my skirt, and my shoes.

I catch the bottle just before it hits the floor, adrenaline-fueled relief pumping hard. I'm just so thankful no one's here to witness this fine example of Rae Jensen's world-famous clumsiness that I'm almost laughing.

"What the hell are you doing, Sunny?" The sound of Grant's voice immediately rids me of every ounce of humor. "Give me that."

He stalks over and grabs the bottle as easily as if it were empty, his biceps barely bothering to bulge as he flips it over and plugs it into the opening, where it gurgles loudly into place.

I'm too embarrassed—and, yeah, maybe annoyed at the way he just talked to me—to fully appreciate the way his thighs flex.

Also, I'm not supposed to be looking.

"Thanks." I swipe an arm across my sweat-slick face.

He grunts something.

"What?"

"You shouldn't be doing that kind of work. Dammit, Sunny, it's not just Dorothy you say yes to all the time, is it?" He seems pissed, which I'm not sure I understand.

"Excuse me?"

"You say yes to everyone. Every single ridiculous request."

"I do my job."

"This isn't your job. You are the HR manager for a tech startup. Human resources. Not bottle-wrestler. Girl Scout cookies aren't your job. Blowing employees' noses isn't your job."

"Well, someone's got to—"

"Where's your sweater?"

"My sweater?" I focus fully on his eyes, blazing dark with something else now, something that makes every muscle in my body go tight. "I don't know where I—"

"You were wearing a sweater. Brown with…" He pulls at his own unbuttoned collar, I guess referring to my turtleneck, although all it does is draw my eyes to his Adam's apple, already stippled with a day's dark growth, the tendons wrapping the sides of his strong-looking throat, that dip in the V of his collarbone. He's removed his tie and undone the top button, and now that I've given my starving eyes free rein to look, I can't pull them back in again.

The man is ridiculously attractive and not in a light *hot on socials* way, but like, parts of my body have literally gone rogue. And that's from that one vein on his neck. The curl of body hair below it? Might as well stick my nipples into sockets.

In a last-ditch effort to drag my mind back, I say, "You noticed my sweater?"

"Of course I noticed it. Have you seen the way you fill—"

The abruptness with which he stops talking, along with the lowering of his gaze and the now almost-familiar expression of annoyed consternation, finally registers. Puzzled, I look down at myself.

Down to where my rock-hard nipples are indeed doing some of their very best work, trying to bust their way out of my now fully transparent lace bra and top with the gleeful enthusiasm of a high school production of *A Chorus Line*.

"Oh shit." I might as well not be wearing a shirt for all the coverage I'm getting. In a pointless attempt at modesty, I frantically grab the soaking-wet white fabric clinging to my middle and pull it away from my skin. "Crap, crap, craphole."

"The shirt is soaked, Sunny," he bites out in a low, angry voice that zaps every nerve in my body. "Take it off."

My nipples go impossibly harder as I stand here, frozen, my brain glitching, unable to tear my eyes from stern Office Grant.

No, actually. This isn't Office Grant, all stiff and polite and eternally irritable. This is Club Grant—this is the General—and every instinct screams at me to obey.

CHAPTER SIXTEEN

Grant

"Your top is wet," I repeat, slowly and clearly.

Rae's big eyes stare at me, the limpid green-blue of her irises much brighter than they'd appeared in the darkness of the club. Her hair is lighter too, the exact color of the leaves on the big maple out in front of my house. Her roots have gone dark where sweat sheens her temples, which leads my gaze inexorably back to the lazy river of droplets easing its way into the intriguingly deep valley of her cleavage.

What does she taste like there? Salt? Perfume? Just how much of that warm, bright scent wafting over her desk to mine would I be able to nuzzle from that sweet-looking hollow? Hell, if she'll just remove the damn shirt, I can taste her skin and—

"Well, hell-*o*." Klaus walks in, large and red-bearded. He's a developer. One of Dorothy's very first hires. She'd *trust him with her life*, she told me, although after the fourth or fifth employee, the phrase lost its impact.

"Let me guess. Slip 'N Slide?" His lens-magnified eyes go from the puddle on the floor to Sunny's top. "Oooooh, wet T-shirt contest? Yes! I'm in. Hose me down, boss man, and may the best contestant win."

"How about you help us out here by grabbing the mop?" I grit out before the big guy does something dangerous, like upend an entire plastic water barrel over his own head.

"Fine." He sighs heavily. "Where's the mop?"

"Door behind you."

He mutters something that sounds an awful lot like "Work Dad's no fun" and marches over to the supply closet.

Meanwhile, my unbearably perky colleague has disappeared into our office, only to reappear seconds later, wet shirt, Mary Poppins bag, empty plastic bin, and all. With a mumbled goodbye, she heads out into the night.

I want to stop her, make her take that damp thing off, and put the sweater on, instead of holding it in front of her like that. I want her warm and safe and not out in the cool night air in that farce of a top.

It is with great difficulty that I hold my tongue.

The second the door slams behind her, I can breathe again.

After mopping up the water and seeing Klaus out, I take a quick spin around the office, which is now entirely empty. Good. I'm alone. I can finally get some work done without the distraction of that woman sitting across from me, not to mention the staff's eight million little interruptions. Data, unlike humans, has a soothing regularity one can depend on. And, contrary to buxom, redheaded submissives with a very obvious bratty streak, they do precisely what I tell them.

Did I really demand that she remove that shirt just now? Out loud?

What the hell was that? I've never—not once in my entire life—crossed that line. And I do not plan to start now. Whatever Dorothy's put in the Kool-Aid here at Sugar, I will have no part of it whatsoever.

After fifteen minutes of staring at the screen, I give up. I'll work from home, where there's no lingering smell of her tempting brew of flowers and baked goods and that scent from the club the other night. If I close my eyes, I'll see her pale neck, feel the warmth of her skin, her goose bumps every time I hit a good spot. The swell of her deep, luxuriant breaths and those whimsical freckles, leading down like a fairy-tale woodland path straight to nipples that I can now—

"Dammit!"

I'm up, my hands fisted, my stomach rock-hard, along with parts farther south. I've never once let myself even think of sex at work, much less permitted my body to get involved.

I'm nipping this in the bud. Now. Tonight. Well, tomorrow.

No, actually. Now.

This requires rules. Clear-cut ones.

The second I open a fresh document and start typing, the tension flows out of me. Rules, like data, fix everything. Black and white. Yes and no. Ones and zeros. Those are the things that make sense to me, along with hammering nails into good, solid wood.

Once I'm done, I print the page out and set it on her desk, relieved at the sense of closure it gives me.

I then grab my computer, lock our shared office, double-check that the exterior doors are fully secure, and take off for home.

It's a moonless night. In Richmond's Fan District, where I live, the only light comes from sparsely scattered streetlamps and the warm glow from the front windows of the row houses on both sides of the tree-lined streets.

I didn't think to turn my exterior light on this morning, which is why I feel rather than see the squish of something disgusting under my shoe. Smack in the middle of my welcome mat. Or where the welcome mat would be if I hadn't trashed it after stepping on last night's batch of animal crap.

I let my head thunk against the thick wood of my front door. "Are you messing with me?"

Someone snickers next door. "Cat shit on your doorstep again?" Dorothy's voice wafts over, along with the scent of whatever new strain of weed she's been growing in the greenhouse I helped her wife build out back last year. Ostensibly for orchids, though by this point I'm pretty sure the entire neighborhood knows better.

"Did you see it?"

"It? You mean the poor little stray that keeps leaving you presents? Pretty sure *it* is a she."

"Of course it is," I whisper. "Next time, could you catch it, please? So I can take it to the SPCA?"

She snorts. "Not on your life. That cat's courting you."

"With turds?"

"Maybe your house used to be her place, and she's just coming home to take a dump."

Dorothy lets out a long, slow lungful. By the time the smell makes it to me, it's mixed with a blend of woodsmoke and autumn leaves that reminds me of the year Mom married that guy from Vermont—Blain something. He took me cross-country skiing a couple of times, just the two of us, in a misguided effort to bond with me. Poor guy had no idea he'd married a serial bride—serial matrimonialist?—and, in the process, taken on a serial stepson. He must have been Mom's fourth or fifth? Who the hell knows. I liked that guy.

That was the last divorce I cried over. The last time I made the mistake of thinking relationships could last past their predetermined sell-by date.

I shake the memory off, annoyed that I let it in at all.

"I've lived in this house for four years," I remind Dorothy. It's the longest I've ever spent in one home, and I immediately get that itchy feeling between my shoulder blades. *Keep moving. Keep going. Don't sit still.*

The house needs work, and until I finish it, I won't be going anywhere.

"Maybe it's like *The Incredible Journey*," Dorothy reminisces. "You remember that movie?"

"No."

"Must have been before your time. I'm getting old." Another drag, followed by a steady exhale. "So. What'd you think? Of my team?"

"You mean the rabid monkeys running circles back at the office?"

"Oh, come on. They're good people."

"But are they good at their jobs? And is one of them responsible for your breach?"

"They're good people," she says, with more force than usual. It gives me pause. Dorothy, on the whole, appears flighty, but she's a fighter. A woman who married early and raised a child. Then she turned a neighborhood matchmaking business into an online success. She is not a pushover, no matter how many times a day she loses her glasses.

"Fair enough." Nodding, I shut my eyes hard before reopening them. "I'm not sure what I think yet." This is a lie, obviously, but being an asshole to Dorothy serves no purpose at this juncture. The whole point of this project is to help her. "For the moment, I've found no specific issues."

"Good. That's good."

"Yeah, well, it's early days. I'll figure it out eventually. There's always a bad apple to root out."

She pauses to suck in smoke. Her next sentence emerges in the kind of tight, half-coughing vocal fry I associate with hard-core stoners. "You are the most cynical human being I've ever met."

"Comes with the territory."

"You ever get tired of it?" Dorothy's voice is wistful.

"Security consulting?"

"Yeah."

"I'll stop when I've reached my objectives."

"Objectives. Shit." Another long drag. "You gotta learn to relax, kid."

Relax. Right. I can't help but smirk. "That's what the club's for."

"Oooooooh, the club. Yeah. I'll bet. Maybe I'll go check it out sometime."

"Oh lord." Picturing her and Malika all gussied up in leather and vinyl is enough to morph my smile into a full-on grin.

She giggles. "I could turn out to have a latent penchant for whips and chains."

Malika, I can absolutely envision wielding a whip in spike-heeled boots. Dorothy's a little harder to picture in anything but flowing hippie dresses.

Rae would look good in PVC, my mind unhelpfully supplies. I think of her eyes, her lips, that little divot in the middle of her freckled chin. The way she'd light up, bright red, if I spanked her just right, and how loud she probably moans when she comes.

My stomach rumbles, snapping me out of it. I toe off my shoes and quickly shove my key into the lock. "Night, Dorothy."

"Hey." She shuffles up to standing and walks over to where our banisters almost touch. "Any more news on our data breach?"

"We've got one guy talking about it over on Reddit. That's it. My dark web monitoring hasn't detected anything from Sugar. No leak sites or data dumps. No sign of it anywhere." I shake my head. "Right now, far as I can tell, the breach is just a rumor."

"You think that little bastard made it up?"

"He might have. I plan to find out."

"I know you believe there's someone on the inside—"

"There often is."

"But my employees are not like that. I trust them. Totally."

"I'll figure it out, Dorothy. And I'll keep it under wraps until I'm sure." I suppress a yawn. "No one will guess what I'm doing at Sugar."

"I know. Thank you."

"Just doing my job."

"You could've gotten a lot more for the office space. I know that."

"I wanted to fill it."

"Grant." Her mom voice shuts me right up. "In twenty-one days, everything I've built could come crashing down because of that parasite my daughter married."

I nod.

"What you're doing is more than just a job. More than renting out an empty office. You're saving my ass."

"Don't worry, Dorothy. I'll fix it." I shove open the door and head inside, grab a beer, and settle in for a long night of work, hoping to god I can keep my promise.

CHAPTER SEVENTEEN

Rae

I stare at the sheet of paper waiting for me dead center on my desk. For a handful of seconds, I think Sam's done this as some sort of practical joke. She's always messing around, so it makes sense, except Sam would have made it about picking boogers and, I don't know, naked things. Also, Sam doesn't know about Grant's link to the club and, now, to me. At least I haven't mentioned it.

"What a prick."

No touching? *Touching?* Really? Have I even touched him once? Nope. I don't believe I have. In fact, he is the one who's done all the touching in our short-lived clustershart of an acquaintance.

I set down the box of cupcakes I baked last night and pick up Grant's list of demands, my hands visibly shaking.

OFFICE RULES
1. NO TOUCHING.
2. DOOR MUST ALWAYS REMAIN OPEN DURING CO-OCCUPATION.
3. CLUB IS OFF-LIMITS.

I'm about to crumple it when I hear the beep of a key card activating the exterior door. My entire body freezes.

I came in early today to prep for a benefits meeting with the department heads. Actually, I'd planned to come in at 7:00 a.m., but I hit snooze twice and finished frosting the cupcakes and changed my top three times, what with that mortifying wet T-shirt moment cycling through my brain on repeat all night. Then I had to swing by Hannah's to bring her emergency diapers and make sure Otty got up for her breakfast shift, so 7:00 a.m. turned into 7:30 a.m., which, when I looked at my phone on the way upstairs, had somehow magically transmogrified into one minute to 8:00 a.m., since literal time is against me and I've never, ever, not once in my entire life managed to be early for anything.

Which means the meeting's starting... crap. Now!

I'm about to chuck Grant's pathetic one-sheeter into the trash when he appears in the doorway, freezing me in place.

His eyes go straight from my face to the paper in my hand. "Dammit," he mutters as his gaze flicks back up to meet mine again.

My eyebrows lift. "Well, good morning to you too."

He does not sound happy when he says, "You found it."

I hold up the list, surprised at how steady my hand is. Is it because he looks suddenly unsure? Is that why the anger's gone?

Whatever the reason, I'm now soaring on a fresh wave of... gosh, it couldn't be excitement, could it?

"You looking for this?" I ask in my softest voice. "Your lil' list?"

He drops his head with a sigh and shakes it before looking up at me. "Yes. I should not have left that for you."

"Says who? This is a great idea. In fact"—I grab my favorite pen from the capybara cup on my desk, set the paper down, and add a fat number four—"why don't I go next? No..." I say, scrawling as quickly as I can get it down. "Glow-er-ing. There." I dot the *i* with a heart. "Looks like we've got ourselves a rule number four."

When I look up, the man's clean-shaven face is creased into the literal definition of a glower. Image search *Glowering Man* and you'll see Grant G. Bowman. Middle G for Glower.

"What are you talking about?"

"That. Right there. You're doing it. You're glowering. It's unpleasant."

The expression disappears in the blink of an eye, his features smoothing out so he's as bland as vanilla pudding. "You can't tell me what to do with my face."

"Really? Well, then you can't tell me where I can and cannot go when I'm not at work." I turn, whip a piece of tape off the *Lion King* dispenser Otty gave me last Christmas, and march up to the storage unit built along the back of the room. After a moment's hesitation, I open the tall, shared cabinet that divides his side of the storage wall from mine and tape the list on the inside, at eye level. "There." I brush off my hands and step back before carefully closing the door. "Easy!"

His exhalation is loud enough to blow the whole damn office down. Ignoring him, I walk to my desk, gather my things, and head toward the conference room.

"Hey!" Samantha calls as she sails into the lobby, tall and slouched, despite years of physical therapy for her scoliosis, wrapped, layer upon layer, in the miles-long scarf I knitted for her early in the quarantine.

Sam, of course, has already got a Blow Pop in her mouth. Watermelon, obviously.

My grin is huge. "Hello, hot stuff."

Her eyes zero in on the big plastic container in my hands.

"What are those?"

"Klaus's birthday cupcakes."

"You're a goddess."

I take in the sallow color of her skin, the puffiness around her eyes, and the sleep lines on her cheek. "You look exhausted."

Avoiding my gaze, she slings her bag onto her desk. "What do you mean? I'm not exhau—" She's betrayed by the yawn that cuts her off mid-word.

"What have you been up to, Sammy? I swear you're being weird."

The innocent look she gives me is as fake as the ID she used to buy booze before either of us was old enough. "What?"

"Hmm." Eyeing her so she understands that I'm unconvinced, I hold up the cupcakes. "These are going in the break room."

"I can take them for you," she offers with the smirk Hannibal Lecter would use when offering to babysit.

"Limit is one cupcake per person. There's a sign." I lead the way down the hall to the kitchen.

"You're so organized."

I don't need to reply. We both know that it is absolutely the case. I am organized AF. By necessity. As the eldest, I basically raised Otty after Mom died. I mean, Dad was a mess, so the lunch packing, and permission slip signing, and grocery lists all fell to me. I'm not mad about it. It's good to be needed, especially if it keeps everyone safe and happy and doing what they're meant to be doing.

Sam rips open the container and bites into a gluten-free chocolate cupcake with vegan buttercream frosting, not even taking the time to admire the little green succulent I piped on top. I'll forgive her since she probably hasn't eaten actual food since yesterday's lunch.

"What's going on, seriously?"

"Ngnh?"

"You're being weird."

"Nghg ngh."

Now I know something's off. Because, yes, her mouth is full, but that's never stopped her from speaking before. The woman knows how to talk and chew. When it comes to food, Sam has exactly two settings. She's either ravenous beyond belief or has forgotten its very existence. There's no in-between for her, and though we've never discussed it, I know it's a direct result of being brought up by a mom who spent time in and out of rehab and psych wards and an absentee birth father.

The first time I brought Sam home after school, she wolfed down every box of cereal in the house, including the desiccated bran flakes from the back of the cupboard. From that day on, I added extra to our weekly shopping lists, and Dad picked it up, no questions asked.

"I'm sorry to have to point this out," I tell her, in no way distracted, "but you've got literal suitcases under your eyes this morning. Like shipping containers. Also, you didn't answer my texts last night. Or my calls." Which I don't think has ever happened.

"Nnngh nigh."

I stare at her through narrowed eyes, ready to get to the bottom of the mystery, when I catch sight of the clock above the fridge. No! I've somehow gone from early to on time to four minutes late. "We're talking about this later."

"This?" she manages to grunt through a mouthful of frosting.

"Why you're avoiding your best friend."

"Okay, fine." She swallows a massive bite and licks her lips. "I've got stuff going on. But if we're laying our cards on the table,

I'm pretty sure there's something you're not telling me, either, missy." Her eyes flick to the side as someone passes the break room door, stops, and backs up to look in at us.

It's Grant. Because of course it is.

"Coming?" It's definitely more of a demand than a question.

I swallow. "Coming?"

Oh god. What's wrong with me? Did I have to repeat that one word aloud? And why does it sound like I made it dirty on purpose?

"To this morning's benefits meeting." The way he snaps out his arm to look at his watch is all business. "You're late."

With that, he turns and walks out, all straight back and starched white collar.

Samantha watches me follow him out, her eyes wide with curiosity, dawning understanding, and more than a little hurt, which stands to reason given that she's the one person with whom I've shared everything for almost my entire life.

Until yesterday, in fact, when I omitted the very relevant detail that Grant Bowman is none other than my Friday-night Dom.

We've both got secrets. Not good. At all.

I'll talk to her, I decide. And I'll fix things. It's what I do.

CHAPTER EIGHTEEN

Grant

Rae has talent. I'll give her that. Although talent isn't the right word. Is it charisma, perhaps? She's somehow managed to make an incredibly dry subject entertaining, which is quite a feat.

It's her ebullience, I think. Or enthusiasm? Yep. That's it. The exact thing that caught my eye at the club on Friday. The thing that kept me eavesdropping on otherwise dull conversations between her and prospective Doms. A couple of the guys mistook her wide-eyed excitement for innocence or naivete, but I knew better.

This presentation, if anything, proves that Rae knows what she's doing and is more than capable of communicating it to others. I can't help but feel grudging respect.

I'm still pissed at myself for this morning. I did not want her to see those rules.

After a late night spent digging through the company's data management systems, I'd planned to get here before her and scrap the damn list, which, with a little distance, was clearly a terrible idea. But then Devil Cat struck again, this time shitting not in front of my door but inside one of the shoes I'd forgotten to clean and bring in last night, which meant my entire morning was screwed.

Those shoes are gone. In the garbage, along with the welcome mat and a pair of my favorite socks. Today I'm wearing Vans, the shoes I usually Dom in. There's some cognitive dissonance happening. Wearing the flat, soft-soled Vans at work feels like a contradiction in terms. My body's confused.

I look up at where Rae's standing by the whiteboard, grinning at someone's question about a new hire, her thick curls up in that clip, her neck delicate and vulnerable without the tumble of hair to shield it. The various chords of dissonance melt together like different colored waxes on skin.

Aw, hell. Don't think about it. Not wax, dripping slowly onto her back. Not the way that nape would feel if I bit her there or how she'd look kneeling on the floor between my splayed legs, begging me for one taste of my—

"Does that work, Grant?"

"Sorry, what?" I blink back to the meeting and hate that it takes actual willpower to turn to Dorothy instead of focusing on Rae's naked nape. Shit, have I been staring?

"You wanted to talk to Jade about gaining access to employee computers? Passwords? I suggested you could chat this afternoon."

"Yes. Absolutely."

"Okay." Jade gives me a look that contains zero friendliness. "Any reason you need to get into—"

"It's for the audit. Let's schedule an exact time."

"Well, as IT manager, I should be in on—"

"Just a routine thing, dear," Dorothy breaks in. "Did I hear someone mention cupcakes?" She looks around as if baked goods might have magically popped into the room in the last few seconds.

Fair enough. There is something sort of fairylike about Rae. If anyone could make a plate of cupcakes appear with the wiggle of her nose, it's her.

Right now she's regaling Sugar's leadership team with details about the succulents—the word frankly sounds dirty when she says it—she spent this morning piping on top of each cake.

What does she not do for these people?

Wait. Does she pay for the ingredients out of her own pocket?

She'd better not. With a staff of just under two dozen, that's a lot of flour and butter and whatever else goes into cakes.

Our eyes meet, and her face goes immediately from animated to... What is that expression? Glaring and mean.

People stream out of the room. A couple give me dirty looks. I guess I cramped their style yesterday when I requested that food no longer be allowed in meetings. Or maybe it's the whole mystery auditor thing. They never like that.

Across the room, Rae mouths something at me. I shake my head.

Again, she opens her mouth and says whatever it is, slower this time. *Howard? Yo, Howard?*

You coward?

I mouth an exaggerated *What?* and watch as she rises in a poof of mustard-yellow skirt and caramel top, gathers her things, traipses over to me, and then bends into my space to stage-whisper, "I said *glower*. You're glowering, General. That's against the rules." Then she sails out.

CHAPTER NINETEEN

Grant

An hour later, I walk into the pumpkin-spice-scented office and do a double take.

Rae's turned her desk around so that, instead of facing me the way Dorothy and I had initially set the office up, she's giving me her back.

Aside from a quick break in her typing and a subtle stiffening of her spine, she doesn't acknowledge my presence. She just sits there, her eyes on the screen, sipping at some fancy-looking coffee and clicking away at her mouse while very subtly bopping to whatever's piping through her enormous, sticker-covered pink headphones.

Ignoring each other. That works.

I settle at my desk, put in my earbuds, and get back to work.

Which would be fine if I could concentrate, but Rae's almost more distracting with her back to me than her front. She wiggles. Squirms. Wait, is she flat-out dancing now?

And what is that top, actually? It's much shorter and looser than what I've seen her wear. Every time she moves, it slides to one side, baring a round, freckled shoulder.

Still typing, she shimmies it in place, bends to grab something from a low desk drawer, and goes back to the wiggling.

Then there's the coffee. Every time she takes a sip, I could swear she sings. There. That little sound. Was that a moan? Is she truly moaning over pumpkin spice?

There is no way the woman's not doing it on purpose. The shimmy, the bare stripe of lower back. The peekaboo shoulders and the pleasure sounds. She's got to be taunting me.

My brow wrinkles as I watch her move, her round figure so soft looking that my mouth literally starts to water. I'm breathing hard, thinking about the ass she's got hidden under that pile of fabric. My palms itch to cup that curve, to absorb the jiggle from a good spanking.

After an especially enthusiastic shoulder shimmy, her curls tumble partway down, and I almost order her to put them back up. Because that throat was made for a collar. For my teeth. The way her tender ass was made for the light slap of my palm, not too rough, enough to make her gasp and make the warm place between her—

With a stunning suddenness, Rae simultaneously taps a pile of papers on the surface of her desk and spins in her seat, throwing a glance my way and catching me, hand in the cookie jar. Or rather, palm, teeth, tongue...

Shit.

My eyes flick quickly away from her magnetic body to my screen. I blink. *Concentrate, asshole!* Finally, it comes into full focus. Numbers, letters, lines of text.

Out of the corner of my eye, I see the prim, closemouthed smile she gives me before traipsing over to the walnut cupboards on the back wall.

She opens the door that contains the Rules—the one that's actually a mini coat closet with a rail I added after polling my Off the Cuff friends on what's missing in most offices. The entire wall of cabinets is made of walnut I reclaimed from a famous hotel that went out of business downtown last year. Half the wood in this place came straight from the Old Coles Inn.

None of that matters right now, though, because all I can think about is the damned list, taped up on the inside of that central door.

Did she add a rule while I was away? I didn't even think to check.

Forget it. With considerable effort, I ignore the sway of Rae's hips and focus back on my review of internal security policies and procedures. On the surface, Dorothy's team is as feral as the cat who ruined my three-hundred-dollar shoes. Hell, Rae here is the closest thing I've seen to the kind of type A personality necessary to run a profitable company, and she's an enabler. As the one responsible for hiring, she should have reined her boss in, not egged her on while Dorothy populated her office with this ridiculous entourage of court jesters. With hiring practices based more on gut feelings, Magic 8 Balls, and mood rings than actual skill, I expected to find one issue after another.

Everything I've looked at thus far, though, appears to be industry standard. Clean. They have processes in place, which is better than a lot of businesses I've audited. Despite how out of control they are in person, their work is professional. Which makes the security breach all the more surprising. If it's even real. I'm beginning to think it's just a rumor started by Dorothy's son-in-law as an excuse for the power grab he's planning.

The quick look I cast Rae's way stutters to a stop when I catch the tail end of a mighty, extravagant stretch, one arm in the air, her other hand massaging her neck. I go completely still. In a flash, I'm back at the club, my fingers digging into the muscles of that neck, those shoulders, that tender-looking back, my mouth drawn to the sweet curve of her ear, the smell of her deep in my lungs.

She swivels her hips as she lowers herself into her chair, and I lose my last thread of control. Before I know what I'm doing, my earbuds are out, and I'm halfway across the space that separates us, cracking my knuckles, my eyes on that neck. I know exactly where to stroke to make her open that plush mouth and moan. I know how she'll sigh when I—

What . . . the . . . literal hell are you doing, Bowman?

I can't touch her. Not only would it be inappropriate. It also happens to be literally rule number one. *My* rule.

Completely unaware that I'm hovering back here, Rae stretches again, letting out a sigh that strums every cell in my body. Halfway through the stretch, she stops abruptly and turns as if she's just remembered that we share an office. Except I'm not sitting six feet away, like she expects. I'm standing right behind her.

Our eyes meet, hers wide. I'll admit this looks very, very weird.

My mind scrambles for something to explain my lurking presence. Anything to offset the kind of creeper vibe that would absolutely get someone kicked out of Off the Cuff.

I'll add a rule to the list. That should fix it.

Rules are what make BDSM safe—possible, even. Rules keep businesses running and networks online. Rules are what we need. What this whole batshit company needs.

In a split-second decision, I veer left toward the closet door, which is halfway open by the time it occurs to me that I don't have anything to write with. I'm about to head back to my desk when my eyes land on the list—unchanged—and beside it, a pen, stuck to the inside of the door with what appears to be Velcro. I hesitate for a few seconds before yanking it off with a loud *scritch*.

She pays no attention as I scrawl a new line in shimmery purple ink.

When I shut the door and return to my seat, I am significantly calmer. Much better. All she has to do is follow that rule, and we'll make it through the next twenty days without a hitch.

CHAPTER TWENTY

Rae

WHAT DID GRANT JUST add to the rules?

I'm dying to get up and look. But maybe he needs to stew for a while.

Obviously, the problem with making him stew is that I'm stewing too, and patience is low on my list of virtues.

When my phone rings, I snap it up with an overloud "Rae Jensen!" The next fifteen minutes are spent going over the final details for our employee retreat, which is just around the corner. I can't wait for it to be over, honestly. It's a ton of work.

"Retreat?" Grant asks after I hang up.

"Eavesdrop much?" I say over my shoulder.

"You weren't quiet."

"Well, forgive me for doing my job here."

"It's your job to plan a retreat?"

"It's HR."

His humming non-reply compels me to explain. With an exaggerated sigh, I say, "Once a year, the Sugar App staff goes to an offseason mountain resort for 'bonding activities.'" I provide a helpful set of air quotes over the last two words. In case he doesn't know what that involves.

"That sounds chaotic."

"Oh, it is," I add with a smile. "So much fun."

"But do you really need to bond?"

"You tell me. Last year, the dev folks, matchmakers, and designers played a game of hide-and-seek that led to one of the app's most successful features."

"Which is?"

"The Wild Turkey Chase."

He just shakes his head.

"It's a scavenger hunt element. Very popular with older folks who want a little more from their dating apps than a right swipe." I lean forward, annoyed that I have to defend Sugar to this guy. "Did you know that we're industry leaders in the senior market?"

"Nice." I hate how good his grudging approval feels. "Okay, then. This retreat is when?"

"Less than two weeks." And then a wild hair makes me ask, "Want to come?"

"No."

"Of course not."

"What does that mean?"

"Just that I'm not surprised." I produce one last artificial smile over my shoulder and turn back to my desk. "We are definitely not to your taste."

His only response is a low growl that, though impossible to interpret, has my pulse thrumming double time.

After that, I reply to a message from my cousin. I somehow got roped into planning her bachelorette party, which is turning into a lot more work than I'd banked on. I call the restaurant where we're having dinner and double-check the number of guests. Then finally, oh finally, I get up and replenish my tape supply, refill the contents of the blood bag, and shuffle a few files around. Nothing to see here. La, la, laaaaa. I'm just happy to have *Wicked* playing in my ears. I'm happy that it's finally autumn. Happy that I can pull out my favorite jack-o'-lantern tights soon and wear them to the office. I'll bet Grant will hate them.

By the time I finally make it to the little coat closet, I'm almost shaking with excitement. I open the door and read.

5. NO DANCING, SHIMMYING, OR STRETCHING.

What? I make myself look it over again, slowly, my face burning. Did I even dance? I don't think so. And any stretching I did was totally unconscious.

I picture Grant glaring over like I'm something he's just stepped in while I innocently go about my day. I'm mortified. Seriously, the man is an absolute killjoy.

Should I add a rule? About his typing? The annoying way he taps his foot under the desk? Or I could make something up. That would irritate the crap out of him, wouldn't it? If I claimed he smelled like, I don't know, cheap cologne or fish or something.

Or... I could leave him hanging. No reaction. No new rules.

Pleased with that idea, I take another deep breath before I do my best to set my face into something neutral and shut the door.

I'm fizzing inside as I force myself to walk unhurriedly back to my desk.

It doesn't take long for me to realize the back-facing thing was a strategic mistake. I am way too conscious of his eyes on me. It's going to be a long day, imagining him watching me like a hawk, following every move I make, judging me. Especially if I can't dance, shimmy, or stretch. I so badly want to.

Wait. Now that I think about it, that is actually three rules. Doesn't seem fair.

I slide my headphones back, turn around, and raise my hand like the approval-seeking fourth grader I once was.

When that gets no response, I wave, and when that doesn't work, I stand and walk the four steps to his desk, plant one hand on my hip, and wait.

The typing stops. Slowly, Grant's eyes scan up my body to my face. The way his dark brows lift sends a fresh wave of this indescribable feeling through me. It's the strangest blend of excitement and irritation and a third thing, warm and liquid and unfamiliar. Whatever it is, I'm obviously the only one feeling it. I mean, look at those eyes. Two pools of sharp annoyance in an ocean of blasé.

Yeah, the man really dislikes me.

With crisp, precise movements, he removes one earbud. "Yes?"

The breath I suck in is a giddy mix of oxygen and pure adrenaline. "We have a problem."

His eyebrows stretch impossibly higher. "Oh?"

From the headphones around my neck, Ariana Grande's rendition of "Popular" pierces the silence, faint and tinny but perfectly clear. "The rules? The line you just added?" The quick flick of his eyes toward the coat closet edges me up and up until I could almost float away on the bubble of glee welling in my throat.

"Rule five?"

"Can we really call it that, though?" With the reckless abandon of a puppy tackling a sleeping cat, I go on. "I feel obliged to point out a problem with rule five."

The brows dip into glower territory. Probably not the best time to mention it. "What are you talking about?"

"Weeeell, I'm pretty sure number five is actually three rules. Not one."

"O-kay...and...?"

"I believe we should make it one rule per line." With a flash of inspiration, I add, "And per person."

A series of reactions passes over his face, from disbelief to exasperation to a stubborn sort of refusal and, finally, oh god, finally, the mouth hardens, the square jaw flexes, and it all—*poof!*—disappears behind that stoic mask.

"Right," he says with a stiff nod. "You're saying one rule per line. And we alternate. Makes sense."

"I knew you'd be reasonable." Is that a faint lift at the corner of his mouth? "Anyway, I've got a rule to add as well. But it doesn't seem right to stick a number six on until you've decided which one you'd like to go with for five." It's almost impossible to maintain a straight face when I say, "What do you think? Will it be dancing, shimmying, or stretching?" I give him my most guileless expression. "Doesn't matter to me."

His breathing is slow and measured as he appears to parse out his choices, everything about him screaming *Businessman weighing the merits of very important business-y proposals*. When in reality, he's picturing me dancing around the office.

I bite my lip *hard* and force myself to stay calm. "Well?"

"I'll fix it." He gives a single nod, all official and serious.

"Great. Thanks."

I return to my desk and, pushed by some absolute imp of an inner devil, give a little stretch as I settle into my chair. Might as well do it while I can.

CHAPTER TWENTY-ONE

Rae

"Okay. Spill," Sam says through a mouthful of fried food.

The two of us are sitting in a back booth at the extremely busy Galaxy Diner, less than a block from work. Over the last half hour, I've watched my best friend down something called a Nuclear Waste Dog, slathered in salsa and chili, cheese, sauerkraut, and several other entirely unnecessary things. She's now plowing her way through our shared Tater Tot basket and guzzling a milkshake while awaiting the fried OREOs she ordered for dessert.

"Spill what?" I reply without meeting her look.

"What's going on with you and *Work Daddy*?"

I almost choke on the bite of hoagie I've just taken, hunch, and look around to make sure no one we know happens to be sitting in a neighboring booth. "Shhhh! Are you kidding me right now? You can't say that this close to the office."

"Oh my god. I'm right, aren't I? You and Work Daddy are banging."

"We are not!"

"And yet your reaction could not be more suspicious." Of course Sam knows I'm hiding something. She knows everything about me, from my star sign to the way I always hiccup after my first sip of soda. "Am I gonna have to flog it out of you? I could use one of those cat tails."

"A cat-o'-nine-tails? Do you even know what that is?" I take another bite, studiously concentrating on my hoagie's crisp outside and melty middle.

"It's a hairy whip."

I set the rest of my sandwich down, working hard to calm my oversensitive gag reflex. "Gross, Sam."

"A wig on a stick."

"Shut up. No. It's a whip with, like, a bunch of thin strips of leather."

She pulls out her phone and searches. "Hm. Okay. Kinda mop-like." Nodding, eyes still down, she asks, "You see any of that at the sex club on Friday? With Work Daddy?"

"No! And it's not a sex club. It's a BDSM club. Also, he wasn't..." I let it trail off, unable to finish the lie.

"Aha! You did see him there! I knew it! You two totally recognized each other yesterday, didn't you? Didn't you? Oh my goddess, you crashing into him like...Wait." She bends close, her dark eyes huge. "You called him *sir*. You never call people *sir*. Shit, Rae. He's your daddy!" Her voice, which has gone from zero to a million decibels, is starting to attract looks.

"Stop it. Shush. Please. Come on!" I whisper, patting the air to get her to quiet. "I've got to go back and work in the same room as him, okay? It's been tense." And we haven't even made it through Tuesday.

"Tell me everything."

My head lowered, I whisper, "Yes. He was the Dom I mentioned."

"Guess the cat-o'-nine-tails is out of the bag!"

"Please, Sam, just keep it down."

"This is amazing. What, was he, like, all done up in leather?

Oh, sweet Jesus, does he wear chaps and stuff? Butt hanging out? No. No, no, please tell me you've seen his wanger. Please. I just wanna—"

"Stop. Now. I can't." I point at myself. "HR manager, remember? It's inappropriate and unprofessional and—"

"OREOs!" our waiter announces as he sets the plate down with a flourish and takes off for another table.

As the smell of deep-fried batter wafts my way, I sit up and say, "Listen. I'll explain, but you cannot mention this. At all. To him, to Dorothy, to anyone. Okay?"

"O ye of little faith." She shoves a huge bite of deep-fried, oozing cookie into her mouth, shaking her head at me in that disappointed way she has. "When have I ever let a secret out?"

Actually, never. She's good like that. A vault. Otty told Sam about losing her virginity the day after it happened, and she never once mentioned it to me. I didn't find out for ages. I'm still kind of peeved that my sister told my best friend something that vital, and she never once gave so much as a hint. In the end, Hannah's the one who spilled the beans. To this day, I don't get why I was left out of the loop. Honestly, it still hurts.

"Speaking of secrets." I eye Sam, that hurt squiggling in my stomach. "You still haven't told me what's going on with you."

Her eyes go round with fake innocence. "Eee?" she says around a mouthful.

"Don't even try it, Samantha. You've got a hickey right there."

The second she slaps her hand to her neck, I give her my evilest laugh. "Aha! I was right!"

"Where is it?"

"I lied. There's no hickey."

"You evil wench!"

"Who are you boinking?"

Her eyes narrow. "I'll spill my beans if you tell me what Work Daddy's wanger's like."

"Can we please not say wanger?"

"Okay. His dingaling? Peepee? Phallus? Man meat? Knob? Oh god, it's an anaconda, isn't it? I knew that guy was packing. Look at his swagger. I mean that BDE is above and beyon—"

"You're dead to me." I sit back in my seat, arms crossed, doing my best to look disapproving when, really, I'm working hard to hold the laughter in. "Seriously, though. There was no nudity. Got it? I saw nothing."

"But did you feel it? Like, in your butt crack? Like at the club, did he nudge it up against your mound? Was there dry-humping? Nothing between you and his impressive dick print but those expensive-looking man pants. I'll bet you could gauge his girth and—"

"Oh my god, Sam." A laugh bubbles out as I shout, "There was no penis contact. No penis! At all!"

Of course, that has to be the exact moment the song ends. In the few seconds before another begins, I swear every single head in the diner turns our way.

The word *penis* seems to echo endlessly as my cheeks burn up.

"No penises, huh?" Klaus marches up to the booth wearing a bright smile behind his giant red beard. He's got on shorts, despite the chill, suspenders over a button-down shirt, sleeves folded up to his elbows, and the usual amount of red chest hair peeking out at the collar. The outfit, I assume, is why everyone calls him Klaus. He looks like he came straight here from nineteenth-century Bavaria. His real name, I know from his personnel file, is Eugene Harvey Echols. Because he's apparently happier with the Klaus moniker than his birth name, HR discretion ensures that his legal name is not something I'd ever divulge. "I'm sorry to hear that."

"No, you're not." Sam scoots over to make room for him. "You wanna hoard all penis contact for yourself."

"Guilty." Klaus watches me while working to shove his middle into the narrow space between the table and bench seat. "Whose penis are we discussing?" Klaus's gaze seesaws between the two of us.

"Nobody's," Sam and I say simultaneously.

"Shame. I was hoping this was about..." Klaus leans in, fanning himself with one big hand. "Work Daddy."

"Oh god." My face sinks into my hands. "Are you kidding me right now?"

"I didn't say a word," Sam insists. "I swear!"

"There is nothing to say!" I look up and bang my fist on the table, rattling dishes and, frankly, myself. "Please stop. This is unprofessional and...uncalled for."

"Sure. Of course."

"But Work Daddy's so evil and hot and—"

"Stop. I mean it." I look at Klaus. "Don't call him that."

"Okay then."

"Either of you."

"Scout's honor," says Sam, as if she ever participated in Scouts in her life.

My skeptical glance slides from Klaus to Sam and back. They're both obviously lying.

"I gotta go." I stand, grab my things, and turn. "Do not refer to him as Work Daddy on Slack. For your own sake. I don't want either of you fired." I look at them again and give them a final, firm "I mean it" before stomping to the counter to pay.

On the way, I'm pretty sure I hear Klaus ask, "How long till they bang it out?" which I choose to ignore.

I'm still seething as I hurry back to the office, turn the final corner, and stutter to a halt when I catch sight of the building where it all started. There it is. The comedy club, the entrance to Sugar, and that anonymous metal door leading straight down into Richmond's sexy underworld.

As if conjured by my thoughts, the door to the club swings open as I come even with it, and Harlow emerges. It takes me a moment to recognize her. Maybe it's because Friday night's sleek black outfit has been replaced with shorts and sneakers and a VCU sweatshirt. More college athlete than intimidating bouncer.

"Hey." She gives me a big smile. "What you doing?"

"I work here." I point at the glass door leading to the small lobby and the stairs and elevator beyond it.

"Yeah? That's cool. You coming back to the club this week?"

"I wish."

"Why can't you?"

"Well, I'd planned to, but..."

I lose my train of thought when the glass door opens, and Grant himself steps onto the sidewalk, all business with his laptop bag and his expensive suit. His reaction, when he sees us talking, is almost comical. Friendly surprise followed by squinty-eyed annoyance.

"Hey. Just the man I was waiting for." Harlow gives him a shoulder bump.

"Ready for lunch?" The second his eyes leave me and go to her, he smiles. Like genuinely smiles. I hardly recognize the expression after being on the receiving end of nothing but scowls.

Oh wow. I get it. They're an item. Harlow must be the reason he isn't in the market for a sub. Strong and beautiful and confident and kind Harlow.

It's probably the fried pickles or flashbacks of the term *man meat*, but I feel sick.

When Grant slides his arm around Harlow's waist and gives her an affectionate squeeze, I wave, mumble something about getting back, and head to the door, feeling foolish for my own disappointment.

Behind me, Harlow says, "So you and Sunny are working together? That must be fun."

I'm halfway across the lobby, exterior door about to close, when Grant snorts. "Fun?" His tone suggests the very opposite. "Try excru—" The rest of his reply is lost when the door shuts, cutting off the sounds of traffic and everything else. Thank god.

Oh, that's nice. Maybe I'm not his dream sub or whatever. Maybe I'm annoying and too distracting at work, but the fact is that we are now colleagues, and the least he can do is pretend not to hate my guts.

That's it, I decide. I'm putting something very, VERY good on that list. I've no idea what, yet, but it'll put him right in his place.

I trudge all the way up the steps to the office, press my phone to my ear when I see Blake waiting for me, and mouth, *Sorry!* As soon as I've shut the office door, I throw open the closet, ready, so ready to show him, because who does he think he is? He's by far the more disruptive of the two of us, so he can…

What the hell?

My mouth drops open as I read the new rule five.

That's it. I am over Grant Bowman's shenanigans.

Entirely out of fucks, I stomp over to my desk, grab the fattest permanent marker I've got, and cross the new line out.

There.

That's better.

CHAPTER TWENTY-TWO

Grant

LATE WEDNESDAY AFTERNOON, I badge open the door to find what appears to be a full-blown party in reception.

"What is this?" I ask the woman seated in a visitor chair, knitting. She is wearing a mustache, like everyone else here, including Klaus, who's pasted a large black one overtop of his own copious facial hair. Covered in purple frosting, it is absolutely revolting.

"Henny's birthday."

"Of course." As if I even know who that is. "Where's Dorothy?" Even as I ask, I recall that she's meeting with one of her investors. With less than three weeks before their yearly meeting, she's attempting to drum up as much support as she can.

I spot Rae through the crowd. She's at the other end of the lobby, her arms full of used cups and plates. Our eyes meet. A long second ticks by. Another. Even from here, I can see that her hair is piled on top of her head, leaving her nape bare. The Dom in me really does not like being disobeyed.

Someone punches a balloon in my direction, and Rae disappears from view. I step out of its path, coming back to the present with an almost physical jolt.

Instead of standing here in the entrance, my lunch in one hand

and a box of cat repellent in the other, I make a beeline for our office, slip inside, and shut out the uproar. My phone buzzes in my pocket.

I struggle to set down my things and pull it out to see that it's my mother. I've got to talk to her eventually. I'm just not in the mood to hear about the new fiancé and how in love she is.

Instead of answering, I head over to look at the list, undeniably curious to see what rule Rae has added in my absence.

The excitement plummets when I see what she's actually done. No new rule. Just a thick, black line through my last one.

I've rarely felt anything so righteous as the anger that fills me, burning through all the *should*s and *should not*s as I go to the door and fling it open. Rae is all I see as I storm across the lobby, ignoring one human resource violation after another, to where she's gathering up the team's dishes.

"Rae."

"Grant," she replies, voice light, eyes huge, that little Betty Boop mouth just begging to be bitten.

"I need a word."

The eyes get bigger.

A voice beside me sings, "Aaaaaaaaw, someone's in trouble."

I turn and glare at the man until he scurries off.

"Can it wait?" Rae asks, eyebrows raised in an expression of polite interest that drives me bananas.

"Now." My lips are stiff. "Office."

"Sorry." She lifts the cardboard box she's filled with dirty dishes. "Busy."

"Kitchen, then."

"Fine." With a prim smile, she leads the way through the unruly crowd and down the hall, into the break room.

I shut the door, cutting the decibels in half and turning everything between us way up.

She sets the box on the counter and watches me, her arms crossed. Is she settling in for a fight or about to bolt? I hope it's the former.

"I saw what you did," I tell her, putting my back to the kitchen door. "To my rule."

"Oh?" More of the false innocent act. She knows exactly what she's doing to me. I want to wipe that bored expression from her pert little face and replace it with something more interesting.

"You shouldn't have done that," I tell her, sliding out of my jacket and carefully hanging it on the back of a chair. Her eyes follow my progress.

"Why would you say that?" Her tone's all casual curiosity as she turns to open the dishwasher and gets to work filling it. "We don't need that rule. It's ridiculous." Her little shrug sends her shirt off one shoulder, and I swear to god I'm going to bite all of it: the shirt, the shoulder, and the bra strap playing peekaboo with her freckles. "What could possibly be wrong with me putting my hair up?"

Does she not get what's happening here?

She tosses her head, sending a few curls dancing around her face. The rest are pinned to the very top of her head, in direct opposition to my request. The very important—absolutely necessary—rule five.

"I decided we don't need the rules." She flashes a look at me, all hot challenge, before returning to her dishes. Like I don't exist. Like it barely matters if I stay or go. "We're civilized people."

"Civilized?" Is that what she thinks? "You've got no fucking idea, do you, Sunny?"

CHAPTER TWENTY-THREE
Rae

Alrighty then. I guess we're not civilized. I guess we're... something else. Something rougher, uncontrolled. A little scary.

What's he going to do? That's the thing keeping me on my toes as I rinse dishes with total concentration. Pretending everything's just hunky-dory and there's not a man behind me being... well, the word *uncivilized* certainly springs to mind.

When he doesn't say anything else, I glance over my shoulder at that face and—oh, crap—my insides clench, my nipples go hard, and I watch, my mouth slightly open, as he unbuttons a sleeve and starts rolling it up.

Mesmerized by his quick, precise movements, I find myself turning to lean back against the sink, eyes glued to those efficient hands as he sets to work on the other sleeve.

His approach, as calm and deliberate as a hunter with his prey, makes my pulse go haywire. The closer he gets, the harder it is to catch my breath, and when he leans in...

What's he doing? Is he going to...?

He reaches around me to shut off the water. I didn't even realize I'd left it running. I never leave water running; it's much too precious a resource. Expensive and limited and... "What are you…?" My words trail off, like the last of the breadcrumbs I dropped to get us to this place have suddenly frittered away to nothing, and it's too late anyway because I'm Little Red Riding Hood from *Into the Woods*, and the Wolf is right here, and I maybe kind of asked for this. No, I definitely did. Who cares, anyway, because with Grant Bowman this close, I'm short-circuiting.

He doesn't reply, and I guess I didn't actually finish my thought. So what is there for him to say as he stands there, three feet away, watching me with eyes that are sometimes black, sometimes brown, and always—always—searing me from the inside out? Like a burning coal in a cold furnace, the man incinerates me without an ounce of warmth.

"We've got a problem, you and me," he says, his tone so conversational that this could almost be a professional conundrum he's come to me to solve.

"Oh?" I manage, soap-slick hands gripping the sink behind me in a way that sticks my boobs out and makes my heavy breathing obvious.

He looks down at my chest and watches a full in-and-out cycle before allowing that sharp-edged gaze to return slowly to mine.

"I think you know exactly what problem I'm referring to." He settles into a position that's somehow both casual and purposeful. Hands at his sides, tension in the thick, corded forearms I can't stop staring at, his legs a little wider than they'd naturally land.

"I…I don't…"

"The rules, Sunny."

Everything clenches between my legs *hard*. "The rules?"

"Don't play innocent now." The headshake, the cynical ghost of a smirk. This man will have none of it. Not for a solitary second. "You're much too intelligent for that."

He thinks I'm smart? That's a shocker. But the compliment

feels as good as his undivided focus. Even the hint of condescension hits a pleasurable note deep inside me.

He looks down, squeezing the back of his neck, and sighs with obvious disappointment. Why, oh why, do I now feel chastised and put in my place and, incidentally, more turned on than I've been in my life? If the sink weren't holding me up, I'd melt to my knees, hug his legs, and beg him to...to...for...if only...

"Turn around." His words are all consonant. The whiplash of a *T*, the final *D* sparking down my spine.

Yes. That. The instruction pings through me, lighting up nerves and cells like the on switch to my circuit board, and yet I can't convince my body to move.

When all I do is stare, he releases another of those annoyed sighs and steps closer.

"Turn...the hell...around, Sunny. Now."

I've never spun so fast in my life. For a blank moment, I stare at the sink, my hands floating above it like birds with nowhere to alight.

As if he knows how directionless I am, Grant guides me. "Hold the sides."

I lean forward and put my hands against the edges, grip hard to keep from sliding...and wait.

Wait.

Wait.

"You know why the rules are there, Sunny?" he finally asks, the question a puff of warmth against the side of my head.

"I...I think so."

"No. I don't believe you do. If you did, you would take them more seriously." There's a little sound from him, half growl, half grunt, and then he's closer, body heat giving his proximity away. "You think it's a game? What we're doing here? What we did down there?"

"Uh..." I don't know. Maybe? Isn't it, though? Kind of a game? I've heard people refer to BDSM dates as play sessions, which makes me think that's exactly what it is, but then for others, it's a lifestyle. I...I don't know what he wants me to say, which is simultaneously the best and worst sensation.

As an eternal teacher's pet, I hate not having the answer. I'd feel unmoored, lost, and on the cusp of failure if he weren't right there behind me. As it is, I want him one step closer. I want more than heat. I want the weight of him, the pressure, and maybe—*what the hell, Rae?*—maybe a little pain too? Like, if he tries it, just once, maybe I'll go to that place he took me to on Friday, and everything—all the overwhelm, the anxiety, the uncertainty—will fade and—

"Stay with me," he says in that low, solid voice.

It's some kind of magic that makes everything suddenly crystal clear. I'm present, in my body. "Okay," I whisper, hypnotized.

"Good. Now listen."

I nod, staring down at the pile of half-rinsed plates, aquamarine frosting running down the drain in a rogue Van Gogh swirl.

"The rules are for your own good. And mine. The rules keep things clear, separate. They keep us safe."

Slowly, my eyes close to the rich, warm velvet of his voice as it radiates from my ear to my solar plexus and places farther south.

I can't help the way my back arches, seeking more from this encounter. A hint of friction, at the very least.

"Look at you." Another annoyed sigh, and he shifts. My breath catches as one arm settles on the sink ledge beside me, the other on the opposite side. I'm boxed in. Trapped. Still, annoyingly, he's not actually touching me. "You need to be contained, don't you, naughty girl?"

I try to shake my head, but I'm not sure it works. Nothing works but my heart, which is about to explode from all the pumping.

"Widen your legs."

I immediately obey.

"You know what I can't stand? What isn't remotely acceptable?"

I hope he doesn't expect a response.

"The way you prance around—"

"I prance?"

"Yes."

"Huh. Okay."

"Stop. Talking." One knee nudges the back of my thigh. "You think there aren't consequences? For disobeying? For sashaying around, all fairy dust and light, like there's nothing bad in the world, when we've got jobs to do."

"What? That doesn't make any sen—"

"And this goddamn neck."

Oh. Oh, that's it. Here we go. The rule. The one that pushed me too far and made me take a big fat black marker to his precious list.

5. HAIR MUST COVER NECK AT ALL TIMES.

"Yeah, about that, I'm not okay with you telling me what I—" I start to turn, and he stops me with that same knee, only this time it's flat against my bottom.

"Don't move."

"You don't decide how I do my hair," I whisper.

"Don't I? You run around with this pretty little nape exposed, Sunny, and expect to be treated like a colleague instead of the little sub you are? Making me sit there and stare at it, hard as a rock while you staple and type and bop around in that chair, with this soft throat out, begging for…"

He loses it here, his voice gone, scraped raw, as if the last few words were wrung from his lungs, the velvet sound from before has been brushed the wrong way, and now the rough's come to the surface.

"Begging for what?" I ask, as his breath heats my nape, sending goose bumps out to the tip of every finger, every toe, prickling so hard that my body can't help but wiggle in response.

"Don't move, Sunny."

It's too late, though. I can't help but shift my weight, and he retaliates by inserting his knee fully between my legs from behind, and suddenly I'm straddling it.

"You see now, Sunny?" he rasps. "We talked about this. In the club, remember? You disobey the rules. You pay the consequences."

I've just opened my mouth to remind him that we're at work and his rules are inappropriate here when… he bites down on my neck. The only sound I can produce is a gasp.

Everything goes blank.

Quiet.

I'm a body. An animal. Caught, strangely calm. Excitement's an electric pulse, thrumming, thrumming underneath my surface.

"Consequences," he mutters against my skin before licking it. "That's all this is. Cause, effect, quid pro-fucking-quo."

He's right. This feels inevitable. Like a chain of events that can't possibly be stopped.

"Use it," he mutters into the crook of my neck. "Use my knee."

Without hesitation, my body obeys. Pushing, cramming.

His hand pressing down on my shoulder, making everything more, harder.

Eyes closed. A slow hip circle.

Good. So good. Pressure at my hip, making me speed up. Grind faster, ramp up the contact. I let out a whimper.

"There it is," he whispers. "Good girl."

Pleasure fizzes through me, sparking in my fingers, my toes. I wiggle, lit up and alive.

He claims both hips and works me up and back over that muscular thigh, up and back, until there's nothing else. And then, there, the press of him against my ass, his erection a metal bar right between my cheeks.

He's as turned on by this as I am. His excitement eggs me on, and I'm arching, reaching for more. Straining. Stretching.

"That's it. That's my sweet Sunny. Give it to me. Show me how you do it."

"Give you... Give you what?"

"The orgasm you owe me." His mouth strokes my ear, the words a harsh counterpoint to the wash of warm breath. "Go on. I know it's in there. Show me."

I don't get it. "Y-you want me to make you come?"

"Oh, Sunny." His dry laugh makes me feel young and naive.

It's a threat, that laugh, coupled with a promise. I lap them both up like mint chocolate ice cream.

"I'm not the one who's going to come all over this knee, sweet subby. You are."

I gasp.

CHAPTER TWENTY-FOUR

Grant

"I...I can't. I don't do that."

I laugh again. Poor Sunny's got no clue how hard I'm willing to work for it. Doesn't she see? "It's not yours anymore, sweetheart. The orgasm's already mine."

"What?"

I breathe her in, stroking my nose along her hairline. She smells good. Like the most dangerous of consequences. Can't stop myself from licking her shoulder for another taste of that heady salt/sugar/sex combination.

No flower and citrus perfume here. Just her. That's the scent I want.

"I don't...understand."

My heart's thrashing in my chest, the same beat pulsing hard in my cock. "You owe me," I say, giving more pressure, more speed, and drawing a gasp from her open mouth. The ache that fills my chest as I work her body and stare at that profile is utterly baffling.

"You ignored the rule, Sunny," I explain. "You crossed it out. I can't let that slide. You know I can't." And then, "You wouldn't want me to, would you?"

Her little headshake isn't enough.

"Say it. Tell me I'm right."

"No. No, you really shouldn't. Let it slide, I mean. You can't ignore that."

Her words make my cock impossibly harder. The way I want this woman...

I suck in a deep breath and shut my eyes. Concentrate on how hot and soft she is. How bad she's been. How right it'll feel when I drag all that pleasure right out of her. "Good. We're on... the same page, then." My breath's coming out in ragged grunts. "This... is the consequence."

"Oh god," she gasps. Her eyes roll back. "But there are people around. They could come in and see us..."

"You'll have to be quick, then, won't you?"

"I... I don't know how."

Everything stills. My pulse, my breathing, even the air around us. And then swerves, like the earth's just moved.

"Explain," I order, letting one hip go to nudge her face my way.

"I-I've never come without my hand." The last two words are quiet, her voice dropping into a whisper when she adds, "Or a toy."

Hell yes.

Slow, controlled, I watch my knuckles brush her cheek and then swipe across her damp mouth. Stare at my thumb as it skims her plump bottom lip, and finally, with excruciating care, presses inside. "I'm your toy. Got it? Use me." Her pupils blow wide. "You're going to come, Sunny," I tell her, my voice low and sure. "Because you have to. It's pure mechanics."

I press my thumb deeper into her mouth and heft her body between mine and the sink, letting gravity and our combined muscles ratchet her higher, and higher, until all that pressure's got nowhere left to go but out.

"You're so good," I tell her, gruff and low. "Look at you fucking my thigh."

With a whimper, she suckles my thumb, her soft, slick tongue sending liquid pulses to my cock.

"Suck harder," I order, knowing full well that someone could walk in here any second. I throw a quick glance at the door.

She obeys, her body losing its rhythm as she focuses on my thumb instead of her goal.

This is what I love. Learning a woman, playing her like an instrument.

"Do it," I urge, my words a dirty counterpoint to her accelerating exhalations. "Come hard for me, sweet girl."

There is nothing better than this—her entire frame seizing, her insides clenching up, and her teeth sinking into my thumb. Rae is so gorgeous in these few seconds that she looks suspended out of place and time, caught inside something that is as much like pain as pleasure. It's magnetic the way she's lost, and there's nothing left in her warm, soft frame but bliss. I could watch her for hours. Her utterly unselfconscious grimace, slowly ebbing until there's nothing but peace on her face.

"Good," I grunt, my voice in tatters. "That's it. There you go." I hug her through her entire climax, soaking it up, feeling it vibrate through me, my dick aching with a need that I could ignore for hours if this is what I get in return. All this syrupy pleasure. Epic and raw and mine. *Mine*.

I'm about to remind her to thank me when, behind me, the doorknob turns. Before it starts to swing open, I've got the water running and a towel shoved into Rae's trembling hands. As if the new arrival's popped our bubble, I'm suddenly assailed by the smell of dish soap and the sound of laughter coming from the lobby.

I pick up a sponge and scrub the first thing I find, a mug with the words *Developers' tears* printed on the side. Finally, I glance over my shoulder to see a woman whose name I can't remember. Taylor? Drew?

"Oh, there you are." The woman's voice is loud after our hushed restraint. "We're all playing spin the bottle, so I need a—"

"Spin the bottle?" Rae throws me a frantic look. "That's a bad idea," she says.

"Pfft. It's fine!" The woman's opening cupboards in search of something. Probably the bottle in question. "We just need—"

"No spin the bottle." I don't turn all the way, given the current state of my erection, but my voice carries, low and resonant, like I'm still deep in a scene.

The woman stops in her tracks. "Huh?"

"No spin the bottle," Rae explains.

"Not now. Not ever," I add. Oh, the irony. The hypocrisy.

With a disappointed *tsk*, the woman throws up her hands. "But I love spin the bottle. We always—"

"I'll bet you also love that you have a job." I've got no problem being a prick when it's called for.

"Are you serious?" She appeals indignantly to Rae. "He can't threaten me like that."

"I…" Rae looks at me for the solid five seconds it takes her to dry her hands on the towel before turning to her colleague. "Actually, Blake, he sure can." Her face is a remarkable study in contrasts. Flushed, but calm. Those cheeks bright red, which could be from the steam rising from the sink. More likely it's from the climax I just caused her to have in the workplace.

"No spin the bottle, Blake," she reiterates.

"It's company policy." I shut off the water and accept the towel from my partner in crime.

"Company policy." The woman's eyes flick between Rae and me. "Really?"

"Yes, Blake." Rae nods. "Please tell the others."

"And if they're unhappy," I add, "they are welcome to come see me."

"Wow. All right, I guess." Blake gives us one last long stare before leaving in a huff.

Without looking at me, Rae says, "Thank you."

My eyebrows lift of their own volition. "What exactly are you thanking me for now?"

Her flush darkens. "For standing up to Blake. She can be... pushy."

Oh, that. "You're the one who laid down the law."

She appears to consider. "Well, then, thank you for supporting me. And, you know, being the bad guy."

"I am the bad guy, Sunny." We share a long look as I step closer, reach around her, and unclip the shiny metal claw holding up her mass of hair. It tumbles around her shoulders like something liquid and alive. "Now, how about we get back to obeying those rules?"

Her glare is perfection. One more thing to add to the list. "After what just happened? You want to go back to the rules?"

"What just happened proved that we need the rules, wouldn't you agree?"

She watches me with narrowed eyes, chin jutting at a stubborn angle.

"If you've got something to say, Rae, I think now's the time to say it."

"Are you telling me that what you... what we just did was all to prove a point?"

"Yes." I can't even tell if this is a lie or not, but it's necessary.

"We'll go back to how things were. We need structure, control, rules, dammit."

"And what? Sweep this whole escapade under the rug?"

"Exactly. It's the professional thing to do."

She huffs out a disbelieving sound and considers me for a few seconds, arms folded over her chest, before finally appearing to come to a decision. I don't trust her sudden smile. "All right. Back to the rules we go."

"Good," I reply.

"Good," she says before stomping out.

CHAPTER TWENTY-FIVE
Grant

It has been a long week. I've done nothing but work, attempt to sleep, and when that failed time and again, I've jerked off thinking about the breathy sound Rae makes when she comes.

So, of course, first thing Friday morning, I step in what looks like mouse entrails as I walk out my door. Another gift from my cat admirer. I'm starting to believe Dorothy when she says there's more to what's happening here than your run-of-the-mill trolling. A haunting? The little bastard's wily.

I should have turned around and gone inside immediately after that, but no. I have shit to do. Sixteen days left, and I've found no sign of the breach. Nothing at all.

Usually, at this point, there is some trace of wrongdoing. But my vulnerability assessment has turned up exactly zip. How can I address the security breach if there's no sign of weakness in the company's systems? No SQL issues, no malware or malicious code. And because Dorothy's business model is centered on a human-centric approach instead of a machine-led one, growth is minimal compared to other tech companies I've worked with.

Against all outward appearances, Sugar's protocols are robust, which leaves very few possibilities. All of which I've got to verify after I go by the hardware store for one of those humane traps. Either there's no breach and this company is squeaky clean, or whoever accessed the company's data is on the inside.

As I leave the store, the smell of a good dark roast lures me into the kind of upscale coffee shop I usually avoid. I get to the counter, and right smack in front of me is a cutesy sign telling me that pumpkin spice is everything nice. Of course I think of Rae. Again.

I order my regular large black coffee, and then, for some inexplicable reason, ask for one of the sickeningly sweet seasonal drinks at three times the price. Then I wait, sipping at my coffee while they dump half a gallon of fancy syrups and swirly creams and powders into a cup and wondering what the hell has gotten into me.

It's a peace offering to a colleague. That's all.

Liar. This isn't about peace.

It's about the sound Rae makes every time she sips at pumpkin spice coffee. I swear I'm not a masochist, but dammit, I want to see the expression that goes with those happy little moans.

That sound is just one of a list of things I've unconsciously compiled this week. So far, it reads:

- When Rae listens to music, her entire body wants to move. (I no longer believe this is purposeful.)
- Is loved by all and feeds them like it's her job. Which it isn't.
- Works her ass off.
- Says *yes* to absolutely everyone.
- Swings her feet under her desk because they don't touch the floor.

- When she comes, her expression is the closest thing I've ever seen to religious rapture. I can't stop thinking about it. This has become an issue.

I'm distracted by that last item as I walk into the office and don't immediately notice that it's Rae seated at reception today instead of Sam. Only after I see her do I narrow in on the man lurking in the lobby, way too close to Rae for comfort—both mine and clearly hers. With her arms crossed, chin jutting, and eyes narrowed, she is the very definition of defensive.

The second she sees me, her expression goes through a gratifying transformation from that one-step-closer-and-I'll-smack-you look to unadulterated relief. "You're here!"

"Yep." I hold up her coffee, ignoring the man, who is unsubtly sizing me up. He's a tall, lanky, stereotypically handsome guy with light brown hair that swoops over his brow and an easy smirk. He's wearing a plaid button-down that looks expensive, a sleeveless, green puffer vest, and khakis with the kind of pristine white sneakers I've only ever seen straight out of the box.

"You want this here or at your desk?"

"You...brought me coffee?" Rae says in the tone of voice I imagine she'd use if I'd shown up with a puppy. I don't hate it.

"Where's mine?" The guy chuckles.

My head swivels slowly his way as I set Rae's drink in front of her. "Have we met?"

"Not yet." He sticks out his hand and grabs mine in one of those too-tight power shakes that Harlow refers to as a Penis Pump. "Dane Wabash," he says in a voice that's salesman smooth.

Well, hell. Dorothy's son-in-law in the flesh. This can't be good. "Grant Bowman."

"Grant! Great to meet you!" He's mid-thirties, but something about him is both old and simultaneously infantile. An aging mama's boy who learned to emulate Dad but never actually grew into a man. He releases my hand and takes in the lobby with an expansive stretch of the arm. "Just here to check the place out."

"Check the place out." I give him exactly the amount of inflection he deserves. Which is zilch.

What I really want is to watch Rae's face when she takes her first sip, but this guy's in my damn way.

When I step to the side for a clearer sight line, he follows. "You know." He leans in to meet my eyes, man-to-man. He's an inch or so taller than I am and is working very hard to use that to his advantage. "Gotta make sure everything's running smooth." His expression sharpens. "I'm concerned."

"Concerned? I don't understand." To my disappointment, Rae sets her coffee on the desk before asking, "Are you hoping to...work here?"

"That's cute," he tells her, giving me a side-eye that's as patronizing as a nudge with an eye roll. "I might."

What the hell is he doing here? This feels like a whole lot more than a random visit.

"Right. See, the thing is, I do the hiring, and we don't have anyone coming in today; nor are there any open positions currently, so..."

"Sorry, hon. My bad." He still doesn't look at her. If I didn't already dislike the man on principle—for Dorothy's sake—I'd hate him now. First, he makes me miss the first latte sip, and now he's disrespecting Rae. My hands clench into fists.

"Dotty didn't mention me?" Dane Wabash *tsk*s, shaking his head and baring his teeth, which I think is meant to look contrite. "Yeah. Granny's forgetting things now." Another *tsk*, and the guy's grating on my nerves so hard it takes a concerted effort to unclench my jaw. He leans in close. "See, Dotty's been goin' downhill, real fast. Age. You know? Rachel's concerned."

"I don't understand," Rae says.

I, however, see exactly what's going on. And I don't like it one bit.

"In a couple of weeks, hon, I'll be your new boss," Wabash faux-whispers, all *aw shucks* and *look at how modest I am*.

Holy shit. He's just declared war on Dorothy. As easy as that. And now we're down to sixteen days to shore up this company's defenses before what's looking like an all-out assault.

"New boss?" Rae looks from me to him and back. "I don't understand what's—"

"The company's in trouble. Did you know that?"

"What? I don't even—"

"Probably above your pay grade."

I'm a second away from grabbing the asshole by the collar and lugging him out when Rae, tight-lipped, steps between us and asks, "Is Dorothy expecting you?"

"It's all good." He winks at her and looks around, clapping his hands a couple of times like he's just rarin' to get started. "I'll just show myself around and—"

"Have a seat," I interrupt. There is absolutely no way this man is getting unfettered access to the offices. None. "I'll let Dorothy know you're here."

"Perfect. Lead the way."

Rae widens her eyes at me. "Maybe I should go see if Dorothy's available. You can hang out with Mr. Wabash."

"Oh. Hey. Before you go..." As Rae attempts to head off, he reaches out and grabs her arm.

Rae jerks to a stop.

Every muscle in my body tenses up.

She looks down at his hand. Her mouth opens and closes.

"How 'bout that coffee, hon?" the man says.

Heat spreads over my body, fogging my vision. I've never once felt this close to ending someone.

"Let. Her. Go."

CHAPTER TWENTY-SIX

Rae

Dane Wabash's hand drops from my arm.

"Sit down," Grant says, so threateningly calm that the hair all over my body stands up.

Oh. My. God.

"Sorry, man. Didn't know you two were—"

The door beeps a few feet away, admitting Dorothy. "Dane? What a surprise." She looks at the three of us, obviously gauging the situation before putting a strained smile on her lips. She's giving Barbra Streisand when she puts out a hand, not for a shake, but for a queenlike clasp.

"Hey, Dotty, I was just—"

"Have you had breakfast?" Dorothy Gold lowers her glasses and narrows her sharp gaze on him, and oh, holy crap, she's not Barbra; she is literally the Godfather when she says, "We're going to breakfast."

"I'm actually here to—"

"The investors' meeting is in two weeks, Dane. We are not open for visitors today."

"Listen. I own half this—"

"Need me to escort him out?" Grant cuts in, big and hard and scary in a way I've never seen him look.

What the hell is going on?

"I don't know. Do I, Dane?" Dorothy asks the other man.

He looks from her to Grant, possibly sizing him up. The threat sizzling in the air between them makes me take a step back.

"I'm good." He grins. "Breakfast with the mother-in-law sounds great." He heads outside, holding the door open for Dorothy, and gives Grant a final stare before following her down the steps.

The second the door closes, I look at Grant. "What just happened?"

Grant shakes his head, breathing hard.

"You okay?" My hand lands on his chest, and he anchors it there with one of his.

"Are you okay?"

"I'm fine."

"Did he hurt you?"

"That's her son-in-law?"

"Are you hurt, Rae?" He looks down at the wrist Dane Wabash grabbed. "Show me."

I blink. "It's fine. See?" I hold out my arm.

Grant takes my wrist gently, turns it over, and runs his fingers across my skin.

The second he sees the red mark, he spits out, "Goddamn it. I should've…"

"What?" Our gazes meet. "What should you have done?"

"When he grabbed you, Rae, I wanted to…I had…"

"What did you have?"

"I had urges."

"Urges?"

"Violent ones."

"Okay." He's so close I can smell soap and warm skin. "What about now?"

"Now?" Our eyes snag, and I see the striations of his irises, as finely detailed as the rings in a tree trunk.

"Are you still having urges?" I whisper, his proximity sending warm, lazy curls to my belly.

Our hands slide together, palm-to-palm, and our fingers clasp. His pupils widen, his eyes lowering to my mouth. I can't help but stare and wonder how he tastes. My head tilts back, suddenly heavy from the pressure of his gaze. His focus sharpens on my mouth, and I swear he is three seconds from closing the gap between us when the exterior door beeps and swings open, letting in the sounds of traffic along with a shot of cold air and a wide-eyed Sam.

Grant and I jump apart. Sam pauses in the open doorway and stares at us. "Good morning?"

"It is," Grant says, his voice low and sandpaper rough.

"Definitely." I nod, looking around like I've lost something.

"I'll, uh…work." On that note, Grant bends, scoops up his laptop bag, and says, "Don't forget your coffee," before heading into our office.

"So," Sam sings as she saunters in, "what'd I miss?"

"Hold on." I grab my things and start to follow Grant.

"No, no, no, you hold on," she says, stepping in my way. She has to bend to line her face up with mine, and whispers, "We're going out tonight. And you're telling me everything. Got it?"

"Only if you tell me what's happening with you."

"Deal."

"Deal."

She moves out of the way and goes to high-five me, giving up when she sees the coffee in my hand.

"What was that about?" I ask Grant as I close the door behind me. "The son-in-law thing?"

He looks at me, appears to consider, and then shakes his head. "Nothing. Don't worry about it."

"Oh, no. You don't get to blow me off like that after the things I heard today. That guy is up to—"

His phone vibrates. He mutters under his breath, grabs his things, and looks at me. "I'm serious, Rae. It's fine. Everything will be okay. Got it?"

Another long vibration from his phone makes him curse. I back away. He starts to take off and then turns to look at me from the doorway. "Don't forget to drink your coffee." His gaze flicks down to my mouth and then up. "It's pumpkin spice," he says, before leaving me standing in the middle of the office, utterly confused.

I take a sip. Another. Dammit, why is this so good? I have tasted a lot of pumpkin spice in my life, and this one is definitely a top ten contender. I'll have to ask Grant where he got it.

Right after I make him explain the Dane Wabash thing. Because whatever is going on here, it's not good.

What I don't get is why it's being kept a secret.

CHAPTER TWENTY-SEVEN

Rae

THAT NIGHT, I AM, yet again, loitering in the street in front of the building. It is a testament to my love for Sam that I am out here in front of the comedy club right now instead of at home in my vintage *Lion King* pajamas, hard at work on my book nook with *The Great British Bake Off* in the background. Probably thinking about all things Grant Bowman, and WTF are we doing?

There's no way to suppress the little spark of excitement that lights me up every time I remember Grant getting all caveman and protective and then looking exactly like he was about to kiss me. I wish I could say that I wouldn't have let him, given that he is still the enemy, but I'd be lying.

I also think constantly about what happened in the breakroom on Wednesday. At work, at home, at my sister's. It's absolute torture, because I know, now, what I want from a sexual encounter. I want that bossiness, the gruff orders. I want a man who tells me to use his body for my pleasure and then goes and makes me do it. I want...

No, dammit. I have got to stop thinking about it. Where's Sam? She's late, and I feel like an ass waiting out here.

"Hey, stranger." I turn to see Harlow leaning in the shadows beside Off the Cuff, all wide shoulders, high cheekbones, and bright red lips. "Didn't know if I'd see you back here."

"Oh, I'm not back," I say, though there's a part of me that absolutely wants to be. I can't, obviously. Grant's rules and everything. "I'm supposed to watch improv with a friend." If she ever shows. Ugh, where *is* Sam? This outing was her idea!

"You don't seem thrilled."

"Yeah. I don't mind it, but..." I shrug.

Harlow grins, a single eyebrow raised. "Unlike last week's visit, huh?"

The groan that escapes me isn't a pretty sound, but it absolutely expresses the way I'm feeling after this past week: stretched taut, like the middle of the rope in a tug-of-war.

"You should come down."

My snort resonates in the suddenly deserted street. "Not a good idea."

Harlow makes a face. "Why not? I'll swing you another trial session if the member dues are scary."

"It's...more complicated than that."

I check my phone again. Sam's thirty minutes late. No messages. No replies to my texts or calls. Coming here tonight was her idea. I'm freaked out. Seriously. Where is she?

"You know what? I'll just take off. She's not—"

"Just couldn't keep away, huh?" Grant saunters up, all big shoulders and dark, edgy annoyance. "What are you doing here?"

His arrival brings the entire night to a head—lurking out on this same sidewalk, getting stood up by the one person I can usually count on, this constant simmer of worry and tension bubbling inside me because of everything that's happened this week. So, instead of the calm, patient response I'd usually manage to dredge up, I snap. "What? You own the sidewalk?"

"I own the building, Sunny."

"You do?" Surprised, I look at Harlow.

She nods and swings open the door with great ceremony.

Grant walks in and turns back to look at me. "Remember the rules."

Sweet Baby Jesus, what is it about Grant telling me things that makes me feel like rebelling? I'm possessed. Wild. And not of the carefree variety. More like dangerous. Proving him wrong is something I absolutely must do. Immediately. Devastatingly.

"Rules?"

"I'm not allowed to go in."

"Excuse me?"

"The club is off-limits to me."

"Says who?"

"Says His Majesty."

"Oh, does he now?" Shaking her head, Harlow swings the door wider. "He is *not* the boss of this place, Sunny." Her smile is devoid of humor. Deadly. Like she snacks on mediocre white men before dinner and picks the gristle out of her teeth. "Tell His Royal Highness that you're my guest." She nudges her head toward the open door, so certain of herself that she practically makes the decision for me.

As if I need help breaking the rules.

CHAPTER TWENTY-EIGHT

Grant

I'M DOWNSTAIRS AND HALFWAY through the inner door when Rae calls my name.

"Hey, Gran... General!"

Goddamn it.

I turn and wait as she stomps her heart-shaped ass all the way to where I'm standing, all thick and gorgeous in high-waisted jeans and little sneakers and a sweater that hugs every curve. I make the mistake of letting my eyes linger too long on her cleavage, and when I look up again, she's gone from angry to downright livid.

"Who the hell do you think you are?"

She's somehow backed me up against the lobby wall.

"I'm the guy who's making sure you don't lose your job."

"My job?" Oh, she's pissed now. "You think this is about my job, you jerk? You're the one who disobeyed the rules at work. I didn't do that by myself."

"Not coming here is a rule. Or did you forget?"

She lowers her voice. "Sure. But making a colleague come at work is just fine, huh?"

"We discussed that. I was proving a point."

"Oh, such bullshit. You wanted to pretend it never happened because you knew you broke your own damn rules."

"Yeah?" I allow myself the luxury of a long, slow, top-to-bottom look. "Then I take it you're here for another taste."

Her eyes narrow to slits. "Oh, you sanctimonious pr—"

Something gives inside me, a dam breaking. I can't wait another second. I dip my head and stop her with my mouth. My hands slide into all that hair as I drag her close.

After a fraction of a second's surprise, she kisses me back, all teeth and tongue and disgruntled little sounds, between which she manages to mutter, "You're an asshole, Bowman."

I growl, apparently less skilled at talking and kissing than she is.

But also my brain's shorted out and my body's on autopilot, and its destination is set for all the way. There's no request for consent, no communication between us. Just this wild, snapping beast that is the sum of our parts. The burn of my scalp where she tugs my hair, twisting my face left so she can nibble at my jaw, but fuck that. We're doing this my way.

"Get your ass over here." I scoop her up, spin, and pin her to the wall in one move. Rae's legs wrap around my waist, and what started off as a joint struggle suddenly morphs into a partnership. "I'll make you come again," I warn, pumping my hips to show her just how ready I am to take this further. "I've seen how you lose it."

She bites my lip. I lick into her mouth. She groans, and I eat that too.

This kiss...it's nothing like what I've done before. It's not a stepping stone on the way to something. Not part of some accepted agenda. It's not even like the big, open-mouthed kisses I've done in scenes, which are more about physically dominating a partner than intimacy. I'm out of control, wild, and I resent her for it. For the way I can't think straight, see straight, can only twist and bite...and want.

"Oh god, Grant," she sighs, and I feel huge. Bigger than the goddamn world. I kiss her deeper, harder, tighten my hold, and—

Someone interrupts. "Geesh, you two. Get a room."

CHAPTER TWENTY-NINE

Rae

WAIT. WAS THAT SAM?

"Seriously, lovers, get a room."

That's definitely her. I'll kill her.

With an irritated grunt, Grant loosens his hold on my butt. I slowly drop to the floor, joints out of order, bones rubberized.

"This is gonna be so fun to watch on Monday morning."

Gasping for air, I stare up at Grant. Who is this flushed, hazy-eyed man? Serious Grant is nowhere to be seen. I like this version. The one who watches me, fierce and lost at the same time, and then presses his forehead to mine to whisper, "You okay?" too quietly for them to hear.

My nod rubs our skin together.

He stares down at my mouth like it's done him dirty, then back up to my eyes, and he doesn't have to say what he's thinking because I feel it clenching deep, deep inside.

Finally, squinting against the light, I catch a glimpse of Sam and Daff over Grant's shoulder. They're watching us with unabashed curiosity. Sam's got her arms folded. Daff's chin's cradled in her hands, elbows on the check-in desk. They're wearing twin smirks.

I glance up at Grant as he finally eases back, looking like he's been sucker punched. *I know exactly how you feel, bud.*

"Fuck." His eyes clear, and his jaw hardens. A second later, he swipes my feet out from under me when he says, "This didn't happen."

"What?"

"You. Me. That... that... *kiss.*" He imbues the word with so much venom he might as well have slapped me across the face. "Never. Happened."

But here's the thing, right? I may look like an oversized Kewpie doll, but I'm no one's pushover. This man can pretend whatever he wants. I am not playing.

"Oh, it happened, Mister," I tell him, forcing my words out as clearly and concisely as I can manage after the once-in-a-lifetime workout my libido just endured. "You lost control."

"Is Mister his kink name?" Sam asks.

We both turn and spit out simultaneous *no*s before returning our attention to each other.

"I didn't lose control."

"No? What about the rules, then?"

"*You* broke them."

"Oh, so that's your excuse? Victim-blaming, now?"

"You have rules?" Sam lowers her voice. "They have *rules*?"

"Of course we do," he says, in the same tone my asshole uncle Bert might use to argue in favor of trickle-down economics.

"It's ridiculous," I snap, my voice overlapping his.

"Y'all are giving enemies-to-lovers so hard right now," says Sam.

"Right?" replies Daff.

"Are they doing a kink scene?"

"Hmmmm. Maybe."

Neither of us even glances at them. We can't, given how intently we're staring at each other. There's a litany running over and over inside me, saying, *Do all the things. Kiss me. Make me. Rub and push and pull and tell me how good it feels. Make it hurt, and then make it feel better, and then—*

With a muttered "I'm losing it," Grant turns, rubbing his mouth with the back of his hand. "You've got to get outta here, Rae. I can't think when you're around." He literally snarls, "Please just go."

I'm vibrating with the aftershock of that request when someone yells "It's the General!" from the steps, immediately followed by the swarm of a big group clogging up the space, and there are way too many people for how raw I feel. We get separated. I twist around, and Grant's glaring at whoever called his name like he wants to punch them for interrupting, which I'd almost laugh at except I wanted to keep doing what we were doing, and apparently, he can't wait for me to *leave*? Because it never *happened*? Hurt whooshes up to clog my chest, my throat, my sinuses.

"Come on, Beanie. This guy's a turd." Sam grabs my arm and shoves me up the steps in front of her and through the crowd, which closes behind us like we were never there. We're almost to the street door when she turns back to shout over the newcomers' heads, "Hey, Mr. *Mister!* I hope you know you're an ugly gherkin-fucker and you don't deserve her!"

"What was that?" I ask as we spill out onto the sidewalk, me blinking like a newborn and Sam on the warpath.

"This way." She drags me around the corner and out of sight.

I stumble to a stop and lean against the brick wall, my breathing as harsh as if I'd just run a one-hundred-meter dash instead of dry-humping my off-limits colleague.

"Geez, Rae. Sorry I was late," Sam says, eyes flicking left and right before landing back on me. "Although, do I really need to apologize?"

"You absolutely do," I gasp, out of breath, out of my mind.

Turning, I start walking, just walking, barely taking in the people wandering by. I feel explosive. Grant's down there in *his* club right now, probably with his real, full-time sub—or girlfriend or, who knows, poly triad?—picking up exactly where he left off with me. And it hurts.

Sam's sneakers slap quietly on the brick sidewalk as she runs to catch up. "Hey. Hey, Beanie. Come on."

I think it's the sound of my family's nickname for me that stops me in my tracks, my shoulders drooping. "Let's go get drunk," I say.

"Fine by me."

CHAPTER THIRTY

Grant

"Take this," Lucas yells over the music from across the bar.

I stare at him for a few seconds before letting him slide a cold beer into my hand. "Thanks."

"Not lookin' so great, bud."

"Fuck off."

He shakes his head and looks out at the crowd. It's busy. Very busy, in fact, which is great. Excellent news.

I swivel on my barstool, eyes searching for anyone who might be in the market for a partner tonight. There. Cute redhead.

Dammit. No redheads. I'm done with redheads.

"What are you doing?" Lucas has come around the bar to stand beside me.

"Checking out the crowd."

"Yeah? What about the sub who followed you down here?"

Immediately, my hackles rise. "What about her?"

"Down, boy. You think I'ma try to steal her off you?"

Just the notion makes my hands tense up, readying for a fight.

Lucas, of course, notices. He's not just a fellow kinkster and a friend. He's a jock, an ex-fighter. The guy knows when someone's gearing up for a tussle and, dammit, that is not me. I've got to release this adrenaline running through my veins or I'll lose it.

"No." I shake my head more to clear it than anything else. "'Course not."

"All right." His eyes flick down to where I'm doing my best to loosen my hands before returning to look at my face. "Mind if I say something?"

Forcing back a sigh, I take a long swig of my beer. "Go ahead."

"Never seen you act like this before, man."

"Great. You trying to tell me I'm losing it or—?"

"I'm trying to tell you to maybe pay some attention to yourself, for once."

"Oh, 'cause I'm usually so selfless?"

Lucas stands up to his full height, folds his arms, and stares me down with those weirdly pale, piercing eyes of his. "Remind me again. How much rent is your neighbor paying for those offices upstairs?"

"None of your business."

"Right." His lips curve up in a slow, knowing smile. "You're not even charging Dorothy, are you?"

"Fuck off."

"Again? Real eloquent tonight."

"Yeah, well, she..." I pause. Am I truly here blaming Rae for the fact that I'm being an asshole? "I can't stop thinking about her, man." The truth comes out in a rush.

"You like her."

"I'm attracted."

He shrugs, a movement that reminds me of some huge geographical feature shifting. Tectonic plates or mountains. "Why are you denying yourself?"

"It's unprofessional. And she'd...want more."

"She tell you that?"

"I know her. She'd want…" I search for some way to express this knowledge I have that Rae isn't a one-and-done kind of person. She's someone you'd have to stick around for, and the fact is, that is absolutely not my game.

I do not do any sort of long-term relationship. Ever. Not with women, not with, hell, houses or jobs or anything. Even my friendships have been pretty short-lived. By choice. Lucas and Harlow are rare for their continued presence in my life.

"How the hell do you know what she'd want? You ask her?"

"I…" My mind blanks. "No. I haven't asked."

"Bro."

"Well…" After a few seconds, I sigh. "Get another beer?"

"Hey, Rogue." Lucas calls the bartender over.

"Yes, Tank?"

"Could you mix us up a couple of your specials, please?"

"Just a bourbon," I break in.

"Come on. You'll love this one."

I groan.

"Two specials for the bosses? Hell yeah."

"I'm not your boss!" I yell as Rogue slinks away, all lean, bare-chested grace. They are very, very popular. As Lucas always says, get a bartender that everybody wants to fuck, and you will always sell drinks. Cynical but true.

Which sounds more like me than Lucas.

Ironic, I guess, given how rough his life was growing up and how easy I had it. Yes, I moved around a lot, but there were years of Lucas's life when he and his siblings were homeless, living out of their minivan, while I always had my very successful dentist mom and some new middle-class white guy to fund whatever I needed.

"Two Sweet Subs for the two hottest people here."

"Sweet Subs?" I choke out, looking over at Lucas.

"Thought you'd like that."

I shake my head.

"Thanks, Rogue."

"Anytime, Tank." After a wink, they turn and sashay away, a little extra sway in their hips.

"Rogue's flirting with you," I tell him.

"Definitely."

"Never flirts with me," I muse.

"Wonder why."

I accept my glass from Lucas, move to take a sip of the orange foam on top, and stop when he says, "Wait, wait, wait. I've got something to say."

"Ah, hell."

"No. Seriously. Listen."

I settle back onto my stool.

"You're a dick, Grant."

I roll my eyes. "Okay. You know what? I didn't come here for—"

"But you're *my* dick. And I take care of what's mine."

"You've got to be kid—"

"As the only guy here who's stronger, smarter, *and* better looking than you—with a bigger penis—I feel that it's my obligation to tell you…"

"Mm-hm."

"You've got to top this woman."

"Come on. Are you—?"

"Denying yourself is making you miserable. And a miserable Grant is a sad sight to see."

"I'm not miserable."

"You're so miserable it's like you've turned into the Upside Down version of yourself."

"What?"

"*Stranger Things*? I know Harlow made you watch it. Remember the bad place? That's you. Like there's a good Grant, and there's a messed-up Grant, and you've transformed."

"You're saying I've gone to the dark side."

"Except not sexy."

"Is the dark side ever sexy?"

"Sure. Darth? The Siths? Adam Driver?"

"Just... put it here." I hold my glass out for him to tap with his and take a sip of the drink, and it is... "Damn."

"See?"

"What the hell's in this?"

"Gochujang, apparently."

"I don't even know what that is." But it's damn delicious.

"You really need to get out more."

"You are aware that I don't have a humiliation kink, right? I did not come in tonight to get insulted."

"Did you come in to smash that cutie against the wall out in the vestibule?"

"First of all, she smashed me against the wall first."

"Oooooh, nice. You find yourself a switch, General?"

I make a face. "Nobody tops me. You know that."

"I don't know. A little topping from the bottom never hurt a guy." He takes a long sip, his eyes smiling as he watches me. "I heard you kissed her first."

"Seriously?"

Lucas's single eyebrow lift is a thing of ironic beauty. And yes, I should know better. Obviously, Harlow and Daff have been providing him with a detailed blow-by-blow since the second I showed up here tonight.

"I have no privacy," I say, to which he just lifts that damned eyebrow higher and says, "You have no private *life*. Not the same thing."

"All right." I take another sip and let the drink expand through me, all spicy, sweet, and salted smoke. It's pretty extraordinary. "You think I should...see her."

"You should at least give it a try, man."

"What if Sunny wants long-term?"

His deadeye stare is effective on most people. Just bounces right off me.

"What?"

"With y'all's chemistry, it'd be a waste not to see where it goes."

"She's just so..."

Lucas waits.

Nothing more comes out of my mouth, but I notice my breathing's gone all messed up.

"How much longer you planning to work up there? Couple weeks?"

"If that."

"Give her that. See what happens."

The idea has appeal. The possibility races through me, bringing with it relief. Peace. Within seconds, I'm calm again, my breathing deep and even, my pulse slow. In control, which is the farthest thing from what I was out there with Sunny in the vestibule. That wasn't a scene. It was mayhem.

Maybe Lucas is right. Being around Sunny without touching her is making me lose it. The solution is obvious: I've got to Dom her, keep a hold of the reins, and maintain control. For both of us.

Piece of cake.

CHAPTER THIRTY-ONE

Rae

"I'm texting him." I hold out my hand for my phone.

"Who?"

"Grant. No, Brendan. No, Grant."

"Bruh."

"He needs to know he's a total prick."

"Which one?"

"Both."

"No. They do not."

"They do! It's vitally important that I tell Brendan how bad he is at kissing. Was. Is. Ever more shall be." I take another sip of cranberry-watermelon slush. God, it's delicious.

"Yes, but not tonight."

"Why not?" I squint at where Sam's backed into the corner of the world's smallest sofa, literally sitting on my phone to keep it away from me. "This is the perfect night for it. Grant's kiss is right here." My hand goes to my lips, my skin still buzzing. "Sammy, I just... Why's it so good with this guy? Like, what is it? I mean, his voice. The dirty talk?" Another swig. I don't let myself think of who he's dirty-talking with right this very minute. *Chef's kiss.* Somehow, I accidentally kiss with the hand holding my glass, which sends a watermelon waterfall over the sofa and me. And Sam. "Oops. Oh. Sorry. Sorry. Let me get you a towel or a—"

"No towel! I'm fine." She wipes herself off, giggling. "Geez, Rae. Give me that."

"No." I steal the glass back, spraying myself yet again with watermelon rain. "It's too good."

"You're gonna throw up."

"I won't." Sitting back down on my side of the sofa, I shake my head, staring at the drink's pretty, pretty color. "I am stronger than that."

"Everyone knows you have a weak stomach." She hands me an open bag of chips. They're jalapeño cheddar, and I picked them out at the little corner market. "Eat."

I reach into the tiny bag, put a chip in my mouth, and consider. "Not bad."

She takes one and crunches down. "Pretty good."

"Ten dollars good?"

"Absolutely not."

"But you bought them anyway."

"I did," she says.

"Because I wanted my favorite Cheetos."

"Which they didn't have."

I sigh. "And you're a good friend."

"I am." She watches me closely. "You okay?"

"I'm sad now."

"What's up?"

"Mom loved jalapeño Cheetos."

"Oh, Beanie, I know. The date's coming up soon, isn't it?"

I nod. "September sixteenth." The day Mom died and left me in charge.

"I'm sorry."

"It's okay." I look over to where Pepe's taken refuge on the chair in front of my workbench. "Pepe loves me."

"He does."

"Dad loves me. My sisters do."

"Yep."

"You too?"

"With all my heart, Beanie."

"Grant Bowman is a dick." I sound whinier than I'd like, but my god, why'd he send me away like that? All, *you've got to get outta here.*

"Pretty much."

"He'd hate these chips."

She snickers. "He'd like them 'cause they were expensive."

"Oooooh, yeah. Definitely. So much that. 'Cause he's a snob."

"Hmm." She seems to consider. "Is he?"

"Maybe. Probably." Another sip. The watermelon's starting to feel too sweet on my tongue. "Berk."

"Here."

Sam grabs my glass and shoves another into my hand. It's cold and slippery with condensation. "What's this?"

"Water. Try it. You'll like it."

"Ha ha." I slug back the full glass. "Oh god, yes."

"More?"

At my nod, she stands and walks the three steps to the sink, where she fills it again, pries a couple of ice cubes out of the tray, plops them into my glass, and returns the tray to my mini freezer.

"You're so good, Sam." I accept the glass. "So nice to me."

"What now?"

"You put the ice away."

"Course I did. Who wouldn't?"

"Brendan."

"Your ex was a turdface."

"Wait. What did you call him?"

"Brendan?"

"No, Genghis."

"Genghis?"

"Bowman."

She laughs, long and hard. "Oh, hell yes. That's what you call him? I love it. The conqueror."

"Such a hard-ass, right?" My eyes land on my workbench. I get up, trip on the blanket that's somehow wrapped itself around my leg, and flop to the floor.

"You okay?"

"Fine. Fine." Once I pick myself back up, I wobble over to look at something I started working on last night. "Look. I just made this."

"A chair?"

"Grant's chair from our office. It even tilts, see?" She whistles when I show her how it adjusts. "I started making our building. *His* building. Did you know that?"

"Know what?"

"Genghis owns our office."

"That seems...unethical."

"Does it?" I consider. "Those two are up to something." I flick a set of tiny handcuffs I put together. They're so cute. So perfect. I'd pictured him putting a real set of these on me and pretending—ugh, no.

"Hey, you made a cat-o'-nine-tails."

"It's a flogger."

"That's amazing."

"I wanted to make the whole building, you know?" I point the itty-bitty flogger at the wall o' book nooks. "With the club in the basement and everything, but…" Emotion fills me like bubbles getting forced into water in one of those at-home soda machines, and suddenly I've crushed the tiny flogger in my hand. I pick up Grant's chair, ready to smash it to bits.

Sam grabs it from me and holds it up high. "Nope."

"You can't do that. It's mine."

"You'll regret it."

"I won't. It'll feel good to break it all." Just like I'll break his rough/handsome face when I get the chance.

"No. You'll hate yourself."

We're circling my chair in a demented ring-around-the-rosy, Pepe's brows twitching as he watches blandly from the seat, not nearly interested enough to lift his head.

Finally, I give up, spin, and fall flat on my bed, which, like everything in my place, is conveniently right there.

"Why'd he have to be so good at the sexy stuff, Sammy?"

She sinks down beside me. "Could be your ex was just the worst."

Grant barely even touched me, and it was better than anything I ever did with Brendan. My mind skips back to the way it felt when his mouth landed on mine tonight. The hungry sounds he made. "His breath was all shaky."

"Genghis's?"

"Yeah. Like…he felt it too."

"Bet he did."

"Why'd he go and ruin it?" Turning with a groan, I hide my head in my pillow. "*This never happened*," I imitate, terribly. And then, "*Please just go*. Asshole couldn't wait to get rid of me. Probably so he could go and kiss someone else against a wall."

"Actually…"

"Actually, what?"

"You didn't see the way he looked at you."

The hopeful, excited little puppy inside me perks up its head. "How did he look at me?"

Sam stares up at the fabric I've draped across the ceiling to hide the fact that I'm literally living in an unfinished shed. "Okay. You remember that dog you guys had?"

"Butterscotch?"

"Yeah, you know how Otty would purposely drop salami on the floor, and he would like go crazy wolfing it down, and your dad would drag him away, kicking and fighting, and Butterscotch would look back with that yearning in his eyes?"

"Yeah."

"Well, that's how he looked."

"Like I was salami?"

"Exactly like that. He's Butterscotch. You are just-out-of-reach floor salami."

"I'm floor salami?"

"Yep," she says with a level of certainty that calms me immediately.

"Why does he have to be like that?"

"Men." She shakes her head.

For a long moment, we lie side by side, flat on our backs, staring up at the intricate nips and folds of fabric. After a while, I turn and look at Sam's profile, which is almost as familiar to me as my sisters' or my dad's. "Where've you been going, Sammy? All week?"

A pause.

"I don't want to tell you."

Hurt swamps me, literal pain in my stomach. "Why not?"

"You'll be mad."

I can't think of a single thing she could say right now that would make me mad. Not one.

So, of course, she goes and proves me wrong.

CHAPTER THIRTY-TWO

Rae

"I'm seeing a guy," Sam says. "And shit, Rae, I think he's married."

Oh. Oh, wow. Okay, there it is. Yep. I don't like that. At all.

I sit up. "Why would you do that?"

"I just...He's kinda sexy."

"Kind of? Sam, that's a terrible reason to sleep with a guy. Especially one who's married."

"We haven't had, like, actual P-in-V sex yet."

I snort. "Great. That makes it better. I mean...who is he?"

"He's just a fuckboy, Rae."

"Ew. Even worse. Why?"

She shrugs. "I've been...lonely."

"Lonely? But I'm here."

"You're busy."

"Oh, please. No more than usual."

"You fill every second of every day, Rae. You're occupied. Doing things. For people."

"Who?"

"Um, Hannah."

"She's my sister."

"Right. So's Otty. And then your dad, who has told you to stop getting his meds. You don't listen. You still do it all."

"He forgets."

"And at work? It's like...the Rae show."

"What?" My stomach suddenly hurts.

"You're busy. And I am...fine with it. But..."

"But what?"

"But my house is crap, and my roommates are a nightmare, and...you know how it is. At night."

I do know. Sam's scared of being alone. And she hates the dark.

"You can sleep here."

She sighs. "Your place is already too small for you and Pepe and the...nooks. I'm not crashing here."

"But you know I'm here. Whenever you need me."

"Between dry humps against the wall and spankings and—"

"I am not accepting spankings at this time, thank you very much."

Her smirk is so skeptical that all I can do is roll my eyes and shake my head and give her one of my own.

"Whatever. Just...You can count on me, Sam. To help."

"Okay."

"I'm serious. And I won't judge you for being a Jezebel."

"Thank you."

"Too harshly." I flop onto my back and stare at a dark stain on my ceiling fabric that seems to have grown bigger since the last time I paid attention.

"I'm ending it anyway."

"With the guy?"

"He's a jerk."

"Grant's a jerk too." God, it hurt when he told me to leave. "What was it you called him? A turtle-fucker?"

She barks out a laugh. "A gherkin-fucker."

"What even is that?"

"A gherkin? It's a pickle."

"I'm pretty sure it's a hairy thing."

"What? No way. Gherkins are pickles in the UK."

"No. No. A gherkin is like a pubic wig or something." I sit up, looking around for my phone.

"Hang on." She reaches under her butt and pulls it from her back pocket. "Uh, you've got notifications. Lots."

My body flushes hot and then stone cold. "Let me see."

She hands over the phone, and I scroll through the long list of texts, all from my sisters.

Otty: There's a car at dad's

Hannah: okay. And?

Otty: Listen, listen. I came over to check on him

Hannah: You mean do laundry

Otty: I've been going commando for two weeks. My entire car's filled with laundry. I can't see out the rearview. but I can't go in.

Hannah: Why not?

Otty: Like I said. CAR in his drive

Hannah: Whose is it?

Otty: FFS, Hannah, I don't know! I wouldn't be freaking if I did, would I?

Hannah: Go spy

Otty: What do you think I'm doing, sitting here in my car right now?

Hannah: And?

Otty: I'm hungry.

Me: What do you see?

Otty: Nothing. No movement at all

Me: Are lights on?

Otty: Living room. Dining. Kitchen.

Me: Maybe he's having a poker night or something.

Hannah: Our father?

Me: Well, go up and knock.

Otty: Absolutely not.

Hannah: Why not?

Otty sends a photo of herself. Under a bright yellow bathrobe, she is wearing a bathing suit and a too-short pair of jean shorts that were mine in ninth grade.

Me: Omg. My eyes. I will never be the same.

Hannah: We all know that washing and drying is *not* her talent.

I chuckle at the *Chicago* reference. It is by far Hannah's favorite musical. I can't help but wonder if the state of her marriage is to blame.

Otty: Now I have to pee.

Me: Pop a squat in the yard.

Otty: Shorts plus bathing suit squat would be a nightmare.
Shit, it's late. I've gotta go, anyway. Working brunch tomorrow.

Me: What'll you wear to work?

Otty: I'll wash something in the sink. Blow it dry.

Hannah: Welcome to adulthood

Otty: Really?

Hannah: No. What you are describing is the opposite of adulthood.

Otty: You're an asshole. Tell her she's an asshole, Rae.

Me: She's telling the truth.

Otty: I hate you both. And I'm leaving. One of you bitches can spy if you want to know who the mystery car belongs to.

Hannah: There are children sleeping in my house. I can't.

Otty: Where's Schaffer?

Hannah: Minneapolis? Memphis? Don't remember.

Otty: It's Friday.

I race over to a different thread and text Otty directly.

Me: Stop it. Leave her alone about Schaffer right now. It's late. She's on her own. She doesn't need us reminding her that her husband's never home.

Otty: You're so annoying

Me: Thank you

Back to the group chat.

Otty: All right, I'm out.

Me: Did you at least try to call him?

Otty: No! Are you nuts? It's three in the morning.

Hannah: Why don't you go over there, Rae?

Me: Glossing over the whole three in the morning thing, are we?

Me: I've been drinking.

Hannah: Oh, well, good girl. For not driving.

I flick through the apps on my phone to check in on Dad's heart on the vitals app.

Me: Heart rate looks normal.

Hannah: Also, he's an adult.

There's a long pause while probably both of us fall into picturing some version of Dad that is in no way adultlike. Banana hunts, kitchen dance parties, air guitar contests.

Hannah: Dad is an adult.

Me: Right.

Hannah: He's alive.

Me: 👍

Hannah: He's fine. Leave it.

Hannah: Night, beeshes.

Me: Night.

When I turn to ask Sam if she can drive us out there, she's dead to the world, snoring lightly beside me. Oh well.

I carefully get up and wobble around, turning off the million little lamps and string lights. I grab an extra blanket, clean my teeth without turning the electric brush on, pee, and drink a massive glass of water.

My eyes land on the tiny flogger. Maybe I'll do the whole building. A minuscule world in which I'm the one who calls the shots, not Grant Bowman or the General or anyone else. A universe where I can play out the scenes inside my head instead of worrying about everyone else all the time. I like that idea. A lot.

As I turn to get into bed, my eyes land on Sam's bag, which has fallen over, half its contents dumped out on my floor. When I bend to pick it all up and stuff it back in, I pause at the sight of a laptop. It looks an awful lot like the ones we have at work. Weird, right? We're not allowed to take those home, as per Grant's new office safety protocols.

Preoccupied now, I get into my bed, turn over, and look at Sam, whose sleep position is as decorous as always, body perfectly straight, hands folded at her chest, face placid. I'll ask her tomorrow. Maybe she got permission. Maybe it was an emergency, and she had to take the computer home to get something done. And maybe that is why she was late meeting me tonight—a subject we never got around to discussing.

Hours later, I wake up to find my bed empty. There's a sickly morning light coming in the window and absolutely no sound but the chattering of a few birds.

"Sam?" I whisper-shout.

Nothing.

I look around, grab my phone, and stare at it blearily for a few seconds before I can focus on a text notification.

Sam: You are the best. I love you. See you Monday.

My woozy head drops back onto the pillow, mind racing with questions of where she could possibly have gone at this time of day. I can only come up with one answer: the married douchebag.

I don't like it at all.

CHAPTER THIRTY-THREE

Grant

The second Rae walks in on Monday morning, I know I'm screwed.

She's wearing her hair up, and I don't mean in a casually thrown-together bundle like before. No, today, it's styled into a glass-smooth roll, so intricately twisted up on the back of her head that there is no doubt the move was purposeful.

"Good morning, Grant," Rae says as she sails into the office, smelling like fall and flowers and the exact scent of woman my body's aching for. "I brought you a coffee."

Her smile is sharp. It says *I'm done with your bullshit*. It says *I came to get spanked*. It says that I am in deep, deep trouble.

She sets the coffee on my desk, turns, and walks over to the closet, her coat falling from her shoulders in a long, slow slide that shuts down at least half my brain.

"Thank you," I manage, sounding strangled.

It would take a team of wild horses to force my eyeballs not to stare at her full breasts, round ass, and soft belly, all lovingly encased in something I can only describe as a long, skintight sweater with a row of buttons down the front.

The way it highlights every gorgeous curve and also manages to be work appropriate is some kind of witchcraft. Between that and her hair and the velvety-looking scarf wrapped around her, she is an autumn goddess. All she's missing is a crown of orange and red leaves.

"What are we celebrating?"

"Oh, you know. Just got a coffee for my office roomie. Figured we could start the week off with a peace offering."

Is that what this? For some reason, I doubt it.

With a flourish, she removes the scarf from her shoulders, revealing the back of her dress, which swoops low. Very low.

My mouth goes dry.

"What uh...?"

She turns with a bland smile. "Yes, Grant?"

"What, what is that you're wearing?"

A torture device, designed to crush my innards and turn my brain to mush.

"A dress." She blinks with pure, sweet innocence. "Like it?"

Yes. The answer is 100 percent yes.

Swallowing provides absolutely no lubrication for my parched tongue. I open my mouth to speak. Close it again.

There is nothing for me to say right now.

Because she's just thrown down the gauntlet.

And I am in no way prepared.

Throughout the longest day ever, she bends over, twice. Once to open a low desk drawer she could absolutely have reached from her seat. The second time, she drops a sheet of paper, I am pretty sure on purpose. Both times are pure hell, especially when, upon closer inspection, it becomes crystal clear that there is not a single panty line on her body.

Do nothing. Don't react.

It's what my survival instincts scream each time Rae moves. Or breathes. With every single inhalation.

It's now after 6:00 p.m., most everyone's left the office, but Rae just won't leave. Right now, she's very subtly swaying to whatever's playing in her headphones and licking the frosting off something chocolaty.

I can't tear my eyes away. From her neck, her back, and the flick of her tongue when she turns subtly to the side like she's not flaunting every part of her soft, luscious body for my benefit.

Do nothing. Don't react.

Not easy when the sight of her makes something inside my rib cage twist *hard*.

She stands and stretches, spins, catches me staring, and blows out a long breath, fanning herself with one hand.

"It's so hot in here. Are you hot?"

"No," I growl.

"My goodness." She undoes a button at her throat and then another, while sashaying over to the printer, all rolling hips and lush ass and—

That's it. The last straw.

The smoke clears from my brain. I know exactly how to handle this. I unbutton a cuff.

"Rae."

Her eyes go straight to the sleeve that I'm carefully rolling up, one fold at a time.

"Yeah?" It's a breathless whisper. The jig is up.

"Close the door," I tell her, quiet, firm. I sound like myself again, which is reason enough to cross this line.

Her eyes widen briefly. "Excuse me?"

"We're done playing games now, aren't we, Sunny?"

"I don't know what you're—"

"Oh, I think you do. You absolutely do. Whatever you're about to say, don't bother. You win. No more rules." I finish rolling up my right sleeve, cross one leg over the other, and relax. "Once you've shut the door, go ahead and grab the list."

A pretty pink flush, beginning somewhere below her neckline, has started to crawl up her throat to her face. I'm going to feel how hot that skin is today. Press my mouth to it. Taste it.

Her expression an almost childlike blend of eager and hesitant, Rae walks to the door at a stately pace and closes it. Then she locks it. The sound makes my cock pulse.

I watch the quick rise and fall of her chest as she makes her way to the closet for the list.

The *fucking* list.

Once the door is open, she looks at me, waiting for instruction.

"Bring it here," I tell her with a gentleness I can afford now that I know what's coming.

Just as she tries to give the paper over to me, inspiration strikes. "Crush it. Make it into a ball."

Her eyes stay on mine as she does it. This time, when she attempts to hand it over, I shake my head, slowly.

Calm. In control.

"Tighter. You'll want it small."

Her expression goes almost comically worried, so I ask, "You remember the club safe words?"

She nods so fast I can't help but smile. "Good. Tell me."

"Red to stop. Yellow to slow. Green to keep going."

"Where are you right now?"

"Chartreuse?"

"Is that yellow?"

"It's green." I hear the shakiness of her inhalation, the nerves, the excitement. "Bright green."

"Okay, then. And what do you do if you're unable to talk and you need to stop?"

She leans over and taps three times on the desk.

"Excellent. Any surface is fine. My face. Your skin. I will hear it, feel it, or see it, and stop. Then I'll check in with you. Got it?"

"Yes."

"Good. Have a drink of water."

"What?"

I point at her desk, where there's a mug with the word *Hamilton* written across it. "There clean water in there?"

She nods.

"Then drink it."

With an annoyed little sigh, she picks it up, takes a swig, and at my patient look, swallows the rest down. Then she shows me the inside.

"Thank you. You may put it down." I suck in a long, deep breath. "Now. The rules go in your mouth."

"What? No, I—"

"Are we doing this?"

After a moment's wide-eyed hesitation, Rae stuffs the paper into that gorgeous mouth, wedging it between her teeth.

I'm hard as nails but also calm. Ready.

With a slow sigh, I press on. "Pull the dress up, over your hips. Show me what you've got on under there."

CHAPTER THIRTY-FOUR

Rae

It's happening. It's happening.

My hands shake as I grasp the sweaterdress and slowly drag it up, up, up, baring tall boots with long socks beneath them, and above that... That's right.

Nothing. It's what I decided to wear to work today.

The moment I woke up this morning, I knew I was done with the silly rules, one way or another. Grant would have to suffer. The fact that I still wanted him after Friday, despite his rejection, really annoyed me. So cute sweaterdress it was.

I'm not sure I'm supposed to hear the whispered "Holy fuck" he lets out as the hem reaches my hips. "Turn around," he says in a quiet, stern voice. "Hands on your desk."

Oh god. Oh god. Oh *gods*.

My brain's a wild thing, flailing around like it doesn't know up from down and side from side, and it is way too much. I'm almost outside of my body with how big this feels.

My body, apparently, doesn't require a brain to function. There's no hesitation before I turn, take three steps, push everything on the surface to one side, and plant my hands on the edge.

"Bend over."

What? No! Yes! Oh god, god, god, god, god. Tell me what to do. Make me, make me, make me, make me.

I'm a hot mess.

The sound of Grant moving closer makes me jump and breathe deeply through my nose and then whimper silently when his hand lands on my nape.

Warm. Dry. Solid.

My eyelids sink closed. A long, relieved sigh oozes out of my lungs.

"That's it. *That's* it," Grant says.

Oh wow. That feels...like a drug. Calming. Steadying.

"Do you want to please me, Sunny?"

I nod.

No pressure on my neck. Just the light rub of rough fingers. "Then you'll bend over this desk."

And I'm down. Was there ever any doubt that I'd obey? But the heavy hand on my back tells me it's not enough. Hands sliding along my desk, I go lower, lower, until my forehead presses to cold wood.

"You don't get it, do you?"

Something brushes against my naked ass, startling me. A heartbeat later, his hand skates over my skin again, and my back arches of its own volition.

"Ge' wha'?" I attempt to ask.

"No questions." He pinches my ass, too gently to hurt, but my god, does it have an effect on my libido. As if I weren't turned on enough by this situation, the quick twist of flesh makes me squirm uncontrollably. "If you want to stop, or if you're not sure, you smack the desk. Got it?" A quick, painless slap of my butt to illustrate, and I'm so far gone, I swear I'll cry if he stops.

"Got it, Sunny?"

I lift my head and give a frantic nod.

He laughs darkly, moves back a step, and, I suspect, just watches the show. "Yeah. That's it. Show me what's mine. What I get to play with."

His? Oh god. *His.*

I swallow around the list in my mouth and turn my head to the side, catching the eye of my capybara pen cup, judging me from the other side of the desk. I reach out and turn it around.

Grant's footsteps recede but then return. He throws his jacket over my copious desktop tchotchkes. "Better?" At my nod, he says, "Shut your eyes."

I obey.

"Good girl." Slowly, barely touching me, Grant runs the backs of his knuckles over my skin. Up and down over one butt cheek, to the other side. After a few slow strokes, his knuckles press in harder, moving my flesh in something almost like a massage. Down, left, a quick dip into the crevice, and up.

"You flaunted this sweet, soft body all day, didn't you?"

I shake my head, and suddenly it's not knuckles anymore. It's a thwack, swift and startling. The sting is quick, bright. Barely registers as pain at all.

"Liar. You wanted me to look."

I react, pressing my breasts against the desk and my ass out.

"That's it. Show me. Look at you, all soft curves and dimples and this…" He slides his hand down, down, and then in to where my thighs press tightly together. It's the very worst place for chub rub. The seat of pain and shame for so many years of my youth. "This curve right here," he says, slipping his hand between my thighs and gently cupping one side. "Just…" A loud exhale. "Turns me on so hard."

Oh god, he is so close to touching me right where I want him.

So close, and yet the jerk won't do it. I try to say his name through my improvised gag, but it comes out garbled.

"I know what you're trying to do. You'll have to be patient, Sunny. I'm not ready to touch you there yet. Remember, your orgasms are mine now."

They are?

"It's what being a Pleasure Dom is about. You heard of it before?"

At my headshake, he goes on, one hand lazily trailing the skin of my back and butt.

"It means that your pleasure is my entire wheelhouse. I want to control your orgasms."

Wow. *Wow.* Okay.

"Sometimes it's easy." He leans in to whisper, "Like in the kitchen. Remember how you gave me that climax? Mm, so fucking good."

At my gasp, he says, "Other times, I use tools. To build you up..." His knuckles rasp over my hip, down to my thigh, around to where they meet again. Close, so close to where I'm needy and aching for his touch. "...and up and up, building it so high that there's nothing left but want."

I whimper, my eyes blurring as I concentrate on that touch.

"And sometimes? That means withholding."

When I whine, he chuckles, comes around the side of the desk, where he squats, and tilts my face so I'm looking right at him.

I don't know what I thought I'd see in his expression. Excitement, maybe, to match what I'm feeling inside. Instead, he looks almost...I don't know, peaceful? It's both unexpected and sort of comforting.

"But here's the thing: When I make you wait for that climax, like the good girl you are, and you're stretched out at my mercy, wanting it so bad you'll cry, then..."

I'm waiting, breath bated…suspended on his words like they're the only thing in the world.

"When I let you have it, finally? You'll come so hard you won't know who you are. You want that, Sunny? Huh?"

I nod, embarrassingly eager for whatever he wants to do.

My mouth's dry, and while some small part of me acknowledges that making me hydrate wasn't a bad idea, the rest of me is gone already, a spinning top, lost to entropy. In it to the end.

His attention shifts back up to my ass as he mutters, "As I was saying, you deserve this spanking, sweetheart. The way you flaunted yourself today? Sorry to say it, but you do."

The feminist inside me wants to scream that I can wear what I want, dammit. It's not teasing. It's living my darn life, and if a man can't control himself, then he's the problem, not the woman.

Given that I wore the dress for the very specific purpose of riling this man up, I decide to let it slide. We're both playing this game, and right now, the rules say that I get punished for looking sexy. I want the rules, I want the game, and I really, really want the punishment.

He clicks his teeth together and moves to the back of my body slowly, like he's got all the time in the world, while I'm bent here, soaking wet and straining, straining for contact. I want it. Now. Now, now, now.

"You deserve a flogging, quite frankly, but I'll go easy on this perfect ass. This time." A pause while he skates lightly—so lightly—over the place he smacked a moment ago, and then—

Another smack. I grunt.

Was that harder? I don't know because, by the time the sound's passed and the sensation reaches my brain, I want to beg for more. So hungry and aching, I'd let him do me right here. I'd let him do anything he wants.

"Shhhhhhh," he says, easing that hand over my sore butt. "Good. Good."

A pause. There's sound, like he's shifting, but nothing more.

I strain back to get a look but see only a slice of his wide frame before he spanks me again.

Oh god. The sound of flesh hitting flesh is quiet, but the feel of this one's a sharp sting that brings tears to my eyes and makes my hips press to the desk in search of some sort of friction.

"Oh, sweet girl, trying to get off before I'm done. *No*. I told you, Sunny, the orgasms…are *mine*." His hand lands on my lower back and presses down, and at the same time, he moves in and pushes his hips to mine, and he is hard and…

For a handful of seconds, I lose all track of reality.

He is big. Huge. Even through his pants, I feel the heft of him. I got a hint of it in the kitchen and then up against the club door, but this position is forcing me to face the fact that it would absolutely be a struggle to get him inside me.

That shouldn't be so exciting.

"Your ass is beautiful," he whispers, kneading with one hand before the other joins in. Kneading, kneading, and pressing with his hips, and then the kneading hands hold me open, and his still-clothed cock is right there between my ass cheeks, and I groan, the sound loud, even with the paper in my mouth.

"No. No, sweetheart, you can't make noise or we'll have to stop. You know that, right?"

I nod, frantic to make him understand.

"Good. Good. Now let me play."

He pumps his hips in a very good imitation of sex, pressing his weight into me, his hands keeping my ass open to him, and I'm in a weird, hovering sort of shock about it all until he says, "Can't stop thinking about this. Constantly."

This? Which part? I mean, is this a scene he's pictured before? Because yeah, I mean, I literally pictured him spanking me over the desk, so my fantasies were pretty accurate, actually.

But the part where he makes me feel like I'm giving up more of myself than I've ever done in bed before…that part's new. There's a vulnerability to it that's somehow intimidating and unbearably sexy.

Out in the lobby, a door slams.

We both go still.

CHAPTER THIRTY-FIVE

Grant

I wait through the sound of footsteps. The exterior door beeping open and closing again.

The plan was to turn Sunny into a quivering mess. That *was* the plan. The second I sink to my knees and look at her pussy, I'm obliged to concede that the plan is flawed.

"Fuck," I hear myself whisper, enthralled. "You smell so goddamn good. Need to taste you."

She makes a little sound of protest. A *don't look at me* sound. A sound that says she likes it and she wants it but she's maybe never had it like this before. Like a sex goddess, the center of the world.

"Look at it. All wet like that." My thumb strokes lightly down her soaking middle, opening her up to my view. "So fucking soft." I've got no choice but to push her wide and dive in, face-first.

Big, big mistake. Because the taste of this woman's pussy, on a scale of one to sell your soul to the devil, is beyond infinity. I'm a man possessed, driven by a need that's insatiable.

It should freak me out, but that's the thing about the best/worst mistakes. When you're in the depths of one, it feels so goddamn good that you don't care how wrong it is.

So, yeah, that's where I am. Halfway to perdition. And fucking glad to be there.

Instead of slow-build seduction, I've gone straight to growling, open-mouthed feast. "Been dying for this," I mutter, forcing myself to pull back and stare at how much pinker she's gone in the last few seconds.

A second later, I dive back in, give her my tongue, my nose, and, hell yes, nip her with my teeth. She's bucking toward me like she wants more. Like she's close.

With effort, I give my hand space to slide in and explore her slickness with my knuckles and then stroke her open, gently, like she's made of soft petals, and what the hell is happening? I've never once thought of flowers when I've done this.

"You'll be quiet when you come all over my face, Sunny," I say, my voice low and gruff, even to my own ears. "If I let you come."

She whimpers, and I immediately make myself stop.

"I said not to make any noise, you little brat. You got that?" I stand up behind her, not touching. "Can't stop thinking of how good it would feel to slide inside you."

Her groan tells me she likes the idea.

"Not today, Sunny." Her whimper makes me laugh, low and wicked. "No. You'll have to wait for that."

Another impatient sound, and I give her ass a quick, light thwack.

A muffled gasp.

"You like that?" I lean over her and line my face up with hers, meeting her gaze as she nods. It's the first eye contact we've had since this started, and it shuts my systems down for a beat.

What was I saying? Right. "You like your punishment?"

Her eyebrows dip into what has got to be a pout. I grin, let my body cover hers, and press my iron-hard erection against her.

"This is how it'll be if I give you my cock. You feel that?"

She nods, each breath frantic, as she cranes back to maintain eye contact.

Fuck me, this woman's beautiful. Dancing, smiling, stretched out on her desk like an offering. I watch her, filled with the strangest sensation. Like there are two of me, this one, running through the motions of a scene I can't stop dreaming of, and my double, hovering somewhere beside me, watching, waiting. For what, I have no idea.

I shake my head, blink hard to pop out of it, and concentrate on Sunny's back lifting and falling, her rear end presented to me like a gift, her hands white at the knuckles where they clutch the far end of her desk.

Then I make the mistake of meeting her gaze again, those big eyes, somehow naive and all-knowing and completely hazed with lust, and that's all it takes to send what's left of my tightly held control slipping like sand through my fingers. Why is that? Why would her lost expression make my stomach go tight and clench my jaw hard enough to break teeth? The skin of her cheekbones a hot pink. That deep divot in the middle of her bottom lip—obvious even with the way they're stretched wide with the paper still inside. Why would *any* of this make me want to swipe everything from her desk, flip her over, put my mouth to hers, and take her, slow and deep?

These urges make no sense. I don't lose it. Not at the club and certainly not here.

Control is everything.

But that little freckle—the one that looks like a perfect little teardrop under her left eye? *That* is my last straw?

I search wildly around us for something—anything—to latch

on to. There's nothing. The rules are gone, rolled up into a ball in her mouth.

And whose fault is that? Shit. No. I will not lose all control because of one solitary freckle.

"Turn over," I order, pushing my voice to the deep, crisp place where I prefer it to be. I ease my aching erection away from where it's dying to be. "Now, Sunny. Don't make me wait."

She obeys.

Good. *Good*. Much better.

"Spread. Wide. Heels on the desk."

She tries to say something through her gag.

"Are you using your safe word?"

She shakes her head.

"Is there something you need to say?"

Another headshake, with a bratty little eye roll.

"Hold your legs. Here. And here. I'll be fucking you with my fingers now." My attention moves down her body. "Gonna make this plump little pussy come. When and how I decide. Got it?" At her eager nod, I use my thumb to open her up again and ease it inside. "That's so nice. So fucking wet."

Her blush darkens, and I can feel by how she clenches that the praise doesn't just go to her head. It goes right here, to this hot, slick place between her legs.

I move in again, slow, deep. She responds with a moan. I give her thigh a light slap. "Quiet. Or I stop. You want that?"

She shakes her head frantically.

"Keep these wide. Stay quiet. This'll be over soon."

Like it's a chore she has to sit through. A duty instead of this intense, illicit pleasure.

I drop slowly to my knees, and this time, instead of the wild, ravenous beast, I am calm, methodical. Yes, my dick's pounding, but that's not an issue. It's not an issue that I'm letting this happen at work either. And how, more than anything, I want to drag her onto the floor, make her sit on my face, and force one climax after another from this sweet, sweet body? Not. An. Issue. Nothing is an issue when I'm in the zone. Calm, clearheaded, controlled.

Slowly, carefully, I work her with my mouth, my tongue. Her clit's a hard, sensitive bead, and every time I flick it, she goes tight around my invading finger. I push her up. Up, up, up, with systematic pressure, using her reactions as a guide, plunging deeper into her with a second finger. Work her up and up, then hold her at the top... Control her orgasm the way I do everything. I calmly give, and I calmly take, and this is where I feel the deepest satisfaction.

I mutter things, monitoring every twitching limb and clenching muscle, as her writhing and panting reach a fever pitch. I then press a third finger inside, right on that G-spot, and suck hard on her perfect little clit, and...

As she starts to fall apart, I rise, my fingers still pumping inside her, drag her up, tearing the wad of paper from her mouth and pressing my face to her neck.

My body soaks it all up—the trembling, the harsh breaths, the quiet way she whisper-screams against my shoulder. It's glorious. And it's mine.

At some point, while my still very turned-on body absorbs her tremors, she flops back and looks up at me. The hazy, lost look on her face makes me want to wrap her up in something warm and feed her one disgusting pumpkin spice drink after another, in a bath, with pumpkin spice candles if she wants. She deserves soft towels and a big, cozy bed.

"Come here," I whisper, bending to nuzzle her cheek, her ear, and the curve below her jaw. Back up to her lips. Before I can think it through, I'm kissing her.

It's the wrong kind of kiss for what we are. I know that. But it feels too good to stop.

CHAPTER THIRTY-SIX

Rae

I AM SHOCKED BY how soft his mouth is this time. How tender.

Just a dry swipe of his lips to mine, careful, though not tentative. He's not asking if he can have me. He's learning, listening, testing. If our kiss at the club was a wild, carnivorous massacre, this is a slow, sensuous feast.

My mouth is so sensitive that just that first touch makes me whimper.

Grant pulls back with a quiet, *shhhhh*, before diving in again, his gaze glued to my mouth like he's hungry. Wants more. Can't stop.

Until the kiss isn't exploring anymore; it's taking. Drinking, then biting, tugging at my bottom lip, and letting it go. His cheek rubs against mine, sandpaper rough. His mouth smells like me, like sex.

With an irritable grunt, he changes his angle and licks deeper, his tongue making the kiss carnal instead of sweet, and so ravenous that I feel echoes of it between my thighs.

My legs, which have found their way around his waist, drag him closer, up against me. While his tongue consumes me, his arms wrap my body tight. Shivers run down my back. My fingers tunnel into his hair. So soft. I'll remember that later. The silky give of each wave. The width of his hips, forcing my thighs wide, the heft of this hot, thick shoulder against my palm.

He bends and buries his face in my neck again, his breath heavy and hot and fast. And after a handful of seconds, like he's shut that part of him off, he straightens, drags his lips over mine one last time, and plants a brief kiss on my forehead.

"Okay, then." He steps back from where I'm still sitting on my desk, legs splayed.

Wait, what? Are we done? No, no, no, I want more!

"Here." His voice is gruff, his eyebrows low. I'd say he's annoyed except for the careful way he pulls my skirt down and reaches up to slide both thumbs along my cheekbones. Raccoon eyes, I'm guessing, which he is kind enough to at least attempt to remove. It's a testament to how hard he made me come that I couldn't care less.

"Thank you," I whisper after taking a sip from the water bottle he's just held up to my mouth.

He nods, lips compressed right back into their usual flat line until he opens them to ask, "You okay?"

"I'm good."

This is a lie. *Good* doesn't cover a single part of this. But a girl's got to have her pride, right? And despite the hopefully reparable damage he's just done to my synapses, there's no way I'm telling this man just how completely he rocked my world. The kissing, the dirty talk...the cunnilingus? And then, because I wouldn't be a Jensen if I didn't stir the shit just a teeny tiny bit, I ask, "So. Are we adult enough to admit that you just licked me to fruition and back right here on this desktop?" My dress falls back into place as I hop off said desk, pluck the wadded-up list of rules from its surface, and, with some regret, chuck it in the trash. I'd probably keep it if he wasn't standing there watching me. Next, I open the drawer containing cleaning supplies and set to work. "Or did this not happen either?"

"Oh, this happened."

Surprised, I look up to meet his steady gaze and then slowly look down to where his erection's tenting his pants. "You, uh, need help with that?"

His eyes narrow, darkening as he takes a step toward me.

At that exact moment, there's a knock on the door.

"Shit," I mouth, chucking a used pile of Clorox wipes into the trash like they're evidence in a murder trial.

Grant, cool as a cucumber, inspects me carefully and tugs my dress down another inch before grabbing a folder off my desk to hide his crotch on his way to unlock the door.

Dorothy looks in at us from the lobby. "Time to head home, kids. Nobody wants you here all night."

I can't look at him. "Oh, just getting my things together."

"Good. Good." Dorothy looks at him. "And you? Did you even go home at all this weekend?"

Surprised, I glance his way. "You worked all weekend?"

"Most of it," he says with a sidelong smirk. "Went out for a quick drink Friday night."

A quick drink? Is that a euphemism for what happened between us at the club?

"Well, good." Dorothy does a funny little cha-cha in the doorway. "You two should have drinks or something. On me. Just to, you know, release this aura of tension in here." My cheeks flaming hot, I focus on the bunches of bracelets jingling from her jazz hands. "Go ahead. Put it on the company. Business dinner. Oh! Take her to La Pierre, Grant. You two should blow up the old expense account and—"

"Probably not the best idea right now, Dorothy."

She pauses, deflates. "Oh, right. Sometimes I forget about... everything." Her gaze pinballs from Grant to me and back again. "You two doing okay?"

"We're fine."

"You sure?" She turns to me for confirmation.

I nod quickly. "Oh, yeah. Excellent. And we are just...so..." Words. Words. Can't think of a single one. Oh, here they are... "Fine with cohabitating in this confined space. Together. Close. I mean, not so close, but close enough to you know...greatness." Shut up, Rae. Shut it. Now.

I look to Grant for help with my verbal diarrhea, but he's just watching me with a puzzled expression, and apparently my brain and mouth are in collusion against me because I'm now saying something about satisfying relations, and holy shit, he literally killed my brain cells with his mouth.

"I'm leaving," I finally manage to get out. Thank god.

Grant growls, "We're all leaving," and literally—shit you not—shuts off the overhead light with the three of us in the office.

After a quiet handful of seconds, during which I wonder if I can locate my bag and coat with just the light from the lobby and the streetlamp's orange glow, Grant slaps his computer shut, picks it up, and nudges me toward the door.

"My...things."

"Here." He hands me my coat, which I take with numb hands. I snag my bag from the drawer and head out. "Everybody gone for the night?"

"Yep. I checked on you when I saw the light under your door."

Nodding, he ushers us out the back door and then down the exterior stairs. I wave and take off down the alley, almost at a run.

It's only once I'm safely locked in my car, headed home in

traffic, that I let any of it affect me, and when it does, I'm hit with an absolute tsunami of hilarity.

I have to pull over to laugh. And laugh. I don't know how long it takes. Maybe two minutes? Five? Whatever the case, I finally get myself together enough to wipe the tears from my eyes, let my head fall back against the headrest, and think about it all.

Oh, the embarrassment. I don't know how to fix this with Dorothy. Maybe there's no fixing it. Or maybe she didn't notice anything wrong? She can be out of it sometimes.

And then there was the rest of it. The nucleus, as it were, of tonight's experience. The reason for the season, or whatever you want to call what happened in that office. At my—no, *on* my—desk. Between my legs.

And all the places he kissed me.

Truly, it can't have been that amazing, right?

CHAPTER THIRTY-SEVEN

Rae

Grant's seated at his desk when I race into our office late the next morning. He's perfectly put together, while I look like I've been rolling in Cheerios. Which isn't all that far from the truth, to be honest.

"Good morning." I sidle by his desk, going for nonchalance— no small feat, considering what we did here last night.

"Rae."

Unclear on whether that was a greeting or an attempt to get my attention, I breathe in, steel myself, and look straight at him. "Grant."

He frowns. "You okay?"

"I'm fine. Why wouldn't I be?"

"You've got…" He motions at his temple. "Something… Right…"

I run my hand through my hair, finding nothing out of the ordinary. I struggle to do the same on the other side, but can't quite make it with my left arm full of the clean, folded laundry that Otty's swinging by to pick up.

"Whatever. It's fine. I'll get it later."

"Don't move." Wearing his patented look of long-suffering exasperation, Grant stands, makes his way over to me, and picks something out of my hair.

I get a little woozy at his clean soap smell and immediately flash back to last night when that stern face was literally buried between my legs. I work hard to concentrate on his closely shaven Adam's apple while he picks through my curls, his expression going from blank to annoyed in a matter of seconds.

"The hell is this?" He holds something out, his grimace remarkably close to the one my nephew Devon wore this morning when I tried to feed him his oatmeal.

"Um." I glance down at the piece of gook he's holding out and then immediately back up. "It's either toddler food...or possibly toddler vomit. Take your pick."

The disgust I expect doesn't make an appearance. Instead, Grant goes to my desk to snag a few tissues and returns to wipe first my hair, and then, after what feels like a pretty superfluous *May I?*, a stain on my sweater.

"That might be cereal."

His mouth tightens at the corners.

"I didn't know you had kids."

"What? No. No, I...not me. They're my sister's."

"Ah."

"Two of them got sick last night. And then she got sick, so I went over to help."

"Is she a single parent?"

"Might as well be. Schaffer travels."

Another nod as he rids me of the laundry I'd been holding and tugs my bag from my shoulder. "Sit." He pulls out my chair, and I automatically comply, sighing the second I land. I watch him set my bag on my desk, open the closet, and slide the pile of clothes onto a high top shelf. "Coffee?"

"Oh, I'll make some. Just give me a—"

He tugs off my trench coat before urging me, firmly but gently, back into my seat. "Have you had your coffee yet, Rae? You look exhausted." He hangs my coat up.

"I'm not…" At his skeptical look, I give up all pretense and flop back. "I didn't sleep."

"At all?" He sinks to his haunches, putting us eye to eye.

"Who knows? An hour? I tried. But there was so much throw-up to clean. I'm not good with gross things."

"You should go home."

That makes me sit up straighter. "Absolutely not. I'm fine. I've got meetings today. And performance evaluations to get out to department heads, the retreat to finalize, and—"

"Stay there. I'll be right back." With a sigh, he pushes up to standing and walks out.

I put my things away, fire up my computer, and pause when my feet hit something under my desk. "What the…?"

It takes me a second to recognize it as one of those ergonomic footrests I've been eyeing online. The adjustable wooden kind, no less. Way out of my price range.

"Cream and sugar?"

"How'd you know?"

One side of his mouth kicks up in a smirk. "Given the pumpkin spice affinity, I figured I'd be safe dumping in lots of both."

"No. I mean, how'd you know I needed a footrest?"

"You swing your legs."

"I do not."

"Rae," he says in the same benevolent, takes-no-bullshit tone

I've heard Hannah use with her boys more than once, "we both know you've got your feet in midair while you wiggle around on that sweet, round butt all day. Now, maybe this way, I won't have to spank it again to make you stop."

And just like that, I've lost every one of my core executive functions.

"What?" he asks. "Am I wrong?"

I manage a tiny headshake.

"What's that?" he whispers.

"No. You're not wrong."

"How is your"—the tiniest of smirks—"backside, by the way?"

His words send warmth curling into my abdomen. My thighs squeeze together. "It's fine."

"Good."

I wait, breath bated, while his warm gaze travels all over my face, lingering briefly at my mouth, before returning to my eyes. He's going to kiss me. And I can't think of a single reason I shouldn't kiss him back.

My eyes find his mouth, gravity pulls me forward...and he stands up.

"Good," he repeats. Nodding, he swipes one hand over his face, turns away, and then back to me, before finally returning to his desk.

CHAPTER THIRTY-EIGHT

Grant

I'VE NEVER EXPERIENCED AS many interruptions as Rae Jensen endures in a day. And I'm not referring to her regularly scheduled meetings.

What astounds me isn't just the number of people who come in here asking for things. It's the things themselves. First off, there are the usual requests for things like tampons and tissues. Then the people coming in asking for updates on vacation days remaining and health savings account balances. The patience with which Rae explains over and over that she doesn't directly access the latter, while giving not only personal codes but then step-by-step instructions, is one of the more impressive things I've seen.

We've now got Blake, nearly in tears because her skirt's splitting at the seam and she's got a date tonight, and what does Rae do but calmly sit the woman down in her chair and sew the damn thing up.

I'm irate enough when Blake leaves that I bark, "Shut the door." At Rae's look of reproach, I tack on a quick *please*.

"Why do you look like that?" Rae asks once it's just the two of us. "What's wrong?"

"You've got to stop that, Rae."

"Stop what?"

"Doing all the things for everyone."

She rolls her eyes. "It's my job."

"Sewing emergency?"

"No. That was because I'm nice."

"Hm."

"What? You don't think I'm nice?"

"I don't know."

She gasps.

"I don't know what I think. Except that half the things you do here could not possibly have been in your job description."

"There wasn't a job description."

"Of course not. Dorothy probably hired you out of the back of her car."

"Oh, sure. So, I'm cut-rate? Is that what you're saying?"

"Not at all. I'm saying you..."

The flush on her cheeks, the light in her eyes, and the way her brows crinkle up all coalesce into an urge. Before I know it, I'm up.

"Any more meetings today?"

"No."

I look around, eyeing the blinds. They're cordless, so they won't do. No extension cords either. Another sweep of the room gives me nothing until my attention focuses on the coat closet, and then I recall hanging her jacket up this morning. A trench coat. Ignoring Rae's protestations, I tug the belt from the loops, test it, and finally drop to my knees beside her.

When our eyes meet, I see understanding dawn, mix with consternation, and turn into that perfect, imbalanced blend of excitement and hesitation.

"Do you need to use the restroom?"

Her *no* is high, breathy.

"Good." I bend, wrap the belt around her legs and the chair's central axis, test that she can still turn, and then tie it off into an easy-to-remove, front-facing bow.

"I can't work like this."

"Sure you can." I spin her forward to prove my point, stand up, and return to my desk, much, much calmer than before.

In fact, I feel absolutely amazing.

"What if I need something?"

"I'll get it."

"Oh, please, that's not—"

"What do you need?"

"Well, nothing right now. But if I do."

"It'll be my problem."

She huffs, glances around, and cranes down in an attempt to look at where I've literally tied her to the seat. "Anyone can see."

Shit. That's true. "I've got it." Back to the closet, trench out and over the back of her chair. It hides everything.

Perfect.

Job done, I return to my desk. Now I can concentrate.

CHAPTER THIRTY-NINE

Rae

I AM LITERALLY TIED to my chair. And...I don't hate it.

Okay, if I'm being completely honest, the way my body's reacting is...shockingly inappropriate for a work environment.

Which is apparently the way Grant and I roll. And, yes, I feel lots and lots of guilt about it. It's just that, at this very minute, the guilt is far outweighed by all the other stuff. Stuff like my nipples, which are currently hard at attention and firmly pro-Grant, and my skin, which has gone prickly hot.

A new email pops up in my inbox. I open it, focusing hard on the words and on controlling my breathing. Okay. I can do this.

I respond to the message with information that I literally gave to the entire team last week. It's fine. I'm used to it.

Alrighty then. Back to updating the employee development file. Behind me, Grant's typing like nothing ever happened, and the sound of it is too much. I shut my eyes, squirm a little in my chair, and test my legs for wiggle room. The belt is loose enough that I can wrestle my way out if I want to. If necessary, I can also just reach down and pull the bow open, but...

I really, really don't want to. I want...

"Sticky notes," I say through dry lips.

When he doesn't immediately reply, I push on the desk to spin his way and wait for his eyes to meet mine. He removes his headphones, looks down at where my nipples are fighting the good fight to get out of this top, and back up.

"Yes, Rae?"

"I, um, I need sticky notes."

"Ah. And where would those be?"

I point at a storage cabinet on the far wall. "Second shelf, left."

He seems perfectly content to walk over to the cupboard and search it, his hand finally finding the big, yellow stickies. When he holds them up, I shake my head.

"I need the *Les Mis* ones."

"The *Les Mis* ones. I assume you mean *Les Misérables*, the musical." At my nod, he returns the stickies and continues his search. After a good thirty seconds, he says, "I don't see them."

"Oh, they're...in the box, actually. There, beside the little clothespin thingies." I smile. "Sorry."

"Not a problem." He takes a long look at the miniature clothespins before handing over the stickies. "Anything else?"

At my headshake, he returns to his desk.

Twice more over the next half hour, I ask for things, and both times, he gets them for me, no complaints. Nothing, really, except for this knowledge—this secret—between us.

When someone knocks at the door, I jolt halfway out of my seat, almost tripping in the process. I sit just as a head pops in and, oh shit, it's Otty. Is it after 6:00 p.m. already? I forgot she was coming. Suddenly, all our subtle, sexy transgressiveness disappears, and I am frantic.

"Hey, Beanie! Nice digs!" she says, casting a quick look at Grant and then back at me with an obvious eyebrow hike. "Hel-lo, there!"

"Otty!" I force a smile, even though I have never fought so hard not to cringe, because I have found one more flaw in this game, and it is that I can't even turn fully to look at her. If I do, she'll see the front of my legs. And she'll know. Hell, she's my sister. She'll know something's up anyway. "Meet Grant! Grant, Otty."

"Grant? It's a pleasure. You must be Beanie's new colleague."

"The pleasure is mine. Otty?" I don't have to turn around to feel Grant's eyes shift to me. "Beanie?"

"Yes. It's my childhood nickname," I say awkwardly over my shoulder. "Otty is my sister."

"Ah." I strain to watch his gaze go from me back to my sister. "I see the resemblance."

"Yeah?" Otty grins, her dimples working overtime. "I'm the youngest, obviously."

"Of how many?"

"Three," I tell him.

"The kids..."

"Not mine. Thank god." She shudders. "I'm still in the sowing wild oats phase."

Grant smiles at her, and I feel the strangest combination of pride and hurt. I'm proud because Otty's funny, and I'll always be proud of my baby sister. The hurt is 100 percent that smile. Grant never, ever smiles at me like that. Only scowls and frowns and glowers for me.

"She's here for the laundry."

"Laundry." Grant looks at me blankly.

"In the closet. The top."

"Ah. Yes. Of course."

The second he goes to grab it from the top shelf, Otty makes an inappropriate—but shockingly apt—two-finger-and-a-tongue motion behind his back, and I swear I almost die a little, trapped here at the very desk upon which he did indeed recently perform possibly the world's best oral.

If only Otty knew.

No. No, hopefully she will never know.

"Thank you, Grant," she says, accepting the pile of laundry, which I belatedly recall prominently features at least one pair of lace panties and... yep. That's me, even closer to dying than I was a second ago.

"Want to go grab a little cocktail, or..."

"I can't. I'm..." I cast my captor a frantic look.

"Meeting," he provides. "Very important."

"O-kay." Otty slides a look between us.

"I'll go for a drink!" Sam yells from her desk back in the lobby, followed by the clop of her shoes across the hardwood floor. And then she's here, too, in the office, where I'm being willingly held prisoner. "Come on, Rae. Everyone's gone home."

"I can't."

"Why not?"

"She's needed." Grant couldn't be more serious.

"Sorry." Avoiding Sam's eye, I give a weak nod. I swear that my heart's about to give out. "Important audit stuff."

"Really." Sam's eyebrows lift almost to her hairline.

"Yes. Really," I say, forcing a tepid smile.

"Fine. Have a good meeting." I can almost hear Sam's air quotes on that last word.

"Bye, guys. Where to, Samuela?" Otty follows Sam to her desk.

"Just so you know, every single person has left the building," Sam calls from the lobby. "Good night!"

"Bye!" I reply as they head to the door, and then outside, their voices fading as they go. They are 100 percent going to spend the next hour talking about Grant and me.

"Did you do your sister's laundry?" Grant asks.

"Oh my god." I drop my head on my desk.

"You washed and folded your adult sister's clothes?"

"Do you think she saw? Does she know?" I ask, ignoring his question entirely in favor of much more pressing details.

He shakes his head. "No. I'll lock up. You stay put." Just before he heads out into the lobby, his eyes do that thing where the humor gives way to that dark, knowing glimmer. That heat.

I spend an excruciating couple of minutes waiting, tied to my chair, while Grant takes his time making sure the offices are empty. When he returns, he shuts the door and leans back against it, watching me.

"Can you take this thing off me now? Please?" I beg, feeling silly and excited. We both know how easily I could remove the belt myself.

"Are you going to stay in your seat like a good girl? Stop getting up and running around and doing everything for everyone?"

"Yes."

His head tilts at a curious angle. "You're lying."

I'm about to deny it when the truth hits me. He's right. I am constantly running. The only time I'm not is when I'm at home working on my book nooks. And even then, I'm keeping busy. Busy hands, busy brain.

"I see what you're doing, Grant."

"Do you?"

"You're trying to get me to…do less extraneous stuff. Just stick to my job?"

"Will you?"

"There's no way my extracurricular activities fall under your purview."

"Actually, Sunny, I've decided to take a personal interest in your extracurricular activities."

Whoosh. All my blood rushes to my bottom half, leaving me lightheaded.

"Oh?" I manage.

When he sinks to the floor beside my chair this time, there's a strange tenderness in my chest and my throat. I feel swollen and full and off-kilter, like there's too much or too little oxygen flowing to my brain.

"Grant."

"Yes, Rae?"

"What are we doing?"

He stops moving, my trench coat belt now stretched between his hands. Only his eyes shift up until they meet mine, the connection like a hit of something illicit. Bigger, better than anything I've ever felt.

He exhales, mouth open, so silently I wonder if my hearing's gone. And then, still quiet, he says, "On the floor, Sunny. Now."

CHAPTER FORTY

Rae

Grant folds his jacket in half and drops it onto the hardwood floor. "On your knees, right there." After locking the door, he goes to my supply closet and grabs a ruler and the container of miniature wooden clothespins I use for hanging little signs around the office. Never once did I picture they'd be remotely kinky. "What are you doing with those?" I ask.

He ignores the question. "Safe word?"

"I...I'm at green."

"You sure?"

"Yes. Yes, sir. One hundred percent." Kelly green. Forest green. The greenest of greens.

He takes a handful of my hair, tilts my head back, and bends for a deep, wet kiss that feels so good I want to climb him like a tree and devour him.

"You're dangerous," he mutters against my lips before dragging our mouths apart and turning to line the supplies up on the edge of his uncluttered desk. "The things I could do to that mouth." His gaze lands on my lips, and I swear something changes in its depths.

"I plan to pull this hair," he says, giving my curls the barest tug.

"Oh god."

"Is that a yes, Sunny? Or a no? Either is fine."

"Yes. *Yes*." Flashback to every single time I've wanted a partner to yank on my ponytail but felt too shy to ask. "Please do that."

"I want to play with those sweet little nipples." He watches me.

"Okay."

His dark eyebrows lift.

"Yes, sir."

"You ready?"

My nod is embarrassingly eager.

"Say it."

"I'm ready, sir."

"Good." He plants himself in front of me. "Take me out."

All the blood rushes to my bottom half. "Wh-what?"

"Take my cock out, Sunny. Now." He yanks his shirt out and undoes a few buttons, obviously seeking an unobstructed view of what's about to happen. If I agree to it, that is.

His hands fall loose at his sides as he waits for me to come to a decision.

This is the precise moment when I understand just what a master this man is. Every order is a request for consent. He's not grabbing my hands and making me. He's looking at me with that steady, dark gaze, and he's daring me to unzip his pants.

"Do I have to?"

His eyes narrow. "Do you want to?"

Right now, there's nothing in this world I'd rather do.

I inhale, letting the moment stretch so I'll remember it for the rest of my life. Finally, feeling oddly bolstered by the realization that I'm in charge here as much as Grant, I shuffle a couple of inches forward, reach up, and unzip him. I'm shaking, eager, and so careful as I work my way slowly over the bulge in his pants.

"Now pull it out. Get it good and hard for what's next."

Every word out of Grant's mouth makes me lightheaded.

"Or what?" I ask him, unsure if it's a challenge—a brat moment, as he'd call it—or a real question.

Bless Grant Bowman for reading that hesitation exactly right because, rather than plowing ahead the way I'd expect some men would do, he takes my chin between his thumb and forefinger and says, "So we're perfectly clear. It's no fun for me if you don't want what we're doing. I need to be the boss—of you, of your pleasure—but I need you with me." His gaze devours my face. "Right now, what I want is to watch those pretty lips on my cock. Taking it deep, maybe a little hard. I want to hold your head in my hands and control the angle, the depth, see how hungry that sweet mouth is." His breathing's as shaky as mine, I notice in a far-off part of my brain. I need to remember that, after. "But all of it is up to you."

"I've got my safe word."

"Of course. I need your consent, though." His eyes drop to my chest. "I want to do other things too. A little light slapping."

I blink over to where he's set the items. "You'd be slapping with…"

His lips curve up into something close to a smile. "The ruler."

I gasp.

"Anywhere you don't want that?"

"On…" I look around. The floor? The desk?

"I meant on your body."

In a flash, my brain gives me one scenario after another. My butt, my thighs, my boobs. All of them just this side of scary. None of them bad.

"Maybe not my toes."

His sudden grin is a breath of fresh air, so open and happy that I imagine it's exactly what he must have looked like as a kid.

"No face, fingers or toes, wrists or ankles," he whispers with a quick kiss to my nose. "Promise. What about your nipples?"

"My…" I swallow.

"I want to play with them."

Ooooooooh. Understanding hits me like a ton of bricks as I remember the office supplies he pulled from my cupboard. "Using those?" I point at the tiny clothespins. "Like, as…nipple clamps?"

He nods. "You like that idea?" His gaze is intent, hungry. "None of it's happening if you're not into it."

"Yes. I like it." I nod. "I want it."

"Good. Clasp your hands behind your back." A last peck on my lips, and he's up, his focus on his buttons, on peeling his shirt off, on the items lined neatly on his desk. Everywhere but on me, where I'm kneeling here on the floor. Waiting. It's uncomfortable. Long. Strangely lonely.

"We didn't discuss choking."

I jolt. A little blast of excitement and fear, so closely entwined I couldn't honestly say if I'm for it or not. "I-I'm not sure."

"Fair enough," he says easily, his lack of disappointment or judgment the most freeing thing I've ever experienced. "Can I touch your throat?"

"Yes." Even in my current state, the irony of finding freedom in rules and bindings isn't lost on me. My mind floats to my book nooks and how creating those tiny little worlds paradoxically feels like it opens mine up. "I like the idea. I'd just prefer it to be gentle."

"Understood." His eyes are steady on mine. "And penetration?"

I scramble through a whole series of *should*s and *should not*s and ask, "You've been tested for STDs?"

"Yes. Regularly. We all are. For the club."

Oh, right. I remember the lab had to send my results directly to the club.

"You have other partners?" I ask him.

"Not currently." A pause. "It's been several weeks." He grabs a cell phone, taps on it a few times, and shows me a recent set of test results, scrolling slowly to the last page.

"Thanks."

"I have condoms with me, but as with everything, I'll get your consent. And you can safe word as needed."

"Right. Yes."

"Let's see where this takes us. Yeah?"

Where it takes us. Like it's a road trip, a thing we're doing together. The two of us. Going places.

At my nod, he shuts off the overhead light, leaving us with just the glow from his desk lamp and the streetlights. He sighs, stretches, and then picks up my trench coat belt, which he twists around the knuckles of one hand and pulls taut with the other. Will he tie me up with it? Do I want that?

His back's still to me when he says, "Hold your hair up."

"What?"

"You like wearing your hair up. You'll have to hold it."

"I have rubber bands in my desk. I could..."

He looks up, his face ice hard. I stop talking and quickly bunch all my hair into a mass on the crown of my head.

"Hold it up with both hands."

I comply, nerves making every part of me shake.

"That's better." He eyes me like something he'd select at the market. Gone is the warmth, the laughter. This man brooks no refusal.

It's hot and it's scary, and it's made my body feel separate from me. I know it's there. I'm aware of it. It just doesn't seem like mine.

I've never felt so on display as I do with my hands planted on the top of my head, folded at the elbows in this sit-up position. My back's arched, my chest up.

"You look good like that, Sunny. So damn pretty."

My cheeks heat from the compliment.

"Open your mouth." He comes close, and I have to roll my eyes back to watch him, and even that is somehow sexual. "Go on. Open."

I let my jaw drop, so hyperaware of his crotch, right there at eye level, that I could swear my mouth starts to water.

"These lips…" He brushes a thumb over my mouth and cradles my face with the fingers of that same hand. "They're gonna feel so good, aren't they?"

Should I nod? Respond? I don't know. But then he slips his thumb inside, and I don't have to, and that loosens something up inside my rib cage. No choices. No decisions. Nothing to do. Nothing to think. Just…be.

"There you go." His thumb presses in, exploring my inner cheek, my teeth and tongue, and the roof of my mouth, and then, instead of letting me suck like I thought he'd do, he tilts my head slightly back. "That's it. That's the angle."

Liquid warmth flows straight to my pussy. And yeah, part of it is that the man looks good. I mean, he's unbelievably gorgeous with his shirt off, and I've barely had the wherewithal to look. He's all thick, broad shoulders, lightly furred chest, and sharply carved abs, but that's not what turns my insides to slush. At least not all of it. The way he's playing with me? Wow, does that hit buttons I didn't know I had. The narration, too, is its own torture. The way he's telling me what he'll do, every step of the way. It has the added benefit of giving me time to adjust or protest. Time to say no. Or to open wider.

Time to wait in agony while he plans his next move. Although knowing this man as I now do, I'll bet he's got it all mapped out in his head from start to finish. The General wouldn't leave anything to chance.

It occurs to me that I'm the chance card here, the unexpected piece of this puzzle. The wild roll of the dice is me. For some unfathomable reason, that is what sends the shiver down my spine. Makes me swipe a lick at that thumb and rake my gaze over every inch of his chest with a lascivious pleasure I'd hardly known I contained.

"There she is." His eyes crease at the corners, and I love the tiny thread of warmth that shines through. "Stay like that."

I don't dare move as he reaches for the waistband of his boxer briefs, just visible where his pants are open, and lowers it, exposing his erection with the sort of slow ceremony usually reserved for religious occasions.

He's watching first himself and then me with the utmost concentration, and it is heady how solid that attention feels, holding me up as surely as the wood beneath my knees. In this moment, there is nothing in the world but the two of us.

And his monster cock.

"Um, Grant?"

He lifts his eyebrows.

"You're...huge."

"Then you'd better open wide, sweetheart."

CHAPTER FORTY-ONE

Grant

RAE JENSEN KNEELING ON the floor at my mercy is a dream. Staring at my cock like she can't quite believe what she's seeing. It's so goddamn good I can't describe it. I give myself a single, explicit stroke—more for her benefit than mine—and step close enough to slide the tip over her lips.

The second my aching cock touches her tongue, I get just how tough this'll be. I recognize now that what we've done here these past couple of weeks hasn't been fighting or arguing. It's been foreplay. I've never experienced anything like it. And while we both know that Rae's come twice in the process, I've done no such thing.

At least not at work. In the shower? Yeah. Every single night, I've had to give in and think of her while I took care of business. And not once did it satisfy the urges that come up when she's near.

"Good girl," I say as I feed just the crown into her mouth. Her cheeks hollow, her tongue works, that addictive blush darkens, and all I can think is how gorgeous she is. I give in to my urge to test the heat of her skin and skate the backs of my knuckles down one side of her face as I ease my length in another inch.

She doesn't seem to notice when half her hair tumbles down her back.

"Sunny," I warn. "Hair up. You wanted it. You got it."

The moan she lets out vibrates all the way to my balls, and though control is what I crave, I'm losing it with this woman, yet again. Fast.

No, fuck that.

"Keep your hair out of my way, Sunny. You have one job here. Just keep it up." This is a lie, made all the more obvious as I stuff her mouth full of cock. But it's all about the narrative, isn't it? Another lie. Who gives a shit about narrative when it feels this good? I press in. Deeper. Her mouth works, struggling to contain me, to take it. All the while, her eyes watch me with the same wide-open excitement that drew me to her from the first.

I pull back so she can breathe and press in again, my jaw tight, my hips working. When she loses control of her hair again, something comes loose inside me. Unchained.

"Come on, Sunny," I mutter, always bossy, always a prick. "Arms up. Hold your hair for me."

She immediately obeys, and I stroke her face again to show her how happy it makes me, and then I let go just enough to bend down, grip her hands and her curls in one hand, and use her own body against her. A quick in and out, deeper, rougher. She takes it like a champion, moaning her frustration with each withdrawal.

"Good. Good girl. So pretty with my cock in your mouth." I continue fucking her, slowly but firmly. With her arms occupied, she's forced to push against me to stay up, and she's working for it, my sweet girl. Working so hard. "There you go." She's squirming, her body writhing like she wants to put those hands to use between her legs, and if she can't, she'll use the floor, her thighs, whatever friction she can get. Her hair? It's a chaotic burst of curls down her back while her hands hover lost in the air.

And that's the thing about my brand of kink: the torment works both ways. Giving and withholding are just two sides of the same coin. So, yes, I could come like this, and it would feel damn good. But if I flip it? Prolong the agony for both of us with a bump of uncertainty and a little punishment for fun? Then everything is multiplied. It's a feedback loop of give-and-take and want so deep I could do it for hours.

After a few more slow thrusts, I pull out, dripping saliva. Rae sucks in a deep breath, following my retreat like she wasn't ready to let me go.

"No, sweetheart. Not yet." I nudge her away. "You dropped your hands."

"I...What?"

"Your hair." I shake my head when she rushes to rectify the situation, alas, too late. "I'm disappointed."

Her little whimper hits me hard in the solar plexus.

I cradle her face in one hand. She leans into it, her eyes shut like she's in pain or embarrassed. "You okay, sweetie?" I whisper.

A nod.

"Tell me what you're feeling."

"I-I just hate messing up."

"Oh, baby. You can't really mess up in here. That's the beauty of it. Even when you're bad, you're good. You get that?"

At her quick nod, I tug her hair back. "Say it, beautiful. Tell me you get how good you are. Always. No matter what you do."

"Yes. Yes, sir." I feel her shiver in my palm. "I'm good."

"You are. Take the shirt off." I plant a quick kiss on her forehead and back away. "And pull down your bra."

CHAPTER FORTY-TWO
Rae

I SCRAMBLE TO OBEY. Not because I want to, but because I have no choice. This isn't about what I want. It's what I must do. The simplicity of it satisfies in ways I'd never imagined.

As if the look and feel of the General weren't enough, as if his smell didn't wrap me in something safe and scary and weirdly wholesome, there's this sense that I'm here for his pleasure. No thinking. No planning. No responsibilities at all. I obey, I react, and I soak up all the praise, and I please him.

I don't think I've ever felt so free.

The second I take my shirt off, the air changes. It's cooler. I'm more vulnerable. The only barrier is my plain cotton bra, which I scramble to pull down, exposing myself as if it's my entire job. Exactly what I was made for.

And the worst part? It's that Grant's not even looking. He's turned his back to me while he grabs things from his desk, and it's awful how badly I crave his attention.

He turns to look at me, and against all expectations, he's holding my trench coat belt and nothing else. "You okay, Sunny?"

I look down at my own body, my explicitly presented breasts, and fight to hold back a giggle that somehow gets out anyway.

"Is this funny to you?"

"I don't know." I shake my head, nerves turning fear into hilarity, bubbling up until a choked laugh shakes my shoulders. "I've never done this."

"You're doing great, sweet girl."

His hand, warm and firm, nudges my chin up. I keep my eyes closed as it lowers to skate over my left breast, strokes the side, the bottom curve. My right breast now, caressed, gently, lightly, the touch an exploration. A message. *This is good*, it says. *This is right*.

Both hands now, just butterfly touches, the backs of his knuckles, the side of his thumbs. No pressure, just skimming, barely there. When his breath hits me, warm and humid, my eyes open on their own, and what I'm staring at is the top of Grant Bowman's head. Big, thick brown waves, messy after a day of running his hands through them. There's a cowlick, a sweet swirl that I'd never have seen without the bird's-eye view, and for some incomprehensible reason, it makes my pulse pick up speed. Like he's shown me a secret part of him. A touch of vulnerability in this fantasy scene. A soft underbelly that I'd never have known existed.

The moment his breath touches my skin, I'm lost to the connection again.

His mouth is hot silk around my aching nipple. My eyes roll back. "Oh god."

Pulling, pulling, and soon nipping with his teeth, and then over to the other one, and his hands are on me, and I am moaning, and my hips have taken on a whole rhythm of their own.

When he comes up for air and tells me I'm beautiful, I believe him. I trust him.

"Here." He reaches around me, and it's only after there's a tug at my hair that I realize it's my belt that he's winding and winding into something intricate and almost solid. It takes a while. Long minutes during which I float, suspended. At the end, he says, "Touch," takes my hand, and shows me the thick rope he's made of my curls, containing them and, if my imagination's anything close to right, also providing something for him to hold. My body likes that idea as much as my brain does.

When Grant rises to gather the rest of the items from the desk, I am full of sensation, my blood pumping thick and warm, my muscles aching for something. Anything.

He's back with the little wooden craft pins, picks one up, opens it, lets it snap closed, picks up another, and then uses them to tease my breasts. Just exploration and touch until he reaches my nipples, presses the clips open, and gives me a long look before letting one, and then the other, close gently over the tips.

I gasp at the pinch. The two tiny pings of pain are enough to send everything else into a hot tailspin.

Another moment of eye contact, Grant's steady gaze gauging my reaction before bending to place a kiss on each gently pulsing point. He frames my breasts, admiring his work, and pleasure sparks through me, as light and airy as bubbles in water.

"All right, Sunny. New rule. You ready?"

"Yeah."

At his side-eye, I quickly amend my response to "Yes, sir."

"Good. No more errors, okay?" He lifts the ruler. "Or I'll have to use this."

"Uh...Yeah..." I nod, spacing out with my eyes on the transparent plastic.

A light thwack to my breast startles me into a squeal and turns the heavy weight in my belly into something hot and syrupy. "Sir."

"Excellent. Now. Suck my cock. And once you've finished me off, I'll give you your orgasm. But only if you're a good girl. No touching yourself, Sunny..." He's so serious, so intense. I'm hanging on every word. "If you touch yourself…" He raises the ruler. "You get this. Got it?"

"Yes, sir."

With that, he rolls his chair close and sits in it, a king on his throne.

It's the most apt description, given that he is all I can see, feel, hear, smell. He's the ground under my feet, the ache in my thighs. He's the tightness at my scalp; he's the clenching at my core. He's every fantasy I've ever had, and the satisfaction is guaranteed.

When he manspreads in that chair, erection proudly framed by his pants, there is not a bone in my body that doesn't crave him like water. Like the last molecule of air in the world.

The man says *down*, and I drop to my knees like they're not sore from the hardwood. Like the pain isn't something I'll carry with me for days. For the rest of my life.

There's a before this moment, and there's an after, and I know I can't go back. There was sex pre-Grant. And now there's this, and I am screwed for everything else.

The worst part is that I. Do. Not. Care.

I let him pull me forward by the hair, and I lick him like a lollipop.

He's not just the perfect weight of this cock, the perfect fit in my mouth; he's the very best smell, an ambrosia taste too rich to be real. His shape, his sound, this feeling. God, the feeling. I'm squirming, my thighs shifting in an attempt to eke out the tiniest bit of friction. Anything to alleviate this ache between my legs.

I know as soon as he pulls me off him that I've been caught.

"Sunny." His voice resonates. "Are you trying to come?"

Uh-oh. My pulse is loud in my ears. Finally, I nod.

"You are aware of the consequences?"

When I nod this time, I'm filled with a bright, hedonistic glee. "Tell me."

"The ruler. Sir." I have to work to hide my grin.

"Not much of a punishment if you want it, Sunny." Another sigh. "What's under the skirt?"

"Tights. Um, panties." I'm breathing hard. "Sir."

It takes him a minute to gather up my skirt and pull my tights and underwear down. I shut my eyes hard as he gives my bottom half a good, long look, and when I finally open them, he's staring blandly at my face. Only there's nothing bland about the pink cast to his cheeks or the quick rise and fall of his chest.

He rolls on a condom and pats his knee. I try to figure out the best angle of approach and let him guide me face down across his legs, until I'm ass up on his lap. Ready for my punishment.

How surreal is this?

A giggle tries to work its way up and out of my mouth, but I keep it in. And wait, stretched here on his lap with his cock against my belly, his hand on my ass, and the other below me, playing with one pinched, aching nipple.

This is exactly where I'm meant to be. Here. Now. It feels like fate. Like the end of my sexual rainbow.

Subspace. The word flits through my mind at the exact moment the ruler lands on my ass, and my entire body flinches. Seconds later, his hand soothes. I sink into him again. Give him my weight, my trust. I am submerged.

"There it is."

That hand fondling my breasts sends shards of pleasure to my pussy, so sharp I think I'll scream.

"Good. Just a few more."

I nod. Agreement, acquiescence, consent, a demand. Call it what you want, I am fully on board.

"Good," he mutters right before slapping my ass again with a piece of plastic that has no earthly business feeling this good. Sharp and angry for a split second before the pain washes into pleasure so wide and deep that my extremities fizz with it when the next smack lands. And the next. And the next. And all the while, he's telling me how pretty my ass is in pink like this. My dimples and curves. How gorgeous I am when I moan. How my pussy's begging for his cock, and I'll get it. But only when he's done. When he's ready.

My breasts are pulsing, my nipples throbbing, and my pussy's this swollen, empty ache, and he's moved on to the other cheek and then shoves my legs wide, and—"Oh god," I moan, when the ruler lands right where I want it, on my clit, and the feeling's so big and bright that I'm going to explode and I tell him, and then he's somehow hauled me up and I'm straddling him, a rag doll in his arms. His erection notches at my entrance.

"Fuck, baby. Fuck, look at you. So wet. So needy."

I whimper.

"I want you to come for me, so hard."

I stare down at where he starts forging his way inside me, slowly stretching me. And it's tight. But it's good. Better than anything, with his thumb teasing my clit and my breasts cradled in one hand and he's back to working my hips and my weak legs lift and fall and—holy shit, he's all the way in and I'm so full, and then...then...

My clit, my insides, a flash of pleasure/pain at my breast. He's taken the nipple clamp off, and I am wailing, except there's no noise because he's soaking up the sound with his mouth. I am detonating.

"Next time..." His voice grates against my lips. "I want to feel this bare."

"Oh god," I pant.

"There it is." He takes off the second clamp, and my whole body clenches. "Oh fuck."

My climax builds to a sharp point...and then breaks.

Everything disappears in the wash of sensation. I close my eyes...and I'm gone.

CHAPTER FORTY-THREE

Grant

Sunny's pussy pulses hard around my cock, but in the end, it's her expression that sends me over that edge into heart-pounding oblivion. The look of sublime pleasure on her face.

I tip my head and touch my forehead to hers. All the control in the world couldn't keep me from muttering how good her release feels as I empty myself into the condom. And even once it's over, the aftershocks ride me in little jerks I've got absolutely no power over.

After what feels like ages, oxygen flows back in, reason takes over, and I lick up the last of those sweet gasps, nudge her slightly back, and take her in.

One orgasm, fully debauched. That was the goal, not this other thing that's taken up residence in the middle of my rib cage.

"Come here," I force out through a throat that's raw and tight with emotion. "You're perfect, Sunny." I cup her face, caress her mouth, her cheek, and let my other hand skim over those insanely hot tits. "I want you like this all the time."

"Limp and used up?" Her half grin is the prettiest thing I've seen in my life. It twists something up in my belly so hard that I have to pull her toward me and whisper *in the best way* in her ear.

Her weight is just right. Soft and warm. I dip and let my mouth wander over her neck, her shoulder, press my face in, smile. I could stay here all night.

"We should...um." Rae nudges me gently away. I've been dismissed with a shy smile. She stands, and we both gasp when my half-hard cock slips from her warmth. I put my hands on her hips and hold her steady.

"You need water."

"Right. Yes. God, I'm thirsty." She turns like she's leaving, and I grip her wrist to stop her. "Wait. Hold on." I check her shoulders, running my palms down her arms to grip her hands. "Let me do it. Okay? Let me."

Rae nods. I stand, pull her bra up and her shirt down, and turn to settle her in my still-warm seat. "Wait here."

When her eyes narrow like she'll protest, I add a quiet *please*, which seems to appease her. After quickly zipping myself up and getting my shirt back on, buttoned and tucked, I grab her empty bottle from her desk, unlock the door, and head out for a refill.

I'm gone all of thirty seconds, but the woman is stubborn. By the time I get back, she's up and fully dressed. Shoes and coat on. Her hair's coming down, and the belt's already halfway through the trench coat loops.

"You're a brat," I tell her, to which she replies with a grimace, holding up her phone, "I got a text. I have to go."

"Someone needs you?"

An eye roll. "Always."

"Who is it this time? Your sister? Your aunt's ex's half-stepchild-in-law?"

"Come on. It's not like that."

"What's it like then, being needed all the time?"

"It's..." She accepts the water automatically, her eyes going vague as she seems to consider her answer. When she doesn't move for a second, I nudge the bottle to her mouth and watch her down half the contents. "It's good to know they're safe."

That answer surprises me. "Safe?"

"My family. The people I love."

"Drink more. Finish it."

She obeys. I wipe a rogue drop and move closer, using her belt to draw her into my body. I feel...unready for it to be over. "You should stay. Let me...care for you."

"Oh. Aftercare." A breezy wave of her hand. "I'm good."

Frustration rips through me, and I cinch the belt further, bringing our bodies in tight. "I'll drive you."

"What?" A laugh. "No. No, I'm fine."

"You can't drive after...that. You need time."

"I drank my water." She holds up the empty bottle like a kid proving she's taken her meds, eaten her veggies, done all her homework, and now can she play? Except with Rae, I know... I just *know* she needs the aftercare. More than that, she needs a shoulder to lean on. Someone to make sure that she's eaten after she's fed half the world.

It pisses me off. "Listen to me, Sunny. This is how it works. If you're going to be my sub, you need to let me take care of you."

"Am I?" Her brows lift high. "Going to be your sub?"

"Do you want that?"

"Yes."

"Then you'll listen. You'll do what I say."

"Okay. But...the scene's over. Right? And I'm...free to go. Unless I've grossly misunderstood the boundaries here. I haven't, have I?"

Dammit. She's right. Why am I pushing so hard? This isn't who I am.

I step back, into the skin of a Dom who uses power exchange to get my rocks off. Nothing more.

The last thing I want is to tie myself to anything or anyone for longer than the time it takes for one of us to get off. This is a messed-up reaction to mixing business with pleasure.

"You're right. Apologies." I breathe deeply, relaxing my spine and my shoulders. "If we're doing this, though, we're doing it right. In the future, no shortcuts. Got it?"

Her eyes go slightly fuzzy, her mouth soft. "Yes. Got it."

"This is the last time you run off without aftercare."

"So, we're doing this? Are you my Dom?"

Yes, my body shouts. "Text me when you're home safe," my mouth says. "We'll discuss."

CHAPTER FORTY-FOUR

Rae

My phone vibrates as I get home three hours later, sore and exhausted. All the adrenaline burned off while I raced over to Hannah's with electrolyte solution and ginger ale and crackers, which I dropped onto the porch when she warned that they're now all sick. Even Schaffer, which is wild, given that he just got home today. Like he somehow magically got the exact same bug while he was in Milwaukee or whatever, and now he's home and it's obviously morphed into the man flu, which is worse than Hannah's and the kids' combined.

Pissed as I am at my brother-in-law, there's still a shadow of that postcoital glow, and let me tell you, I have not yet stopped trembling. It's the glowiest I've ever felt from sex. Or foreplay. Or... well, if I'm being honest, anything at all.

I'm all cleaned up and ready for bed when my gaze settles on my Carytown book nook. While I'm still basking in the aftershocks of what we did, I sit at my table, turn on the light, and rummage through a bin of clear plastic bits in search of the perfect material to make a ruler.

I've never put myself in one of my models, and I'm honestly

not sure I can do so now, but the urge to immortalize the way I felt tonight is strong. So I set to work.

My body's humming low and constant like a high-voltage power line, so the vibration of my phone doesn't immediately register.

When it does, I scramble to get it out from under me. Too late.

A second later, a text comes in.

Grant: It's Grant. Answer the phone.

My pulse flicks up into overdrive.

Me: Bossy much?

Grant: Part of my charm. I'm calling you. Answer.

The annoyance that drums up is nothing compared to the excitement I feel as I answer his call.

"Hello?"

"Are you home?"

"Yes."

"When did you get there?"

"Oh, maybe half an hour ago." A look at my screen says it's been longer. "I kind of lost track of time."

"You didn't text, Rae."

Too busy thinking about you. Well, and cleaning up after sick people. And making the world's tiniest spanking ruler. "Oh, shit. I forgot."

He growls. "You'll have to do better than that, Sunny."

I go instantly pliant at the sound of my kink alias.

"Okay, sir."

"First. We should go over the club checklist you filled out."

Whoa, okay. I can do that.

"I need a response, Sunny. Yes, you're fine with it, or no, you'd rather not?"

"Yes," I rush to reply. "Absolutely."

"Good. And then we'll discuss your punishment."

"Punishment?" I whine, like the good little brat I apparently am. Wait. Are brats good or bad?

"For not texting the second you got home."

"I'm sorry."

"I'm sure we'll find a way for you to make it up to me."

"Okay...sir." Way too worked up from the direction the conversation's going, I turn off my desk light and get into bed. "Should we do that now or...?"

"Checklist first. Punishment after."

"So, we're doing like an official Dom/sub thing?"

"Isn't that what we discussed?"

"I thought you didn't do long-term."

"I don't." There's a gap of a few seconds before he says, "This will be until I leave the company. That's it."

Disappointment floods me. It stinks because I don't want to feel these things. I shouldn't feel these things. I mean, if nothing else, I should hate this guy whose job is in such direct opposition to what I stand for. But after tonight...yeah. Who am I kidding? This is totally happening. "You'll be my starter Dom."

That seems to surprise a huff of laughter from him. "Sure. I like it."

I'm smiling as I snuggle deeper under the covers, and for a happy moment, all I feel is a heady glow.

"The checklist you had at the club? Is that still current?"

"Yeah. You have it?"

"I remember your choices, but if you can share the list with me, we can make it official."

"Oh. Wow. Okay. Yeah. I think. Hold on." I go over to my worktable and scrabble around in my drawer until I find where I've hidden it, pull it out, and start reading. "Do, um, *you* have a list?" I ask, putting him on speakerphone in order to take photos of the list to send over to him.

I hear the smile in his voice when he says, "You don't need my list."

"But what if—"

"My list is what you want."

I think about that. "Like, are they identical?"

"No. But remember the Pleasure Dom thing?"

"How could I not?"

"Okay. Got it." A pause while he's no doubt reading. "Let me see this. This first section? Where it lists bondage and suspension experiences?"

"Yeah," I reply, reading the long, very detailed number of things I would or would not do. Quite a few are hard *no*s, like mummification and all-day bondage. Cuffs, harnesses, ropes, chains, restraints. All of those are things I'm curious about but wouldn't do with just anybody. With Grant, I realize, it's a huge *hell yes*. Hair tie is on there. I move a mental check mark from *no* to *yes* on the Tried It column, skim down to nipple clamps and do the same. My eyes land on ball gag, which I'd entered as a very light *maybe* with a low rating. I think of how I shoved our list of rules into my very own mouth, and suddenly my rating's moved up a point or two. Or fifty.

"Another thing we haven't discussed is birth control. Do you want to stick to condoms?"

"I, ah. I have an IUD." Excitement fizzles through me. "We could forgo condoms. If you want."

"Understood. And yes. I want," he says, that all-business voice a couple of notes deeper. "Okay. I'm printing this out. On the bottom, I'm handwriting that I will adhere to the items provided on my submissive's checklist. I will obtain your consent before embarking on an untried activity, and I will take care of my submissive's every need. Are we clear?"

"Yes. Sir."

"For the duration of the term."

My belly swoops, this time not in a good way. "That's right."

"To the end of my current assignment, which will not exceed three weeks."

Three weeks, tops. I am devoid of oxygen. Of everything.

"Rae?"

I clear my throat, croak, and then clear it again before I can manage a weak "Y-yeah."

"You okay?"

"Yes. Great." I look down at my list again, which features such treats as anal training and...oh, there it is, orgasm control. Suddenly, I'm a little woozy from this late-night libido sneak attack, not to mention the evening's main event.

"I'm signing this. I'll scan and send, and you can do the same."

"Wow. Official."

"That's the point."

Right. "You are nothing if not a stickler for rules."

"Exactly."

Neither of us mentions the fact that we had literal sex on his office chair tonight.

His voice gets quiet, private. "Can you turn on your camera?"

"Is this the punishment? Making me show you my pj's? Because I can assure you, this outfit's a libido killer. The punishment would be all yours."

"Your pj's got little flowers or something? You wearing one of those eye masks?"

It's absurdly close to the truth.

"Show me. I want to see your face when I tell you the consequences."

Ooooooooooh.

Caught halfway between turned on and shy, I tap the camera button and give him a close-up shot of the undereye patches I slapped on in an attempt to combat my lack of sleep.

"I knew it." Grant looks tired too, his eyelids heavy. This close up, there's something softer about him. Sweet. "Now, show me the pj's, Sunny."

I hold the phone out so he can see the entire ensemble, which consists of thermals and a fuzzy bathrobe. It's cold and damp in here, so warm is where it's at.

"What's that pattern?" He's squinting. "Looks like little turds."

I laugh. "Hey! No! They're hedgehogs. They're cute."

"Hm." His eyes are smiling now. "You're cute."

"And these are ranunculus flowers. They're my favorite."

"They're beautiful." His smile disappears. "Like you."

"You're making me blush."

"Your blush, Rae, is one of my very favorite things."

"Oh. Um, thanks?"

"Another one of my favorite things is when you come on my cock. Like you did tonight."

My pussy clenches hard.

"Did you like that, sweet Sunny?"

"Yes," I whisper. "Sir."

Something about his serious expression tells me I'm not going to like his next words, and oh boy, was my Spidey sense right.

"You'll have no more orgasms until I say so, Sunny." A hard stare. "Understood?"

"Wait. What?"

"Tonight, you do not come. No touching yourself. No getting off. At all."

"Why not?"

"Because I said so. See how it works?"

"How will you know?"

"Because you'll tell me."

The jerk is right. I want to wipe the smirk off his face.

"Well, guess I'd better go, then," I say in my brattiest voice.

"Good. Get some sleep."

"You're bossy."

"That is the sum total of my charm, sweetheart."

Not true, but there's no way I'm telling him that. Instead, I ask, "When am I allowed to come, then, huh? In three weeks?"

He goes serious. "You'll come when I say so. Got it?"

With a whoosh, my entire body goes hot and heavy and so darned needy that I wonder if I can even sleep without taking care of myself. Which, honestly, is a first.

"I don't like you right now," I lie.

"You'll thank me later."

I growl and he chuckles and we both end on a sigh.

"I have one more request, Rae."

"You giveth orgasms and then you taketh them away... What more could you possibly ask for?"

He grins. "I want to put your desk back to where it was."

"Why?"

"So I can look at your face while there's still time."

Of everything he's said to me, that's what makes me blush the hardest.

CHAPTER FORTY-FIVE

Rae

I'M WEARING A GARTER belt to work on Wednesday, along with pale pink, gossamer-thin thigh-highs. Also, as it happens, no panties.

Because if I'm going to suffer from this no-orgasms nonsense, Grant had better suffer too. I may be a Very Good Girl who enjoys pleasing her Dom, but I also, without a doubt, enjoy a good dose of comeuppance.

My Dom. Just thinking those words warms me as I walk up the exterior steps. I enter Sugar's lobby, where Sam's at reception on a call. She lifts a hand, and I stop beside her desk.

I really need to talk to someone. Badly. But she makes a face and waves before tucking her head down and whispering into what I realize is not the office phone but her cell.

Oh my god. Is it the secret fuckboy?

With a smile, I mouth, *Can we catch up?*

She replies with a silent, *Lunch?*

I give her a thumbs-up and brace myself to go into the office. Is Grant even in yet?

Just then Klaus and Blake round the corner from the kitchen.

"Look, Rae." Klaus stomps right up to me. "This has got to stop."

"This?"

"Work Daddy," Blake says, like I'm a fool. "We need him gone. Stat."

"Uh, why?"

"We'll all be out of work soon 'cause of him," says Klaus. "I saw the investors' meeting in Dorothy's schedule."

"He's here to screw us." Blake sounds as certain as I've ever heard her.

"I don't think—"

Klaus leans in and stage-whispers, "He's a hedge fund guy, isn't he? Dammit, Rae, I really wanted to see you two get dirty, but…"

"We're shutting down the office pool," says Blake.

I look from her to Klaus. "The what?"

"You know. The betting. You and Work Daddy."

I groan. "Listen to me, you two. Grant is not here for your jobs."

"How do you know?" asks Blake.

I open my mouth and shut it, look down at the outfit I chose today—to tease this ostensibly bad guy—and make a decision. "Have either of you done something wrong?"

Blake looks abruptly down at the floor, guilt scrawled all over her features.

"Define *wrong*," says Klaus.

"Something fireable." When that doesn't have an effect, I roll my eyes and add, "By Dorothy. Have you done anything that our boss, Dorothy, would fire you for?"

"Uh, no."

"Obviously not."

"Well then, you're good. Relax."

"Really?" Blake eyes Klaus, who looks over at where Sam, still on the phone, shrugs.

"You sure?"

I swallow, remembering the sweetness of Grant on the phone last night, the affection in his voice, and come to a decision. "I'm sure. Grant's a good guy." A pause, and then I jump in feetfirst. "I promise."

I need a minute in the restroom after that confrontation. When I walk back through the lobby, Sam is still on the phone. Something's going on there. Something more than just a married guy. Which I'll be getting to the bottom of, as soon as she and I get a chance to talk.

She ignores my look.

Okay, then. I guess there's nothing left for me to do but face my office mate.

Grant looks up as I walk in. Just his eyes move as he continues typing, watching me cross the room, put my jacket away, and finally take in the room's new arrangement. It's official. We're face-to-face again.

I do my best to ignore him, sit down, and open my computer. But let's be honest, anyone with eyes can see that I'm not entirely myself right this second. I'm an amped-up version. My butt, sore and oversensitive from where my wool skirt's rubbing against the vestiges of last night's spanking, is a constant turn-on.

Headphones on, email inbox open.

I sneak a glance, sure I'll catch him staring. Nope.

My nerves continue to fizz as I go about starting my day. Dani swings by asking for sticky notes, and another colleague wants printer paper. Both times, as I'm about to respond, Grant cuts in and tells them to look in the storage closet, down the hall. While it's not great for his already poor reputation with the staff, I rather enjoy not being the one to tell them. He is, after all, already considered the bad guy.

Unlike my colleagues, though, I no longer see Grant as a threat. Would I like to be let in on what, exactly, he expects to find at Sugar? Yes. Of course. But I trust him in a way I didn't before. He's not a man who'd go and fire people for no reason. Deprive a poor, horny woman of her rightful orgasms? Absolutely. Of a job? My instincts say that he would not.

I check the time. A little before noon. Seems as good a time as any to start my campaign to make him regret the orgasm embargo.

I gather a few files from my desk drawer and head to one of the cabinets, where I get down on my knees and then move to all fours to slide them all the way back.

Behind me, all typing stops.

Grant can't see my sore bottom. I know that. But I specifically chose this length of skirt to play peekaboo with my garters.

No orgasms, he says. Well, no orgasms, my (well-spanked) ass.

It doesn't take long for him to clear his throat. "Do you have lunch plans, Rae?"

My mind goes blank. "Do I?"

"We should, ah, meet. About…"

"The thing," I finish.

"The thing."

"Yes, sir." We stare at each other through a silence that is positively throbbing with subtext. "I mean, Grant," I amend. "Oh, actually, I have to check with Sam."

I duck out into the lobby, where my bestie's madly tapping at her phone.

The second she sees me, she slams it face down on her desk. "Rae!"

"Hey. You mentioned lunch, but I've got the…"

"Yeah, actually, I can't. Not today. There's…"

"Retreat coming up, so lots of…"

"An event," she finishes, nodding.

"Meetings." I end at the very same time and immediately feel bad about lying. "You good?" I ask.

Sam's hand flies down to still her buzzing phone. "Great. Awesome. Just..." Her shrug is so painfully casual that I know for a fact that something's off.

"Hey. Maybe we should cancel our..." I wave a hand in the air. "Events. And have lunch after all, you know?" I cast a quick look over my shoulder before leaning in and whispering, "I have so much to tell you."

"Me too, Rae."

"Let's do it. Lunch. Come on. My treat."

"Yeah, I—" Her phone buzzes again. She picks it up, reads whatever it says, and I watch in real time as her face morphs into a look I never thought I'd see again. The expression's only there for a split second, but it's enough. She looks young and scared, like the Sam I first met back in middle school. The Sam who didn't have enough food at home, whose mom was never around, and whose dad was a one-weekend-a-month kind of father.

The second she opens her mouth, I can tell she's going to turn me down. What I don't expect is the sudden wide grin and whispered, "Booty call, baby." She lifts her chin toward my office door. "You do yours. We'll compare notes, okay?" Her secretive giggle makes me think I imagined that whole look on her face. "You've got a lot of talking to do, lady."

A wash of heat floods me. It's equal parts embarrassment and excitement, and when Sam shoos me off with one hand while tapping on her phone with the other, I decide that thing I saw was just my own guilt for not being as present as I should be when she's obviously got as much going on in her life as I do.

With a smile of my own, I head back to the office.

"Now?" I ask Grant.

He takes his time to finish whatever he's typing, his lips turning up only slightly when he responds with "Now."

Sam's nowhere to be seen when we leave together, heading downstairs in silence. A quick check of the sidewalk, and he lets us into the club and then down another flight.

It's totally different here during the day.

"I'll show you around." Grant tilts his head toward the low table where we first met. "Bar area here, which you are familiar with. Cocktails and chill out over there." The sofas are soft, buttery leather. Easy to clean, I imagine.

"These are semiprivate play areas." He pulls a heavy velvet curtain aside to show me one of a dozen small nooks.

"I had no idea these were here."

"That's the beauty of it." He opens the next one, watching me. "Exhibitionists can open it. More private people leave it closed."

"No peeking?"

"Those peeking—without prior approval—are given a warning and then thrown out. Come on." He takes my hand and leads me to a door, which he unlocks. "The front is fully clothed. No nudity allowed."

"And back here?"

"Private rooms through there." He walks me into a smaller area filled with wooden crosses and benches, seats, and cages. There's a stage to one side and another door at the back. "This is the members-only dungeon. Hold on." He does something on his phone, and music floats out of speakers that I can't see.

I stare around, taking in details and cataloging them in my head for use in the book nook. "I thought the whole place was members only."

"Yes, well, there's a ranking system."

"That seems elitist."

"Not really. Given what happens back here, we require longevity and trust before opening these doors."

"Would I be allowed back here?"

"As my sub, yes."

"And after? When I'm not your sub?"

His expression goes dark. "The club owners would all have to be in agreement."

"Would you vouch for me, Grant?"

He watches me, head angled as if to get a fresh perspective. "Well, that depends, doesn't it?"

"On what?"

"On whether or not you were a good girl."

"I was," I reply with embarrassing speed. "I am. I promise."

"I'll be the judge of that." A pointed look at his watch. "I've got thirty minutes." He's already rolling up his sleeves as he leads me over to a bench in the corner. "Lie down."

"But, I don't know, it's, like... lunchtime."

"Yep." He smirks. "And I'm hungry, sweet girl."

CHAPTER FORTY-SIX

Rae

I SETTLE BACK ONTO the shiny, padded black surface, staring up at the pressed-tin ceiling.

Grant grabs my thighs and drags me to the end of the bench, slowly slides my skirt up, and lets out a low, gravelly sound as he reveals first the garters and, above them, my complete lack of underwear. The man usually knows what to say, so I'll take his inability to find words as a good thing.

A deep inhalation and then the snap of one garter. "You know, when you got down on hands and knees in the office, I had an inkling? I pictured a thong."

The leather's cold under my ass, the sensation of lying back like this almost clinical until the rough pads of his fingers stroke me, and then it is anything but.

The music is slow, the beat heavy but subtle. Sexy. Warm.

"Now, tell me the truth, Sunny," Grant says as he kisses my neck and my cleavage before moving down to my lower half. "Did you come?"

My whispered *no!* feels wrenched from my lungs.

"Hmmmm." I see the doubt written plainly on his face. "Last night? This morning?"

"No, sir."

His grunt is pleased. I think. I can't tell. I want to ask him if he came, but I'm not sure I'm allowed, and then he's cupping my breast and my linguistic skills fly the coop.

My hands flail out and land on handles apparently meant for grabbing just like this.

Grant's now making his slow way up a leg, down the other, ignoring my aching pussy like it's not the objective here.

When we both know it is.

"I want…"

"What, sweet girl? Tell me."

I shake my head.

"If you want it, say it."

"Touch me," I beg.

"Where? Here?"

At my eager nod, he gives a touch, light and quick, on my mound. Strokes and applies pressure to my abdomen just above it. I curl up, but he urges my legs down. "No. No, no, no. You don't move. At all."

I squirm, and he slaps me between the legs, making me go perfectly still. I don't want any more slapping. Or do I? I think I do.

Crap, it's all mixed up. The pleasure, the pain, the simplicity of taking whatever he gives. I was already wet with want when I left the house this morning. Now I'm absolutely soaking.

"What about you?" I finally ask, dying to know. "Did you get to come?"

"What do you think?"

He sweeps my right leg back, presses my other thigh to mirror it, and I'm spread wide open in this dark, cavernous place.

"I…I…don't know."

The laugh he lets out is devoid of humor. "I came three times, baby. Twice last night. Once this morning to take the edge off." The graze of his thumb over my entire pussy is too light to satisfy, but the aftershocks it sets off light up nerve endings I had no idea were there.

Again. Again. And each time, I bow up off the bench for just a touch, a taste of whatever he'll give me.

His laugh turns wicked because he knows exactly what he's doing. I have a sudden fear. Is he toying with me?

"You'll let me come now, right?"

No answer. Just the warm hint of a mouth close to where I want it.

"Please. Please, sir. Touch me. Please."

"I jerked myself in bed last night, picturing you on this bench. Begging."

"I . . . I'm sorry."

"Sorry for what, sweetheart?"

"For . . . for wanting it so bad."

"Don't be sorry for that." The words are puffs of heat, teasing my sensitive flesh. I spread my legs wider, arch higher, for just one touch of his lips. His tongue. He could bite me and I'd be happy.

"I'm not. I think it's mesmerizing, how hard you're trying to work your body on my face."

A long, lazy hum brings his lips right where I want them. Almost. Almost. So close, I'm dying.

"God, you smell good. Ripe and warm and sweet." Another tease, more heat, a hint more contact. The man's an expert at pushing me to the brink. I hate him for it. I want it. I need it.

"Maybe you don't need to come right now."

I sit up straight. Pissed as I've ever been, and the bastard laughs at me before his face goes stern. He walks up behind me, wraps a hand around my throat, and tugs me back without a hint more pressure than that.

The anger of a second ago turns into something else. Almost frantic. I'm desperate, needy, Sméagol with my precious. I'm dying to bargain. "I'll do what you want," I tell him. "Anything."

"Oh, baby. No. No, no, no, no." He's beside me, that hand stroking my throat, the hint of threat more forbidding than a choke hold. His other hand's traveling down me, over my clothes, like he's got all the time in the world, and we're not in a rush to see this through before lunchtime is over. "No. You don't give consent like that. Not when I'm standing here, hard as nails, thinking about all the ways I could take you. Here." He caresses my throat. "Here." An insinuating nudge of one breast toward the other has me picturing him between them, the way I'd struggle to make it good. The way he'd use me for his pleasure. The way I'd let him.

A light slap on my hip, under the edge of the bench, to my ass, which he palms *hard*. "I'd take you here."

Finally—oh god, finally—he's spreading me wider, stepping between my legs, and dipping his head down, down, and his mouth lands on my lips, and…

"Higher. Please. Lick my clit."

He laughs, slaps my inner thigh, and tongues my opening.

"Sir," I beg. "Please. General. *Grant*."

Another lick. Another. "I don't think so."

"What? What? You can't—"

"I can." He steps back. I crane my neck to watch him unzip his trousers and pull himself out, step close to me, and—holy mother of all gods—take himself in hand. "I'm coming on this pussy," he warns, his look telling me to speak now if I don't want that or forever hold my peace.

"Green," I whisper, which puts a smile on his mouth.

A dozen strokes, and he's doing exactly what he threatened. It is mesmerizing, the way he loses it, right at the end, his hair a mess, sweat beading at his temples. It's when our gazes connect that the switch fully flips.

The first hot jet stripes my inner thigh. He grunts with every warm pulse, his eyes flicking from my face to where he's painting me with his pleasure.

I strain for contact. I'm so close, it wouldn't take much at this point.

Finally, he finishes with a long, satisfied sigh, and I want to scream from frustration.

And Grant, my god, he must be a sadist after all, given how placid he is. How easy, how pleased. He cleans me up, cleverly avoiding direct contact with my neediest bits, presses my legs together, drags my skirt down over my hips, and helps me up to sitting.

"Good girl."

"You asshole."

"No, no, no, sweetie. You'll see. It'll be so good when it's over."

"Over? What? When is that?"

A kiss pressed to my temple. "Later."

"No. Oh my god, I hate you so much."

"Do you?" A smirk. "Come on. Let's get you hydrated."

I growl. The jerk just laughs.

Twenty minutes later, I'm back at my desk, fed, watered, and coddled within an inch of my life. I'm also angry as a wet hen that he won't put me out of my misery.

Nonetheless, I don't once consider going to the bathroom and taking care of it myself. That would be cheating. And Grant knows as well as I do that I'm a rule follower at heart.

CHAPTER FORTY-SEVEN

Rae

GRANT IS DEAD TO ME.

He left for his emergency meeting with Dorothy around 5:00 p.m. and hasn't come back. Now, at almost 7:00 p.m., I've just finished up payroll. I am tired, hungry, and...yes, horny as a horndog in heat. I want that orgasm he promised, dammit! It's mine!

But no way in hell am I going to ask him for it.

Because submissive in bed I may be—or on the floor, the desk, chair, and sex bench—but I'm not running after the jerk for this O. I just won't do it. I'll take care of the deed myself.

So instead of going to my dad's or my sister's or by the store for something to eat, I rush home, pour Pepe an extra helping of food, and climb up on my bed.

It doesn't come, though. Or, rather, I don't.

Maybe it's the lighting. I reach over and turn my lamp off. Nothing.

The music?

I dig through my music app for something resembling the dark, bass-heavy background music he'd played today at the club, run my hands up under my skirt...and...nope.

Sighing, I pull my toy chest out from under the bed and grab my favorite suction clit stimulator. Turn it on...

And can't quite get myself to press it to my body because...

"Can you believe it, Pepe?" Pepe meows a reply. "He told me not to...and now I can't."

Ignoring that last bit, the cat yawns, and nonchalantly stretches a leg out to fully clean his belly. I hate him too. I hate all of them. Everyone.

And then my phone buzzes.

I pick it up, see Grant's name, and hit accept. "Hey, Sunny."

"Don't *Hey, Sunny* me," I nearly shout into the phone.

"Aww, you suffering, sweetie?"

"You're a monster."

"Let me see you."

I turn on my camera and glare. But then I see how exhausted he looks, dark smudges under his eyes and a five-o'clock shadow that looks hours over the limit.

"God, you're pretty, Rae."

"What's wrong. Why do you look like that?"

"Just tired."

I snort. "At least you're not aching like a—a—a..."

His smile's oddly soft. "What, Rae?"

"I don't know. I can't think like this."

"Why not?"

"Because you left me, wet and worked up, and...and covered in your..."

"Spunk?"

"Argh! And you were right there all day! With those burn-y eyes and that...hair!"

"Bernie? Like...Sanders?"

"Oh, stop it. Show me the orgasm, Bowman."

He bursts into laughter. "That's my line."

"Well, it's mine now. I want it."

"You can't have it," he says, his voice low but rich. Bossy as hell and so rough I feel it on my skin.

"Sadist," I hiss.

"Brat," he replies, his eyes warm as he watches me. "Show me. Show me how turned on you are."

"No."

"Sunny."

It pisses me off that my body races to obey when my brain's this irate. But he looks good and he sounds good and he's tired and…

"Show me your face. Move the camera back."

I obey.

"Now the rest of you."

I pan down over my wrinkled work top and the skirt I've got hiked up already to my hips.

"Hold on. What's going on here?"

"I tried."

"Tried."

"I was gonna do it. I'd decided to."

"What's that yellow thing?"

"My lemon?"

"Rae…" How he gets disappointment and excitement so perfectly wrapped up in that one syllable is a mystery to me, but it's all there. "Baby, you're not supposed to try. You're supposed to wait. That's the rule."

"I hate the rule. The rule sucks."

He sighs and lies back, and the moment I realize he's probably in bed too, all the pent-up frustration loosens, and I'm turned right on again. Only the good kind of worked up, not the kind that's like a too-tight knot I don't have the tools to loosen.

"Show me your bed," I say. It takes a second, but he finally does it and what he shows me is a plain white room, navy sheets, and a dark bed frame. "It looks big."

"It is."

I don't say anything else about that bed, that room. It's got no place in this relationship, or whatever this is, and I'm not about to push any boundaries between us.

"I want to come now, Grant."

"I know, sweetie." He sighs. Smiles. "But you can't."

I suck in a breath. "You're pure evil."

"Maybe." He nods. "But let me tell you something. Your next climax is going to be something to behold. And I wouldn't miss it for the world."

CHAPTER FORTY-EIGHT

Grant

It's Friday. Less than two weeks to the investors' meeting. I've been working my ass off all week to finish the audit, but the deeper I get into the company's security protocols, the less I find. And the less I find, the more worried I become. We're either looking at someone who's very good at what they do or... there's something else going on here.

And that worries me too.

Meanwhile, Rae is in a mood.

Her patience wears visibly thinner and thinner as the day goes by. I'm not an actual sadist, but I find real pleasure in watching her frustration make her meaner. Or, at the very least, less servile. No, that's wrong; she would hate that word. Let's say... less accommodating. She's just so cute when she's mad. If I'm not careful, I'll develop a fetish for bossy little subs, and then I'll be in real trouble.

It is such a pleasure to watch her turn people away at the door, using the word *no* like she means it and—in one particular instance—telling a coworker to refer to her email dated yesterday, which Rae then printed out and gave to her, before closing the literal door in her face. Gently, of course. With a smile.

"What?" she barks when she catches my look.

"Nothing, Rae. You are very..."

Her squint makes me want to go over there and wrap her in my arms, make her come, and then tuck her in bed, where we would—

No. None of that. Just the coming part. The rest I'll take or leave.

"Tell me about this retreat you're planning."

"Why? You wanna come?"

"No."

"You should. They apparently got the count wrong and reserved an extra cabin. Give you a chance to see how great everyone here is."

"When they're not driving you nuts, you mean?" I ask with a smirk.

"Don't look at me like that."

"Like what?"

"That's an *I-told-you-so* expression if I've ever seen one." She narrows her eyes. "This is your fault, Mister. If you hadn't decided to—"

My phone vibrates in my hand. I scramble to answer, so flustered that I put it to my ear without checking to see who it is.

"Granty! There you are! I've been trying to get you for ages!"

I keep my sigh silent, turn in my seat, and press the phone tighter to my ear. "What's up, Mom?"

"What's up? You know what's up. I've left you a million messages! Do you even check anymore, or are you too busy for that?"

"I'm busy."

"Oh."

"But also, I...uh. Don't think I can make it."

"Oh."

"Sorry, but this is the thirteenth one, isn't it, Mom?"

"Is it?"

"Yeah. I counted. Don't you think you should walk yourself down the aisle?"

"Well, I prefer to stick with tradition. Besides, it's important to include you in the ceremony. I just adore Henri. You're gonna love him. He's a pro golf player. Can you believe it? Retired, of course, but I met him at the club and—"

"I'm not going."

"I could... We could change the date, I suppose, to accommodate your—"

"No, Mom. I don't want to go."

"Oh. Well, that's just unkind."

"Is it? Or is it unkind to give the guy false hope? Hm? Maybe instead of marrying him, you could, I don't know, do like the rest of the world and date for a while, you know? Maybe you could—"

"Okay. Fine. That's it. Thanks. If you want to act like this, I'm done for today. I'll stop asking. Bye."

She hangs up.

"Wow."

I look up at Rae. I can't believe I forgot she was there.

"That didn't sound fun."

I huff. Fun and my mother are polar opposites. Except maybe to the men she marries. For a while, at least.

"Yeah." I don't consider telling her about it, exactly. I just open my mouth, and it pours out. "She's a serial bride."

She gasps. "That's what you meant when you said *thirteen*?"

"Yep." I sit and roll my stiff neck. Between work and Rae, I haven't had time to run these past few weeks, and my body's feeling it. "She thinks this'll be the one, you know? Get a clue, man."

"That is a lot. Did you have like a ton of stepdads?"

I nod. "Yeah. My dad was number two."

"Where's he?"

"Florida. With his third wife."

"Wow. Sorry. That must have been rough on you. As a kid."

"You stop believing after a while, you know?"

"Have you been married?"

I jolt. "Uh, no." Subtext: And I never will be. I don't know why I don't say it. "Growing up with a rotating door of stepfamilies doesn't exactly motivate when it comes to settling down."

"So... not into long-term relationships."

"Long-term anything. This building? My current house? These are my longest-term commitments, probably ever." I shrug. "Except college. Four years." It occurs to me that I've been in my house now for nearly that long. The itch I usually feel to get up and move on to the next thing just hasn't pushed me out yet. It will. I know it.

"My parents were one-timers."

"Yeah?"

"I mean, who knows, right? Maybe time would have changed things, but..." Her smile is warm but a little distant. "Nah. She's been gone twenty years, and Dad's still in love with her."

I fight the urge to pick her up and cuddle her on my lap. While I struggle for something to say, she asks, "What about the club? How long have you been involved with that?"

"Well, it's only a few months old now, but I've been working on the project for a couple of years. Fundraising and crowdsourcing and so on. I've enjoyed taking a more active role in getting them up and running, but as soon as they're well established, I'll sell. What'll the long term do to my friendships, you know? What'll I even want in just a few years' time?"

"What do you want now?" she asks.

I open my mouth to give the usual reply, which is that I want freedom and a decent income, my own business, the ability to choose whatever I want whenever I want. A place to play. Partners to play with.

It all feels... wrong in this moment.

"Hell if I know." And then, because I'd rather not dwell on it, I ask, "What about you? You in the place you want to be? Here? Where do you even live?"

"I have a tiny house."

"You do?"

Her smile tugs at my belly, says *come here* and *kiss this mouth*. "When I left my ex, I moved out right away. There was, like, nothing available in town. So the Mole Hole came up and—"

"Mole Hole?"

Her smile melts away. "That's what Sam calls it."

I suddenly don't like the idea of Rae in a tiny place. She should have space. A manor to parade around in like a queen. Then again, I can see how she'd like something cozy. A sweet little cottage.

"No bathtub, right?" I ask, apropos of nothing.

"No. Sadly."

"You should come take a bath at my place sometime."

We're both stunned into momentary silence by the unexpected invitation.

"Oh. Sure. I'd, um, I'd really like that."

"I'll get the bath salts ready." It's meant as a joke, but now I stare down at my computer screen and see nothing but Rae naked in my bathtub, slick and soft and covered in bubbles, and then—oh, hell—I slide in behind her and...

"Anyway!" Rae appears to search for something to fill the long silence. "Um. My family. We're kind of eccentric. We are obsessed with musicals. And, uh, weird snacks. We've also got strange traditions, like hunting for bananas on New Year's Day."

"What?"

"We're very close. Sam calls us the von Trapps. My dad and sisters and me."

"You mentioned your mother being gone?"

"Oh. Yeah. I was in middle school when she got cancer. Hannah's a couple of years younger than me, and Otty was tiny."

"Otty. I still don't get her name. Is it like Audrey?"

She snort-laughs. "Nope. Her real name's Hazel. Otty is short for Otter. Or in her case, Sweet Baby Otter. Because she was so little and so lost and blind-looking and just had, like, flappy little hands, a little open mouth, and she's just Otty."

At my expression, she giggles. "I told you. We're weird."

"Must have been hard, losing your mother at that age."

"We figured it out. Eventually." She's silent for a moment and then goes on, eyes vague. "I remember drowning in toddler food and kid stuff, homework, laundry. Hannah disappeared into books. Otty cried and cried and cried and never, ever slept. She'd wet her bed and cry some more. Dad was in a deep, dark hole." She huffs out a sound that's possibly intended to be a laugh but is so full of pain that I have to fight the urge to take her in my arms. "It's all so foggy. I remember the tightness in my belly every morning when I woke up. My head full of the things that had to happen in order for us to just survive. There was food, sleep, pee. Clothes so tight they chafed my underarms and dug blisters into my heels. My English teacher, Ms. Barcom-Tancredi..." She smiles. "She was the best. She'd give me sandwiches and make sure I actually ate them." A grimace. "Another teacher slipped me deodorant. So embarrassing. And then there were the times I'd snort awake in biology to find half the kids staring at me."

"That sounds hard, Rae."

"It got better. The third year, I think, after…" She waves her hands, and I nod. "It was Thanksgiving, and Dad came home with this huge, overcooked turkey from the supermarket deli along with lumpy mashed potatoes and mushy peas. We had cranberry sauce straight out of the can, and to this day, it's the only way I like it. Anyway, we were a unit that day, the four of us. A family in a way we hadn't been for over three years. We talked about Mom and cried together. Otty nearly suffocated on mashed potatoes. We made our own, self-contained bubble. We just hunkered down until the outside world barely existed." Rae blinks at me like she's just waking up from the memory. "And then Sam came along. She's the only person to ever burst the bubble. Actually, she sort of climbed into it."

"So, you're close, then, the two of you?" I don't know why I'm asking these questions.

"Very." She glances at her phone and jumps. "Oh, crap. I have to go."

"Where to?"

"None of your business."

"Fair enough." Smiling, I watch her gather her things, waiting for her to say something about the climax denial. Instead, she only gathers momentum, getting more irritable as her purse falls and her jacket gets caught on her chair.

When I get up to help her, she puts a hand out. "Don't come too close, Genghis. I'm grumpy enough to bite."

"We're back to that nickname, are we?"

"If the shoe fits…"

"How about you meet me at the club, and I'll put you out of your misery?"

She glances at her phone and groans. "I have plans."

"Bad ones?"

"Didn't seem bad when I made them."

"What is it?"

"Paint and Sip with my sisters."

"Oh, really." I reach for her hand and set a heavy silk pouch in her palm.

"What is this?"

I'm grinning widely when I say, "Please wear it tonight."

Her growl is so cute that I want to bottle it.

"You'll need to download the app. But it's worth it. I promise."

"Better be good."

"Also," I say, just before she opens the door, "while I appreciate being compared to a famous Mongol leader known for his ability to both conquer and unite, I think you might find that Grinch is a more accurate G-letter comparison."

She laughs suddenly, hard, all animosity gone, and my chest expands with what feels oddly like pride.

"You're right, that's perfect. So irritable. So angry."

"Except I'm not a thief."

"Well..."

"What? What have I stolen?"

"Holiday cheer?"

"Please. Christmas, like most holidays, is an entirely commercial invention. Nobody actually believes in the... What are you laughing at?" I smile, knowing exactly what she's laughing at and feeling like a million dollars for making her smile again when she's spent the whole day as mad as a snake.

"Actually. Wanna know what you stole?" She leans close, every fantasy I've ever had wrapped up in one plump little package, and says, "You took all the orgasms in Whoville." The door opens with a swoosh. "I better get them back."

"Just wear what I gave you," I call, watching every move as she struts out.

This, right here, is the moment when it occurs to me that I am in way over my head.

CHAPTER FORTY-NINE

Rae

It's a vibrator. Remote-controlled, of course, and, according to the instructions and the app I've downloaded, it works from anywhere in the world.

Do I plan to wear it to the Paint and Sip session with my sisters? Hell no.

But then he texts me, right as I'm leaving.

Grant: Wear it, Sunny. I'm counting on you.

Dammit.

I send back a selfie of myself sticking out my tongue and, after a moment's consideration, head back into the bathroom. I switch the thing on, sync it with my phone before putting it in my panties, and use the magnet on the outside of my underwear to hold it in place. Oh, wow. Okay. This is not going to be easy.

Grant: Show me.

Feeling feisty, I take a quick full-length snap of myself, fully dressed.

Grant: Sunny.

Me: I guess you'll just have to find out, won't you?

Grant: Fine. Who's driving tonight?

Me: We all are.

Grant: Take a rideshare. Please. On me.

I sigh, halfway to my car, and call him. "I'm driving."
"I'd rather you not."
"Yeah, well, this isn't up to you."
"Sunny…"
"I'm late, Grant. And a rideshare will just make me later."
"Fine. But call me when you're done. Please."
"You're being awfully bossy for someone I'm not in a relationship with."
"You're my sub."
I sigh.
"I'm a protective bastard, okay?"
"I'm getting that. But it's Paint and Sip, not a dive bar."
"Please?"
"Yes. Fine. I'll call."
"Thank you. Have fun."
"Bye." I hang up and race off to meet my sisters.
An hour later, halfway through our wine flight and elbows deep in a floral still life that is pretty cute, if I do say so myself, I feel a tickle between my legs.

Oh, crap.

I glance up to where Otty's got her tongue out as she taps

brush to canvas, easel dancing with each pointillist strike. Beside me, Hannah's given up on the painting entirely. She and half a dozen women—and one man—of varying ages, including our instructor, Jazz, are recounting their birth experiences. I tuned out when they started getting into the nitty-gritty of afterbirth.

Another vibration, this one stronger, has me curling in on myself. Checking to make sure no one's looking, I put my brush down and pull out my phone to see a message notification.

Grant: One.

Oh my god.

Me: This isn't fair.

Grant: Are you safe-wording?

A look around shows absolutely no one paying the slightest bit of attention to me.

Me: Green

The second I hit Send, it buzzes again.

"Nice, Amy!" Jazz calls from the other side of the room. "The shapes are really gaining dimension with that shadowing there."

Me: Let me go to the restroom at least.

Grant: Stay where you are, Sunny. And be very, very quiet.

My mouth drops open at the next vibration, and I take a frantic look around. Can they hear the slight buzz?

The music's loud, so maybe not. And Hannah too, with her raucous wine laugh and that stage voice. Another longer, harder vibe and all I do is turn to my canvas, shut my eyes, and take it.

I collapse back onto my stool and pant, much the way Hannah's new friend is panting through a description of her wife's twenty-four-hour home birth marathon. I block them out, pick up my brush, and focus on the feeling. Oh, oh, it's good. Uncomfortable, strange, and also really, really hot, but oh my god, if he doesn't stop soon, I'm going…to…

My hand squeezes the brush, my eyes shut *hard*, every muscle tightens up, and I climax.

Wow. Wow. Wow.

I scrabble for my phone, tap out a message, and collapse back into my seat, relieved when the vibe stops.

"Interesting choice, Rae," Jazz says over my shoulder.

"Wha…?" I jump, blinking at the thick, black slash of paint bisecting my canvas from left to right. "Oh."

"Truly exceptional, actually." She turns. "Y'all should come see this. Rae has pushed limits here, folks. She's working with style and composition in a way I rarely see in these classes."

"So avant-garde," comes a voice from beside me.

I give the woman a weak smile.

"What made you think of that?"

"Oh, Rae's always been the artist," says Otty, nodding sagely from where she's sidled up beside me.

"So talented," says someone else.

"So realistic and then…slash."

"I know, right?"

"Jealous, girl."

The buzzing starts up again.

"You should see her book nooks."

"What's that?"

"Show Jenny," says Hannah.

"I…I…"

"Here. Give me your phone."

"No." I hug the phone to me as the next round of forced pleasure ramps up between my thighs.

"What? Come on. Don't be embarrassed. They're pure genius."

"Oh my god," Otty adds. "The one she's doing right now?"

"The Carytown one?" I ask.

"What Carytown one?"

"Nothing, it's just…" I look around at the expectant faces, wheezing like I'm running for my life while Grant's off somewhere, like some diabolical Wizard of Oz, turning this moment into something it really, really wasn't meant to be, and I am about to… "Gotta pee," I half shout as I race for the restroom.

Door shut and locked, and there's just enough time to collapse against it, and, oh, oh, there it is.

My mind goes blank as pleasure starts between my legs and radiates out to my fingers and toes.

Just as I start to come down from what might be the biggest orgasm of my life, the vibe starts up again, and… Oh god. Oh god. It's too much. Too big.

Holy. Shit.

I squint at the phone and wildly type a text.

Me: Two. You have stop. They want phone. Can't. Can't do more

Another whoosh of warmth makes me collapse onto the closed toilet seat, phone forgotten on my lap while I writhe.

Finally, the buzzing stops.

Panting, I pick up my phone.

Grant: They?

Me: Sisters. Need phone. Photos.

I shut my eyes, gasping for breath, half laughing at what I've just done. What we've done. How on earth did I come so hard here, of all places? It had to be the slow build, the way I've had to hold it in and hide it from everyone out there. The secretiveness to this orgasm somehow magnified my body's reactions, until...

Me: Wow.

Grant: You okay?

Me: That last one makes three.

Grant: I'll bet you've got one more in you.

A knock at the door.

I type out a quick thumbs-down, exit the messages app, and say a nonchalant, "Be right out," tucking my phone into my bra.

"Beanie? You all right?"

"Fine. Fine." I fish the vibrator out of my underwear and, with nowhere else to put it, shove it into my other bra cup. The darn thing's starting to weigh me down.

"Sorry if we pressured you."

"Yeah. Sorry."

"No. No, I'm fine." I run water over my face, step back, and stare into the mirror. Pink cheeks, eyes at half-mast, lips trembling.

"We didn't mean to, Beanie," Otty slurs. Definitely drunk.

I look at my hand. Shaking.

Okay. Calm. Deep breath.

"You guys. I'm fine. You didn't pressure. I'm good."

"We love you, you know," says Hannah. Also drunk.

"I love you too."

"We know it's hard for you to share your book nooks. We just want the world to see your talent."

I sigh. "I know. And I love you for it."

"Need a huggle?" Otty asks.

"No, I'm fine."

"Hey, I want a huggle!" says Hannah.

What can I say? A huggle request, in our family, is a call that cannot be denied. So, with one last inhale, I pat my face dry, open the door, and accept the big fat group hug from my sisters.

The problem is when the buzzing starts up in my bra.

"Wha's tha'?" Otty says against the top of my head.

"Sorry. Work thing."

"Work?" Hannah steps back. "In your boob?"

"Just hold on." Turning, with my sisters hovering behind me, I scrabble to grab my phone. If I pull the vibe out now, I will be oh, so busted.

The buzzing ramps up. My sisters crowd me.

I hunch over, typing frantically.

Me: No more. Done. Over. Red. Red. Red.

Immediately, the buzzing stops.

"Who's texting? Is that Dorothy?" asks Hannah.

"New mean boss guy?"

"No. No, it's..." I read the text chain and see that instead of the thumbs-down I'd intended to send Grant from my perch on the toilet seat, my fingers had accidentally done a thumbs-up.

Grant: You okay?

Me: Yes. Yes. Sisters. Gotta go.

Grant: Got it, sweetheart. Have fun. I'll leave you alone.

"It's a retreat thing."

"I want to go on your retreat," says Otty.

Hannah says, "We should do a family retreat."

I nod and smile, returning my phone to my bra as I lead the way back to the main room. I transfer both electronic devices to my bag the second no one's looking and take a long sip of wine before returning to my painting.

At the end of the night, woozy from too much wine and way too many orgasms, not to mention my first nonfamily book-nook commission—scary, but yay! I did it!—I stumble out onto the sidewalk with my sisters. We take out our phones only to discover that there's not a rideshare to be found.

"There was a basketball game tonight."

"No way," I say, staring down at the hour-long wait. "I can't drive like this."

"Uh-uh," Otty says, shaking her head. "Not safe."

My phone buzzes with a new text.

Grant: Everything okay? You have fun?

Me: Yes. But a game just got out. Can't find a ride.

Grant: You're at the Paint and Sip? Downtown?

Me: Ya.

Grant: Be right there.

CHAPTER FIFTY

Rae

So. Here we are, just me and my two very drunk sisters, toting our still-damp masterpieces as we climb into Grant's gigantic truck. I feel like a teen who stayed out past curfew.

"Look!" Otty shoves her painting into Grant's face.

"Nice. Very... classic." He throws me a look that I feel right where that vibrator sat for half the night.

"Not as good as Rae."

"Rae's is amazing!"

"The teacher gave it a name!" Hannah says. "Juxta—"

"Juxtaposition!" Otty yells. She clearly drank a lot more wine than I did.

"May I?" Grant tries to get a look at the painting, which, in my mind, shall forever be known as *Orgasm #2*.

Since he'll see it eventually, I turn it around.

"Nice."

"You should see her book nooks!"

"Otty, please," I beg.

"Book nooks?"

"I'll tell you later."

"All right. Let's get you all home."

We climb in.

"Why is it you have a truck like this if you're a corporate consultant?" asks Hannah with the narrow-eyed intensity of a prosecutor at a murder trial. Even drunk, Hannah's as sharp as a tack.

"I do construction. On the side."

"You build things?"

"Renovate."

"You should stop by my place sometime. All the half-fixed crap could use an intervention." His only reply is a smile, and she goes on. "So, that's your hobby?"

He shrugs, slides me a secretive look, and says, "One of them."

Otty snuffles and lolls against the back window, fast asleep.

"Huh." Hannah leans forward. "Like what do you renovate?"

"The building we work in," I tell her.

"Really? What else?"

"I've also got a property in the Fan."

"You're flipping it?"

"I live there." He sucks in a slow breath. "For now."

Shock pricks me in little waves as I realize how little I know about this man. "Are you moving?"

He doesn't turn, doesn't look my way. "That's the plan."

I nod. Right. There's a deadline for what we're doing.

"I have another building downtown. I'll start renovating it as soon as..." He casts me a quick glance. "As soon as I'm done with my current contract." Another deadline. So many deadlines.

"Cool."

"Yep."

"What'll that one be?"

"Mixed use. Condos. Shops."

"But you still own the Carytown building. Where you work."

And do other things. If only she knew what he and I get up to in the basement.

"I do."

"Not flipping it, then?"

He sniffs. "Not for the moment."

Hannah sits back. I know her well enough to realize there's at least one *what are your intentions with my sister?* question hovering on the horizon, and I cannot take that right now.

Maybe I don't want to know. I mean, what are *my* intentions, even? A few days ago, I'd have wanted him gone and said good riddance. But now? I like Grant. Only *like* isn't the right word. I turn and look at his profile, and all the things that come up are way stronger than like. I like Dorothy. I like Harlow. What I'm feeling for this man is nowhere near that.

"Stop the questions, Hannah."

She snorts.

"Hey!" Otty mumbles. "We passed my place!"

"You can stay at mine."

"Ew. In a kid's bed? No, thanks, Hannah." Otty's up and fully awake. "Take me home, please, Angry Hot Man."

"I'm not angry."

"His name's Grant."

"Grangry," Hannah whispers.

Otty leans forward to stare at his profile. "He's so serious."

There's a pause while we all appear to consider that.

"He mostly is," I concede.

Grant glances over at me and then back to the road, the subtlest smile in his eyes.

He puts a hand out and covers mine, which feels, oddly, more intimate than anything else we've done.

Uh-oh.

I don't look down at it or acknowledge the overture, other than turning my hand and clasping his back.

The rough, comforting hand, the warm truck, my sisters safe in the back seat.

This, probably, is when I really start to fall for him.

CHAPTER FIFTY-ONE

Grant

IN SILENCE, WE WATCH Hannah walk to her porch, turn to wave, and disappear inside the kind of suburban cookie-cutter home I would never have pictured for her.

Once she's in, I look at Rae. "Where to next?"

"Um. Got to backtrack. I'll get my car."

"You seem tired, Rae. Let me take you home. Please."

"You're right," she says, literally yawning to prove my point. "I'm in Byrd Park."

"Wow. Swank."

"Meh. You'll see."

"Not so swank?" I set off toward the ritzy Richmond neighborhood.

"It's *smaaah*." The word turns into another yawn, which in turn makes me yawn, and we both laugh, and then the silence is this soft, golden glow around us, part awkward and part easy.

"Pepe's gonna be so mad I was out late."

I go instantly taut. "Who?"

"My cat."

Muscles loosen. "Ah, the angry Frenchman."

"What?"

"You mentioned a Halloween costume. The first time we met."

A giggle bursts out of her. "Oh, right. Forgot I told you about that."

"You end up picking one?"

"No." She throws me a look. "Been a little busy."

After a few minutes, she guides me down a dark street. "This is it." She points at a big Victorian, possibly painted blue, although it's hard to tell in the dark.

"Nice."

"Not really. I live in back."

"Back?"

"Want to come see it?"

I really do. I want to fall into her world, arms wide open.

Which is precisely why I say, "Better not."

Then a car drives slowly by, and no part of me is okay with her heading into that dark yard on her own. "I'll walk you, though."

"I'm fine." She opens the door and turns back to say, "Good night," before setting off across the grass.

I can't let her leave like this.

"Wait. Hold up."

She doesn't stop walking. I hit the lock button and run after her.

"What? I'm fine," she stage-whispers, hurrying even faster. "I do this all the time."

"Walk in the total dark to get home?"

"Not usually at two in the morning, but yes."

She ignores my muttered *Jesus* and plows on. There's a path, I think, under the unmown grass, which is wet and damn cold.

Her poor feet must be frozen in those pointy shoes. I can't stand the idea.

"You need lights back here."

"Tell that to my landlord." She tromps straight back to a small, cinder-block cube. Possibly a garage. It starts to rain, and it is cold.

"You live *here*?"

"Yes. Anyway. Thank you for taking me home. And for my sister. And for…" It's sprinkling heavily. "You can go, Grant. Don't stay out in the rain."

"I'll wait."

She shoves her key in her lock and pushes the door open. It's pitch-black inside.

"Might as well come in for a minute."

I step through the door and look around while she turns on lamps of all colors, shapes, and sizes, lighting up what is literally the smallest place I've ever seen. There's room for one person to walk between living room furniture, kitchen counter, bed, and a little workbench, covered in tiny objects.

"This is a garage."

"It's my home."

"It is a shoebox."

"If you came here to insult me, you can—"

"No. No, sorry. It's…" I take in details I hadn't initially noticed—paintings on the walls and swaths of cloth covering the ceiling. Bright, chaotic colors everywhere, and at my feet, a fluffy white cat. "It's cozy."

She fills an electric kettle and sets it on to boil. "Close the door, please."

Does she mean with me inside or out? Where do I want to be? In or out?

The cat rubs and rubs against my legs.

"He'll make a run for it if you don't close it."

I reach out and shut the door before wandering over to look at her tiny creations. "These are amazing. What did your sister call them?"

"Book nooks."

"What do you do with them?"

"Make them. And I guess now I'm starting to sell them."

"Really? This is so cool. What's this one?"

"It's a workshop."

"Like your workbench."

"I call it my Barbie Dream Workshop. All the shelving. All the space."

"This is so...you."

"Thank you."

"Dream workshop, huh?"

"In an ideal world."

"What about this one?"

"That's the set of *Into the Woods*."

"Ah."

"You even know what that is?"

"A musical?"

"Good guess."

"You're into musicals."

She snorts. "Into them is minimizing the way my family relates to Broadway shows. But yes."

"You sing?"

"Never, if I can help it."

Smiling, I bend and pet the animal. It's so soft. It bumps my hand when I start to back away, so I scratch it behind the ear, and then its front paws cling to my legs, so I bend and pick it up. I stroke the cat's chin, and it pushes back. Moving on to the ears, I marvel at the deep, calming vibrations from its body. I look up from the warm, furry armful, faced with an irritable Rae, hair down now, arms akimbo.

"Are you kidding me?"

Both Pepe and I stare at her. "You want me to go?"

"No!" Sighing, she folds her arms and looks us over. "It's just... This never happens."

"Sorry. Should I put him down or...?"

"Not now, you can't. You'd better sit."

I look around and opt to sink into the big armchair.

Pepe snuggles deep, filling the cracks of my lap like warm liquid.

"He's never done that with anyone but me. He hates all people."

"Really." A deep scratch behind the ear makes the cat's green eyes disappear under heavy lids. "Huh."

"Do you even like cats?"

"No." He squirms and rolls and finally settles with his face in the palm of my hand. "I don't know, actually."

"What do you mean you don't know?"

I watch, mesmerized, as she pulls her dress up and off, hangs it carefully on a hanger, and puts that on a hook by the door.

The place is cluttered but really neat. Everything seems to have a spot.

Pepe pushes his face harder into my hand, and I rub the side of his neck. "Never had a cat."

"Any pets?"

"No. I moved too much." And I really don't want to talk about it. "Can I get up?"

"With a cat in your lap? Never."

I look down at the creature who has literally taken over my entire body. "I can just... push him off."

"Against the rules."

"What rules?"

"Cat rules."

"Cat rules?"

"Yep. Cat rules are not the same as human rules. For example: cat on lap? Can't move. You are out of play for the foreseeable future."

"That's ridiculous. What if you have a job to go to?"

"Call in sick."

I snort. "What are other cat rules?"

"Are you allergic?"

I shake my head.

"A cat will always go to the allergic person in the room. Cat rule."

"What else?" I ask, my voice as light as I can make it while watching this beautiful woman wipe makeup from her face, each swipe revealing glowing skin, covered in more freckles than I'd even guessed at. "More ridiculous rules?"

She yawns and the sound sends a shower of sparks down my spine, and I've got no idea why that would happen. There's nothing sexy about a yawn. Except with Rae... there kind of is.

"Hey, I'm not the one who makes the rules." She walks over to the boiling kettle, grabs a teapot, and fills it. "I just enforce them."

"Tell me about tonight."

"You mean the Paint and Sip Orgasmathon."

I grin. "Yes. I want details."

"Give me a sec, and I'll tell you all about it." She disappears again into the bathroom.

I shut my heavy eyes for just a few seconds and settle deeper into the very comfortable armchair, hands sinking into soft, warm fur. I smile at how cute Rae is. Laugh at how she manages to twirl between her bed and her kitchen in such a small space. Feels so good here. With her...

Something wakes me up with a start.

Oh shit. My neck hurts. What the hell?

Groggy, I look around, taking in unfamiliar shapes.

A pair of tiny bright slits reflects the dim light coming in from the only window in the place.

Cat.

Chair.

Smells like chocolate and spice and... Rae.

Slowly, quietly, I push myself up to standing, stiff in all the worst places.

Over on the bed, there's a shape that has to be Rae. The cat is somewhere around her head region. I shove back the urge to go over and make sure he's not cutting off her air supply. He lives here, for fuck's sake. She'd push him if she had to.

As quietly as I can, I check my pocket for keys and sidle over to the door.

It's got a handle lock, which is good, since I can shut it on my way out, but really not okay for a woman living alone in a glorified shed.

Every cell in my body wants to stay. To slide into the bed beside her. Or just sit here until the sun's fully up, guarding her while she sleeps.

Which is exactly why I have to go.

I cannot for one second explain, however, why I stop at a gas station on the way home and buy cat food for the Devil Cat that's been shitting in my shoes.

Except that Rae made me do it.

CHAPTER FIFTY-TWO

Rae

I'm floating as I walk up the street to work on Monday. And it's not just from my Friday-night paint-gasms or the way Grant made me feel when he held my hand, when he took my sisters home and then walked me to my house, and Pepe liked him, and...

Ugh. Okay, it's mostly that, but there's other stuff too. The book nook I'm working on is flying. I posted a short process video, hashtagged the kink community, and got more engagement than I ever have—like close to viral views, actually, which is amazing. BookTok, apparently, really likes cozy/kinky mash-ups.

Another relief was when Dad FaceTimed my sisters and me last night and explained that the reason he's so busy is that he just got cast as Herr Schultz in a local community theater production of *Cabaret*. Surprise!

I couldn't believe it. Dad, acting again, after all these years? He hasn't sung in a musical since he and Mom used to do community theater together. Hannah and I would go to rehearsals with them, and they'd joke about being the von Trapp family, except I could never sing. Or act. Which was what led me to stage management and from there, well, to human resources. Not that I studied it or anything; turns out stage managers are good at everything.

Anyway, we get now why he's had an elevated heart rate and why costars are coming by to run lines and all of that stuff. Car mystery solved. I'm happy for him, and yes, it's a bittersweet happiness because Mom should be up there onstage with him. But that sadness is always there. It's just a part of my makeup since she died.

I pull into a rare free spot in the alley behind the building and allow myself ten seconds to think about Grant. It makes me giddy every time. Because Friday night, things felt different. More intimate. Which is possibly the very reason he took off from my place when he did.

So, yeah, I feel giddy and a little nervous. Aside from one check-in text and an offer to help me get my car, I haven't heard from him since he passed out on my sofa.

I'm halfway up the exterior stairs, grinning like a fool, when the door to Sugar opens. Sam comes out. She stomps down the first few metallic steps, her arms full of things, and jolts to a stop when she sees me.

"Hey, stranger!" I call out. "Where've you been all weekend? I keep calling you and texting and you're..." I catch sight of her puffy red eyes and her wet cheeks. "Are you crying?"

Her only response is a sniffle and a headshake.

It's obviously a lie. "What is it? Who do I kill?"

"Nothing. No one."

I turn around as she brushes past me. "Hey! Seriously, stop. This isn't nothing. You never cry. What's going on?"

"Why don't you ask your *boyfriend*?" she throws over her shoulder.

"My what?"

"I've been fired, Rae. That's what, okay? Ask the gherkin."

"Fired?" I follow her down the steps. "What happened?"

I start to chase her down the alley, and she turns, one palm flat out toward me. "Stop. Truly. Just...give me space right now. I mean it."

"I—"

"This is not a joke. I for real need a minute."

"I can wait here if you want me to—"

"Ugh. More than a literal minute, Rae. For god's sake. I need space. To figure things out."

"Figure what out?" A buzzing starts up in my head, and I feel suddenly sick. "What's going on? Seriously. Are you serious?" She's stomping off, and I might throw up. "Please, Sam. Let me—"

"No. No, whatever you're about to offer, it's no." She throws up a hand. "I'm leaving. Don't follow me. Please." I stand there, blinking in shock. Just before she disappears around the corner, Sam turns back and yells, "You know what you can do? Tell that dickhead to go and screw himself!"

The second she's out of sight, I grip my bag and go. Up the steps, through the door, and into my office. It's empty, but Grant's jacket's here. I race down the hall. No sign of him in the conference room or the kitchen. Dorothy's door's closed. I'm so mad that I knock just once and then barge inside before coming to a stop.

There's Grant, sitting across from Dorothy. He's holding her hand, and that really pisses me off. Like how can he find room in his tiny heart to be nice to Dorothy after destroying Sammy's life?

I stomp up to him, my chest heaving. "What did you do?"

CHAPTER FIFTY-THREE

Grant

"Ask your friend," I say.

"I did." Rae deflates. "She won't tell me." Immediately, she reinflates, staring daggers at me. "I get it, you know? Sam's been distracted lately, but is there no grace? She's good at her job." She appeals to Dorothy. "Come on. Tell him! Remember the slow dating campaign? And the whole silent dating thing? The Bring Your Mom to Date Night meme? That was legendary, Dorothy. Why'd you let this guy fire her? We got industry recognition for those campaigns. They put Sugar on the map."

"Yes, dear, but..." Dorothy throws a pleading look my way. "It's complicated."

"Obviously. Since I am head of human resources for this company, and someone was let go behind my back."

Rae turns to glare at me, and gone is the woman I drove home on Friday. This one is on fire.

"You did this. I know it. You know how I know? Because Dorothy cares about people."

No shit. And look where it's gotten her.

"Did you know, Grant, that Sam is a morale booster? She's funny and kind and would never—ever—do anything to hurt this company." Rae's stare is as close to X-ray vision as I've felt. "Who else, Grant? Huh? Who else are you planning to get rid of?"

I get up to close the door and offer Rae my seat with a sweep of my hand.

She rolls her eyes at me. "I'll stand, thanks." Her cheeks blazing bright red, she swings back to look at Dorothy. "Just how many heads are going to roll? At least tell me that. Is my job on the line here too?" She points at me, without looking. "Because of him?"

Dorothy's shoulders sag. "There was a leak, Rae."

"What?"

"A breach. And Grant's here to fix it."

Rae shakes her head like she's looking for clarity. "Are you even an executive consultant?"

"No. It's a cover," I say, guilt swamping me like it's never once done before. And I've been doing this job for over a decade. "I use it to—"

"Sam accessed data from her computer," Dorothy says.

"What?"

"She's been taking the computer home, Rae." Dorothy's face shows nothing but regret.

"Oh, crap," Rae says.

"Grant planted fake data, linked to everyone's log-in, and...it was accessed this weekend."

"This weekend..." Rae looks at me, all the luster gone from her eyes. "Seriously. Sam wouldn't do something like that."

"It came from her computer, hon. Her log-in." Dorothy's expression is pure compassion. "She admits that she took it home when we've expressly told everyone not to."

"The data was released," I tell her.

"On the internet?"

"On the dark web."

"He's lying," Rae says to Dorothy, who's already shaking her head.

"I'm afraid not. What Grant's done has saved the company, Rae." Dorothy stands and walks over to take her hand. "Remember my son-in-law? Well, Dane's using what he considers poor security protocols as the perfect excuse for a power grab."

"But the company's yours."

"My daughter is also a shareholder. And there are investors. Dane's been working on Rachel to hand him the reins. Then he finds a data breach..."

"It's why I'm here. The supposed breach. The first one. He claimed he found it on the dark web, said you had security issues, and it was time for Dorothy to step down."

"He's been saying I'm inept for the past couple of years now. But with this breach, I asked Grant to come in and help."

"And I requested that the staff come into the office," I add. "And that Dorothy tell no one about my actual role."

"Grant is here to keep Dane from taking over my company and..." She looks at me, obviously thinking about Dane's latest announcement. "Outsourcing every single job overseas."

"What?"

"He'd fire you all."

"He can't do that!" Rae turns to me.

"He could. But I have yet to find a single security issue. The protocols are solid. Your team was irreproachable." I exchange a look with Dorothy. "I don't believe there was an actual breach. Until now."

"Sam wouldn't leak anything. She wouldn't know how."

"She wouldn't have to."

"What?"

"She's been taking her laptop out of the office."

"We've all done it."

"Not right now, you don't. Not without authorization. I've drummed it into you."

"She's had personal stuff come up. Maybe she missed security meetings or didn't read emails."

"Accessing the network without the VPN."

"Oh, come on. Everyone makes mistakes." She turns to Dorothy. "Is that all? You cannot possibly fire her over something that everyone's probably done at some point. Did you warn her first?"

Dorothy's sigh is long and heartfelt. "She's been purposely bypassing security, Rae. The firewall, the VPN. There's no way it was an error."

"No." Rae folds her arms over her chest. "I don't believe you. That's ridiculous."

"We have proof."

CHAPTER FIFTY-FOUR

Rae

I HATE HOW THICK my voice sounds when I say, "Show me."

I watch in numb silence as Grant turns his laptop around so I can see it and hits Play. On-screen, Sam enters the Sugar offices, clearly at night. She grabs her laptop and takes off again.

"That's it?"

"There's more." He clicks over to another screen, showing what I can only assume are log-in times and IP addresses, followed by a series of names. He scrolls through data, explaining access times and locations and how the customer data dump was offered up for sale just last night.

"It's been monitored. The alarm sounded the minute the post went up."

"Could it be...spoofing or something? Is that what it's called?"

He shakes his head, and I want to kick him. Or punch or make him react in some way bigger than this. More than this. Doesn't he see that he is wrong?

"There is other foolproof evidence that I'd prefer not to go into right now."

"You sure like your secrets, don't you?"

For the first time, Grant looks away.

"What did Sam say?"

"Claims it wasn't her. She took the laptop because her home computer was broken." They exchange a look. "She needed it for...gaming."

"Gaming!" I almost scream. "What? She doesn't game. This is ridiculous. She said that?"

They both nod, and I'm struggling to figure it all out, and nothing makes sense to me at all. I look at both of them. "Frankly, I would have appreciated a heads-up."

"Oh, honey, I didn't want you to have to choose sides."

"I appreciate that, Dorothy. I do." A deep breath in. A slow eight count out, and then I turn to my boss. "But I am an adult. I'm a professional."

I do not glance for one second at Grant, lest he see any hint that I'm thinking of what the two of us have done over the past couple of weeks. Because you know what? We were totally unprofessional, and it won't happen again. Then I do look at him, and I say, "In fact, I should come clean and tell you, Dorothy, that there are things I've...done in the past." I swallow, hating my white Irish skin for the blush I know I'm currently sporting. "I should probably let you know that Grant and I, um, we..."

"Have a previous relationship," he finishes, giving me that stern look with its annoyingly sympathetic undertones. The look that says, *I'll smack your ass raw, and then lick your pussy and make you come, and then put you in a bath, and then—*

"Oh, I know all about it," Dorothy says with a casual wave of her hand. "You two." She is smirking like we're two kids who got caught shoving Halloween candy in our mouths after bedtime, and not two consenting adults engaging in highly inappropriate workplace behavior.

"Us two?"

"Do what you want." She snort-laughs. "I trust you both. Implicitly."

I must look panicked when I meet Grant's gaze because he shakes his head, somehow conveying that she's not aware of details. I hope.

"What next?" I manage to ask instead. "Are you... involving law enforcement?"

"Oh, no. No, honey."

"If we need to," Grant amends.

"I'd rather not." Dorothy is firm.

"Understood."

"What about you? Are you done here?" I ask Grant, hoping that's the case and also unsure I can survive a single day here without him. *Are you done with me?* is the other, unspoken part of that question, and it's the part that hurts the most. But I have my pride. And most of my heart's still intact. So maybe the question should be the other way around. Am I done with him?

The answer's yes, I guess. I mean, it has to be, right?

He fired my friend. Yes, based on evidence, but it can't be the truth. How can I trust him now? Our entire... thing... came out of a lie.

"Can people know why you're really here?"

"Pretty sure a few already do."

"I didn't know."

"I haven't been tearing apart your code in search of issues, though, have I?"

I stare up at him, and he stares down at me, and, god, hasn't he, though?

"I've asked him to stick around through the investors' meeting. We need to give them the facts."

"The results of the audit."

"Next week?" I ask, needing an end date for this mess.

"Yes." Dorothy nods. "Grant's here until then." She throws him a smile. "Trying to convince him to come to the retreat with us too. Maybe celebrate that our security's in top shape, do some creative team brainstorming before we head in to see the investors."

The retreat. No. No, god. I don't want to go now. But I have to. I planned it, didn't I? What I want is to run home and hide my head in my blankets. Disappear, like I did in subspace, but I want this man nowhere near me when I do.

"Sounds great," I lie, unable to look him in the eye.

I know Grant's never promised me anything, but I feel so betrayed. It's odd, I guess, given that I barely know him, and I've worked for Dorothy for years, but his betrayal feels so much bigger than hers.

How long have you known? I want to ask him. *Did you have any inkling that you planned to fire my best friend when you gave me three orgasms on Friday night?*

"So, what are the next steps?"

"I meet with the investors. Explain the breach. Tell them it was Sam all along. Grant will present his findings on security and explain the beefed-up protocols."

"Will that be enough?"

"It has to be," Grant intones.

CHAPTER FIFTY-FIVE

Grant

IT'S EARLY EVENING BY the time I look up from my laptop and realize I've missed lunch. I'm knee-deep in cleanup. There's the audit report to put together and Samantha's computer files to double-check. I'm also bolstering the systems already in place.

Rae's desk is empty. She spent the afternoon in reception, which is no doubt as much about avoiding me as it is watching the door. It's amazing how much I've been able to get through without having her right there to distract me. It's also gut-wrenching, which makes no sense.

I should be happy to be getting out of here. Job well done. Case closed.

I stand and stretch, walking around my desk to check on Rae. Looks like she's out. Maybe she's gone for the day.

The printer in our office is out of ink, so I head down the hall, noting how quiet everything is for once. Most of the staff are probably at their desks with noise-canceling headphones on. Or gone, actually. They're all gearing up for this retreat thing. And it's after 5:00 p.m.

The supply room door is ajar. I open it the rest of the way and jolt when I see Rae inside.

She jumps about a foot in the air and drops a ream of paper.

"You okay?" I bend to pick it up and hand it to her.

She starts to nod, and then it turns into a headshake, and then—ah, hell—she's crying. "Rae?"

Her tears are silent, her body tense, the paper pressed hard to her chest.

"Come here." I grab the ream and set it aside, and after the briefest of struggles, she's in my arms, shaking.

It takes a while for the tears to work themselves out from silent, racking sobs to calm to hiccuping, and, finally, a few long, shaky breaths.

"I'm okay," she says against my chest. "Just let me..."

I tighten the hug. "Stay. Stay."

The way she relaxes in my hold tells me she needs this.

Damn, she feels good.

"I got you," I whisper. "Stay right here."

"I hate crying. Sucks."

I let out a quiet huff of laughter. "I know. I know. What do you need?"

I cradle her warmth to mine, set my cheek on her head, and listen.

"What I need? For Sam to answer my calls. And, and you know, for the company I work for not to be in trouble." A shaky exhale. "And my dad is doing a play, which is good, right? No big deal. But he's got this...condition. His h-h-heart."

Dammit. I slow my breathing, soak up her shaking.

"He's not supposed to get his heart rate up, but the app keeps beeping, and he's acting like it's fine, but what if he's actually getting sicker and just hiding it? Because the thing is, we lost Mom, and I can't...I can't...I can't do it again, Grant. I can't lose him too. And did you know it's September sixteenth?"

"It is. Yeah. It is."

"Mom died twenty years ago *today*..." The last word's basically a hiccup. "And I missed the date because of you!"

"Because of me?"

"You, distracting me with your dark eyes and big hands and the way you say my name." The accusation warms me. "And Dad's busy acting, so he doesn't care, and Otty's working, drinking all the time, Hannah's barely making it through with her shitty husband, the kids don't have their father, and because of you, I forgot to buy Mom flowers."

"Oh, baby. Rae. Sweetheart." I touch my lips to her hair, her temple. "Come here. Come here." She tilts her head up, and I lean down to meet her.

Her mouth is warm against mine. So soft. So damned sweet.

She pulls away, sniffling, runs her hand across her nose, and says, "I can't keep them all safe if they're running around like that, can I?"

"They're okay, sweetie. They're safe." I kiss her again and press my forehead to hers.

She clenches my arm and yanks at my shirt. The stroke of her hot fingers on my skin makes my muscles jump. My arms tighten. It's a struggle, and I'm losing. I'm trying to calm her, but she'll have none of it. I haul her up and push her back against the shelves, thinking I'll tamp down all this wildness, give her another kiss, and help her figure it out. But then she's got her leg up around my waist, and what started as comfort is a frantic grabbing of hands.

Our breathing is wild, our movements chaotic. She's undone my pants, and I've got her skirt up and—"No panties," I breathe. But also, "Fuck, you're not wet enough."

"I'm fine, Grant." She tears at my fly, yanking it down. "Just do it."

Next thing I know, my cock's pulsing in her hand. I can't think. Can't function with how hungry she is. How hot.

"You want this?" I ask, against her mouth.

"I need it," she says. "Just this. Just this."

Gathering the very last bits of my wits, I grab the supply room door and drag it shut.

It's completely dark. Even with my eyes wide open, there is nothing but the weight of her curves in my arms, the clasp of her hand on my erection. I tilt my hips forward, give her a taste of what she wants.

"Oh, please. *Please, sir.*"

My breathing. The slick, intimate sound of my aching cock swiping up and down against her warmth. I scramble for a thread of control. "Keep quiet, Sunny, or we'll have to stop."

"Okay. Yes, that's it. Sir."

"Spit in your hand," I order, my chest full of things I'm not used to feeling. "Get me good and wet."

"Oh god. It's big."

"You know it fits, Sunny. Now do it. Don't keep me waiting."

"I...I don't..." An awkward huff as she tries to slide me in. "Doesn't fit."

For a handful of seconds, there's nothing but shaky inhale-exhales and the careful press of my cock to her entrance.

"Careful," I whisper. "Don't force it. Slow."

"Don't want slow."

"You need slow, sweetheart." I release a long, anguished *oooh* into the air when just the tip eases in. Clench my eyes, grit my teeth. "Fuck, Rae."

She's whimpering, high and quiet, little panting gasps that set my entire fucking world on fire. "That's it. Let me in."

"Y-y-y-es. Yes, god. Please." An almost silent whine that sounds as much like pain as pleasure and then, "Please, sir, please fuck me."

"Shhh. You'll take what I give you. Just hold still." Patiently, one fraction of an inch at a time, I pull back and press inside. Back, in. The sounds are absolutely pornographic. I hope to god everyone's left for the day.

"Please."

"You'll get the whole thing when you're ready."

"I'm ready."

I wrap a loose hand around her neck. "In my own good time, you little brat. Fuck," I grit out, "you're so goddamn tight."

"Oh god."

"Shhhh." I put my mouth to hers to stem her throaty hums and sink in an inch, another.

I hardly notice the way she's pressed up against the shelves, her ass in one hand, my other hand collaring her like the good little sub she is. My cock thick inside her.

"Fuck."

"Grant?"

"Don't talk. Don't…move, Rae. You move, and I'm done."

"Oh. I…Okay."

I tip my hips back, sliding out almost to the tip and thrusting back inside, bottoming out so hard we both let out deep, guttural groans.

Too loud.

All her weight gets shifted to one side as I put my hand to her mouth and give her another deep pump. Another.

After no more than a dozen thrusts, I feel the pressure build up in my balls and the clench of her hot pussy, and she's gasping into my mouth, "I'm coming. Oh god, I'm coming."

It's more than I can take, the frantic gasps, the way her body squeezes mine. I bury myself deep and let go.

CHAPTER FIFTY-SIX

Rae

My entire body tenses up in the first seconds of orgasm. Clamped so tight I couldn't move if I had to.

This feeling...it's not just sex. It's warm and right. Like a hug. But fucking. I'm also angry, though for just this moment, I can't remember why.

A second after I go, he pushes deep and pulses inside me.

It's remarkably quiet, I realize after floating in my brain for a while. Quiet and safe.

Probably reeks like sex in here, which isn't something that I'd mind except we are...Oh god. At work. Again.

I pat Grant's head. After a second, he lifts his face from where it's been buried in my neck. Still breathing hard. Still quiet.

"Uh...Thanks," I say, awkward and weird and also, like, rocked from another Grant Bowman orgasm.

"Huh?"

"Could you...?"

"Yeah." He tightens his grip on my ass for a handful of seconds before slowly releasing me to the floor. "You okay?"

I nod, adjusting to the feel of solid earth beneath my feet.

Oh god. What did we just do?

"I should go," I say, shimmying my skirt back into place.

He doesn't reply, but I imagine his brows lowering.

"No glowering," I say.

"You can't see me."

"I can hear it."

He snorts. "Those rules are gone, remember?"

"I'm reconsidering that." A weak smile cuts through the tears clogging my throat. He bends and takes my lips in a kiss that's deep and wet and so intimate there's no way I can pretend we didn't just do this. Any of it. All of it.

"You go first," he finally says, giving me one last kiss for good measure. "I'll take my time."

With a nod, I straighten my clothes, open the door, and, once I confirm the coast is clear, head back to the front desk like nothing's happened.

On the outside, at least. Inside, I have no idea what's going on. I'm a mess. A mixed-up ball of confusion.

I'm ashamed of what I've just done, and guilty that I did it with the man who fired Sam.

Worse than that, though, is the part of me that wants him again. And not just until he leaves Sugar, but forever.

Yeah, that part's bad news.

CHAPTER FIFTY-SEVEN

Rae

After trying Sam, yet again to no avail, I walk into work on Tuesday to hear Dorothy's boss voice coming from our office. "You're coming."

"That's ridiculous," Grant replies. Sounding all stern and Grant-y.

I repress a shiver that's trying to work its way up my spine because the one thing I decided, last night when I ignored his messages, is that I'd nip this whole thing between us in the bud.

"I need you there. In case..."

"In case what?"

"Of a confrontation."

He sighs. "Yeah. You need me to be the bad guy."

"I'm sorry. You're also part of the team now, right?"

He scoffs. "Not permanently, Dorothy. This is just until the investors convene."

Dorothy dips into the very rare, very scary mom voice. "You are coming to the retreat, Grant Bowman. And that's final." She bursts out of the office, sees me, and waves stiffly over her shoulder as she carries on walking.

"Hi." I stick my head in.

"Hello, Rae." He gets up and follows me into the reception area. "You okay?"

"Just great."

"No replies last night. What's that mean?" He watches me for a second. When I don't answer, he runs a frustrated hand through his hair, looks around, and says, "Tell me about this retreat."

"It's fun." Usually. No guarantees this year.

"I was afraid of that."

"Maybe not *your* sort of fun."

He looks me over, clearly reading all kinds of things into my comment, and I can't even deny that I meant them, because I did. Even when I try to ignore the man, he's all I think about.

"What is my sort of fun, Rae?"

"Oh, you know. Tightly controlled. Sedate." His brows go up. "Lots of rules."

"Always."

"Anyway." I open my computer and click on the email icon. "The retreat is nothing like that. You'll hate it."

He groans, turning around like he's going to head back into the office, though he's slow to move.

I ignore his retreating back and concentrate on the many messages from staff asking questions they already have the answer to. I'll need to start hiring for Sam's position.

I'm just creating a folder when Phil pops around the corner and smiles at me. "Quick question."

"All ears."

"First off, are you free evenings next week?"

"Sure—"

Grant pops out from our office, eyes narrowed, mouth open, and I rush to add, "—ly you jest?"

"What? No. You'll love this. So, you know in the Glen Allen

office, how we turned the break room into a haunted house, and had everyone—"

"No," I interrupt, my eyes on Grant, who isn't even pretending not to listen.

"Wait, I didn't even—"

"Is this about benefits?"

"No."

"Hiring?"

"No."

"Professional training? A problem with a colleague?"

"No, bu—"

"This doesn't sound like an HR problem."

"It's not. It's a—"

"No, then, Phil. The answer is no. Whatever it is, it's a no."

"But you made it all so perfect last time."

I nod, a little bit hating the wash of pride I get from those words, but the truth is that the haunted house was, in fact, perfect. I spent a ton of time on it. I recruited staff to help and used up every second of my day outside of work to get it done. For like, three weeks. Truly, the scream room was pro level. And the sensory boxes? Amazing.

But that's not the point. The point is that it's not my job. Grant was right. I can't run around doing all this extra stuff. I am so tired right now. And still, I have to fight the urge to give in.

"I am not a party planner. I am not a chef, or a cleaner, organizer, office manager…" I stand at Sam's desk and let my voice carry a little farther. "I'm not the receptionist or the marketing manager. I'm not in charge of office supplies or events, and above all…" Every deep breath I suck in brings me more than just oxygen. This is justified. This is the truth. *I am right*, my brain is telling me, and, right there to back it up, Grant watches from the door to our office, his eyes bright with approval.

So when the last words come out, I don't have to scream them or even look at Phil. I just open my mouth, meet Grant's eyes with all the ferocity I feel, and say, "And I am absolutely no one's work mom." I give Phil a quick, close-lipped, no-nonsense smile. "Is that it?"

"Y-yes."

"Good." I'm all benevolence now. Placid, kind. "Thanks for stopping by. I'm here should you need any help with subjects pertaining to human resources."

I look back at my computer; Grant's attention is still on me, a warm, wholesome glow.

It feels way too good.

That evening, the entire staff rushes out to get ready for tomorrow's retreat. I finish up preparations at the front desk and ignore the impulse to rush out too. I've packed my bag, along with everything I could possibly need over the next few days. Ironically, given everything that's happened recently, I am more relaxed about this year's retreat than I've ever been.

I've just turned off my computer when the exterior door buzzes open, and Grant, who I thought had left for the night, walks in. He's got a big, beautiful bouquet in his arms. It's green and soft pink and puffs out like a cloud.

"Rae."

I say nothing.

"These are, um..." Why is he embarrassed right now? What is happening? "They're for your mom. For her..." He huffs out a frustrated sound. "You said you forgot, and it was my fault and..."

"They're ranunculus flowers," I say as he presses them into my arms.

"You had them on your pj's."

"You remembered."

"Yeah."

I nod. Swallow. Stare at the bouquet, which is somehow light and sweet with all that pink, but there are also warm, earthy greens. It's the perfect bouquet. I don't know how else to say it.

"Mom would have loved these," I whisper, meeting his gaze from my hiding place behind the flowers. "Thank you."

He nods, looking more awkward than I've ever seen him. "I could, uh, drive you? To her...you know."

"That's okay. I...We don't put them on her grave. We put them in water, usually. And...you know. Look at them. To think of her."

"Ah. That seems nicer."

"Yeah."

Another nod.

"Anyway. See you tomorrow."

"See you tomorrow," I reply, hoping he'll leave soon so I can cry all on my own.

CHAPTER FIFTY-EIGHT

Rae

Grant, who has literally been forced into coming to the retreat, looks unhappier than I've ever seen him. Comically unhappy, actually.

First was the ride here. Ninety minutes in a converted school bus. I miss Sam so much. She should be here, dammit, screaming out "Kumbaya" with the rest of the crew. Not Grant scowling in the back like he'd rather be getting a tooth pulled.

Grant. Ugh. I am...conflicted.

It was obvious from the glimpses I got from my front-row seat that he hated every second of the trip, from the X-rated but alcohol-free game of truth or dare being played in the back of the bus, to sitting next to Doreen, who probably told endless stories about her married gay son—a point of pride—and his three children, for whom she is constantly knitting things.

We've been here for less than half a day of bonding activities, and Grant looks like he's seriously considering murder. I'd laugh if I didn't feel so raw about everything.

I tried calling Sam about eighty times yesterday. Finally, this morning, I woke up to a text telling me she loved me, and she's fine, but she needs some alone time. Alone time? Sam?

I want to cry.

Then there are the death glares the others are giving Grant. They hate him, and I feel kind of... bad about it? I mean, he's only done his job. Could he have done it without making some enemies along the way? At this point, I honestly don't think so. I want to cry about that too, a sentiment I have no desire to explore further.

At least it's pretty here. The lodge is essentially a castle surrounded by cabins on a mountain west of Charlottesville, close to the national park. Outside is a forest and a small lake, and inside, there are literal suits of armor and fireplaces you could roast a wild boar in.

I love it. The very best part is that I don't have to lift a finger now that we've arrived. The venue's event planner organizes almost every second of the time we're here.

It's after dinner, and we're all sitting around in this gigantic ballroom. I feel Grant's eyes on me, but every time I look up, he's talking to someone or watching someone else.

Maybe it's just wishful thinking. Because, yeah, despite everything, I still like him. I really, really like him. I like how serious he gets and how warm he can be. I like the low, fierce, constant burn of his presence. His confidence. The steady way he watches me, the solidity of him. He's a good man. And apparently, good does things to me.

He's also competent and solid with an underlying layer that warns, *Watch out. Anything can happen here.*

So yeah. I might be a little too into him for my taste. Or probably for his.

Yet again, I'm staring, and yet again, he looks up, and I tear myself away, only to meet Dorothy's openly curious gaze. When she winks, I roll my eyes, groaning inside.

"Hot potato!" squeals the organizer, Trish. She's very enthusiastic. In a good way, mostly.

We circle up, and I turn to see Grant beside me. We share a quick smile, and my insides melt.

The game's fast and hilarious, and at least two people fall. Grant passes the ball to me, and I catch it and feel his hand on my hip. I just barely manage to pass it along to Doreen, and through all the commotion, somehow Grant's hand gets forgotten, and it stays right where it was, on my hip.

A second. A few more. I don't look at him right away, but when I finally glance up, he's watching me with this intensity that turns everything inside me liquid. I've got no idea how long we stand there, his hand on me, my eyes eating him up.

It takes Trish screaming "Talent show!" to snap us out of it, and when that happens, I look around and wonder how long we've been lost in our little bubble because hot potato's apparently done, and everyone's clearing out.

I'm in a dream as I follow the sound of Trish's voice. Like the others, I've already been so programmed to follow her orders that I immediately move. "Now, every single one of you is scheduled. So let's not get behind, shall we?"

First up, Klaus lumbers onto the tiny stage and blows us all away with a very brisk soft-shoe performance.

"Next! Remember, everybody goes! Nobody skips it. I've got you all on my list, and I know your talents, people." Yeah, Trish is frightening.

It's a long night, featuring such amazing talents as Dorothy's bizarre crying baby imitation and one of the younger guys spinning a pen over his knuckles for a solid minute. By the time my name is called, I'm ready to present the very rare talent that Trish convinced me is worth sharing.

I sit on the edge of the stage and apply lipstick with my toes to a loud round of applause. I can be a bit of a show-off like that.

Grant, of course, goes last, and I have no idea what to expect. What's obvious is that he's not thrilled to have to step up onstage.

Trish hands him a microphone, and someone plucks a few chords on the piano, and then—holy shit—Grant opens his mouth and sings the first line of "My Way," like the gruff, stern Sinatra the world didn't know it needed.

I am floored. We all are. For the first time all night, every single person here is utterly silent, and a lot of those who've spent all day glaring at him suddenly soften. Such is the power of a good song. I know this in the depths of my soul. I know it when I think about Mom and the way she'd sing me to sleep before my sisters were born. When I remember Dad singing us all out of some of the deepest, darkest moments of our lives.

This man is a triple threat. And I don't mean in the usual theater way of act, sing, and dance. That would be my dad. No, the problem here is that Grant is kinky, smart, and he can sing. My father would love him. Okay, not the kink part, per se, but the musical part? There is literally nothing my family loves more than karaoke. Their one biggest disappointment is that I am tone deaf and can't sing my way out of a paper bag.

This man, however, with his low, rich voice, could sing the pants off... well, anyone here, judging from the expressions on most of their faces.

My skin breaks out in goose bumps as he croons about approaching the final curtain, and then—good lord what witchcraft is this?—he ups the tempo and intensity, and something happens in my chest and my throat, and I am so close to crying again that I have to get up and leave before I do it in front of everyone.

I hear the thunderous applause through the hallway wall, and all I can think is, *No. Please, no.*

But it's too late. Obviously. I wouldn't be hiding here behind a suit of armor, crying into my hands, if I didn't feel this way about the man.

And when I say *this way*, I'm pretty sure it's more than like. Or lust. Or kinky curiosity. Yep. I've finished falling, and I am solidly in love with a man who's got no interest in the long term.

So basically, I'm screwed.

CHAPTER FIFTY-NINE

Grant

I KNOCK ON THE door to Rae's cabin, listen to a scuffling from inside, and then knock again.

She opens it a crack. "Hey. What's up?"

"You alone?"

"Yeah. My roommate got fired."

"Got a second?"

"Oh, um... I was going to sleep."

"Ah..." I lift blankets and a bottle I pilfered from the open bar. "I was hoping you'd come out. With me."

"Where?" She sniffles.

"Are you sick?"

"No. No, I'm fine."

Unconvinced, I watch her for a few seconds. "You see the lake out there?"

"Yeah."

"Thought we could take a boat out."

"Now? It's like midnight."

"Exactly."

Her smile is slow to come, but once it's there, it lights up her entire being.

Hell, it lights me up too. You could power something big with Rae's smile.

"Give me a sec," she says, going back inside and reappearing a moment later with her coat, hat, and scarf.

We head along the well-marked paths for a bit and then strike out through a dark, forested area that smells like pine needles. I take her hand. Just to help her navigate the dark, obviously.

At the lake, she settles into a canoe. I take off my shoes and socks and roll up my jeans, walk into the water to pull the thing out, and sputter as I get in.

"You okay?"

"Can't feel my feet."

As I struggle to dry my feet with the blanket, Rae picks up the oars and rows us in circles, giggling madly.

Finally, she hands them to me and slides forward to warm my toes with her soft little hands.

A couple of long strokes and we're away from shore. The cabin lights grow smaller and smaller. A few more strokes, and the night forest noises go faint, the smell of lake water overtaking pines and wet dirt and dead leaves.

I'm sitting in the back of the boat, and she's facing me on the wooden bottom, my feet in her lap, one blanket covering us both and another around her shoulders.

At about the middle of the water, I set the oars down and just sit. Breathe.

The air is still and cool. "Smells like Vermont," I say, out of the blue.

"Is that where you're from?"

"No."

She doesn't reply, and I don't plan to add more, but then I do. "I was born in New Jersey. Summit."

"I've never been there."

"I don't remember it. I then moved to Pennsylvania and then back to New Jersey. Boston. For a while. Then Vermont." My favorite. Calm. Simple. "My mom's a dentist. Well, she was. She's retired now."

"She picked up and moved you that much?"

"Yep." I don't bother adding the obvious: that each and every move corresponded to a new husband. "What about you? Always Richmond?"

"Midlothian."

"Ah."

"Don't look like that."

"Like what?"

"Like you've cataloged me into a Midlothian-shaped life."

"Okay. So, how was it?"

"Well, you know Midlothian's kinda fancy. Safe neighborhood. Good schools. Great place to grow up. All the euphemisms."

"Right." I envision massive brick houses, huge yards, and tasteful landscaping. Nice, if that's your thing.

"Yeah, well, ours was the eyesore. A little seventies split-level. The family car was a decade old. And, yes, I said car. Singular."

"Ah."

"All around us, it was executive dads, and moms who stayed home during the important years. But my family? Artsy was the nicest description of us I heard. My parents were both elementary teachers, so that should give you an idea of the income divide. Anyway, when I went to college—a state school—it was like I had finally found my people. Artsy and poor." The way she says this, it is clearly more compliment than insult. "I got a scholarship, lived in student housing, and rode my bike all over the place. Sam and I went to VCU together."

"To study theater?"

"I was a theater major. She did art."

"Wow. VCUarts has a great reputation."

She considers me for a moment. "And she's a great artist. She just..."

"I'm sorry, Rae."

She nods. "I know."

I grab her hand and hold it tight. "I mean that. I didn't... When I realized it was Sam, I... Fuck. I really didn't want to hurt you."

"I realize that." A long, deep sigh. "I love her as much as I love my sisters, you know? She just... I just... I lost my mom, and still I had the best family I've ever known. Sam really, really wasn't lucky."

"Well, she had you."

"Yeah. Yeah, she still does." After a long silence, she sniffs. "Someone's having a campfire."

"Smells good."

We slip into silence.

After a few minutes, I search for something else to say that won't hurt and land back on our previous conversation. "Where'd you live when you went to school?"

"Little place near Monument. I loved it. My favorite part of Richmond was the Fan. Still is. There's this one street I used to ride down all the time."

I root around in the blankets and pull out the bottle of Virginia bourbon I pilfered from the party. "Yeah? Where?"

"Grace Street."

"No way."

"What? Why?"

"That's where I live." For now.

"You're joking."

I hand her the bottle. She sniffs, takes a tiny sip, and passes it back to me. In the light from the moon, I can just barely make out her grimace.

"Nope." I take a long swig, enjoying the bourbon's smooth descent. Nothing goes better with this woodsmoke smell than whiskey. I listen to the very faint song of the season's last crickets. "My place was abandoned when I bought it. At auction. They almost took it down."

"You fixed it up?"

I nod.

"I always had this fantasy of living in one of those houses. Picking paint colors and finishes and making it mine." I can hear the smile in her voice. "Like my very own Barbie Dreamhouse."

"So, bright pink?"

"No. Although maybe a couple of interior rooms in a classy, demure pink. It was just a daydream. Like one day, I'd save up and make enough to buy a row house with my ex." The puffed-out sound she makes isn't exactly a laugh, but it's not entirely sad either. Somewhere in the center of bittersweet. "Never mind."

"What happened?"

"I thought my ex and I had more in common than we did."

"That why it ended?"

"I just don't think we loved each other all that much. I broke it off when it occurred to me that, like, in a fire, I wasn't sure if he'd come back to grab me or his PlayStation."

What the hell? "Are you serious?" The desire to hunt this guy down immediately and beat the crap out of him is sudden and shocking.

At her nod, I tamp down the unexpected flash of violence. "I'm sorry, Rae." I reach out and push a curl behind her ear.

"It's all right. I'm much better off without him." She shivers, and I realize how cold it's gotten.

"Here, move up."

She scoots toward me, and I edge forward to the middle of the boat, drawing the blankets tighter around us. I bend into the little cave we've made and breathe. "You smell so good."

She exhales. I inhale. Our breath mingles between us, whiskey and smoke and her toothpaste.

"Were you about to head to bed when I knocked?"

"Yeah." A sigh. "No regrets."

"Hey. Why'd you leave during my song tonight?"

Her breath catches. I wait for a heartbeat, another.

"It made me emotional."

"Sinatra?"

"You, Grant. It wasn't kinky. It wasn't sexy. It wasn't work-related. It was just...you."

I swallow *hard*, no idea what to say.

"I know you're moving on soon. I get it. I mean, given your past and..." Her eyes are shining when they meet mine. I really hate the idea of being responsible for putting the tears there. "I didn't mean to fall in love with you. I didn't mean to." She shrugs those sweet, round shoulders, and I have to fight very hard against the urge to wrap her up in my arms, keep her safe, and give her every last thing she wants. Even if that thing is me. Not just now, but always. Forever.

And then, she looks up at me, the sheen of tears overflowing into two thin tracks bisecting her cheeks, and there's this moment...or realization...or premonition—I don't fucking know. Just this feeling that if I don't take care of this woman the way she deserves...If I don't take on the burden and the...the...

the honor of her tears, her emotion, and all that love; if I don't make them mine, right this minute, then I am not the man I was meant to be. That's the feeling.

I've got no fucking clue how to express it. All I can do is lean in and kiss her.

CHAPTER SIXTY

Rae

His lips are cool, his tongue hot. The kiss is slow, warm syrup.

It's different from before. No power exchange, no flirting. It's a kiss. Just a kiss.

Except not. At. All.

It's a kiss the way the Sistine Chapel is a painting. Yes, it's lips and tongues sliding together, but there's more than technique involved. There's something deeper. Understanding or artistry, or a sensitivity that I've never experienced before. Maybe it's our connection that makes it so much more.

He changes the angle, licks deeper, and I'm slammed with lust. Only it's not the adventurous lust I've experienced with him before. It's not sneaky or taboo or *oh-my-god-get-in-me*.

It hurts. That's the kind of want I'm feeling. Want that's like pain because it's from somewhere deeper than I'm used to, and what we have will be over at some point, and just knowing that feels tragic and wrong.

A little sound escapes me as I shuffle forward to get more. Grant urges me onto his lap, and then the lust takes over, bigger, deeper, more urgent than anything we've done, and I'm scared.

This isn't just Grant the Grump anymore. He's not just a sexy guy I share an office with. A Dom I play with. He's this man. A little wild, a little nostalgic. Good at reading people. He has friends who love him and a heart of gold that he would never, ever admit to.

I'm shivering slightly from the cold, from his kiss. He urges me closer, and we're pressed so tightly together, and this closeness doesn't just feel sexy; it feels necessary.

This. Here. It's what we're meant to do. Aside from what we did in the kitchen at work, I haven't experienced this kind of dry-humping since I was a teenager. And let me tell you, it is underrated. His hands on my ass, guiding me, his erection turning me on, and his mouth making me lose my ever-loving mind. That's how it is when I come.

Out in the wild. With no one around but an owl, hooting from the woods.

I pull back, my pulse flickering at the back of my eyes.

"I love that."

"What?" I pant, like I've just run a marathon.

"When you come. Each one is different. This time, you scrunched your face up, and bit your lip, and made this little noise." His thumb swipes my mouth. I try to catch it, but it's already gone.

"What kind of noise?"

His teeth flash in the moonlight. "You'll just have to pay attention next time."

"How am I supposed to do that?"

"Should I record you?"

"No. Absolutely not. I hate everything about my voice."

"Really?"

"Yes. It's like a foghorn."

He barks out a laugh. "No, it's not. It's sweet. I like it. I...I love it."

The way that word vibrates in the air between us feels like it means more than it does. I'm so raw from what I've admitted tonight that I bat all the feelings back and turn to humor for distraction. "Yeah, well, you should hear me sing."

"Oh, I'd like that."

"Actually, you wouldn't. I guarantee it."

"Bullshit. Come on. Sing."

"Nope."

Grant leans forward and tickles me on the stomach, and I attempt to roll up like an armadillo. He gets through, though, and tickles harder, which makes me laugh like a hyena.

Now he's laughing, and I'm howling, and we're sort of wrestling in the boat, and then, I've got no idea how it happens, but I go from ridiculous, teasing fun in the warmth of the blankets to holy shit, I'm about to fall in.

He catches me just as the boat starts to tip, pulls me into his chest, and uses his weight to counter the move.

"You okay?"

I nod slowly. Tears pop, unbidden, into my eyes. Ugh. I really need to stop all the crying.

"Hey. Hey, what is it? What?" We're on our sides in the bottom of the canoe, and it's cold, but his arm's tight around me. The boat's floating, the water just an occasional splash against the side.

"I haven't done this since I was a kid."

"Kissed in a canoe?"

I gently smack his arm. "Been in a canoe at all."

"Are you, uh, okay?"

I nod. "I'm good. Really good."

"I'm glad." He puts his lips to my forehead and presses a kiss there that I will feel for the rest of my life.

"We should get back," he says.

I snuggle deeper into him, in no way ready to face anything else but this.

"Breakfast at eight."

"And then the daily icebreakers."

"The ice has melted," he growls, which makes me laugh again, and then he tightens his hold and makes this pained sound. "You fucking fell me, Rae."

I have questions, but I wait. He lets go of himself so rarely. I know better than to interrupt what he's about to say.

"What is it with you?"

I don't dare reply. My answer's definitely not what he's looking for.

A shuddery sigh against the top of my head, a kiss, and then the press of his cheek. "I've never wanted...this. All of it. I'm not made for it, you know?"

I nod. Not that I agree, but still.

"When you're around, I get this...this..." He lets me go long enough to thump a palm to the top of his chest and then pulls me back into his arms again. "It's like a...Hell. I can't even explain. Like a pain. That feels kinda good?" He shakes his head and starts to move. "We better get back."

"Wait."

He looks down at me from where he's now sitting.

"I, uh...I feel it too. The..." I awkwardly hug myself. It's the only way I have to show where the feelings reside. "The good-pain thing."

"Yeah?"

I nod. "And I'm not a masochist."

"We'll see about that." After a second, he smiles, helps me up, and shifts over to his seat. "Because you haven't let me paddle you yet."

We dock the canoe and go back to the cabin in silence. At the door, when I think he might kiss me good night, he just pauses and stares and then runs the tip of his finger down my nose to my lips. I kiss that finger. His eyes darken.

"Want to come in for a sec?"

We share another long look. I open the door wide and wait.

"Yeah. Yeah, I do."

CHAPTER SIXTY-ONE

Grant

RAE'S CABIN IS A replica of mine. Small, with lots and lots of plaid.

Suddenly awkward in a way I haven't been since I was a kid, I put the blankets and bottle on the desk and take a stroll around the room, adding a log to the woodstove.

It's rustic. Antlers on one wall. A patchwork quilt on the bed. "They've sure got the country cabin thing down, haven't they?"

Rae's *mm-hm* is muffled. When I turn to see why, she is halfway out of her T-shirt.

I can't help but laugh. I love this. The big blast of want and excitement and live-out-loudness that is Rae Jensen.

"What? What is it?"

I help her out of the shirt, put my arms around her, and pull her in tight. I'm hugging her. That's all this is. Two bodies pressed tight. Even after what she said, it shouldn't feel like so much more. Fuck, am I scared? Is that what this is?

"Why'd you laugh?"

"Because you're so delightful, throwing off your clothes like that."

"Don't embarrass me."

"No, no, no, Rae. Don't be embarrassed. Please. God, you are so..."

"I'm a lot. I know."

"No!" I'm dead serious when I pull away and stare. "You are just the right amount. Of... everything."

"You think?"

"I mean it. You're lovely. You're kind. You're... maybe a little too helpful, we've established." I bend and press a kiss to her collarbone, her bra strap, her shoulder. "And you are perfect."

"I have to be helpful."

"Why?" I let my nose wander down to the valley between her breasts. Kiss her there.

"I'm not..."

I pause in my descent. "Not what?"

"Never mind. Keep doing that."

"I'll keep going if you keep talking."

"Oh, come on," she groans. "Are you serious?"

I breathe against the side of one breast. "Yep." Nudge my nose into her throat and then stroke my cheek against her arm. "Talk. Or no more of this."

With an annoyed huff, Rae goes on. "Fine. So. My point is that I'm not anything special. *And*... before you rush to contradict me. This isn't bad. We can't all be wildly exciting people. My family, I mean... My mom was a star, you know? She sang and danced and charmed the hell out of everyone. And Dad, he's like that too. Sort of the softer version. Hannah's just a powerhouse. I wish..."

As I bend and kiss her soft belly, her voice fades away. "Go on," I say against the skin there.

"Otty is incredibly talented. She'll be the next Taylor Swift. If she ever gets her act together. And she will. I'll make sure of it."

I smile against her warm, fragrant waist, flush with affection for this woman. "You, however, are nothing special."

"Right. And, honestly, I've gotten where I am because… I give people what they need. And if they… Oh, oh, that's nice."

The woman enjoys a tongue in her belly button. Good to know. "Keep talking."

Another irritated sound, and she's off, sounding almost unaware of what's coming out of her mouth while I taste, lick, and bite every part of her I can. "Listen, just, here's the thing. If I don't help and do extra and give people what they need, then who am I?"

"You're Rae. Rae Jensen. You are a star." When she snorts this time, I stand and look down at her. "What?"

"Look, I know I'm not particularly, I don't know, notable. But that's the point, right? You've got the stars of the show, like my mom and dad and my sisters. And you've got the folks backstage. I'm a stage manager. That's my strength. My worth is in what I can do. Supporting others."

"Bullshit." I pick her up and chuck her onto the bed.

"Hey! Don't do that."

"Why not?"

"Because I'm heavy."

"You're just right."

She apparently sees the truth of this and stops talking.

"Take it all off," I order while I do the same with my clothes. "And listen. I've got something to say. You are more than what you can give. So much more that I can't believe you think that." I pull at my sleeve, and a button goes flying. I move on to the other. "Don't you see how much you bring to every room you enter?" I work at my pants and watch, anger warring with fascination, as she struggles out of her jeans and leans forward to work at her bra. "Stop choosing other people, Rae. Choose yourself, for once. You are pure delight. You're not just some person who makes the best cookies in the world or helps people." I rip off my jeans, toe off my socks, and stare down at her, in all her glory. "You know what I see when I look at you?"

Her skin's creased from the bra and jeans, and the freckles I knew I'd find everywhere are scattered as randomly as the stars we stared at a few minutes ago.

Only I didn't pay nearly as much attention to that sky as I'm paying now to her body. Her face. Her beautiful, beautiful being.

Slowly, full of that good pain I described, I crawl onto the bed and over her. "Rae," I grunt, because her skin under mine isn't just soft; it's exquisite. I want to rub myself. To sink in. I want to share all of it, all of her, all of myself. I've never once felt this open to someone else.

I stiffen my arms and look down at her, doing my best to ignore the snug perfection of my erection against her belly, the deep pleasure of just the points of her breasts against my chest. The sheer joy of so much skin pressed flush to mine.

"I see..." I swallow, staring down at eyes that have lost all but a thin circle of blue. "A woman whose love of life, whose enjoyment of the little things, lights up the world around her." I can't bring myself to carry on, to tell her that she is pure, sweet, hedonistic pleasure. That I've never felt so alive as I do while taking care of her.

I bend my head and kiss her. There's too much sensation to take my time. I could do it out in the cold, on the water, but here, with all this heat and touch and solid, undeniable connection, I am lost to her. To this. To us.

The way our mouths work together in harmony is such a turn-on, I get lost in the deep, aching kisses.

I don't know how long we kiss and writhe together. At some point, her legs go wide, and my hips settle, and I push back up, staring at her.

She reaches for me, lines us up, and I'm pressing in. Slow, taking my time because this thing has an end date, and there's this feeling—this absolute certainty—that this is it. The last time this will happen. The one time like this. I don't even know what this is.

Her. Me. Us.

I'm gasping, pressing into her, taking every thrust she gives me back. Staring into those endless wells of... what? What is that emotion in her eyes?

I... I can't...

Oh, wow. This isn't... I don't...

She tightens around me, and I press deep, arms around her, and I'm coming. I'm coming so hard.

And it hurts. In my chest, my throat.

It is the best fucking pain.

CHAPTER SIXTY-TWO

Grant

THERE'S A THUMPING. I ignore it and turn to press a kiss to Rae's warm shoulder. She wiggles and lets out a sleepy/happy sound, and I dive under the blanket to kiss her collarbone, her breasts.

Fuck, these nipples. How did I live without them for all this time?

This is the best I've ever felt. Solid, raw, real. It's that happy pain thing, times a million.

We fucked all night. Three times, at least. I've been inside her fast and furious, a little rough. Oh, hell, then the wild, twisty feel of her going tight around me while I tickled her through an extended orgasm. Laughing, playing. Things I've never done quite like this.

Then I spent at least an hour under the blankets playing with her body, exploring her. Tasting and sucking and breathing her in until I'd memorized every muscle, freckle, and curve.

Even now, after all that, I want more.

It should scare me, but it's like my body's taken over, and the control's flown the coop, and oh, yes, she's wet again, and pliant and smiling and ready.

Sex has never been this easy, this bright. Happy.

Dawn light was seeping through the curtains the last time. She arched into me, and I spooned her tight, nudged her leg up, and slid into her swollen, soft, slippery body. Slow, barely moving.

I don't know what to call what we did there. Or the feeling expanding in my chest, a raw, open thing, pumping quick and hard.

With my knee, I ease her wide again and cover her with kisses first, then crawl up and give her my weight. My whole body.

She mutters something about the door, giggles, and hides her head under the pillow.

Door? Knocking. Shit. Who the hell is that?

After a final nip at her nipple, I stumble out of bed, snag a blanket from the floor, and wrap it around me. Groggy, happy, I open the door and go still.

"There you are," Dorothy huffs, stamping on the porch, her breath puffing in the cold. "Figured if you weren't here, we'd have to drag the lake for your body."

"What is it?" My mind's still back in that bed, and my body wants nothing more than to join it.

"We've got to get back."

My brain shifts, refocuses, and slowly wakes all the way up.

"What happened?"

"He did it. The selfish little bastard got a hold of our data." She grinds her teeth. "The *real* data."

The floor shifts under my feet. I put a hand on the doorframe to steady myself. "Tell me everything."

"I'll tell you on the bus." Over my shoulder, Dorothy yells, "Get up, buttercup. We're heading back to Richmond."

The bus ride back is a hushed, unhappy affair, full of exhausted campers complaining about their retreat getting cut short. When one of them attempts to start up a round of campfire songs, I turn and stare, and within seconds, the happy camper's shushed. There will be no more messing around. They might not be aware of the threat, but all their jobs are at stake.

I'm on my phone the whole way back, trying to get more information. According to his early-morning phone call with Dorothy, Dane claims to have caught another Sugar App data leak on the dark web. He is, quote, "very concerned."

What a prick.

When the bus pulls up in front of our building, I'm the first out.

Dorothy and I head upstairs. I barely notice the others, although I feel Rae on the periphery.

Rae. Dammit. Rae. I'll think about her later. Right now, my mind's a litany of *I should have caught it*s and *This is my fault*s.

My fault, dammit. Never should have left or let myself get distracted or cared about something other than what matters here.

This company. My job. My responsibility.

The fury running like poison through my veins is as much toward myself as it is to the prick sitting in Dorothy's office when we get in, his face a mask of false concern.

"Real sorry to drag you all back from your little vacation. Staff must hate me right now."

"It wasn't a vacation, Dane." Dorothy's jaw looks like it'll crack if she doesn't loosen it. "It was work. Team building is an important part of what puts us head and shoulders above the competition. It's like a think tank."

"Oh! Wow, really? 'Cause... I've been loving these pictures up on Insta." He shoves his phone in our faces, so annoyingly smug.

There's photo upon photo of people having fun. Dorothy with a wineglass, head thrown back in laughter. Klaus collapsed on the floor mid-limbo.

I go hot and then cold when he gets to the last one, my body turning to granite. It's Rae and me, during hot potato. Her head's tilted back as she looks up at me, and she's wearing this smile, so warm and full of affection. My hand's on her hip, like it belongs there. And yes, it was in a public place, with other people, but nothing about the way I'm looking at her says work buddies or just pals or people who just share an office.

Looking at this photo is like staring at a naked picture of the two of us, and though it may be irrational, I want to break the man's face. Just for seeing the photo. For holding it in his hands.

Clearing my throat, I look up at him. "What is your point here?"

"Well"—Dane sets his phone down, eyeing me with sly intent as he stretches in Dorothy's chair—"like I said, you've been hacked. I thankfully caught the leak in time. And...you're fired." He turns to Dorothy and points at me. "He's fired."

"On whose authority?"

"Mine. And the investors'."

Dorothy sucks in a deep breath. "You spoke with my investors about this without me?" The fool might not be able to tell that he's released the kraken, but he is the only one. Dorothy is livid. I've never seen her face this hard. This is a woman not to be messed with.

I glance at Dane and see not one ounce of terror when he says, "Well, of course, Dotty. What d'you think I'd do when I found all that sensitive information on the dark web?" If this man knows how to access, much less utilize the dark web in any meaningful way, I will eat my fucking shorts. "You think I was just gonna throw up my hands and wait for the *professional* to take care of it?" He points his thumb my way.

"Dane. I want you to leave. Right now."

"No."

"If you don't get out in the next thirty seconds, I am calling the police." She points to me. "This is still my company. Also, this *professional* happens to own the building, so, yes, we are fully within our rights to kick you out. Go. Now."

Dane looks from me to Dorothy, half laughing like he can't believe it. "You're not serious."

"As a heart attack. Which, thanks to regular visits to the doctor, I will not be succumbing to anytime soon. Sorry to disappoint." She stands, as unyielding as Margaret Thatcher, and points one rigid arm at the door.

"I'm telling Rachel."

Dorothy blinks. "You're pathetic."

"I know about the leak. I know you've had employees literally stealing from you."

Dorothy's staring him down like he's a snake about to strike.

"I know about everything, Dotty. Everything you've been trying to hide." He's chuckling outright, and it is pretty weird. "I know that this dude's just a buddy. Next-door neighbor. I know that this contract is a way to siphon money over to him. I know that you've been skimming off the business for ages. All-expenses-paid luxury holidays like the one you just had over in the valley." His laugh becomes ugly. "The investors aren't happy about that. Yeah." He throws the door open and turns back. "Enjoy your last few days here, Dorothy. By this time next week, you'll be out on your ass." Dead serious, he says, "Tell your little employees they'd better update their résumés, because I've already found their replacements."

He slams the door *hard*.

"This is my fault," I tell her.

"Of course it's not. He's an evil toad." Dorothy sinks into her chair, looking tired. Her head tilts back as she watches me pace to the door. "Get your ass back here. We've got work to do."

"You mean I've got work to do."

"No, kiddo. We do. You're not alone here. That's what it means to be part of a team. Now, come on. Let's figure this shit out."

I know she means well, but I've never in my life felt less deserving of a person's respect or of being part of a team.

I know exactly how the situation got this out of hand, and it's because of my unprofessionalism. "I screwed up, Dorothy."

"Oh, shut up, Grant. Please shut up and help me figure out how to get rid of that little shithead. Bonus if we can keep his name from ever making it onto the permanent family tree."

CHAPTER SIXTY-THREE

Rae

It's near the end of the day when Grant finally emerges from Dorothy's office. He knocks on the open door of our shared office before sticking his head in. That alone is odd.

The second I see him, I know it's bad. He looks exhausted, like himself but more deeply carved. An exaggerated version of the scowl. I can almost see the extra weight that's settled over his thick shoulders.

"Hi," I say when he doesn't immediately speak. I'm tired too. Neither of us slept much last night. Even with the dread hanging over us, memories warm my belly.

He steps inside and closes the door.

"What can I do to help? You've been in there all day. I just want to pitch in."

"There's nothing you can do. This is my problem to fix."

"No, Grant. This affects all of us. We're a team and—"

"Someone fed him intel, Rae."

"You're sure?"

"Yeah. Maybe Samantha? But it can't be. She didn't have access anymore."

"Can he prove there's a leak?"

"He doesn't have to, Rae," he says a little too loudly, but then lowers his voice as he goes on. "He's brought Dorothy's investors into it, already convinced them that he's the better fit for CEO. She's been on the phone with them all day, and they are not happy."

Worry clenches my teeth and tightens my throat. I feel sick with it. Grant must feel a million times worse. I stand up from my desk and walk to where he's hovering on his side of the room. I reach out to touch this man I spent the night with. Whose hands were gentle and sweet and also rough when I wanted it, whose eyes burned into me with so much affection. He was boyish and warm, and the connection we shared was stronger than anything I've felt before.

Ever.

He backs up a step.

I blink, sitting with incomprehension for a few seconds before the rejection kicks in.

It hits me hard behind my eyes.

I blink back a painful rush of tears.

It hurts. I can't describe it, can barely understand how it could be this bad. Breaking up with Brendan was a scraped knee. This is a gaping wound. This is my insides pouring out.

I get out a pathetic little "Are you...?"

"We need to talk."

Take a breath. "Okay."

"This was a huge mistake."

Exhale. Slow. "This?"

"Us." He sweeps his hand to encompass the office. "All of it."

For another handful of seconds, I can only stare. My hand goes to my cheek like he's slapped it.

I turn and look at my desk, the cupboard. I look at all the

little items I bring in to pep up my life here, and the only desire I can drum up is to swipe it all off my desk. To smash everything. Make it loud. Make it count.

"Rae?"

I look up at him, and there's worry in his gaze, also pain, both quickly replaced by that *nothing* he's so good at wearing.

"Yes, Grant?" I force out, sure of only one thing in this moment: If I let out just one drop of this grief inside me, I won't be able to stem the flow. Keeping it in is the only solution.

"Uh. You okay?"

I smile. "You're an idiot."

It's his turn to blink in surprise. "Excuse me?"

"You're a fool if you think you can stuff it all away and pretend it never happened."

"Stuff what—"

"Oh, please." Oh. Oh, wow. Okay, that's out. This is happening. "You just stop it. Now. Because you're lying, and I'm tired of liars."

"I'm not lying about—"

"You're lying that what we did meant nothing," I tell him.

"I didn't say that."

"You said it was a mistake."

"We shouldn't have let things—"

"It was *not* a mistake." My finger's jabbing the air. "None of it. It was good—no, it was great—and you're lying to yourself if you think—"

"You're a perfect sub, Rae. It's just—"

"Are you kidding me? You are being so unserious right now. I am…I'm…" Beyond livid. *Burning* with the rage. "Can't you see that the only thing driving you is fear? After all that talk about me choosing myself, this is what you do? Well, guess what? I'm choosing. And it's what I want. You. Me. Us. I am choosing me. You, Grant. You, sir. Sex and kink and love, they don't have to be mutually exclusive. Not everything in life is so neatly compartmentalized as you'd like to think it is."

"I can find you another Dom. You deserve someone who can—"

I step back, my eyes wide, a fresh wave of shock running through me. "A new Dom? You think that's what I'm after?"

I can see the lie trying to form in his mind—and the resistance to it. Because no matter what he might think, Grant Bowman is actually human after all. Before he can get a chance to say more, I shake my head, grab my coat and my bags, and look at him, so angry now that the hurt's taken a supporting role.

"You lie to yourself all you want, big guy. Sure. I can find another Dom. But we both know this isn't about that. It never was. Maybe one day you'll grow up, face your fears, and figure that out for yourself."

I swoosh out the door, almost trip on my own coat, and finally gather my things back to my chest with all the dignity I have. Then I take off into the night.

I don't let myself cry until I get home.

CHAPTER SIXTY-FOUR

Rae

It's Friday night, and I feel like doing nothing.

I sit down in front of my massive, elaborate book nook, grab my tweezers and glue, and wait for the bad feelings to subside the way they always do when I get working.

It doesn't. I can't.

It's not doing the trick.

I stare at my hands. There's no hiding anymore or distracting myself from the mess I've made of my life. Especially not when everything about this damn model reminds me of Grant. The little library nook I've added with its jacquard-painted wall and the bench I made after our lunch excursion to the club.

I sink back in my chair, eyes shut hard against the feelings trying to swamp me—again.

Pretty sure I've said *no* more times in the last two days since the retreat than I have the entire time I've worked for Sugar. It felt really good until it occurred to me that I'm not actually that into HR. I'm tired of being here for people. Tired. Just tired. Then there's Samantha, who finally reached out and explained that she and her mystery man gamed on her computer. That's why she brought it home with her.

She's still fired, though. It was a rule she ignored, and I get it.

The guy has since completely ghosted her. Jackass.

I drop my forehead on my folded arms. I'm wallowing. I know that. But I can't seem to find the silver lining, the flip side, the tiny spark of hope that's always kept me going. It's not there.

My phone chirps. I ignore it. It goes again. Again. God, can't anyone leave me alone?

I pick it up and read.

Hannah: Have you heard from Dad?

Me: No.

Hannah: Are you home?

Me: Yes.

Less than a minute later, there's a knock at my door.

I type: Is that you?

"Yes, you ding-dong!" Otty yells. "Open the damn door!"

I trudge over, unlock it, and before I've gotten it all the way open, my sisters are shoving their way inside. "Let's go," says Hannah in her bossy mom voice.

"What? Where?"

"Dad's." From the way Otty sinks onto the world's smallest sofa, I can tell she's been drinking.

"Get up, Otty! No lazing around!" Hannah turns to me. "She's had three edibles. I can't make her worry about this, and we need to be worried."

"About what?" I am, of course, immediately worried.

"Shoes on. Grab the key to Dad's. I'll explain while we drive."

I throw pants, shoes, and a coat on over my *Sweeney Todd* T-shirt, grab Otty by the arm, and follow Hannah out the door.

"I went by the house," she tells me as we take off down the quiet street. Otty, as usual, has piled into the back. I'm in front, and let me tell you, the minivan is nasty. Every seat is crusted with some kind of crumb. I'm hoping it's Cheerios.

"Is that throw-up?" I point to a stain on the dashboard.

"Of course not."

"What is it?"

"I don't know, Rae, do I? Let's solve one mystery at a time, okay?"

"Fine." Annoyed now, I turn to look out the window.

"So, Dad was home. Or at least his car was there. Lights on."

I check the time. It's only 9:30 p.m.

"Mystery car was there."

"Running lines, then?"

"Maybe, but he didn't answer when I knocked."

Annoyance gives way to my first real niggle of worry. I check the vitals app.

"Why didn't you go in? His heart rate's up. He could be on the floor."

"Fallen and he can't get up!" yells Otty from the back.

"Exactly!"

"I lost my key." Hannah's driving fast, taking corners like the F1 racer she once dreamed of being. "That's why we needed yours."

Funny, I can't think of a single fast-paced job Hannah didn't fantasize about at least once when we were kids.

"Where'd you lose it?" Otty asks.

"What part of *lost* don't you understand?"

"I got mine, Otty. Remember?" I hold up my key chain. "Besides, there's always the Boyfriend Window."

Hannah snorts. "Have you seen that branch recently? It doesn't look strong enough to hold one of my kids, much less me. I'm a lot bigger than I was back then. Nobody wants me in the hospital."

"Amen," says Otty.

The car slows as Hannah turns into the quiet, wooded street we grew up on, past the sedate brick Colonials. Our split-level is in dire need of renovation, but I love it the way you love something you can't imagine ever living without.

This is home. As far as I'm concerned, Dad will always live here. He and this house are symbiotic, or whatever the word is that means they need each other to survive.

Hannah starts quietly singing "Home" from *The Wiz* under her breath, and unlike when I sing, her voice sounds amazing.

Otty joins her from the back seat, her harmony pitch-perfect despite the edibles.

I get goose bumps.

"Lights are out now," Hannah says as she shuts off the engine.

Worry washes over me, so familiar I barely notice it. "No porch light, no bed light, no TV. That car's still there."

Tension fizzles through my body as we topple outside. I've never seen it this dark. Not once. At the top of the short flight of stairs, I look at both my sisters, insert my key in the lock, turn it once, twice, shove at the door, and—

"Ooof."

It won't budge. I turn the knob and try again. Nothing. I

fiddle with my key, rattle the knob, pull the key out, and do it all again, and then I'm banging at the door with both hands. It's the dead bolt. And we all know that key was lost years ago.

"Dad? Are you in there?" Hannah screams. Our fists barely make a sound on the thick wood. "Dad!"

No response. No movement. He has to be home if his car's here. Maybe, maybe he's at rehearsal or something, but Hannah says the lights were on earlier. This is a nightmare.

"Let's go around back."

Shaking, I put my phone on flashlight mode and start down the steps, picturing Dad on the bathroom floor, unable to move. If we can't get in the basement door, I'm calling 911.

We're halfway across the yard when the front porch light comes on. The door swings open. As one, we fly back to the porch.

"Hannah? That you?"

"Dad? What's going on?" Relief pours through me as we retrace our steps around the house to the front. "Are you okay?"

"Rae? What are you girls doing here?"

"What's going on, Dad?" I hear that I'm yelling. I just can't seem to rein it in.

"What? You're all here?"

Our steps slow as we near the front stoop. Even in the crappy light of the single bulb, I can tell there's something off about the way he's standing, half inside, half out, and he's wearing the holiday robe. Again.

"Holiday robe?" mumbles Otty, too low for Dad to hear.

"Yeah. It's weird."

Hannah sniffs. "Is he burning a fire in there?"

I smell it too. Woodsmoke, like when we used to have fires around Christmas. It was a rare luxury because wood cost money and didn't actually heat the house.

"Dad?"

"Kiddos!" He smiles, wide and fake.

We make it halfway up the steps before it becomes clear that he's not going to move out of our way to let us into the house.

"Come by for a late-night snack?" Why's he being so weird?

"A snack, Dad?"

"No. No snack!" yells Otty. "We were worried."

Hannah and I exchange a look. The concern I've felt for Dad these past few weeks shifts. Is this dementia? Please, please, please let it not be dementia.

"Aw, well, you girls are really so sweet, but I was just—"

"You've got to tell them, Nate," a woman's voice says from over Dad's shoulder.

We watch wide-eyed as she comes into view.

"Ms. Barcom-Tancredi?" we all three whisper.

"Heh. Yeah. Well, you can probably call me Laura now."

Nope. Not happening. I will absolutely never be able to call her anything but Ms. Barcom-Tancredi.

Dad deflates from his weird defensive posture and turns sideways to let us through. Ironically, now that he's inviting us into the house, none of us seems all that excited to enter.

"So, you're fine, then."

"I'm good." He glances back at Ms. Barcom-Tancredi and smiles. When she smiles back at him, emotion wells up inside me, so strong that I can't quite catch my breath for a few seconds.

Maybe it's shock? Or maybe, maybe seeing my sweet father look truly happy for the first time since Mom died has made me see just how hard it's been.

Not just for us. For him too.

"Dad."

He looks at me.

"How did you and my English teacher meet?" My favorite teacher. The teacher who let me eat in her classroom and brought sandwiches when I didn't have time to make them for myself.

"We're doing *Cabaret* together. She's amazing as Fräulein Schneider."

"We hope you'll come to the performance next month!" Ms. Barcom-Tancredi throws into the mix.

"Hey, Rae! You'll love this part! So, I tried out your app, Honey," my dad says.

"Sugar."

"Right, well, Laura was on it, and we were a ninety-eight percent match. I clicked on her, and she said yes. We auditioned together on our first date, and, well...the rest is herstory."

"Ourstory," adds Ms. Barcom-Tancredi, smiling at Dad.

Hannah surreptitiously squeezes my hand. I squeeze back.

"Want a hot chocolate?" Dad asks, as if this were a regular Friday night and not the night we discovered that Dad has an actual life. Not only that, but he's safe and healthy, and his heart's probably just dandy.

"I want vodka," says Hannah.

"Don't have any of that, honey."

Otty asks, "Edibles?"

"Well, we were about to go to bed."

"Oh, no. I'm out." I step back, bash into the still-open screen door, and catch myself on the frame. "We need to split."

"Yep." Hannah's shoving at me to move out of her way so we can get out of this place right this moment.

"What? Why?" Otty's clueless.

"You don't have to go, girls!"

"You know what, we'll talk soon!" I say over my shoulder.

"Want to come for coffee in the morning?" Dad's grinning when he yells out the door.

"I'll make sure to be gone!" Ms. Barcom-Tancredi calls from behind him.

"We're good!" I yell as Hannah and I each grab one of Otty's arms and run like hell.

CHAPTER SIXTY-FIVE

Grant

I'VE DONE THE RIGHT thing. I know this.

Yet, for the rest of the week, through the hours and hours I spend going through data, meeting with Dorothy and her staff, and then the investors, I can't stop being pissed.

How the hell can Rae possibly think we could be more?

That's what annoys me the most. She knew what we were. I was clear with her from the start. What we had was a power exchange, not romance. It was a game. A way to get our rocks off and enjoy ourselves.

It's Friday evening, and the meeting with Dorothy and her investors was a huge waste of time. It was painful to watch her defend her decisions and management style to a group of people who have no idea what this company even does.

Thankfully, no major decisions have been made. In the meantime, the work I've done here feels ineffectual at best. How the hell did the information leak if no one broke into the system? Dane Wabash still hasn't sent us his proof, so there's still a chance he's bluffing.

I'm at home, looking over videos of the lobby and building

entry logs. Literally staring at lists, times, days, and black-and-white videos of every entrance to the building.

Nothing.

My mind wanders to Rae's laugh out on the canoe. How it started high and light but then evolved into this belly laugh when she passed a certain point. Just the most joyous sound I've ever heard. I feel it, even now, in my body. When I blink my computer back into focus, I have to literally wipe the smile from my face with my hand.

Not for the first time today, panic settles over me.

The job that I took on as a favor to a friend has turned into a nightmare. A failure.

And Rae. Every time I think of her—which is way too often—the panic comes back. Like forgetting something or missing a last plane out. Shit.

I stand up from my desk, which overlooks my front porch, and a slice of Dorothy's porch to one side. Back in the kitchen, I go to make another coffee and then realize it's probably ten o'clock at night and decide to switch to beer.

Through the wide window, I can see lights on next door. Malika and Dorothy are probably getting ready for bed.

Rae's probably at the club. I should go. Check in on her. Make sure she's being taken care of. Or call Lucas, at least.

I've got my phone in hand before it occurs to me that she is none of my business now. I know this with absolute certainty. Except the idea, when I let it come, of finally finding someone to commit to, well, it doesn't make me panic nearly as much as the notion of losing her. Am I just too chickenshit to follow through?

No. No, I'm bad at relationships. Commitment. I'm not capable of loving someone like that. I never learned how.

Beer in hand, I head back to my desk and sit down. If I can't fix what I had with Rae, I have to at least get to the bottom of whatever bullshit Dane Wabash cooked up. It's taken me too long to unravel this mystery. The guy isn't all that smart. What the hell am I missing, dammit?

I can only blame myself for this getting as out of hand as it has. I got distracted. Carrying on with Rae was the most unprofessional thing I've ever done. Hands down. I crossed a line, both professionally and personally, and this project has only suffered from it. I'll let Dorothy know I'm resigning. Recommend a few colleagues to take over from me.

As I pull up my laptop to type my resignation letter, an email from Dorothy pops up. She finally received the so-called data breach details from Dane and has forwarded it on. It is, according to his message, just a sample of the user information he found on the dark web.

My pulse picks up as I look over the sample. I recognize this data. I know this data. Hell, I planted this data myself. And I know exactly where. It makes no goddamn sense that the data got out, unless...

I turn and look through my side window, straight into Dorothy and Malika's place. I've been there enough times to know that my desk points right at Dorothy's home office. Even now, the monitor's glow is visible through their curtains.

This is it. I know it.

I grab my phone, glad that the lamps are still on next door. I start to send her a text but then call instead.

"Evening, neighbor."

"Saw your email."

Her only response is an angry hum.

"I've got a question for you. Well, a couple."

"Shoot."

"That computer you have at home. The one in your office?"

"Yeah. You need to use it?"

"Nope. Thanks. No, but...it wouldn't happen to be a work computer, would it?"

"What do you...? Oh. Oooooooh."

"Can you access the office intranet from that machine? From home?" This could be something. I'm buzzing with that familiar tingle that tells me I'm about to close a case.

"Of course."

"Please tell me it's password protected."

"It is."

"A decent password. Like I taught you."

"Well, I haven't changed it recently, but it's good. It's Rachel's birthday and her middle name."

"Rachel? Your daughter, Rachel? The Rachel who's married to Dane Wabash? The guy who's after your company?" I inhale in an effort to control my annoyance. "You know, Dorothy, I'll bet Dane knows her birthday."

"Oh, shit."

Bingo. This is it. I'm on the right path. Now I just have to prove the asshole did it himself.

CHAPTER SIXTY-SIX

Rae

"This stuff is disgusting." Hannah pours herself another watermelon vodka and settles back into the blanket fort Otty built in my house. It's actually pretty cool. You can go from the sofa to the bed without being seen. I'm impressed.

"You wanted vodka."

"This isn't vodka. This is melted plastic in alcohol."

I don't bother replying. Right now, all I want is to stop thinking about what Ms. Barcom-Tancredi meant when she said they were headed to bed.

They. She and Dad? Together?

"They're kind of cute together," Hannah says, vodka glass already half-empty. It's her second one.

"Dad and Ms. Barcom-Tancredi?"

"You mean his new girlfriend?"

All three of us stop to let those words sink in.

"Laura," I say.

"Laura," my sisters repeat, like we're just down from outer space and we've never encountered human speech before.

A knock at the door makes all three of us jump. We don't

move under the blankets, because who the hell is at this door at midnight?

"It's Sam! I know you're there!" A pause. "I've brought offerings." Another couple of seconds go by. "And explanations."

Otty and Hannah both give me considering looks.

"Go ahead," I whisper to Otty, who crawls to the front door and opens it. "What kind of offerings, Tank Girl?"

"Vodka."

"What flavor?" yells Hannah.

"They didn't have watermelon, so I got plain."

"Hallelujah." My sister clambers her way to the entrance.

"What else?"

A sheepish, exhausted-looking Sam squats down so she can see me. She's carrying two huge bags, which she sets down like a tribute to the local beast.

That's me. I'm the local beast.

"Cranberry, limes, soda water. Diet Coke..."

I open my mouth to ask which kind, and she quickly says, "Gas station. Also, those lemon sandwich cookies you like."

One of the bags disappears from view, clearly carried off by one of my scavenging sisters.

"Clementines, pickles, chips, special cocoa...and...three bags of jalapeño Cheetos."

Oh, she knows she had me with those Cheetos. They're hard to find nowadays, and they are my absolute favorite junk food. Also, the clementines were a master stroke because there's always a moment when we're tired of eating the crap and need something fresh.

"Fine. You can stay."

Her grin is huge as she passes the other bag off to my sisters.

I relinquish a piece of blanket fort, and without hesitation, Sam's got her shoes and coat off, and she's ducked down and squished in with me.

"Nice digs. You've managed to make the smallest home in the city seem even smaller."

"It's cozy."

"Sure is, Beanie."

Otty's opened a bag of Cheetos and already shoved a handful into her mouth when she joins us. For once, I don't even give a crap about getting the orange stuff on my couch. Who cares? Truly, who gives any part of a shit about stains when life is just one big shit stain anyway and nothing—nothing—makes sense?

Especially the part where Dad has a new girlfriend.

Except... I kind of like that part.

"Dad's got a girlfriend," I inform Sam.

"Nice going, Mr. Jensen."

"It's Ms. Barcom-Tancredi."

"No freaking way."

"Yes, way," says Hannah as she slides in beside us.

"Hey, you okay?" asks Sam. Which is hilarious, right? I mean, she's the one who's gotten fired and disappeared and was gallivanting lord-knows-where with some married guy.

"I'm fine, you wiener face. What about you?"

"Wiener face?"

"Penis breath."

"Oh my god," Hannah sighs. "Eighties insults?"

"Vintage eighties insults," Sam replies. "The very best kind."

"Picturesque."

"Gross." Otty takes back the Cheetos and hands Hannah a cocktail. "Here."

"Ew. It's nasty."

"Needs more cranberry."

"I need a cup!"

"I'll get it!" Sam squeezes out, turns to the kitchen area, scuffles around, and goes silent.

"Oh, wow. Rae."

"What? What is it?"

"Your nook."

I snort. "Stupid nook."

"No. No, it's good. It's really good."

"Right?" Hannah yells, giving me a look. "I told her she needs to charge more."

"It's just a pathetic fantasy."

"The hairy whip thing!"

"For the love of all that is holy, please just call it a flogger."

My sisters snort-laugh.

Sam's laugh stops abruptly.

"What's wrong?"

"The... You..."

Now it's my turn to get up and out, only I do it like a blanket fort Godzilla, dragging three different chenilles and a twinkle light with me. "What is it?"

"That's me." Her voice is nothing but a scratch. "The little person sitting at reception. You stuck me in there."

"I've missed you."

Sam lets out a sob and reaches for me, and we're hugging. After at least a minute, I let out a long, shuddering exhale and draw back.

"That's what you get for having secret boyfriends."

"Pot, meet kettle."

My sisters pop up to standing at almost exactly the same time. "Secret boyfriend? Who? What?"

"I was seeing a guy." Sam glances quickly at Hannah and back at me. "He was married."

A weird buzzing starts up in my head. She wouldn't. She really wouldn't.

"I've got something to tell you. About him."

"Oh god." I'm pretty sure my whole face collapses. Was my best friend sleeping with my brother-in-law? She's pretty weird when it comes to men, but...no. No way. No.

"I was pretty sure he'd given me a fake name, so I looked in his wallet the last time I saw him. His real name's Dane Wabash."

Shock hits me so hard I can't think.

"Who's that?" Otty pipes up from where she's collapsed back on the love seat.

"Our boss's son-in-law?" I can't help but grimace. "Ew, Sammy. Ew."

"I know. I just...you know how I am about assholes."

I shake my head and sink down next to Otty. It's a tight fit.

"I called Dorothy. Talked to...Grant. Look, I'm sorry. I wanted to tell you that. I just...My taste in men sucks balls."

"You suck balls!" yells Otty, the way she used to as a kid. Minus the balls part.

"Nothing wrong with it," Sam replies.

"Your choice," I add.

"No judgment," Hannah pipes in.

"Yeah, we've sucked worse," Otty finishes.

We all look at her.

"Have we, though?" Hannah asks.

"Well...I mean..."

All eyes switch back over to me.

"What?"

"You're the adventurous one," Sam says. "With your hot Dom."

"Dom?" Hannah looks at me.

"I'm not really adventurous. I'm a scaredy pants."

"You're the bossy pants," says Hannah, poking me. The whole evening feels like a return to childhood. I don't hate it.

"Mom," Otty intones.

There's a weird silence.

"Yeah. About that." I stand back up and look at each of them. "I can't do it anymore. I can't take care of everyone all the time."

"We're over it too," Sam says.

"Wait." I'm immediately defensive. "Over what, exactly?"

"Taking care of us all the time. Get a life, man." Hannah, as always, finds the humor.

"No, but seriously. And now, like Dad's got a girlfriend? Is she gonna check his vitals app, or do I keep doing that? And what about you guys? Have you got it all figured out too?"

"Schaffer got an assistant," says Hannah. "And less travel."

"Really?" Hallelujah.

"I also gave him an ultimatum: help out or get out. We'll see how it goes."

"He bought her flowers," Otty pitches in.

"This has all happened, like, this week?"

"Yep. And I'm moving to Charleston," announces Otty.

"What? Why? Is it safe there? Where are you gonna...?"

The three of them exchange a look, and I stop dead.

"I've got a place, a job, and already booked a couple of local singing gigs."

"It's so far."

She nods. "That's kind of the idea. A little change of scenery, a little distance from the prick who just fired me."

"Wait. You were fired?" I ask.

"We don't need you, Beanie."

"I do," says Sam, her grin lopsided because of the Blow Pop she's just stuck in her mouth.

"No, you don't."

"I need you as my best friend. And an HR person with experience reading résumés."

"Hm. I'll help with the résumé." I crunch on a Cheeto and stare them all down. "You know we'd have gotten here a lot sooner if you'd all just done what I said over the years?"

"Whatever. I think it's time for a sweet baby huggle!"

"No!" I scream. "No huggles! Please, no huggle!" It's too late. My sisters are smothering me with hugs and kisses already. It's one of those family traditions that you love to hate, or hate to love, or whatever it is when it's wonderful but also might kill you from literal lack of air.

"I love huggles!" yells Sammy as she jumps right on top.

I'm laughing and laughing, and I love them so much, and then I just burst into tears. Again.

CHAPTER SIXTY-SEVEN

Rae

GRANT'S DESK IS EMPTY when I get to work on Monday.

This is no surprise. He spent most of last week either in Dorothy's office or in meetings. Sam apparently spent half the day with the two of them yesterday. And with the police...which is wild.

Literally, his side of the room looks like no one ever occupied it, much less sat there and watched me like a horny hawk. I hate it.

Unable to stand being in this office for one more second, I hurry out into the lobby and become aware of how chaotic everything is.

I turn as a smug Dane Wabash saunters into the lobby from the front entrance, chatting with a group of people who, it turns out, are the investors. Holy shit. What's happening? Is that Dorothy's daughter, Rachel?

"Rae!" Dorothy comes out of her office. "I'd love for you to sit in on this. We might need your input."

"Oh. Of course. Sure. Sure."

From the moment we file into the conference room and sit down, Dane lords it over Dorothy.

"Dotty's the best," he tells the three men and two women who make up the group of investors while his wife looks on. "She's been begging us to give her grandkids." He reaches out to chuck his wife under the chin but stops when he catches Dorothy's death glare, instead smoothing his hand over his fresh-looking haircut. "Can't wait to retire and be the doting granny she was meant to be, right, Dotty?"

"Let's begin." There is not an ounce of bonhomie in Dorothy's expression as she looks around the conference table.

"Right. Well, we all know Sugar has been in a downward spiral for the last few years."

What? This is patently untrue. The company's profits have steadily grown. He's flat-out lying now?

Dorothy, usually not one to keep her mouth shut, folds her arms across her chest and settles deeper into her chair to watch.

He attacks her leadership skills, her lack of innovation, her limited capacity as manager, and then he attacks her character. When he mentions that she's an old-fashioned matchmaker with the heart of a homemaker, the rage pushes me up to standing, ready to protest, like someone in an old courtroom drama. That's when the door opens.

I'm literally half standing when Grant walks in, followed by two women in suits. He nods at Dane.

"Mr. Dane Wabash?"

"What is this? What's going on?"

"I'm Detective Rosa Ortíz, Richmond Police, Cyber Crimes Division. This is Forensic Accountant Bethanne Wilson. We'd like to ask you a few questions, sir."

Dane's smug, corporate a-hole golfer tan turns a sickly gray. "Can't you see I'm in a meeting?"

"I'm afraid it can't wait, sir. We are in the middle of a serious criminal investigation." I squint at the woman she introduced as Bethanne. Forensic accountant? Have I seen her before? I swear she looks familiar.

"Well, I'm not going. This is bullshit. You can't make me. This is an extremely important meeting. My investors have come all the way from—"

"I'm sure we can answer all your questions here, Detective," says Dorothy, wearing her first smile of the day. "The investors won't mind, will they?"

Everyone shakes their head aside from Rachel Gold—or is it Wabash?—who pushes her chair slightly back from her husband's.

"Thank you." Ortíz turns to Dane. "Please tell us where you were, sir, last Wednesday night, September eighteenth, between the hours of ten p.m. and two a.m."

"What? Why? No. I want an attorney."

Ortíz shares a long look with the accountant. "You are welcome to an attorney, sir, but we're just asking questions at this point. We spoke with your wife this morning, who confirmed that you were not home at those specific times. Nor on September tenth at ten p.m. We are currently investigating alleged bank fraud, wire fraud, identity fraud, computer fraud, computer invasion of privacy, and you are a person of interest in those—"

"Fine! Fine. You win. I'll come. But you'd better get ready because I will not sit back and allow you to perpetrate this witch hunt. This is harassment. I'll be talking to my lawyers."

Lawyers? Plural. My god, this man is really atrocious.

He turns to the investors, who are looking decidedly queasy now.

I glance at Rachel, and she looks pissed. She also looks like she might have known this was coming.

"I'm not responsible for any of that. If anyone's guilty here, it's him." He points at Grant. "And her." His attention moves to Dorothy. "She's mismanaged this place like you wouldn't believe. Treats employees better than her own daughter. Than us!"

Rachel rolls her eyes. Wow. Okay. This is unexpected.

"Do you know what their end-of-year bonuses are like? It's insane. Highway robbery. She's stealing from you to pay those. It's robbery! Fine, though. *Fine*, I'm coming. I'll come. We can pick this back up later. Just let me—"

"Now, Mr. Wabash."

Dane stomps out, followed by the two women. Bethanne Wilson throws me a sly wink as she makes her exit, and in a flash, I know exactly where I've seen her: at Off the Cuff. I think I recognize her from my first time at the club.

This is wild.

"What's going on?" asks a woman about Dorothy's age, who's been following the proceedings wide-eyed. Company legend says that Dorothy reached out to friends for seed money back in the day. I'll bet this is one of the people who loaned it.

"This is Grant Bowman," Dorothy announces to the room. "He's the corporate security expert I called in when my son-in-law first mentioned rumors of a Sugar App data breach."

"Apologies for the interruption." Grant nods at the assembly, plugs in his laptop, and turns to the screen.

"I'm sorry to inform you all that you have been lied to, repeatedly, by Dane Wabash. I've compiled the evidence proving his embezzlement from Sugar, as well as funds he siphoned from Ms. Gold's personal accounts. Mr. Wabash has worked to tarnish both the company's and Ms. Gold's reputation. His efforts to oust Ms. Gold as CEO have potentially impacted the company's image as well as team morale. I also want to lay your minds to rest regarding the breach of user data. While data was accessed—illegally— it was not disseminated."

Grant's eyes flicker as they briefly meet mine. He looks exhausted but strong. Unbeatable.

"The data stolen from the Sugar servers was not, in fact, user data, but a dummy list uploaded for security purposes."

A list of names appears on-screen. I scan it, expecting to find nothing special, and then cough out a shocked sound. If there'd been coffee in my mouth, I'd have spit it all over.

> Jean Valjean
> Betty Rizzo
> Velma Kelly
> Eliza Hamilton
> Percy Blakeney
> Henry Higgins

They're all musical theater names. Every single one of them. With email addresses beside them and, past that, credit card numbers. Those all fake, obviously.

> Matilda Wormwood
> Agatha Hannigan

The list goes on.

"This is ridiculous," one of the men cuts in.

"It would be." Dorothy looks at the people who came today to watch her fail. "If Dane Wabash hadn't used my personal computer to access this list while both my partner and I were away. On business."

"When was this?"

"This week," Grant replies, moving on to another slide. This one is a video. "This footage is from the camera on the house next door to Dorothy's residence. Taken while the entire Sugar staff was accounted for."

"At retreat," I whisper.

"At the yearly retreat." He gives me a look. "We were prepared for the possibility of an inside job. We had not, unfortunately, considered that it might happen at Dorothy's residence instead of remotely, or here, in the offices. However, we now have log-in times and footage of Mr. Wabash arriving at the location, as well as his fingerprints on Dorothy's home computer. That, along with the multiple dummy payments made on his behalf, is more than enough for a conviction."

"And here"—Grant hands folders out to all five investors—"are your buyout packets."

Someone gasps. Dorothy's ex-bestie looks sick to her stomach right now. Good. She should be. This is what betrayal looks like.

"Thank you, Grant."

"Thank you, Dorothy." Grant picks up his computer and gives the room one last look before heading out. Do his eyes linger on me a split second longer than the others? Maybe. But I can't think about that right now.

"In light of the events leading up to today, as well as the clear breakdown in communication between us—dear investors—please understand that this is a onetime, formal buyout proposal from me. Please get back to me within the next twenty-four to forty-eight hours. I urge you to accept what are excellent terms." She's standing there, giving Patti LuPone as *Evita* vibes, and it takes every bit of my restraint not to slow clap. "Thank you for coming. Please see yourselves out."

Cue the standing ovation.

CHAPTER SIXTY-EIGHT

Grant

OCTOBER

It's late. I'm trudging up my porch steps when Dorothy speaks from the porch next door. "You regret it yet?"

"Regret what?"

"Don't play stupid. I'm so tired of stupid men."

I sigh, turn, and look over at where Dorothy's quietly sitting in the dark, waiting to pounce. She lights a joint now, confirming that she has indeed been lying stealthily in wait for me.

"Yes." I sink heavily into my porch chair. "I regret losing her."

"Yeah, well, I was sad to lose her at Sugar." A pregnant pause. "We had lunch today. She seems pretty good. Rae's got chutzpah," she says.

"She does."

"You know I lost two good people because of you?"

"How do you figure?"

"Well, we lost Sam, though she's back on as a consultant. Much better for everyone this way. Hourly work. A little freedom. And we don't need to worry about her internet security at home."

"I'm glad."

"And then you made my jane-of-all-trades start saying no to everyone."

"About time."

"Yeah. I should have nipped it in the bud earlier. I waited too late. Now she's gone."

"You're blaming me for this?"

"Nah. I'm just teasing you. Don't blame you for either one. Although the way you've been slinking around lately, you'd be an easy target if I wanted to."

I laugh, though there's not much humor in it. I am bone-tired after a long day at the house I'm renovating over on Floyd. It's a good one. Not as big as mine and nowhere near the bigger projects I'd planned to take on, but it's got details that'll make someone very happy. The downtown building's progressing with a big, professional crew, but nothing's quite as satisfying as working with my own hands. I stayed extra late tonight, hoping to block out the fact that Rae might be out, just a few blocks away, dressed to the nines, the brightest, most beautiful person in the entire club.

I guarantee she's got a string of Doms by now. I *hope* it's a string and not one. The day she finds a Dom she wants to stick with... That'll just about kill me.

There's a light trill at my feet, and Devil Cat bumps my leg. I bend and pick her up, smiling at the little bite she gives me before allowing me to scratch her ear. From the incredibly bizarre calico pattern on her body to her creepily mismatched eyes, she is flat-out the ugliest creature I've ever seen.

"Like I said, Rae seems pretty happy now that she's off doing her own thing."

"Does she?" I can't help hoping it's her work making her happy and not a man. Devil Cat's purring gets extra loud as my scratching gets harder.

"I'm sad she left us, but making those little doohickies has just lit her right up."

"The book nooks."

"Yeah. Love those things. She's killing it. Too busy to make one for me."

I picture Rae in her tiny home, making her little book nooks. My chest hurts, the way it does every time I think of it. I'll admit that I've watched her socials exploding in real time. As of her last post, she's closed to commissions. Too busy. Too popular. Too everything.

Something drops with a thud on Dorothy's porch, followed by a second thud. "My dogs are barkin'."

"Pretty tired myself. I'll just head in and—"

"I love my kid. You know that, right? Only good thing to come out of my marriage. But I sometimes wish she had a little of that Rae magic, you know? That..."

"Zest for life?"

"Yeah. Some of that. Ambition and... the other thing."

I know exactly what she means.

"She rubbed off on you for a minute there," Dorothy says.

"What?" I look over.

"At the retreat. You were fun. I liked that Grant."

"So, what am I now? Chopped liver?"

"Ah, you're all right." She exhales. "But you were better as part of a couple. With Rae."

"I'm not a couples guy."

Dorothy scoffs. "You are the very definition of a couples guy, kid."

"How so?"

"First of all, you're boring."

"Jesus, Dorothy, don't hold back."

"You need Rae."

"I don't *need* anyone." This feels so much like a lie that I have trouble getting the words out. Sensing my weakness, Devil Cat nips at my finger. I move my scratching to her chin.

"You do. She elevates you."

She does...No, did, dammit. She made me feel...so much bigger. So much more than what I'd set out to be.

"Seriously, though. What are you doing with yourself? You look like hell."

"I work."

"Right. Anything else? Do you even have a hobby?"

"Making money."

"Not a hobby. Not even, in my opinion, a valid use of your time, much less your humanity."

"You make money."

"I matchmake. Money's a side effect. But Rae? She's...a spark. For a guy like you, who's held himself in check so long, if you'd just let her light you up, you'd be able to...to..."

"Live."

I can't believe I've said the word aloud. It feels simultaneously like the most pathetic admission I've ever made, and the most freeing.

With Rae, I was alive.

Am I even living right now? Is this how life's supposed to feel?

Dorothy hums a long, low sound. There is zero judgment in it, and for some reason, that makes me feel even worse.

"I can just picture the two of you. You'd be happy, kid. Like you were at the retreat. But also a wreck, running around after Rae, working hard to keep her happy while she fixes up the world. It's what you want, isn't it?" She laughs a silent, stoner's laugh. "There's a damn hobby for you."

I shake my head, shut my eyes hard, and then open them, craning my head to catch a glimpse of stars through the glare of streetlights. Nothing. Not a one.

"Listen, Grant, let me tell you what you've got going for you. One: You've got a nice house, and despite what you claim, it's more than just an investment. It's obviously been a labor of love. Those corbels. The reclaimed brick. That's not investment-level stuff."

I put out a hand and run it over the railing I sanded by hand, painted twice before finding the right color. "So, I've got a house."

"Two: Though you work hard to hide it, you're a decent human being. Better than decent."

"Oh, please."

"I swear you've got a radar for when Malika comes home with groceries. You're there, ready to carry them. The other day, we both realized that neither of us has taken the garbage to the curb once this year. What is up with that?"

"I like to help."

"Yeah, well, I appreciate you. And you know how I feel about men."

"Not great," I concede with a smile.

"Yeah, not great. You're a natural caretaker, fighting those instincts tooth and nail, and you know, it's funny because Rae was forced into the caretaker role through circumstance. She's only slowed down now thanks to you. You helped her snap out of it."

"You're matching our traumas."

Even in the dark, I see the glare of her eyeballs as she gives me a long, sarcastic Dorothy stare.

"No way," I say as realization hits. "That's the key to your algorithm? Your big trade secret? Holy shit, Dorothy. I can't decide if you're a genius or a creep."

"Not mutually exclusive."

"That's some evil mastermind shit."

"Glad you recognize the genius at work."

Her front door swings open, and Malika sticks her head out.

"Ah, my sidekick calls."

"It's late. You coming?"

"Yes, madame." Dorothy creaks to a stand, reaches out, and hands me her half-smoked joint.

"Refer to me as your sidekick again, Dorothy, and I will sidekick you out of bed." Malika looks over at me. "Night, Grant."

"Night, you two."

I watch them go in together, to sleep. To live. To be a couple. Two such different people from entirely different backgrounds who make each other happy.

My phone buzzes in my pocket, and I scramble with the joint and the phone, pull it out, and read a new text from my mom.

> Mom: Sorry it's late. Wanted to say you are right. You are right and I am so sorry. I broke it off with Henri tonight. I'm...being single.

And just like that, my entire perspective shifts.

If Mom can be single for the first time in forty years... maybe...What if...?

I stare at the joint in my hand, consider finishing it off, and decide I've got way too much to do if I'm gonna do this right.

I stomp down into the tiny front garden and put the joint out in the dirt before standing and looking up at the sky again. From here, I can see a few stars. Not the millions that blinked in the sky above our canoe that night, but a few. Enough to show me the way.

Perspective. That's what I was missing. Well, that and the

motivation to change. Now, somehow, in the few weeks since I met Rae, I realize exactly how much she gave me of both.

She changed my life. Changed my whole world. Why couldn't I see it? Or at the very least admit it?

My perspective was off, that's all. Now I've got to show her that I'm worth taking back. Worth loving. That's all.

Please, I think, staring up at the only three stars twinkling hard enough to cut through the city's glare, *please, don't let it be too late.*

CHAPTER SIXTY-NINE

Rae

NOVEMBER

Every year for as long as I can remember, I've come to the Harvest Festival Market as a customer. The day I left Sugar, I signed up for a slot to sell book nooks here, but even before today, I was all sold out. In fact, business is absolutely booming. It's been less than two months, and I'm already making what I made full-time. Plus, I get to pick my projects, work from home, and not think about Grant day in and day out.

The biggest miracle is that, thanks to a big social media influencer who took an interest in my work, not only did I break a couple hundred thousand followers almost overnight, but I'm officially booked out for the next eighteen months. The down payments on those alone filled my savings account right up.

But one of the promises I made myself when I left Sugar was to make sure to get out of the house. I know how easy it can be to stay stuck inside, cozy and warm with my little worlds. The fact is that I like people. I just don't want to be at their beck and call.

"These are adorable. How much is this one?" A woman's standing at my table, arms full of shopping bags from the various vendors. Her clothing says Old Richmond Money as clearly as her hair and face.

"Oh, sorry." I point at the little sign leaning up against the finished Carytown building model, featuring the miniature Off the Cuff and Sugar. Beside it is a book nook I made with my parents, my sisters, and me singing around the Christmas tree. It's our last Christmas together before Mom died. I will never sell either one. They're like time capsules of times I never, ever want to forget. "These are not for sale. I'm commission-only now."

"That's a shame. I've got a friend on the architectural board who would love a Richmond original."

"Please give them my card." I hand it over.

"Listen, I need one of these. My daughter follows you on TikTok. She's obsessed. I really would love to order one. Or two? Could you do me two?"

"I'm booked up." Even now, refusing people isn't easy. "But feel free to reach out, and I'll add you to the wait list."

"I'll triple your price. Quadruple it."

Okay, this is wild. I swallow back the urge to capitulate and smile. "No. Thank you." Saying those words is like a drug. I swear. I hand her the clipboard with my interest form. "Go ahead and sign up here. I'll reach out when commissions open up again."

"Wow." She gives me a disgruntled look, and I'm convinced she'll walk away without signing up, but then she doesn't. Instead, she fills in the form, thanks me, and leaves.

The power of saying no. It astounds me every day.

A text comes in a little later. It's from Harlow, asking if I plan to come into the club again soon. She's been actively trying to get me in there, and I can't tell if it's because she's honestly trying to find me another Dom or if she's trying to get Grant and me back together again.

It's something I might consider, at some point. But I can't walk into that place anytime soon without thinking of Grant. Even now, just hearing from Harlow, I am swamped with emotion.

How long does it take to get over a thing that didn't last more than—what?—three weeks?

It's been two months since I last saw him, and I don't feel any lighter. All I feel is this ache.

I actually tried to play with a Dom that Harlow recommended way back in the beginning. It was fine. Like, fine. I very clearly laid out my limits and told the guy that I wasn't interested in anything sexual. He was okay with that.

I hated it.

In the end, I think that kink, for me, *is* inherently sexual. Sadly, I also think it's inextricably linked with Grant. Which sucks.

Maybe that'll change. Right? Yeah. Sure. Definitely. I learned how to say no, didn't I? Every person who's come up today has gotten a *no,* and that includes some really pushy individuals. I can learn. I can change.

I have 100 percent kept my nose out of my family's business these past few weeks. That's a learned behavior. I'm not saying it's easy to sit here and be strong when Otty's homesick and begging me to come down to Charleston for a sleepover. I'll probably give in to that offer, eventually. But for now...saying *no* is kind of my superpower.

I type out a quick message to Harlow, thanking her for thinking of me and letting her know I don't feel ready to spend time in the club, but I'd love to have lunch with her at some point if she's up for it. It feels good to hit Send.

I shut my eyes, breathe deeply, and listen to the distant strains of a local bluegrass band and the hum of happy chatter. I suck in the smell of smoke and caramel apples. If there's a bittersweet twinge, I don't mind. That's life, I guess.

Something new enters the mix. Cinnamon. Cloves. My pulse picks up like it knows something I don't.

I open my eyes. Blink.

Grant is standing at my stall, a smile creasing his gorgeous eyes. Is he thinner? He looks sort of chiseled out around the cheekbones in a way he didn't a few weeks ago.

"Hi there," I say, sounding like a premade recording of Happy Rae. Sales rep Rae.

"Hi, Rae." His mouth relaxes, but the smile's still there in his eyes while they take me in, slowly, top to bottom. When his gaze returns to mine, there's that deep, warm flicker, but not as intense as I remember it. The burn not quite as bright.

Has he mellowed? Have I? Oh my god, am I hallucinating?

"What's up?" I chirp, way too upbeat for this reunion. Whatever this is. Why is he here? Grant's not a Harvest Fest kind of guy.

Maybe he's not here alone. He's with a woman. Of course. What else could drag him to an event that is so clearly not his thing?

"You been busy?" he asks, then laughs, shaking his head. "Never mind. I, um, I know you've been busy. I, uh...get news. Pretty much hourly from Harlow and Dorothy. I know you helped Sam get her job back at Sugar."

"She'd have done it on her own."

"Right. Well, your builds are unbelievable too. I follow your socials and...The Ice Queen one for that kid at the children's hospital? Blown away. You're an artist, Rae. Anyway...has Sam told you she texts me pictures?"

"What?"

"Yeah. She's a real pain in my ass." He pulls out his phone and scrolls through photos. "I've got the diner. Sushi. Indian food." He holds it up. "This one is you baking cookies in your tiny little kitchen."

He drops the hand holding the phone and looks at me, a little…dumbstruck, maybe. "Sorry. I, um…This isn't how I wanted to do this."

"Oh, yeah?" My nerves spark. "What is it you're doing?"

CHAPTER SEVENTY

Grant

I'M SCREWING THIS UP. Big-time.

Rae's staring at me, wide-eyed, like I'm a stalker, which... hell. I kind of am, right? Why'd I even mention the Sam photos, which I in no way asked for? Of course, that hasn't stopped me from staring at them. For hours.

I spot a clipboard with a list of names, bend, and scrawl mine at the bottom.

"Great. I'll, uh...get on this list...of"—I squint at the top again—"commissions. When they open. Yes. I saw that. On..." Slowly, I stand up straight. A kid bumps into me, full of chocolate, which I'm sure he's managed to transfer to my pants. I cannot drum up an ounce of give-a-shit for anything but the woman sitting there staring at me like I've lost all my marbles.

"I'm trying to..." I shut my eyes, open them, and allow myself to feast on the sight of her. "Listen. You know how you helped Dorothy and pretty much everybody at Sugar? And Sam? And...I heard you helped Harlow with some spreadsheet. I also saw the sick kid on social media who..." I have got to get a hold of myself. *Concentrate.* "I thought you should know that you've helped me too."

"I have?"

"Yes. That's what I came here to say."

"Okay." She stares, clearly dazed by my off-the-wall performance.

"Uh, you are the brightest, best thing that ever happened to me, Rae. But, you know." I manage a weak shrug. "I was too dazzled by your light. And scared. I figured I wasn't what you need, but then...Dorothy mentioned something, and my mom's not getting married, for once. She changed her mind, would you believe, because of what I said to her." I pause, look at the little book nook on her table, and recognize exactly what it is. It's us. It's Sugar and Off the Cuff. Right beside it is her family, including the mother she lost as a kid. I look over at her and force the words out. "I figured, if my mom can change after twelve marriages, maybe I can too?"

"Wow. *Wow.*"

I lean in slightly. "I thought maybe you'd..." I swallow. "Sorry, I'm messing this up."

"You're not." Are those tears in her eyes? I don't want her to cry. I reach up, hesitate, and then, when she moves closer, I give my knuckles one tiny taste of her skin.

"I love you, Rae."

A tear slips from her eye. I let my finger catch it.

"I love you more than...than...Shit!"

"Hey! Watch it!" says a passing mom, covering her child's ears.

"Sorry. Sorry. Shi...Dammi...Ugh..."

"Come here." Her sweet face tilts up, one finger lands on my chin, and we are...kissing. Deep and wet and thorough. I fist her hair and open my mouth, lick into hers, desperate for more. For all of her. "I fucking love you," I mutter against her, and then she's dragging at me, and me at her, and—

"Dude. Come on. We've got kids here."

"What?" I turn to see a man with three children, all staring up at me while I maul Rae.

"Fu—I mean...Argh! Sorry. Apologies." I swipe an arm over my mouth and glance at Rae, who is giggling behind her hand. "I just...I love her, man."

"I get that. Congratulations."

"Thanks. I think?" A glance at Rae. "Would you, um...? Can we...start over? Would you...?" Dammit, what am I supposed to say? Go out with me? Go steady? By my girl? No. No, I've got it. "Light up my world again?"

Her laugh is instantaneous, messy, and teary. She nods and mouths *yes*, and then says it aloud and, suddenly, there is applause.

Oh no. There is now an audience of maybe eight people, including the three kids, who have no idea why they're clapping. Their dad rolls his eyes and leads them away with a final grin.

Someone's filming us, I think, which I hate.

"This is private," I tell them. "You don't have our consent for that."

"Free world, old man," says the kid before taking off, and when I think about what they filmed, I guess it's not the worst thing to have immortalized.

The crowd moves on, leaving us more or less to ourselves. "Sorry. I...I know you're working."

"Worth it." Rae's grin is pure delight. It is everything.

"Would you, um, consider coming back to my place? Maybe? After this?"

"Your place? Like where you live? I thought that was a no-woman's land?"

"Really? No. No, I mean, yeah, you'll be the first, but, I, um, I made something. For you."

She blinks. "Okay."

"Don't be scared. It involves no whips or chains or...nothing dirty. I mean, you can make it dirty, but..." *Shut your trap, Bowman.* "Never mind."

"Sure. I'll come over."

CHAPTER SEVENTY-ONE

Rae

I TRY TO WAIT out the end of the event, but what's the point? All I can do is make googly eyes at Grant. The few people who walk up to my booth end up leaving confused, because I'm clearly making no sense at all.

"Let's go."

Grant helps me pack my things into my car and gives me his address. When I pull up in front of his row house, all I can do is stare.

It is gorgeous. Skinny from the street with a bay window up front. The tiny pocket garden needs work, but the porch is deep and wide, and the front door has been painted the perfect blue, the brick the perfect off-white. I love everything about it.

He opens the front door and lets me in.

"Grant, your house is amazing." If a little sparse inside. I don't have time to remark upon the serious lack of decor or soft furnishings because he's pulled me through the massive great room and the ginormous kitchen in back, out a rear door, and the most lavishly beautiful screen porch I've ever seen, into the backyard, where there is a...

"Um. This looks a lot like my..." *Dream workshop?*

I can't quite finish because I am no longer entirely in my body. I glance up at him and back down at the shed. It's painted a light almost-white that veers more toward pink than the white of his home's exterior. It has windows with dark gray shutters and a dark gray door with a little pitched roof. "What...what did you want to show me?"

Even when he tugs at my hand, I don't want to move because I know what this is, and it's too much. Too huge a thing for Grant to do. Grant of the rules and lists and eight brands of scowl.

"Come on." Another tug and I sail down the steps, along an adorable, cobbled path to the door, which has a tiny mailbox beside it. And a bell just like the one on my dream workshop. How closely did he look at that thing?

"What'd you do?" I ask, almost frantic at the idea that this man—who already went against his very grain by opening himself up to me at the market today, in front of a crowd, no less—would spend time and money and the effort to do this.

"I thought you were building houses."

"I was. I am. I do...Open it."

"But..."

"Go ahead."

I slowly turn the handle and push the door. It opens so easily that I know it's well oiled. Of course it is. Grant Bowman is a man who oils hinges. Inside is a wonderland of space and supplies. There are more shelves than in the miniature version. Of course he'd think of that. And cupboards. Everywhere.

"I...I'm not sure I understand."

"It's for you."

"Grant."

"If you want it. You don't have to. No pressure. Dammit! I knew it was too much. It's too much." He reaches for the door and starts to pull it closed, and then I see the cat lying on the tiny, plush white sofa, which is actually tufted velvet and probably cost more than my car.

"Who's that?"

"How the hell'd you get in here?" He walks over and picks up the cat and then slings it over his shoulder like a newborn. "This is Devil Cat. I've got no idea how she gets inside."

"She's cute."

"You think?" He pulls her back, puts his nose to hers, and wiggles it a bit. The cat swipes a cheek to his and then stares me down like I'd better not mess with her man. Or else. "She grows on you."

I already love him. I know that. The mini-me house? Incredible. I mean, a little extreme, as far as grand gestures go, though I am in no way against letting Grant Bowman spoil me.

But the cat? Ooooooh, boy, does he have me with the cat. I am signed, sealed, and officially delivered.

"Don't you hate cats?"

"I do."

I nod. "Makes total sense. You all right, Grant?"

"I don't know. Do you think you could love me? 'Cause I love you so fucking much."

"I could." I laugh, half crying. "I could love you. I mean, I do."

He nods, all stoic and stiff, that muscle flexing in his jaw. "You staying?" The cat's strangely mottled eyes follow every move I make.

"Is there a list of rules someplace I should know about?" I lift my chin to indicate the giant wall of cupboards to my left. "Maybe hiding in there?"

"Not yet."

"Any predetermined boundaries? Specific instructions? Ways I can and cannot behave? Dress code?"

"No. Unless you want that." He glances down at my skirt and then back up, one eyebrow raised. "I'm working really hard on keeping things...unplanned with you. I hope the two of us can take things a step at a time."

"Oh. You mean, we'd be doing it totally..." I smirk. "Off the cuff?"

With a shout of laughter, he leans in to kiss me, and I kiss him back, and nothing's ever felt so much like home.

When Devil Cat gives a high-pitched shriek and dives from his shoulder into the yard, we are both way too busy to look. Or care.

We've got much more interesting things to do.

CHAPTER SEVENTY-TWO

Grant

APRIL

I'M IN THE KITCHEN when Rae comes up from the yard, so I hear the screen door hinges and then her steps. She comes inside, and I've already got her glass out. It's pink. White wine with blackberry liqueur.

"Oh wow," she says with a sigh, accepting the glass and my kiss.

"Your bath is ready."

"Really?"

"Piping hot. Bubbles. Candles lit."

With a happy smile, she takes the drink with her up the stairs to the bedroom I've just finished renovating. It's more luxurious than before, with some custom built-in features that we're nowhere near done exploring. It'll take years, I figure, to run through the full gamut of what Rae and I can get up to in that room. The new tub restraints alone keep us entertained night after night.

"You coming?" she calls.

"Be right there." I throw some parsley on the plate, grab radishes from the fridge, and make my way up to where the woman I love is living out my wildest dreams.

"Snacks," I tell her, settling the tray across the tub. It's a deep one with room for us both. Tonight, though, we're not playing. We've got somewhere to be. "We need you fed before the show."

"Oh, the show. I'd almost forgotten."

"Your dad hasn't let me forget it for a second."

Rae is fucking gorgeous. Lying back in the bath, bubbles everywhere. Her breasts bobbing, pink nipples right at the surface. She's got her lavender face mask on, and the drink's in her hand, and she is luxuriating. Just the way I envisioned her from that first moment she walked into the club.

I take my time rolling up my sleeves, letting her hear every snap of my cuffs. "How was work, sweetheart?"

"It was good. I finished a commission, sent another one out."

"Good job." I pluck at one pink nipple, and Sunny gasps. "Shhhhh. Don't worry. Relax." My fingers dip into the water, find her belly, skim down, down, to where she's slick between her legs. "Fuck, Sunny."

"I thought about us."

"Did you touch yourself?"

"That's a trick question. I wasn't allowed."

I slide two fingers down, splaying her wide. "But did you?"

Her breath catches.

My fingers press inside. "You're soaking wet."

"Of course I'm wet. I'm in the bath."

"You've been bad, Sunny."

Another gasp. "I couldn't help it. I thought of what you promised and—"

Her phone buzzes from the shelf. I shut my eyes *hard*, fully aware that we don't have time for this anyway. "We'll talk about it later."

"What? I want to talk about it now, sir."

I flip up her mask, lean in, and give her a warm peck on the lips.

"It's your sister. We have to go."

"No fair."

"*Fiddler on the Roof*, baby. Tell your dad to stop auditioning, and then we can stop going to his shows and just stay home and play."

"Never."

"I know." I bend and kiss her deeper, warmer, letting my tongue show her just how explicit I wish I could be. "I'll need to punish you later, though. You know that, right?"

She grins. It's cheeky, a little wicked, and the most beautiful thing I've ever seen.

Later, while her dad is tearing up the stage as Tevye and her sisters and the kids sit on her other side, I catch Rae's smile in the darkened theater, tighten my hold on her hand, and kiss each knuckle.

She responds with a brief G-rated leg rub, and beyond all expectations, this moment, with her, is the best thing I have lived.

It's wild how often this happens.

EPILOGUE
Rae

NOVEMBER

"Why did we decide to do this again?" I ask Grant from the warmth of the massive bed he insisted on getting and then adding all kinds of bells and whistles to. It's silly to have so many restraints because we can always go to the club, but actually, Sunday morning is kind of my favorite time to be kinky. So I'm not complaining.

"To celebrate." His smile's wide and warm and so familiar now that it's less of an ache when I see it and just pure joy.

"Ugh, Thanksgiving."

"You love Thanksgiving."

He's right. I do love it. The way I love every single opportunity to celebrate. "But I also love this." I lean in and kiss the side of his pec, a ridiculous bulge of muscle, tipped with its even more ridiculous tight brown nipple. I say ridiculous, but really I mean wonderful. Beautiful, perfect, divine.

"And I love this too."

"You do?" I ask, bending to kiss the slightly furred center of his abs and then lower, to where the hair gathers darker and curlier, right at the base of his absolutely glorious cock. "What about this?" I ask, letting my breath play along his shaft until it's again at full-mast.

I say *again* because we have just literally finished what Grant calls *making love* and I call a good, hard *fucking*. Mostly to mess with him.

"I know you love that, you little brat."

"Do you? How?"

"Because you let me put it deep inside you."

"Mmmmmm. What else?"

"You let me fuck you with it. Tease you."

With a sigh, I lick gently up the length and force myself to hover at the tip, tenderly stroking with my mouth. "How else do you know?" I ask, already squirming with the desire to give and take and feel, feel, feel. I am constantly ravenous for this man.

And he knows it.

"I know, sweet girl, because when I do this..." He slides his fingers into my hair, and with a moan, I pull back just enough to show him I like it. "And this." Grasping himself at the base, he feeds his long, hard cock inside my mouth, holding me in place.

For a few beats, I let the taste and smell of him—of us—overwhelm me. The feel of him, thrumming hard and thick against my tongue, the heft of him so perfect for my body. He pushes deep, and I struggle to open my eyes and meet his, watching him watch me in the perfect feedback loop we always create.

Once he's firmly rooted inside me and I'm close to tearing up from how good it feels, he says, "You take it like the good little sub you are. Don't you?"

And I do my best to nod. Because I do love this and want it and also... we've only got, like, thirty minutes before people start arriving, and my dad is always early, and—

"Whoa, whoa, whoa…"

"What?" I ask as he pulls back. "I didn't stop. Why are we stopping?"

"I heard car doors."

"No! No, dammit! Tell them I am sucking my man's cock, and I am not to be disturbed. Come here."

He backs away, taking his absolutely glorious erection—still wet from my mouth—with him and rolls off the bed. "Can't, sweetheart. Let's go."

I pout. Which is a thing I do now. He loves it. I kinda like it too, in a sceneing kind of way. Honestly, outside of playing, I have absolutely no reason to pout. The man is…

"You're amazing," I say.

"No, you are."

"Stop it. Let me compliment you, Grant. Take it gracefully."

"Fine. Thank you." He gives my body one last, lingering look. "Now get up and shower. You smell like sex."

"You smell like sex."

"Which is why I'm showering."

"What about Dad?"

"Are you saying you haven't given him a key yet?"

It is a valid question. I have, after all, given keys to Sam and to Hannah. Malika and Dorothy also both have keys, as do Lucas and Harlow.

"No. I draw the line at him walking in on us. I mean… ew. It was enough to have to see Ms. Barcom-Tancredi in her underwear."

"Laura."

"Whatever. You didn't know her before." I follow him into the enormous dual-head rain shower that literally doesn't even seem like it should be in a home. It's like a spa in here. Or a hotel or something. He turns on the water, and I just stand here, and the sprays do pretty much the rest. Including the one at waist level that the man utilizes for wicked, wicked things. "This is like a car wash for humans."

"Don't complain." He soaps up his hand and laughs. "You do know that I'm the one who washes you in here, right?"

"You mean it's not a built-in robot?"

"Nope. Just your man."

I sigh. My man. Oh my god. He really is my man. Which is wild. And beautiful. And…

"What? What is it? Are you crying?"

"Just hormonal. You know how it is." And I always miss Mom in the fall.

"I do, sweetheart. I do." He wraps his arms around me and pulls my back tight against his front. "I love you," he whispers into my ear, "but I can hear your dad talking down there. And I swear if he walks into this bathroom right now, there will be words."

"Didn't you just suggest I give him a key?"

"Suggest it? No." He's grinning. "This is how rumors start."

"You said I should give him a key."

"I said I thought you already had."

"Oh. Hm. Well, I won't."

"Thank god."

"Crap. Is that him on the steps? I'm going!"

I race to get dressed and swipe on mascara before heading downstairs to find literally a dozen people here. And four animals.

"Hey, hon!" Dorothy calls from the living room, where she's pouring champagne into the glasses I set out earlier. "I let your dad in."

My dad and Laura are in the kitchen, covering the counter with pies. "I brought the bananas!" Dad yells.

Otty and Hannah and the kids swarm in. Sam is here, and also Harlow with her Frenchie, Augustus, who, along with Malika and Dorothy's dog, McGruntcakes, are a perfect buffer between Hannah's kids and the cats.

The only ones missing today are Lucas, and Rachel, who sold the home she had with Dane and took off to Europe, funded in part by her mother, who was more than happy to see her sow her wild oats. Go on and get some European action, girl. After being married to that creep, I'd say the woman deserves a break.

Grant's mother, who came to visit us for a week last summer, decided to stay in Florida. I honestly think it's best for everyone. We are a lot, and she's clearly had her fill. She likes a quiet home. Without animals. Preferably without mess.

Oh, and we don't talk about Schaffer at all anymore. But I'll leave that story for another day. Also, we do not discuss kink with my dad here. I mean, he possibly knows, given the club and all, but… I'd rather the two never shall mix.

What we do talk about is work and theater and how Grant spends every weekend building things for our house. First, there were the ceiling-high library bookshelves, complete with ladder, that I'd fallen in love with. He then refinished a stunning apothecary cabinet for my itty-bitty book-nook supplies. Now he's putting a mini screen porch on my workshop, which I told him was overkill. What can I do, though? The man lives to make me happy. We talk about our animals and the kids' teeth, and how great Dad sang "Mr. Cellophane" in the recent production of *Chicago*. Otty has given up music and started working in this really fancy French place over in Charlottesville, and… yeah, I think Devil Cat's expecting kittens.

"You were both amazing," I tell Laura every time I see her. Because it's true. *Chicago* was really good.

And though she's not my mom—and she'll never replace her, either here or onstage or in my heart or anywhere else—she makes my father happy.

The way Grant makes me happy.

In a home way. In a real way. In the way that good couples don't complete each other but lift each other up.

What we have gives me hope.

So when I look around and see Otty yawn and check her phone for the millionth time, and Sam, separate from what's actually happening in the room, surreptitiously grimacing at the kids, and Hannah sitting in the corner, downing her third glass and looking as strained and exhausted as I've ever seen her, I have hope.

Maybe they'll find love too.

I know they will. Seriously. The world had better provide. I refuse to take no for an answer.

ACKNOWLEDGMENTS

THE LIST OF PEOPLE who were there for me throughout this one is long, dense, and probably should include every single one of my friends and family, not to mention the bakery next door, the people who make my favorite wines, and the contestants, crew, and production team behind all twelve seasons of *The Great British Bake Off*. But because no one has all day, here's the TLDR.

My first thank-you goes out to the Bittersweeties: Julie Murphy, Mary Kole, and John Cusick. Not only were you the seed and the spark for this project, but you fanned my flames with undying support, and for that, I will forever be your person. John Cusick, you are the dreamiest, kindest, most delightful individual. To have you as my agent is just beyond. Thank you.

To Alex, thank you for your deep, exhaustive edits, for sticking it through to the very end, and for believing in this project. I know it was a leap of faith, and I appreciate that.

To all the good folks at Forever, I am so thankful for all your hard work. It has been a dream to work with you. ☺

Michelle: Thank you for taming my chaos, keeping me in line, and showing me kindness while you do it. You are the Best PA in the World.

To Rusty, you were not only the absolute best alpha, beta, and omega reader... you're just my sister. Love you.

Molly O'Keefe: a real-life heroine for reading, rereading, and believing in me all along. I'm your forever fan.

Sierra Simone, I'm so glad I met you. None of this would have happened without you. Also, you are a font of wisdom and a delight, and I want nothing more than to drink whiskey and eat canned duck with you on some misty moor... all day long.

To Leeyanne Moore, who is there every single day, thank you, my friend. I mean it.

A special thanks to Elizabeth Safleur for sparking off the water bottle scene.

Andie J. Christopher, Annika Martin, Amanda Bouchet, Adriana Herrera, Theresa Kaye, Joanna Bourne, Tracey Livesay, Alleyne Dickens, Mollie Cox Bryan, and the many other friends who've read, blurbed, chatted, brainstormed, and talked me off so many ledges, thank you for being my people. Without your support, there wouldn't be a book at all.

To Lou, who, many years ago now, gave me my first true foray into the wonderful world of kink, you're one of the best people I know. Love you.

To my parents: Thank you for supporting what I do, even when you're (definitely) not my target reader.

Mon Nono: T'es franchement le meilleur. Tout ça serait impossible sans toi. Je t'aime.

Finally, to my readers, who've followed me from small-town angst, through Antarctic mayhem, kink camps, and sexytimes galore, all the way to this sweet and spicy romp: OMG, thank you for sticking with me. I am neither consistent nor organized, but I will always bring you the HEA with the feels that you deserve. So much love to you all. I am blessed to have you.

Do you love contemporary romance?

Want the chance to hear news about your favourite authors (and the chance to win free books)?

Kristen Ashley
Ashley Herring Blake
Meg Cabot
Olivia Dade
Rosie Danan
J. Daniels
Farah Heron
Talia Hibbert
Sarah Hogle
Helena Hunting
Abby Jimenez
Elle Kennedy
Christina Lauren
Alisha Rai
Sally Thorne
Lacie Waldon
Denise Williams
Meryl Wilsner
Samantha Young

Then visit the Piatkus website
www.yourswithlove.co.uk

And follow us on Facebook and Instagram
www.facebook.com/yourswithlovex | @yourswithlovex

PIATKUS